SOFT TACO ISLAND

LYLE CHRISTIE

This book is dedicated to all who have faced adversity in terms of health, work, relationships, or even a really disgusting public restroom, and now desperately need a FUCKING literary, if not FUCKING literal, break from this crazy thing we call

life.

•Please excuse the use of profanity and be warned that there will be more to follow, as well as some traditional humor, bathroom humor, and a goodly amount of spirited sexual encounters, though it will all be delivered tastefully and with the intent of conveying a deep, rewarding, and soulful catharsis.

CHAPTER ONE-PROLOGUE: **Trouble in Paradise**   **9**

CHAPTER TWO: **Living the Dream**   **22**

CHAPTER THREE: **A New Hope**   **36**

CHAPTER FOUR: **So That Others May Live Happily Ever After**   **50**

CHAPTER FIVE: **The Flight of the Yeti**   **70**

CHAPTER SIX: **The Honey Pot**   **93**

CHAPTER SEVEN: **Warm Milk**   **110**

CHAPTER EIGHT: **Where Eagles Dare**   **127**

CHAPTER NINE: **Bathing and Feeling Dirty**   **147**

CHAPTER TEN: **Paradise Found**   **159**

CHAPTER ELEVEN: **The Sea Makes Men Hard**   **195**

CHAPTER TWELVE: **The Island**   **218**

CHAPTER THIRTEEN: **Dressed for Success**   **235**

CHAPTER FOURTEEN: **The Drunken Pig**   **255**

CHAPTER FIFTEEN: **Vanishing Point**   **269**

CHAPTER SIXTEEN: **Into the Blue**   **281**

CHAPTER SEVENTEEN: **Back Door Man**   **293**

CHAPTER EIGHTEEN: **Déjà Vu**   **309**

CHAPTER NINETEEN: **Night of Future Past**   **328**

CHAPTER TWENTY: **The Gilded Cage**   **353**

CHAPTER TWENTY-ONE: **The Long and Winding Road Less Traveled**   **374**

CHAPTER TWENTY-TWO: **A Boat Too Far**   **390**

CHAPTER TWENTY-THREE: **The Sarsarun**   **406**

CHAPTER TWENTY-FOUR: **The Ace in the Hole**   **425**

CHAPTER TWENTY-FIVE: **A Better Tomorrow, Today**   **444**

CHAPTER TWENTY-SIX: **The French Connection**   **469**

CHAPTER TWENTY-SEVEN: **Ugly Americans**   **488**

CHAPTER TWENTY-EIGHT: **Old Friends, New Beginnings**   **499**

Topless Agenda   **513**

Acknowledgements   **515**

Origin of the Mantasy Genre   **518**

About the Author   **521**

BOOK ONE IN THE

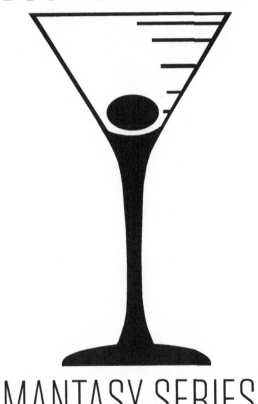

MANTASY SERIES

CHAPTER ONE:PROLOGUE
Trouble in Paradise

It was nine fifteen in the evening as the Eurocopter EC 155 flew north over the dark waters of the Caribbean, with the island of Martinique an hour behind and its destination only a minute ahead. The person at the controls, a former Navy pilot named Lux Vonde, glanced over at the very important attache case in the empty copilot seat and felt her pulse quicken as she contemplated the fact that it's contents would determine the fate of thousands of innocent lives. The helicopter bucked slightly sideways, and she turned her attention back to the horizon and made subtle adjustments to her course to account for the crosswind. It was always a little disoncerting to fly over the ocean at night, but she wasn't the least bit nervous, as she had done this particular flight two times a day and five days a week for the last six months. Of course, she ususally had a full compliment of VIP passengers, but tonight her only company was the case, which was to be delivered to her employer, a man named Adrien Babineux, who was the president of the oddly named Soft Taco Island.

She would be flying directly to the world famous casino, but the first visible landmark was the presidential palace. It resided on the southernmost tip of the island and was a glowing white beacon of light in the darkness below. Beyond it, she passed over a vast expanse of untamed jungle until the flashing lights of the helipad atop the casino came into view. She banked right and came down in a clockwise circle, adjusting the collective until leveling out and dropping down the final few feet to land perfectly in the center of the pad. She shut down the engines and flight systems then picked up the case and stepped down from the helicopter, nodding at the ground crew who were going to prepare it for its return flight to Martinique—a flight that one of her fellow pilots would be taking over. She reached the elevator, stepped inside, and hit the button for the bottom floor. The doors slid closed, and she took a moment to calm her nerves.

This mission had been six months in the making—six long months of determined effort, only to have it all unexpectedly come to a head tonight with the arrival of the attache case. She had picked it up from a courier in Martinique and was supposed to deliver it directly to President Babineux in his private office, but she had other plans. Babineux might have been her immediate boss, but her real employer resided about two thousand miles away in Langley Virginia, as Lux was, in actuality, a deep cover operative for the Central Intelligence Agency. The elevator dinged as it reached the bottom floor, and she stepped out and casually scanned all the people around her as she made her way through the crowded casino. The security men stood ever watchful on the periphery, and none of them gave her so much as a second glance. She reached the entrance to a private corridor and nodded at the sentry, who waved her through as he had on every other occasion. She was a trusted employee and, as such, enjoyed fairly unrestricted access to the majority of the island. Babineux's office was through the set of double doors at the end of the hallway, but her meeting was still about thirty minutes away, and, having just gotten off a flight, she needed to freshen up. That meant a detour into the ladies room.

This particular bathroom, as well as the mens on the other side of the hall, was for executive staff members and included a dressing room, showers, and even a lounge. After stepping inside, she went straight to the second stall, the only one that had a window. She did indeed need to pee, but when she was done she proceeded to open the window and climb out onto the ledge that ran along the side of the building. With the case in hand, she set off, eventually passing by Babineux's office windows, where she glanced inside. The room was empty, as he had yet to arrive, but just thinking about him filled her with a sense of urgency, and she quickened her pace. She reached the back of the building and lowered herself onto one of the dumpsters before dropping down into the alley that ran behind the casino. She continued walking and glanced at her watch to see that she was right on schedule. She'd practiced this route on several occasions, always keeping careful track of her times so that it would be perfect if she needed to make an impromptu escape from the island. She rounded a corner and came to the casino's delivery ramp to find her friend waiting in the little delivery truck exactly as he'd promised.

"Hello, John Parker," she said, ever happy to see him.

John Parker was a fit, good-looking man with dark skin and short well-kept dreadlocks common to the people of the Caribbean.

"Hello, my darling. Just sit back, and I'll have you at your hotel in no time."

She held the case on her lap as they sped along through the warm Caribbean night and passed the various landmarks that had become a part of her daily life. The casino was now well behind, but the rum distillery was just coming into view, and it was crowded as usual with tourists starting the night at the free tasting room. Just beyond it on the right was the faux lagoon and the tiki bar, while off to the left was the walking path as well as the main beach, and, all around, people were enjoying themselves, completely oblivious to the dark and deadly secrets lurking beneath the surface of this tropical paradise. A little over a minute later, John Parker pulled the little jeep up to the front entrance of Lux's hotel, and she leaned over and kissed him on the cheek, the gesture making him smile.

"What was that for?" he asked.

"To thank you. You've been a big help," she said.

"Not a problem, and if you see Bridgette, tell her I'm free tomorrow if she wants to do some snorkeling."

Bridgette was Lux's younger sister, and she had come to visit for a week, but enjoyed island life so much that she decided to stay on indefinitely. It wasn't a good idea to have a family member along on a covert operation, but it did have the unintended side effect of adding some legitimacy to her cover.

"I will," she lied.

John Parker was a good man and deserved to know the truth, but she was in the business of keeping secrets, and that meant lying to her only real friend on the island. She gave a final wave as he pulled away, then she turned and walked into the entrance of her hotel. As usual, it was crowded with people from all over the world, and a cacophony of foreign accents filled the air as she approached the elevator. While she waited, she instinctively had a look around the lobby and locked eyes with a man she didn't recognize, and he held her gaze a little longer than was comfortable. It was probably nothing more than attraction, but something in the back of her mind made her pause for thought. As a spy she learned to trust her instincts, and, right now, her instincts were telling her to proceed with caution. She stepped into the elevator and pressed the button for her floor. The doors closed, and she found her anxiety growing exponentially with each second her stop grew closer. The elevator came to rest, and, when the doors opened, she paused, deciding at the last second not to exit. A security man appeared at the end of the hallway, and, upon seeing her, called out as he started walking in her direction.

"Stay where you are!" he said, as he drew his pistol and began running towards the elevator.

Something had gone seriously wrong, and, now, she needed to come up with an alternative plan, although that would necessitate time—something she didn't have at the moment. She hit the button for one of the lower floors, but the doors remained open, making her wonder if the man would make it before they closed. In a panic, she reached over and pressed the close door button, unaware that it was nothing more than a cruel psychological ploy to appease type A personalities. In truth, that button only worked when a key was inserted to activate its functionality, so, as hard and frantically as she pressed it, nothing would happen until the elevator's preprogrammed timing came into play. The doors finally started to slide shut, but she could see the man was close enough that he'd likely make it in time. That left her only one alternative. She waited until he was only a step away then adjusted her stance and threw a kick through the opening, landing it in the center of the man's chest. He wasn't expecting the blow, and it doubled him over, allowing her to slip her leg back inside with only inches to spare as the doors closed. The elevator started moving, and she used the time to form a plan that would entail achieving two primary goals. The first was to hide the case, while the second would be to get her sister off the island. Both would be challenging, but the first was critical to her mission.

The elevator came to a stop, and the doors opened, but, before she left, she hit several buttons in the hopes that it would make it harder for security to figure out where she had exited. She stepped out into the hallway, entered the stairwell, and headed down to the ground floor. Arriving at the bottom, she opened the door only a tiny crack to see that there was a security man in the hallway standing guard only a short distance from Bridgette's room. She slipped back into the stairwell and headed for the other door that allowed direct access out onto the resort grounds. She went out into the night air and tried to think about where in the hell she was going to hide the case. She could bury it in the jungle, but that would be time consuming, especially without a shovel. She needed something that was closer and faster. The deep thrumming sound of dance music was spilling out of the nightclub on the other side of the building, and she found herself smiling as she realized that, sometimes, hiding something in plain sight was the best option.

She set off for the nightclub, ever watchful for island security, but, thankfully, the number of people milling about allowed her to easily blend in with the crowd. As she neared the entrance she could see the doorman screening everyone entering the club, though his goal didn't appear to be looking for potential dangers, but rather to enjoy the parade of flesh. A group of drunken women, likely a bridal shower, were in line, and she managed to join their entourage, allowing her to slip easily past security with her attache case. Three minutes later, she was on her way out, the case now safely hidden and her mission, at least temporarily, accomplished.

Now, it was time to deal with Bridgette. She walked to the other side of the hotel and entered the same stairwell, taking a minute to peek through the other door and see if the island security man was still outside her sister's room. He was there, vigilantly standing guard, which meant she needed to get creative if she was going to reach Bridgette. The answer was actually quite simple, and she found herself smiling as she headed back up the stairs to the second floor. Upon arriving, she walked along the hallway and looked at the room numbers until she came to number two-forty-two. Bridgette was in one-forty-two, so it stood to reason this room would be directly above. Now, all she had to do was get inside. She was versed in all manner of techniques to bypass locks, but electronic ones were tricky because there wasn't physical access to the tumblers. The other more obvious problem was the possibility that the room might be occupied, in which case this would come down to some clever subterfuge. She knocked on the door, and, a moment later, it opened to reveal a pleasant looking, middle aged man, likely northern European judging by his light blue eyes and blond hair. He looked rather surprised to see his guest and smiled bashfully.

"Hello, how can I help you?" he asked, in accented English that revealed he was indeed from Northern Europe, specifically, one of the Scandinavian countries.

"I'm here to give you your massage."

"Oh, but I didn't order one."

"It's complimentary. A little thank you from the resort."

"Well, OK then," he said, stepping aside and motioning for her to come into his room.

He took a second to eye the woman, probably realizing she didn't exactly look like a typical masseuse in her grey short skirt and fitted black shirt. Still, she was remarkably beautiful, and he found himself excited about the prospect of her giving him a massage.

"Where would you like to do it?" he asked, enthusiastically.

"The couch would work, but I think the bedroom would be more comfortable."

"Whatever you think," he said, his face flushing with color.

"Excellent, now why don't you take a shower, then make yourself at home on the bed, and I'll come in and begin once you're ready."

"Perfect!" the man said, as he left the room.

Once he was gone, she went out onto the deck and looked down to see that she was directly over her sister's room, but there was a small problem—namely, another man standing guard just beyond the patio. Fortunately, he was looking away from the building, so success would depend on her ability to pull this off as quietly as possible. She stepped over the railing and carefully lowered herself down until she was hanging from the upper balcony. It was at least another five feet to the ground, and any kind of sound would alert the guard, which meant calling upon both her Agency training and her youth spent in gymnastics. She let go with her hands and dropped, but, the minute she landed, she absorbed the impact by bending her knees and rolling off to the side, a feat not easily accomplished in a short skirt. She managed to pull it off without a sound or any major injury or wardrobe malfunction then took a second to dust herself off and adjust her clothing. With everything back in place, she stepped into her sister's room to find her sitting at the nearby vanity, where she was wearing a lovely evening dress and applying the finishing touches to her eye makeup.

"Bridgette, I need to talk to you!" she said.

Bridgette was so startled by the unplanned incursion that she nearly applied mascara to the entirety of her forehead.

"Holy shit! Where the hell did you come from?" Bridgette asked, looking surprised.

"The patio, obviously."

"Why the hell didn't you come through the front door like a normal person?"

"Because there's an island security man guarding it."

"Excuse me?" Bridgette asked, looking particularly confused.

"Island security is looking for me, but I don't have time to explain everything right now. What I can say is that you have to pack your things and leave the island on tonight's final flight to Martinique."

"Why?"

"I'm in some serious trouble."

"What did you do?"

"It's better if you don't know."

"Fine, then, I'm not going anywhere."

"Bridgette, we don't have time for this. You need to leave."

"Then tell me what's going on."

She decided to keep her answer vague.

"I took something."

"So, give it back," Bridgette responded.

"I can't."

"Why not?"

"It's not that simple."

"Then explain it to me!"

Bridgette could be particularly stubborn but also particularly perceptive and would know right away if she were lying.

"OK, here it is. I work for the CIA."

"You're a spy? But, I thought you were a pilot."

"I'm both, and the thing I took tonight is critical to the success of my mission."

"What the hell is it?"

"Doesn't matter."

"It matters if it's still on your person and they take it back."

"Don't worry, it's cleverly hidden where they won't find it."

Bridgette looked confused as she tried to process her sister's unexpected news.

"But, what happens if they capture you?"

"I'm not sure, and they might also come after you, which is why you need to leave."

"So, why don't you come with me?"

"I'd never get past security."

Bridgette thought for a moment.

"Assuming I get off the island—what happens after that? Do I contact the CIA and tell them what happened?"

"No, they already know something went wrong."

"So, they'll send help."

"No, they'll maintain plausible deniability."

"So, you're just going to stay here and get arrested? That's ridiculous! Don't you have some kind of escape plan?"

"Well, if things had gone the way they were supposed to, I would be on a boat on my way to rendezvous with a Navy cruiser."

"Wait a minute! You were going to leave me here?"

"No, I was obviously going to take you with me."

"So, why not get on the boat, now?"

"It's gone. I already missed the meeting time, and they had strict orders to leave and send an alert to my superiors in the event anything went wrong. That's how I know the Agency is aware of my situation."

The room grew quiet as Bridgette tried to come to terms with her sister's predicament.

"OK, I'll leave, but not until you come up with some kind of plan to get yourself off this island as well."

"There isn't time."

"What about your husband for God's sake? Why can't he help?"

"I'm afraid there's nothing he can do in this situation."

"Well, what about someone else at the CIA or perhaps even an old military friend? Come on! Think! There must be someone out there who can help!"

That was the million dollar question, and one she didn't know how to answer. She needed time to think this through, but she was in panic mode, and the adrenaline coursing through her body was only making it harder to consider her options. Then, when she thought all hope was lost, the perfect person came to mind.

"Finn, I need you to find Tag Finn. He's the only person in the world who could get me out of this mess."

"How do you know he'll help?"

"Because that's the kind of guy he is—plus, he owes me a favor."

"OK, but who is he, and how do I find him?"

Lux smiled and got a faraway look in her eyes.

"He's probably the most unique and capable man you'll ever meet."

"Is he an ex-boyfriend?"

"More or less."

"Well, I'd say the look in your eyes says it was a lot more serious than more or less."

"That doesn't matter right now, but what does matter is that you find him. The last I heard, he was living in Northern California in a little town called Sausalito, where he's supposedly become some kind of private investigator."

That little piece of information was not actually heard but, rather, discovered only a month ago when her fourth glass of Pinot Noir brought on a moment of nostalgic reminiscing that led to some cyberstalking of her former love. After a quick search on Google, she was combing Facebook, Instagram, and his personal website for pictures and details of his current life.

"Private investigator? What you really need is a real life James Bond."

"Don't worry, Finn was in an elite special operations unit and the CIA, so he's the closest thing in real life we're going to find."

"OK, got it. Tag Finn, private investigator in Sausalito."

"Oh—one more thing," Lux said, looking a little troubled as she chewed on her lower lip.

"What?" Bridgette asked.

"Don't tell him I'm married."

"Well, then it was definitely a lot more serious than more or less."

"Whatever, now pack and get ready. The final flight to Martinique leaves in less than an hour."

"What about you?"

"I'll evade capture as long as I can, but we're on an island, so they'll eventually find me."

"Then shouldn't you tell me where you hid this thing you stole?"

"Absolutely not. If they caught you, it would only give them a reason to torture you until you revealed its location. Believe me, you're a lot safer not knowing anything."

"Oh..."

"Yeah."

Bridgette started throwing her various items into her suitcase until she had her things packed and ready to go.

"OK, I'm ready. Are we leaving via the back patio?"

"No, there's a security guard out there as well, so that way is useless unless you can climb like a monkey and feel like giving the guy in room two-forty-two a massage."

"I'm going to have to say no to both of those options."

"Yeah, which means we need a distraction, so we can leave via the front door," she said, as she picked up the phone and called the hotel's front desk.

"Hello, this is room one-forty-two, and I'd like to report a fire."

"Excuse me, madam, did you say fire?"

"Yes, the blowdryer shorted out and started a fire in the bathroom, and the flames seem to be growing quite rapidly."

"I'll alert the island fire department and emergency services immediately!"

"Thank you."

Lux hung up and Bridgette looked at her curiously.

"Isn't your little distraction going to fail when they arrive and find out there isn't actually a fire?"

"No, because we're going to make one. Now, where is your cigarette lighter?" she asked, as she looked around the room.

"I don't have one. I quit smoking, remember?"

"Where is it, Bridgette?" she asked, in a more assertive tone.

"Fine, but just so you know, I only keep it around to light candles," Bridgette said, as she rolled her eyes and went to her purse.

Lux took the lighter from her sister then lit the edge of a hand towel and placed it in the sink. With the flames growing ever higher, she tossed the blowdryer in the sink and wafted the smoke towards the detector on the ceiling until the little device went off, and its shrill siren filled the air.

"Now what? Die of smoke inhalation?" Bridgette asked.

"No, we wait until they arrive and then slip out while they deal with the fire."

Smoke was filling the room, but, thankfully, about thirty-seconds later there was a knock at the door, and Bridgette opened it to allow an entire team of fire and emergency personnel to come rushing in—the security guard who had been in the hall leading the way. In the ensuing chaos, Lux and Bridgette slipped out of the room and exited the building to follow the paved pathway around to the front of the hotel. There were two fire trucks parked directly in front, and just beyond them was one of the island's little three-seat shuttles waiting at the curb.

"Perfect! You can take the shuttle to the casino and catch the last helicopter flight to Martinique."

Lux helped Bridgette place her things on the luggage rack, then the two sisters turned to regard each other.

"Lux! I really don't want to leave you here."

"You have to. You're my only hope."

Bridgette's eyes filled with tears as she hugged her sister.

"Stay safe," she said.

"I will," Lux responded.

"It's time to go, madam," the driver said.

Bridgette took a seat on the vehicle, and, as it began driving away from the hotel, she heard some kind of commotion and turned back to see a contingent of security men surrounding her sister. Lux appeared unfazed, however, and kept her steely gaze on Bridgette, mouthing the words—*find Tag Finn*.

CHAPTER TWO
Living the Dream

Sausalito, California — three days later.

It was eight fifteen in the morning as I sat, book in hand, with a cup of coffee that I'd just reheated in the microwave. I was with the only friend who liked taking shit more than giving it and had no problem kissing my ass. That friend was my toilet. It wasn't the most expensive piece of porcelain in the world, and it didn't heat up, talk, or clean my backside with soothing hot water like those fancy Japanese models. Instead, it was white, comfortable, modern, and had one of those spring-loaded seats that floated down slowly rather than crash onto the bowl. I would have decorated it with racing stripes, but I didn't want to do anything that might speed up the special time we spent together. A little cold at first, its contoured plastic seat quickly warmed up to my body temperature as I put down my cup, picked up my book, and let the end of the digestive cycle begin. My bathroom was my personal kingdom, the toilet my throne, and within these four walls I could relax, read, and reflect on life.

I stared at the page of my latest adventure novel, but the words could find no purchase, as my thoughts kept returning to the events of the previous evening. I had spent it working on my latest and last paying job, which entailed being perched on an old jungle gym in the park just across from the window where my two subjects were enjoying a romantic candlelit dinner consisting of pasta, salad, and red wine. The woman's name was Jessica Green. She was beautiful, just under thirty, a little over five foot eight, and worked hard to keep her figure flawless by spending two hours a day in the area's most exclusive gym. Her husband Steven was forty-eight, almost twenty years her senior, but he was still in good shape in spite of his hectic work schedule as a full partner at a well-known law firm in San Francisco. They were the perfect couple and seemed to have it all: wealth, looks, and an idyllic life in beautiful Marin County.

The problem, however, was that the guy sitting across from her at the moment wasn't her husband. The man in question was Tony Strauss, her personal trainer and likely the reason she spent so much time at the gym. The two had been hooking up for at least as long as I had been watching them, which was a little over two weeks. Her husband, my client, was in Los Angeles on a business trip, which left her especially free to meet up with Tony, or as I called him—Tarzan. That was his official nickname because his musculature and height, combined with his propensity for animal print undergarments, would make him an ideal candidate for a life in the jungle. My exciting job at the moment was to compile video and picture evidence of their adulterous activities, so that Steven could use it against her when he served her with divorce papers the following week.

So, there I sat, outside Tarzan's house in the quiet Sausalito night, with my ass frozen to the cold metal bars of the jungle gym while above me the fog stretched over the hill like a bad combover. I was taking the last sip of my lukewarm latte when I heard a sound off to my right and turned to see a family of raccoons ravaging the park's only trashcan. One of the little ones had found a used diaper and was tearing into it enthusiastically. I couldn't help but feel a little bad for the youngster, as I had inadvertently torn into plenty of shit burritos over the years—this case being one of them. Live and learn, I suppose that's all we can do in this life. I turned my attention back to Jessica and Tony, who were still enjoying their wonderful evening together on the other side of the glass, and I had to wonder what the hell I was doing out here.

The longer I worked the case, the less I liked it—or my client for that matter. He was kind of a dick when we first met, but now I realized he resided about three inches around the corner and was, in truth, a full-blown asshole. I could only imagine what it must be like for Jessica living with the fucker. He was a self-centered egotistical bastard who was obviously more emotionally invested in his elliptical trainer than his wife. It's no wonder she cheated on him, as it was probably the only way she could keep her sanity. The hypocritical prick even had a mistress, which he'd inadvertently revealed when he called me from her apartment landline. Thirty-seconds on Google and I had learned her name, address, and the fact that she was a law clerk at his firm. One night I followed the two of them and managed to get some pretty revealing footage of their hasty hump session in the front seat of his brand new Porsche 911 Turbo. Not too surprisingly, Steven's performance that night was a little subpar, and the entire video was only one minute and ten-seconds from foreplay to finish. Still, it couldn't have been an easy feat in such a small space, least of all for Steven, who wasn't exactly the limber yoga type. One wrong move and he could have easily ended up in the emergency room getting the shifter removed from his anus, which would have been pretty convenient, as the doctor might have been able to remove the stick that was already tightly wedged up there. I had crossed an ethical line by spying on my own client, but I refused to sacrifice my personal integrity for an asshole's money.

Inside, Jessica and Tony had moved to the living room couch and were enjoying more wine in front of the fireplace. They were sitting side by side and talking as Jessica gently caressed the back of his neck with her perfectly manicured nails. Tony said something, and they both laughed, then Jessica's demeanor changed as she turned towards Tony and kissed him passionately. It was her very obvious signal that she was ready to move on to the more exciting activity of the evening. She finished the last sip of wine before straddling Tony, unzipping his fly, and playfully reaching for his member, which was already hard and didn't come out of his pants without a fight. She looked at him teasingly, with a formidable grip on his manhood, as she slid down and took it in her mouth. They hadn't had anything to eat since dinner, so I guess this technically counted as dessert—more so for Tony in my opinion.

Jessica wasn't shy when it came to matters of the flesh, and she set about freeing the cream filling from Tony's cannelloni with such inspired enthusiasm that I feared watching her efforts might be enough to bring forth release from my own manhood, which was already swelling and pressing against the inseam of my pants. Only minutes passed before the pleasure appeared to be too much for him to bear, and he pulled his wood free and frantically undressed her on his red leather couch. She returned the favor by pushing him back onto the cushions and removing his trendy jeans and Abercrombie and Fitch T-shirt. Now that they were both properly naked, she proceeded to ride him like a bucking bronco—only the roles were reversed, and she was the one doing all the bucking. Not to be outdone, I took hold of my date, a cold honey-ham sandwich, and lustfully tore off the cellophane that held it in such a tight little package. I greedily took a bite, and it was obvious that Tony had the better companion this evening, as my sandwich virtually fell apart in my hands. In my haste to get out of the house, I had forgotten to layer the tomatoes between the lettuce and meat, and they had, unfortunately, soaked through and decimated the nine-grain sprouted whole wheat bread that I didn't enjoy but ate anyway because it was healthy. I took one last look at Mrs. Green's spectacular breasts before turning away to give them some privacy.

As I sat eating a cold and unsatisfying dinner, I realized that

I'd reached an all time low in my professional life. Adultery was very likely the lowest common denominator in the private investigation field other than finding lost pets, and, while there was at least something noble, if not mundane, in returning a dog or cat to its distraught owner, adultery had no winners, least of all the messenger. When people hired me to follow their wife or husband, deep down they wanted proof that their suspicions were unwarranted, that they had the perfect marriage, and life would continue happily ever after. I got to be the person who told them otherwise—a veritable harbinger that their life as they knew it was about to fall to pieces. This was my job now, and it was hard to believe how different my life had become in five years. The things I used to do changed the world and made it better, but now I took pictures of people fucking.

I glanced back inside the window for a second and saw that they were still going strong and hadn't changed positions. Normally, they were pretty experimental and would switch it up every few minutes with the precision of Chinese acrobats. Not tonight, however, as she was still on top, enthusiastically rocking up and down while Tony kept a firm hold of her breasts—even going the extra step of keeping a nipple between each thumb and forefinger. It was a good grip, one I used myself. He certainly put out more sexual effort than her husband, but then he obviously cared about her. They were disgustingly in love, and it showed in everything they did, whether it was dining, shopping, or testing out the sofa cushions on the couch in Tony's living room.

I can't say I wasn't a little jealous, as I had been single for about two months and was encountering a bit of a dry spell with the ladies. It's not like I couldn't go out and try to meet someone, but I had been busy working on a mildly interesting, though mostly pro bono, lost pet case. I say mostly because I was paid with baked goods—specifically, chocolate chip cookies. My neighbor, a widow and formidable baker named Joyce Kransky, had somehow lost her behemoth of a cat, Mr. Pickles. He had been her sole companion after her husband Harold passed away the previous year, and the two had been inseparable ever since. Strangely, the tubby tabby appeared at her doorstep the day after Harold's funeral, and I suspected that she believed Mr. Pickles was some kind of spiritual manifestation of her dearly departed husband. It didn't seem that far-fetched when you took into account the timing, and the fact that both Harold and Mr. Pickles were morbidly obese and had an almost pathological penchant for tuna fish.

Poor Joyce was devastated by the loss of Mr. Pickles, and so it fell on me to reunite her with her thirty-eight pound companion. How the hell did she lose a pet the size of a baby hippo—it's not as though the little fucker could actually walk any real distance. Considering Mr. Pickle's sedentary nature, it stood to reason that there was a possibility that he may very well have been catnapped—especially when you took into account that he had become a bit of a celebrity of sorts after winning the local Whole Foods Cutest Pet Contest. So, out I went onto the particularly un-hard streets of Sausalito where, after weeks of work and hours of following up leads, I eventually paid a sketchy anchor-out guy at the local Laundromat twenty bucks to learn that the tub of love had been spotted aboard one of the more active floating meth labs out in Richardson Bay. Few people, least of all the thousands of tourists who visited Sausalito, knew of the great divide that existed amongst the residents of this highly affluent community, and Richardson Bay, while being the sole body of water between two multi-million dollar hamlets, was littered with all manner of boats inhabited by an odd collection of misfits, ex-cons, sailing nomads, and, apparently, an obese feline named Mr. Pickles.

It wasn't the smoothest rescue operation I'd ever performed, but after disarming the meth lab's owner-operator of his Colt forty-five automatic pistol and knocking out his few remaining teeth, I was able to save Mr. Pickles from his pickle, and return him to his quiet former life as an overweight house cat. We'll probably never know exactly how the hell he got out there, but he did seem to have lost a few pounds and gained some energy upon his glorious return home. That had been my exciting job before meeting the illustrious asshole, Steven Green, and now I had the irritating job of watching his beautiful wife make sweet love to Tarzan. Wonderful—all I had at home were the twins, my right and left hands, and, if all went well, I'd get drunk and let them take advantage of me when I got home later tonight.

Tony and Jessica finished and lay entwined in each other's arms on the couch in front of the fire, and it certainly looked warmer and more inviting than my shitty perch in the playground. Eventually they got dressed and headed into the kitchen to clean up their dishes from dinner. I climbed down and walked around the block to the front door and realized that this was going to be awkward, but I felt I owed it to them after spying on them for the better part of two weeks. It was ten-thirty and not a polite hour to be ringing a stranger's doorbell, but it had to be done. I pushed the button and heard footsteps approaching from inside, and the door opened a second later. Tony stood there with Jessica hovering just behind him, and both looked surprised to see a complete stranger standing on the doorstep.

"Good evening, how would you like a personal relationship with Jesus Christ?" I asked.

"Excuse me, but it's a little late."

"It's never too late for Jesus."

"Goodnight," Tony said, as he started to close the door.

So much for my wacky icebreaker.

"Wait, I'm just kidding. I'm actually here to speak with Jessica. Nothing to do with Jesus, I promise."

He turned to Jessica and asked her if she knew me, but she shook her head.

"I'm here regarding your husband, Steven Green."

She looked concerned as she stepped closer and stood beside Tony in the doorway. It was my first time seeing her up close and personal, and she was even more beautiful than I could have imagined. She was nearly thirty but could have easily passed for twenty with her baby smooth skin, bright blue eyes, and long light brown hair. She also smelled particularly good and happened to be wearing the same expensive Chanel perfume that my ex had worn. I liked the perfume but hated the ex, so I suppose those two facts kind of cancelled each other out. I could see that she was wondering who in the hell I was and what news I might have concerning her husband, so I cut to the chase.

"My name's Finn. I'm a private investigator, and what I'm about to tell you is going to come as a little bit of a shock."

"What is it?" she asked, sounding concerned.

She was probably hoping that Steven had been hit by a bus. I was kind of wishing he had been as well, as it would have made it a lot easier for both of us.

"Your husband hired me to follow you and get proof that you're having an affair with Tarzan—I mean Tony."

"Are you fucking kidding me?" she asked.

"No, sadly, I'm not. I've been watching you for the last two weeks, and I'm sorry to say that I've got more evidence than I could possibly need—pictures, videos, pretty much everything except a signed confession and a semen sample from Tar—eh—Tony."

I could see her heart begin to beat faster, her face reddening as her world turned upside down in the space of a few words.

"You've been following us around? Filming us? What kind of sick asshole would do that for a living? Why don't you get a real life? Better yet, why don't you go fuck yourself," she said, angrily.

Truer words had never been spoken, and later tonight I would probably be doing exactly as she suggested. I glanced at Tony and saw that his face was turning red, and he was clenching his jaw, which meant his anger was steadily increasing, and it was only a matter of time before he did something we'd both regret.

"What the fuck do you want from us, asshole? Are you trying to extort money? See if we'll pay you more not to tell Steven anything?" he asked.

"No, I'm not here for anything like that."

It was too late, as Tony was already halfway out the door, winding up to take a swing, and moving like an enraged bull storming out of the gate at a rodeo. He was a big guy, easily six four, with a lot of gym time under his belt and enough muscle to make the Incredible Hulk look like a big green pussy. I wasn't exactly small at six foot, but I had been watching Tarzan from afar and only now realized just how big he was in person. They say the camera adds ten pounds, but, at this moment, I would say it takes away about forty as Tony was looking a hell of a lot bigger than he did through my camera lens. At least he wasn't much of a fighter, though he probably didn't need to be, as his size and strength would be more than enough to deter any sane person from tangling with him, and any insane person could easily be ground into protein powder if he foolishly managed to get within Tony's formidable grasp. Fortunately, I brought with me the tools of a lifetime spent in the martial arts, military, and clandestine services, and I'd had the displeasure of using them more times than I could recall.

Tony was slow, and it was like watching a fight scene at half speed as he came at me with a big right roundhouse punch that couldn't have been more obvious had he called me the week before and told me it was coming. People never expected you to move towards an attack, as it went against human instinct, but, in this instance, it was the best way to gain the advantage with a big guy like Tony. I stepped forward, inside the arc of his punch, and blocked his swing with a heel palm strike to the middle of his bicep—the goal being to traumatize the radial nerve and create a mild muscular paralysis. It lessened the force of his attack, especially when combined with a simultaneous slap to his face. The bicep strike was meant to hurt and temporarily disable the arm while the slap was more of a psychological inroad just to get his attention. He was basically a nice guy, so I wanted to get him under control without actually putting him in the hospital. The slap worked, and, while Tony processed the strike to his face, I was able to easily lift his now deadened right arm and take his balance, allowing me to guide his head down and roll the oversized garden gnome gently onto the grass, where he landed on his back beside his beloved azaleas—shaken and a little stirred. His ego and his bicep might be bruised, but he was technically still unharmed. Jessica, however, obviously felt otherwise, for, after seeing our brief exchange, she ran from the house to comfort Tony as he lay on the ground.

"I'm calling the police," she said, angrily.

"That's not a good idea, as there will be a police report. Both of your names will appear on it, and your husband will be able to use that as evidence against you as well."

"What the hell do you want from us?"

"If you and Tarzan would just listen for a minute, I could tell you why I came here tonight. First, and most importantly, I'd like to affirm the fact that your husband is a complete asshole, but I'm sure you already know that. Secondly, I wanted to warn you that the afore mentioned asshole hired me because he's about to serve you with divorce papers."

She stared at me, unsure what to say as she tried to figure out what motive I may have in telling her this news. At last, her expression softened, and she held her hand out towards the door.

"Do you want to come inside and talk?" she asked.

"What about the ape man? Are we going to have to give him a banana or something to calm him down?"

"He can play with Cheetah while we talk."

"Very funny," Tony said.

I reached down and offered Tony my hand. I had put him on the ground, so it was the least I could do to help him back up. He reluctantly took it then followed Jessica and me into the house. We went into the kitchen, and she asked if I wanted something to drink. I never turned down a beautiful woman offering alcohol so I, of course, said yes, and she made us both a vodka tonic. She neglected to make one for Tony, who poured himself another glass of wine, which seemed kind of dainty for a guy who swung through the trees with a monkey companion. We went into the living room, and I purposely avoided the couch, not sure if they had cleaned it up yet, and, instead, sat on the edge of the fireplace.

"So, what's your story? Why are you telling me all this if you work for my husband?"

"I don't anymore. I'm quitting tonight, and I'm erasing the pictures and returning his deposit. He's going to be mildly fucked when I destroy all the evidence, but I can't give it to him in good conscience. Now, you'll at least be on an even playing field and have the time to get yourself a good attorney and be ready for the asshole."

"So, you don't want anything from us? You're telling me this just to be a nice guy?"

"It probably sounds silly, but I got into this business to help people, and, right now, I think you need my help more than your husband."

"But, he paid you."

"It's not always about money. You seem a lot nicer than Steven, and I don't want to help him ruin your life."

I glanced out the window at my hiding spot in the playground and realized it was certainly nicer to be on this side of the glass, where I could feel the warmth of the fire and be in the direct company of the beautiful Mrs. Green. I hoped Tony appreciated what he had here.

"Thanks for the drink. That's all I wanted to say, so I should probably get going. Your husband will be calling any minute, and I have to give him my final report, and, needless to say, he's not going to be too happy."

"I'll walk you out," she said.

We stood up and walked to the front door and stood there awkwardly, neither of us sure what to say, until she broke the silence.

"I know it doesn't matter, but he cheated on me first."

"I know, and the shitbag is still cheating on you. Speaking of which, I have a little gift for you to make up for invading your privacy for the last two weeks. It's a number of files I put together on his mistress, and it includes a detailed report, pictures, and a short video of your husband screwing her in the Porsche. It should help when you go to court," I said, as I pulled a flash drive out of my pocket and handed it over to her.

"Thanks. The video must be short if it's Steven."

"It is. One minute and ten-seconds. Oh, and a word of advice. In case he hires another private detective, you guys need to keep a lower profile. No more holding hands in public or having sex in the living room."

"You saw us?"

"Yeah—sorry. It's a sleazy but necessary evil of the job. I try to maintain as much professionalism as I can but..."

"But you're filming strangers while they have sex."

"Yeah, sometimes I feel more like an avant-garde adult movie director. No direct contact with my actors. Lots of improv—very cutting edge."

"Maybe there's a new career in there somewhere."

"God no. It's not very fun to watch other people have sex when you've been single for a while."

"I thought that's why men watch porn?"

"Yeah, but I like my women real and in person."

"That's a good thing."

"Eh—time will tell. Well, I better be going."

"Hey, thank you for coming to me. Not many people would do that. My husband is the type of person who believes that he can buy anything, including people. It says a lot about you that you didn't take his money."

"We'll see how noble I am when I'm destitute and homeless."

"Don't worry, I'll put a dollar in your cup, if it comes to that," she said.

"Good to know. Well, I hope everything works out for you

guys."

She held out her hand, and we exchanged one of those awkward male to female handshakes that usually was the way a woman would end a date if she had no intention of ever seeing you again. The only thing you were ever going to get to touch would be that hand. Jessica's handshake, however, was warm and obviously more appropriate than a hug considering we hardly knew each other. I started to turn towards the front gate, but she kept hold of my hand and, instead, pulled me back around so that we were face to face again.

"Hey, Finn, you won't be single for long. You're a nice guy in spite of your job."

"Thanks," I said, smiling as I thought about her compliment.

She smiled back, and I realized that the lovely soon to be *Miss* Jessica Green would haunt my dreams for many a night to come. I was about to leave when the phone rang, and I looked down to see who was calling.

"Guess who?" I asked.

"Say hello to asshole for me," she said, as she turned and walked back towards the house.

It took me five rings to get into my car and hit the answer button.

"Well?" he asked, in an irritated tone.

I knew from previous experience that Steven, or should I say, asshole, could be a little testy at having to wait so long for me to answer. He thought that paying for my services meant I was at his beck and call, and, therefore, expected me to answer within two rings. It would have been too funny to answer the phone with *hello, asshole*, but I refrained and tried to keep it all very business-like considering the delicate nature of what I was about to tell him. Of course, it was only fitting to at least fuck with him a little bit.

"Tag Finn Investigations, how may I direct your call?"

"Not funny, dickhead, now, stop fucking around and give me

the final update."

I gave it to him just like he did his mistress—hard, fast, and without lubrication.

"I'm sorry, Steven, but, as far as I can tell, Jessica isn't having an affair. She seems like the perfect wife to me, and, might I say, you're a very lucky man."

"Bullshit. You know as well as I do that the bitch is fucking around. Are you trying to drive up your fee? Fine, but you better fucking deliver the goods."

"It's not about the money. I'll be returning your retainer, and we can end our agreement effective immediately."

"Fuck you! You're going to finish the Goddamn job."

"I'm trying to keep this professional, Steven. It's over. Our contract states very clearly that I can terminate our agreement if I decide that you're too much of an asshole."

"Look here—if you fuck with me, then you can forget about ever working in this town again. I will ruin you, and let me tell you, fuckface—you better pray you don't run into me when I get back into town, because I will fucking take you apart."

"Those are some strong words coming from a guy whose entire sexual encounters last one minute and ten seconds. That's not a lot of cardio, so you better wait until you can go at least two minutes then give me a call, tough guy."

"Fuck you, I'll bury you, you son of a bitch!" he screamed, just before I ended the call.

CHAPTER THREE
A New Hope

It was a hell of a way to end a night and likely the beginning of a personal financial disaster if I didn't find a new client soon. It had been easy to take Steven Green's money, but it was even easier to return it once I discovered that he was a complete asshole. I realized there was no point in trying to read my book, and I put it down and took another sip of coffee. I needed to clear my mind and let the dump be my spirit guide to a better place. Everything would work out. It always did. I regarded the four walls of my personal sanctuary, exhaled, and let the anxiety pour from my body like water from a snow pack in spring. Things started to move down in my intestines, and all was well with the world. I couldn't see from inside the house, but I'm sure there was a rainbow touching down on it at this very moment—my toilet the veritable pot of gold. I'd find a new client and, in the meantime, have a damn good dump. Then, my phone rang.

"Goddammit."

Now? I didn't expect fate to intervene this quickly and shouldn't have even brought my phone into the bathroom, but I always did. It was some kind of obsessive-compulsive thing like checking to make sure the stove was off before I left the house. Why couldn't my phone have rung even five or ten minutes later? Fate was obviously a cruel mistress and knew that I really couldn't afford to miss a call and have it go to voicemail, as, in my experience, people who didn't reach a live person often called someone else.

"Ahhh farts."

I thought it might be my ex-client Steven calling to berate me about my lack of professionalism, but I didn't recognize the caller's number. There was no way I had time to finish up in the bathroom before I answered, so I was in a bit of a conundrum. It might be the new client that I desperately needed or, quite possibly, a stupid telemarketer telling me I'd won a cruise. I'd never know unless I answered.

"Double fucking farts!"

I mustered my resolve and hit the answer button.

"Tag Finn Investigations," I said, as pleasantly as possible.

"Hello?"

"Yeah, hello."

"Hi, my name is Bridgette Vandenberg. I got your number from your website. Is it a good time to talk?"

Perfect. It was a work call, and I wasn't even halfway through my dump and could only pray it would be quiet and uneventful. The last food item I had eaten was that ham sandwich outside Tarzan's house last night, and I was hopeful it wouldn't cause a gastrointestinal symphony at an inopportune moment. You only had one chance to make a first impression, and I didn't want to make this one getting caught dropping a deuce. Sure, everyone goes to the bathroom, but what kind of professional would even think about taking a business call on the crapper—besides me, obviously. So, now, I had something important to consider—namely, acoustics. It's hard, if not impossible, to disguise a call in a bathroom because of the natural reverb created by the hard surfaces. I was lucky that my girlfriend, one girlfriend back, said this bathroom needed more style and made me buy an IKEA rug, candles, and some knickknacks to dress it up. It looked better because of her feminine touch, but the real advantage was sound deadening. I wouldn't even consider answering a phone in a public restroom. They were even larger and had more reverb, which easily carried the grunts, groans, and bathroom sounds to the person on the other end of the call. Yet another reason I avoided public restrooms.

"Yeah, how can I help you?"

"Well, it's complicated."

There was that word—complicated. I had grown to dislike it over the last few years, because I had heard it so often from my prospective clients. It was such an annoyingly vague term, and whenever I asked people about their case, they would all tell me it's complicated, and it didn't matter if it was money disappearing from their business account, a cheating spouse, or a lost cat. It's not usually that complicated. People's problems generally stem from the most basic of human frailties: pride, gluttony, greed, sloth, wrath, envy, and, of course, lust. Why did your wife cheat on you? The answer is usually simple. Either you're an asshole, she's a bitch, or the pool boy has a twelve-inch penis, and now you know why your pillow smells like chlorine every night. Money disappearing from your business accounts? It's your asshole partner spending it on nooky parlors or a new Porsche. In the case of the cat, if it's not living at a meth lab, it's usually at the neighbor's house because they feed it better. Oh God—something was rumbling down below, and, as I tried my best to keep the back door locked down, a loud voluminous fart escaped and echoed off the bowl.

"Hello? Are you there? What was that noise?"

Fuck you ham sandwich! I'd forgotten about the nine-grain sprouted whole wheat bread, and now I needed to think fast.

"Oh, that was just some guy on a sailboat blowing his horn as he left the nearby yacht harbor. It happens all the time."

"Oh, well, should I tell you my story now? Do you want to take notes?"

Fuck no! All I've got is my iPhone, and there's no way in hell I can type and talk at the same time without the risk of dropping it in the toilet. I really needed to get out of the bathroom.

"Um—just a second, as I'm in the kitchen cleaning up, and I'll need to go to my office."

I tried to sound casual as I finished up, but every noise seemed infinitely louder, and wiping my ass sounded as though I were sanding a table. I could only hope that she thought I was scrubbing burnt food off a skillet. I stood up and was about to flush, but I realized I couldn't, as the noise would be a dead giveaway. I'd have to come back and do it after I got off the phone. I gently closed the lid, washed my hands as quietly as I could, then went into my office and grabbed a notepad.

"Alrighty then, let's hear your story."

"You know, I'm actually outside your place right now."

"Um—what?"

"The address on your website was the harbor office, and the guy there was nice enough to give me directions to your place, so, is it OK if I just come in and we talk in person?"

No way in hell.

"Yeah, great, I'll be right there."

My bathroom was only ten feet from the front door, which meant I couldn't go flush the toilet, because she'd hear it and know that I had been in the bathroom. Shit. I really shouldn't be this paranoid, but this was a potential new client and the most likely way I would cover the house payment this month. She might be a wealthy heiress willing to pay big money to track down a long lost family member, though, with my luck, she'll probably turn out to be a crazy woman who has lost one of her nineteen cats. Still, a paying client was a paying client.

I set off down the hallway, and my anticipation grew with each step until I placed my hand on the knob, took a deep breath to calm my nerves, then opened the door. Holy shit! Shock, fear, and lust were only a few of the emotions to cross my mind in the first instant of seeing the woman standing outside. She looked completely out of place on my doorstep and would have been more at home on the cover of one of the fashion magazines at the checkout stand of my local grocery store. She was probably in her late twenties and drop-dead gorgeous with her long brown hair, perfect skin, and spectacularly light blue eyes. She was also wearing tight fitting exercise clothing, and it adhered nicely to her curves and showed off her figure, which was athletic and toned but still curvaceous in all the right places. It was strange, but the longer I looked at her, the more familiar she seemed. It was kind of like when you ran into someone from high school who you hadn't seen in years and had trouble remembering his or her name and face. I have an almost photographic memory for people, and I was pretty sure, however, that this was our first meeting.

My heart was now racing as I stood there and smiled stupidly, entranced by her beauty and the sweet scent of her perfume as it wafted over me on the light bay breeze. At long last, her mouth abruptly turned up in a questioning smile, and I realized it was probably about time to stop staring and start talking.

"Morning," I said, at last breaking from my stupor.

"Morning. I hope I didn't catch you off guard. I didn't realize you worked out of your home. I wouldn't want to disturb your wife or family."

"No—no problem there. No wife or family. No one here but me."

"Girlfriend?"

"Not at the moment."

"Strange, you're a good-looking guy. Are you damaged or gay?"

"I'm wearing Crocs. What do you think?"

"Damaged."

"Good guess. Come on in."

She laughed, and I realized she looked even better when she smiled, as her perfect white teeth glowed brightly behind her full sensuous lips. Goddamn this girl was attractive. I motioned her past me into the house and almost had a heart attack when she stalled outside my office.

"Should we talk in there?"

God no, it's too close to the bathroom. Instead, I suggested we go to the back deck. The view was nice, and it was a better place to meet and allowed me to take advantage of one of the few fogless sunny days we managed to get this time of year. I hustled her through the house and out onto the deck, where I offered her a seat at my weather-beaten patio table. It was only a year old, but the constant cycle of sun, wind, and fog made it look years older. I really should have gone to Costco and gotten new stuff so I could impress the clients, but my budget was already strained by the more important necessities such as food, alcohol, and toilet paper. Fortunately, Bridgette didn't seem to mind its appearance, and I was relieved to see the deck didn't have the usual accumulation of bird droppings. It was nice living on the water, but it meant sharing your space with a lot of wildlife, mostly seagulls. I shit in my bathroom, while they shit on my deck. Fortunately, the larger animals, like the sea lions, which sunned and slept on the nearby breakwater, did their business in the bay. We sat down and everything seemed to be going along perfectly, until she asked if she could use the bathroom. Oh shit—not now. She started to stand, but I got to my feet first.

"Oh, don't get up. I'm old enough to go all by myself," she said.

"Um, why don't you use the bathroom on the bottom level. The one on this floor has a broken toilet. Just head down the stairs, and it'll be the third door on the right."

"Thanks."

Now was my chance. As she headed downstairs, I raced into the bathroom, flushed the toilet, then sprayed a tiny spritz of air freshener. The amount was critical, because if I sprayed too much, the spring potpourri scent would travel into the hall and be as obvious as a trail of shit leading to the toilet. Satisfied I had done a decent job, I had a quick peak at myself in the mirror and frowned at my haphazard appearance. Damn it—I hadn't even gotten to my shower yet, and I looked like a jackass in my board shorts, T-shirt, and crocs. How could she have possibly thought that I might be gay, when no self-respecting gay man would ever be caught looking this bad? Clearly, I needed to have a little talk with the harbor office about indiscriminately giving out my address to prospective clients. I took a moment to steady my nerves then stepped out of the bathroom only to run into Bridgette as she arrived at the top of the stairs.

"Did I hear a toilet flush?" she asked.

"No—well—yeah. I just fixed it."

"Just now? You're a handy guy."

"Yeah, I suppose I am."

She took a moment to sniff the air then looked puzzled as she regarded me.

"Is that potpourri?"

Yeah, and the remnants of that Goddamn traitorous ham sandwich.

"No idea. Maybe it's my neighbor's flower garden," I said.

"On a houseboat?"

"Yeah, it's in a planter box on her patio."

She raised an eyebrow, half smiled, then turned to walk back outside to the deck. So much for first impressions. We sat down, and, as I looked at her from across the table, I once again couldn't shake the feeling that she looked familiar.

"I saw all those pictures in the bathroom," she said.

"Oh yeah, the wall of shame."

She was referring to the pictures of my days as a United States Air Force Parajumper or PJ: the last remnants of my glorious youth sadly adorning the walls of a gloomy downstairs bathroom—the one I should have used today.

"That's a pretty manly decorating style. Guys really have a thing about their bathrooms—like it's a temple or something. My ex-boyfriend would have never read if he didn't sit on a toilet. Honestly, I don't get it."

"Me neither—I never really spend that much time in there," I lied.

She didn't look as though she believed me, and we sat there in awkward silence until she asked if I had any coffee. Shit, I should have already offered. What a lame host. This girl had me off balance.

"Excellent idea. How do you like it?" I asked, as I stood up and headed for the kitchen.

"Weak and sweet—like my men."

I stopped and turned back towards her not sure I had heard her correctly.

"Seriously?"

"No, I was just kidding. I like my men strong and sweet."

"So, like me."

"Yeah, like you, but without the Crocs," she said, with a little smile.

I turned and continued on my way, unconsciously making a last second detour into the bathroom to grab my coffee cup. As I reappeared, I realized the error of my ways when I saw that she was watching my every move.

"Kind of strange to bring your coffee into a bathroom that doesn't work," she said.

"You always this observant?"

"You always take your coffee into the bathroom?"

"I'm pleading the fifth on this one."

"Good idea."

I'd only known this woman ten minutes, and she was already giving me shit. Might as well get a late breakfast and go ring shopping. I turned and chugged the last sip of lukewarm coffee in my cup then walked to the kitchen, where I brewed a fresh pot, poured two cups, and headed back out to the deck. I handed her a cup as I sat down at the table, and she eyed it suspiciously, with one eyebrow raised as she held it before her pouty lips.

"This isn't the cup from the bathroom is it?" she asked.

I waited until she took her first sip before I responded.

"No, but I'm sure you'll tell me if the coffee tastes like shit."

She stifled a laugh, and it caused her to nearly spit out her entire mouthful of coffee—which, in turn, made her laugh even harder.

"*Touché*," she said, when she finally stopped laughing enough to swallow.

I took a sip of my own coffee and had to smile, as clients were rarely this fun and never this beautiful. Unfortunately, the deck we were sitting on was in dire jeopardy of returning to the possession of the bank that technically owned it, so it was time to get down to business. I asked her how I could help, and she sat for a moment, collecting her thoughts before looking directly into my eyes and speaking.

"I need you to rescue my sister."

That was the last thing I expected to hear, and I had to wonder if I heard her correctly.

"Excuse me?"

"I said—I need you to rescue my sister."

"That's a pretty unusual request."

"Well, it's a pretty unusual situation."

"Interesting. Do you and your sister happen to look fairly similar to each other?"

"If you're asking if we look alike, the answer would obviously be yes, as we're sisters."

"Then I can only assume that she was taken captive while on location shooting the latest Sports Illustrated Swimsuit edition."

"Afraid not."

"So, she's a Victoria's Secret runway model who was spirited away by a dashing, though diabolical, billionaire with a penchant for bondage."

She laughed.

"Wrong again, and, while I appreciate the backhanded compliment, I'm afraid you're way off the mark. As I said before, it's complicated."

"Are we talking kidnapping complicated, because I primarily do investigative work like background checks and cheating spouses," I said, as I spied Mr. Pickles on the adjacent deck, where he was busy licking one of his chubby paws.

I wasn't about to tell her that I also worked the occasional lost pet case, as it seemed to detract from my credibility.

"If it's really kidnapping, then that's something you should be talking to the FBI about."

"The FBI can't help. The United States has no jurisdiction where she's being held. In fact, nobody does. She's in the Caribbean imprisoned on a little speck of land called Soft Taco Island."

I couldn't help but laugh as I stood up and walked to the railing. I always thought better on my feet, and I decided I needed to stand to hear this story. Soft Taco Island? I'd never heard of it. Perhaps it was owned by Jimmy Buffet and was the location of his fabled *Margaritaville*.

"It's not a laughing matter," she said, taking on a serious tone.

"OK, I'm sorry, but Soft Taco Island?"

"Yeah, and it's not as innocent a place as it sounds."

I didn't think it sounded innocent. It sounded more like a brothel or a sleazy version of Club Med. It might as well be Vagina Island, or best case scenario, it could be a fast food chain down on the water in Florida. Guys in Speedo's with lots of body hair and oily skin could pull up to Soft Taco Island in exotic speedboats and order the daily special, which would consist of two taco's and a gordita—the gordita being an overweight Latina hooker. All three would come with extra cheese.

"This is serious. My sister's life is at stake," she said, in a more pleading tone.

"Have you spoken to the State Department?"

"Trust me, they can't help."

The girl who had been smiling and giving me shit only moments earlier set her coffee cup down on the table and gripped it with both hands as though it were the only thing holding her up at the moment. When she looked up, I could see tears forming in her eyes. Oh, Goddammit. Women often used crying to manipulate men, and, while I was good at reading people, I couldn't tell if the tears were real or not. I'd have to give her the benefit of the doubt for now.

"OK, explain it to me."

She wiped her eyes with her sleeve, took a long breath to gain her composure, then continued with her story.

"It's more complicated because Soft Taco Island is a sovereign nation in the Caribbean. No one has any jurisdiction there, and the so-called president is just a criminal with a nice facade who pretty much does whatever he wants with total impunity."

"So, why are they holding your sister? It wouldn't exactly promote tourism if they imprisoned their guests."

"She was more than a guest."

"Meaning what? Employee?"

"In a manner of speaking, but it would be more accurate to say she was there working for her country."

"Peace Corps?"

"Hardly—her employer is a bit more proactive."

Proactive? What the hell was that supposed to mean? What would a woman, very likely smart and sexy judging by her sister, be doing working abroad for the United States? And then it hit me—like a swift kick to the balls.

"She works for the CIA," I said.

"Yep."

"So, why on God's green earth are you talking to me?"

"Plausible deniability."

I knew that term only too well and had also lived under its ominous specter. Every agent knew that the CIA would disavow any connection to them should they be detained in a foreign country, and, if that were the case with Bridgette's sister, then she was indeed quite fucked.

"So, what the hell was your sister doing on Soft Taco Island?"

"Working as a helicopter pilot. At least that's what I thought until she came running into my room and told me she worked for the CIA and was about to be arrested for stealing something."

"What did she steal?"

"No idea. She wouldn't tell me, because she said it was safer if I didn't know."

"That's probably true."

"Yeah, so, just before she got arrested, she told me to leave the island and go get help."

"I hate to say this but getting someone out of a foreign country is no small task—regardless how small the country happens to be. It can take some serious money and resources."

"No need to worry about either of those things, as my family will help with that part."

"I assume they're wealthy?"

"Very."

"Why don't they use diplomatic channels? Do it the easy way?"

"Have you heard of the Vandenbergs?"

The name was familiar, because I had read about them in an exceptionally boring business magazine that I'd picked up in the waiting room of my doctor's office. If I remembered correctly, the Vandenbergs ranked pretty close to Larry Ellison on an America's wealthiest list.

"Yeah, your family is loaded, billionaires many times over. They could probably just call the president and ask for his help."

"We don't exactly have a normal family."

Bridgette went on to explain the unusual Vandenberg family dynamic. They owned majority shares in everything that mattered including software, aerospace, oil, mining, and media companies. Their father, Daniel Vandenberg, the eldest of identical twin brothers by three and a half minutes, had used his unique business acumen and fearlessness to grow a moderate fortune into a multi-billion dollar empire. Sadly, the girls' mother died in a car accident when they were teenagers, and their father remarried a few years later. The woman in question was a beautiful oil heiress named LeAnne Boone, who he had met while on vacation on the island of Kauai. Her family's oil money, however, was disappearing faster than the toilet paper in the porta potty behind an all you can eat taco truck, so it wasn't exactly a stretch to assume that she hadn't married Daniel for love alone. The new Mrs. Vandenberg never warmed to her stepdaughters and, instead, used her diabolical mind and magical vagina to drive a wedge between the girls and their father. Needless to say, Bridgette and her sister would rarely make it home to visit after leaving for college.

They would grow to regret this, however, when their father died in an untimely manner in a helicopter crash while on his way to inspect a new oil rig in the Gulf of Mexico. All control went to their Uncle William, a divorcee with no children who had been in his brother's shadow his entire life. He was, therefore, more than happy to take hold of the empire and, shortly thereafter, his late brother's wife. The two exchanged their vows in a quiet ceremony on Maui since Kauai supposedly brought back too many memories of Daniel—something I found particularly ironic considering the fact that she was marrying his twin brother. With their uncle in charge and their wicked stepmother fucking their uncle, the girls had apparently become mostly estranged from the Vandenberg family.

"It's a family tale befitting of a Shakespearean tragedy," I said.

"Yeah, but, unfortunately, it's our actual life."

"I don't get it. If your wicked ex-stepmother and uncle are too lame to help your sister, how can you hire me?"

"My uncle doesn't want the family name connected with any of this, but he will pay all your expenses and add a substantial bonus if you get her off Soft Taco Island unscathed and without any kind of media circus."

"What kind of bonus?"

"One million dollars."

Holy shit. A million dollars wasn't all that much these days, but it would sure go a long way towards rescuing me from my current financial disaster. She took hold of my hands and stared intently into my eyes, her expression desperate, and I couldn't help but feel a little intimidated by her touch.

"Will you help me?"

I certainly could use the money, and it was a hell of a story, but my intuition was contradicting all the good stuff my penis and wallet were chattering about. I hadn't been very happy when I left the Agency, and the thought of bailing out one of their agents wasn't all that enticing. I think she could tell I was wavering because she delivered the *pièce de résistance*.

"There's another thing. You know my sister. Well, she at least knows you, and she told me to find you specifically. She said you were the one person in the world who could get her off Soft Taco Island—and she said you owed her a favor."

What the hell did that mean? I sat there thinking about the words I had just heard from this intriguingly beautiful woman, and then it hit me. I finally understood why Bridgette looked so familiar, and I should have already put it together when she said her sister was a helicopter pilot. My stomach turned inside out, and I felt dizzy like the first time I had parachuted out of a C-130 back in my military days. I had to sit down and take a moment to steady my nerves. It didn't matter what my intuition, penis, and wallet were arguing about because my heart would have the final say. There was only one person in the world that I owed that kind of favor.

CHAPTER FOUR
So that Others May Live Happily Ever After

MARCH 2005, BAGRAM AIR FORCE BASE,
AFGHANISTAN—TEN YEARS EARLIER.

It was seven thirty-one in the morning, Operation Red Wings was in full swing, and I was just trying to enjoy my morning dump when I heard the unmistakable voice of Lieutenant Wallace calling my name. He was a fellow PJ of Scottish descent who was supposedly related to the illustrious Scotsman William Wallace, but, regardless of his potentially regal family history, he was ruining the beginning of my day.

"This is my quality time. What do you want, Corn?"

I called him Corn because his first name was Cornelius. Plus, he was from the Midwest and, therefore, basically corn fed, thus making his nickname work twofold. He went to Notre Dame on a football scholarship and joined the Air Force after graduating. He was tall, good-looking, nice to a fault, and, typical of most farm boys, strong as a bull. I considered him to be my best friend in the

Air Force, and I could always count on him when the chips were down. If you got into the shit, you would always find Corn, literally and figuratively. We were both Lieutenants, but rank didn't exactly matter in special operations and even less so in our little corner called Pararescue. Real respect came down to two critical factors: giving each other shit and job performance. I excelled at both.

In some ways, I found a career in the military to be an odd fit and kind of contradictory to my independent nature. I had always been a freethinker and major league wiseass, but neither of those qualities were exactly tolerated or condoned in the regular military. Fortunately, I was in special operations, and it was either by divine intervention or my considerable inner strength that I had been able to keep my mouth shut long enough to make it through one of the toughest training programs in the United States military. Of course, every branch in the service will claim that their particular training is harder and their units more elite, but, from what I'd seen out in the field, they were all good at what they did. Every unit had its unique specialty, and Pararescue's was saving people. Like SEALs, we operated on sea, air, and land but had the added benefit of intense comprehensive medical training. It didn't matter if you were out in the ocean or pinned down by enemy fire in the middle of the desert, because we'd find you and get you out alive. So that others may live. That was our motto, and we lived by it every day.

"Need to see you in the situation room ASAP. The operation that went out this morning went to shit, as the entire area was overrun with fucking Taliban. There's more, but I'll wait until you pinch it off and get the hell out of there."

Shit. I had friends on that mission. You never wanted to hear news like this during a morning dump, as it was a bad omen. I finished up, washed my hands, and followed Corn outside.

"I can't believe I actually got you to cut your special time short," he said.

"Hey, I consider spending time with you special as well."

"Since taking a dump is technically number two, I suppose that makes me number one by default," he said, with a smile.

We walked across the base and into a very tense situation room filled with the usual muckety mucks and assorted team leaders. It was bad news all around, as we had a SEAL team in trouble and a downed helicopter. The helicopter, however, was the bigger problem at the moment, as the pilot happened to be Captain John Matheson, the son of a very powerful and influential United States Senator and, therefore, far too valuable an asset to let fall into the Taliban's hands. He was also a close friend, stand up guy, reasonably shitty poker player, and, unfortunately for the rest of us, annoyingly good with the ladies. I liked him. He could have had any posting in the world with his family connections, but he was here in the shit with the rest of us.

His mission had been to drop off a SEAL Team on top of a supposedly deserted ridge in the Korengal Valley. He got the team in, but the area turned out to be overrun with Taliban and Al Qaeda forces. He tried to go back in for a pickup, but his chopper's main rotor was damaged by a RPG, and he was forced to make a crash landing. A predator drone confirmed the location of the downed bird, and Matheson, according to his last radio report, was, apparently, the only survivor. The SEALs, dealing with their own shit storm were unable to reach him and requested the assistance of the US Army Ranger quick-reaction force stationed at Bagram. This was officially now a rescue operation, which meant that Corn and I, as part of the Joint Special Operations Command, were also a key component to the plan. The Taliban had just ruined my dump, and someone, probably a recreational goat herder with bad teeth and a penchant for stoning teen girls to death, would hopefully pay for it later tonight. Operation Lost Sheep was about to begin, and our unit code name was Little Bo Peep.

Not wanting to lose another helicopter, the brass decided to deploy the Rangers west of the ridge to establish a secure landing zone, while the SEALs would wait for nightfall and travel under the cover of darkness to rendezvous with the Rangers. Corn and

I would parachute in directly to the downed helicopter's position, establish a safe perimeter, then treat any survivors and exfiltrate to the landing zone before first light. It wasn't the greatest plan for us, and, in a perfect world, I would have liked a larger team. Unfortunately, the brass believed a smaller force had a greater chance of success, because it could get in and out more stealthily, and should anyone catch wind of our presence, having only Corn and me running around the mountains would belie the true importance of the mission. It was going to be a hell of a tough night, but saving people is what PJ's do for a living. After the mission briefing was over, Corn and I went back to our barracks to prepare our gear, which entailed packing our chutes, checking our weapons, and making sure we had a shitload of medical supplies. It was a lot of items to bring into combat, but it was also the difference between life and death for the people we went to help.

With everything ready to go we had a little downtime to sit, reflect, and mentally prepare for the mission ahead. I generally preferred the more quiet meditative zen approach, though I suspect that was a product of my age. At twenty-seven, I was an elder statesman in this group, and PJ's, who were generally a bit older than the average soldier due to the length and difficulty of their training, were still a tad bit younger than I. The Rangers were even younger and generally spent their pre-mission free time watching movies or masturbating. I suppose I did a bit of that too, but I think my age and wisdom made my sessions more prolonged and meaningful—or at least that's what I kept telling myself.

The end of the day finally arrived, and I turned my gaze out the window and saw that the sun was just setting behind the distant mountains. That meant we were approaching go-time, and Corn picked up his pack and asked if I was ready to roll. I nodded then grabbed my goodies, and we headed out to the tarmac for the final briefing. The Rangers were clustered around the two Chinook Helicopters, and the Lieutenant Colonel in charge of the Joint Special Operations Command was giving them some final words of encouragement. Once finished, he came over and spoke to Corn and me.

"Good evening gentlemen! I hope that you're ready to find our lost sheep," he said.

"It shouldn't be a problem, sir, as Corn here is a midwestern farm boy and finding sheep in the dark was how he spent most of his puberty," I responded.

"Let's hope so, as bringing this man home is of the utmost urgency. If the Taliban captured him and discovered his identity, they would have leverage into the highest levels of the United States Government."

"And Skull and Bones would be missing a member," I added.

John Matheson had gone to Yale university, and, considering his esteemed family background, most likely belonged to Skull and Bones, one of the oldest and most elite of its secret societies. Its esteemed members included presidents, governors, senators, supreme court justices, journalists, barons of industry, star athletes, and now, apparently, one very unlucky helicopter pilot.

"No shit, and considering his family background, John Matheson might even be our president one day."

"It doesn't matter what his shitty job prospects are. He's one of us, and we make a lot of money off that privileged son of a bitch at our nightly poker games, so, trust me, we'll bring him home, even if we have to drag him kicking and screaming,"

"That's the spirit," the Lieutenant Colonel said, as he smiled and slapped us on the back.

We picked up our gear and headed for our ride, and, on the way, passed more of Operation Lost Sheep's helicopters. Their crews were busy performing their pre-flight inspections, and the lead helicopter's pilot, Lieutenant Lux Vonde, or Jugs, as I called her, was just coming around from the far side and into our view. She was amazing from head to toe, and, if you asked her to show you her best side, she'd have to turn in a circle. She had the unlikely physical dimensions of a swimsuit model, lustrous brown hair framing the face of an angel, and light blue eyes that radiated an energy that was sexual and mischievous, or at least that's how they made me feel each time I gazed into them. She was proof that God, on rare occasions, put all his eggs into one basket—she was smart, sexy, and could swear like a sailor.

The majority of the base thought she was a lesbian, because no one had yet to score much more than a smile and a quiet apology after asking her out. It wasn't her intention to be mean, as I suspect she was just picky, or, perhaps, didn't want to mix business with pleasure. Regardless, she was well respected as a pilot and cool as a cucumber when the shit hit the fan. She had flown more dicey combat missions than any other pilot on the base, and, when your life was on the line and you needed to get the hell out of Dodge, Jugs was the one you wanted at the controls.

We spent many evenings together, and she was by far my closest friend other than Corn and John. Just last night, the four of us had been hanging out, drinking, and giving each other shit over a game of poker. Conveniently, it ended up with just Lux and me at the end of the night, the two of us talking as we shared the last beer. The conversation turned intimate, or at least it did in my beer-goggled haze, and I sort of alluded to the fact that I might like her in more than just a friendly way. She looked distinctly uncomfortable, gave me a hug, and then said that she had to hurry off to bed for an early flight the next day. Lame. I should have known she was way out of my league and kept my thoughts to myself. Oh well, that just meant it was yet another night of masturbation, but at least I could take solace in the fact that my sexual muse was alive and breathing. Unlike the other people around me who used magazines and the Internet, my fantasy could walk, talk, fly a helicopter, and make world peace with a front-mounted Vulcan machine gun. Hopefully she had forgotten what I said last night, and we'd be able to continue on with our one sided masturbatory friendship.

She was just finishing her pre-flight inspection when she noticed us and waved us over. She was wearing her usual flight suit, which, on most people, was about as flattering as a potato sack. On her, it was an entirely different story, as her curves filled out all the parts that would have been boring on a normal person. We both gave her a smart salute, and she returned the gesture by proudly holding up the middle finger of each of her hands. It was the infamous double bird, and I had to admire her efficiency at finding the best way to say fuck you to both of us at the same time.

"Hello, Jugs," I said.

"Hello, boys, I hear you two get the hard job today."

"Every job here is hard. I wouldn't want to be a pilot. Way too big of a target flying around in that garbage can," Corn said.

She rubbed the front of her helicopter affectionately.

"Don't be talking shit about my girl here. She's gotten me through some pretty hairy situations, so I wouldn't trade her for anything."

"I know how you feel. I wouldn't trade my ol' tub o' love here for anything either," I said, as I rubbed Corn's belly.

Lux laughed, and I was happy to see that she still had her sense of humor after I stupidly blurted out my feelings last night. The three of us suddenly became awkwardly quiet as we all looked at each other and thought about what lay ahead. It was a strange existence living in a combat zone, always hopeful that you and your friends might survive another day—a fact made all the more obvious when one of you was miles away in a crashed helicopter surrounded by ruthless enemy forces. Lux hugged Corn first then stepped over and put her arms around me.

"Be careful up there tonight. I mean it. It wouldn't be the same around here without you," she said.

"Don't worry, I'm always careful. I even packed a condom—the ribbed kind because Corn prefers them."

"I mean it, Tag," she said, softly into my ear.

Tag? She never called me by my first name—nor was she ever this openly affectionate, least of all, out on the tarmac for all to see.

"You be careful up there too—and feel free to forget any of the drunken dribble I might have mumbled last night."

"It wasn't dribble, and I haven't forgotten a single word."

It felt particularly magical to be in her arms and the longer she held me, the more aware I became of the feeling of her breasts pressing against my chest and the sweet flowery scent of her hair. My head was spinning, and I was, therefore, completely blindsided when she suddenly pulled her head back, looked me in the eyes, then kissed me straight on the lips. Where the hell did that come from? The moment I'd dreamt about, that haunted my waking thoughts every night before I fell asleep, was happening right before my eyes. Suddenly, my knees felt weak, and I could detect an instant throbbing below my waist as blood started rushing into my gentleman region. I kept expecting her to pull away, but she continued to keep her lips firmly locked on mine. I was in shock, but my brain, fortunately, continued to function, so, when I felt her mouth open, I reacted in kind allowing our tongues to meet in the middle and play like a couple of amorous dolphins. It was glorious, and we continued for what felt like an eternity before the sound of the world crept back into our reality, and the bubble of our own private universe receded. We parted lips, pulled back, and stared into each other's eyes, lost in the other worldly magic of our first kiss. That was when I realized the strange noise coming from behind us was the sound of applause from the young bucks of the Ranger Team. Apparently, they had caught our little tête-à-tête and were celebrating the fact that someone had finally broken through to earn the affections of the alleged lesbian. At least that rumor would be put to rest—along with a few male egos as well. We smiled at each other a little abashedly.

"Life is too short—we should have done that a long time ago," she said.

"I agree. We'll have to continue it when we get back."

"It's a date."

"What about me?" Corn asked.

Lux patted him on the shoulder.

"You'll get your chance with Finn when I'm done with him."

I gave a heartfelt wave to the Rangers, then Corn and I continued on, and I was ever thankful my harness and abundance of equipment kept my partial erection mostly concealed. We walked up the back ramp of the C-130, and, just before I cleared the door, I stopped and turned around for one last look at Lux. She was in her seat with her flight helmet on but had her visor up, so I could still see her face. I smiled and blew her a kiss, and she caught it and held it to her heart. Then she blew me a kiss, and I caught it and placed it over my heart. Corn had been watching and shook his head in disgust as we stepped inside the plane and took a seat.

"You never blow me a kiss," he said.

"That's because you're missing the requisite hardware—a stunning smile, pouty lips, eyes like limpid pools of blue, and, of course, some big jugs."

"I have something better—a big heart."

"Fine."

I kissed my hand and blew it to him. He pretended to catch it, but the fucker only held it over his heart for a split second before dragging it down his body and making quite a show of cupping his manhood.

"That's why I don't blow you kisses you big tease," I said.

We buckled in and felt, as much as heard, the engines revving up, and the big plane started to vibrate as we taxied out to the runway. I was realizing it had been one hell of a day, possibly the best one of my life, when, suddenly, a dark thought flashed across my mind. Why now? Why after all these months of purely friendly interaction did it happen now? Life only throws you a bone like this if something terrible is about to happen. Did Lux kiss me because she sensed some kind of impending disaster with her powerful female intuition? Was I going to my inevitable death? Was she? My usual pre-mission adrenaline rush was now replaced with mild terror. As a PJ, I lived for the moment I jumped out of that plane or helicopter. I brought order into a world of chaos and life to those who would otherwise perish. I was an angel of mercy when the world went to hell, and it was a rush like nothing on this earth, but, now, for the first time in my career, I was afraid. Shit, I really liked Lux, and the thought of not seeing her again was terrifying. Maybe I was just being paranoid, and it would all pass once the mission got underway. Connecting at last with the girl of your dreams and ending a long and torrid affair with your hands was obviously a big step. The plane finally left the ground, climbing and bucking on the air currents while the g-forces pushed us firmly sideways in the C-130's longitudinally mounted seats. Try as I might, I couldn't shake the feeling that my destiny had somehow been changed by that kiss.

We spent the majority of the flight in silence, quietly breathing from our oxygen masks, until Corn, like any good friend, sensed my unease and spoke.

"Don't worry, it's fairly common for a man who's unsure of his sexual orientation to have conflicting feelings after kissing a woman for the first time."

"I guess you'd know."

He laughed and patted me on the back. He wasn't Lux, but he was all I had at twenty-five-thousand feet, and all I would have for the next twelve or so hours if all went well. The rear ramp opened, which prompted us to unbuckle our seat belts, stand up, and begin moving towards the back of the plane. The noise of the wind was deafening the closer we got, and we only waited a moment before the green light turned on and the jump master nodded and gave us the thumbs up. Corn and I looked at each other and smiled.

"Maybe we should kiss now in case something bad happens on the way down," Corn said.

"Do you really think I'm going to fall for that again?"

"Why not? You did every other time."

"True."

With our pre-jump banter complete, we bumped fists, then I turned on my night vision goggles and jumped off the ramp, leaving Corn to follow a second later. The wind hit me hard, and I extended my arms and legs into position to stabilize my descent.

We dressed for the weather, but the cold always found some little path through your clothes and straight to your core. Jumping out of a plane into the night air was kind of like jumping into an ice-cold mountain lake. You felt that same kind of mind numbing shock and wondered what in the hell you were doing. Unlike the lake, however, where you could easily climb out and be free of its cold embrace, the bone chilling night air at twenty-thousand feet was with you until your feet touched the ground.

We were doing a HAHO, or high altitude-high opening, jump, because it would allow us to silently cover the majority of the distance to the target by parachute. This would keep the bad guys from hearing the plane, and subsequently make our arrival a hell of a lot more stealthy. The downside, however, was that the crash site was above nine thousand feet, and the thin air made it more likely that our chutes could get fouled up when they opened. I checked my altimeter and GPS then decided it was time to pull my rip chord and test fate. My parachute popped open without a hitch, and my body rapidly decelerated into the harness, making me feel the familiar crushing of my testicles which were in the unfortunate position of being between the earth and the straps that kept me from plummeting to my death. Maybe there would be something left for Lux if everything were still intact when I reached the ground. I made a quick visual reference for Corn. He should have been about fifty meters off my six, but there was no Corn. Shit! We were radio silent at this point, but I decided to check in anyway.

"Corn—where the hell are you?"

"My fucking chute got tangled, so I had to cut free and open my reserve, but I'm fine—thanks for asking."

Corn had just dealt with the worst case scenario of a high altitude jump and was, unfortunately, well below our minimum altitude to reach the target. In order to hit a ten thousand foot mountain from five miles away you had to open at a minimum of eighteen thousand feet, give or take wind conditions. That meant I was officially conducting this rescue operation on my own in an area overrun with enemy forces. Lovely. It wasn't exactly comforting but those were the breaks when you were a PJ. I thought about giving Corn some shit, but he was probably already mad enough that I didn't want to add to his misery. I, therefore, went with a different approach.

"I guess I'll find the sheep all by my lonesome, but maybe we can meet up later for brunch," I said.

"Sounds good. What should I bring?"

"I would suggest an appetizer, but that would imply your penis, so let's keep it simple. I'll take care of the food and you can bring the Champagne, orange juice, and toilet paper."

"Toilet paper?"

"Of course—everybody shits after brunch."

"Wouldn't that depend on what you eat?"

"No, it doesn't matter if you have eggs Benedict or waffles—everyone shits after brunch."

"Anyone ever tell you that you might be a little fucked in the head?"

"No, but I have been called insightful."

"I think they were just trying to make you feel better about your neurosis."

"I'm sticking with my answer, but, either way, I suppose it's time to get to work."

"Roger that."

"Yeah, so, this is lone wolf Little Bo Peep saying roger and out—but not out of the shit, unfortunately."

"Damn right. Now find our sheep and get your asses safely to the rendezvous point," Corn said, before clicking off.

I checked my GPS and made the appropriate course corrections to make sure I was still headed for the crash sight. Everything was going perfectly according to plan, and the apparent wind was actually helping me reach my target. I had a rare moment with nothing to do but enjoy the scenery, so I rotated my night vision goggles off and enjoyed an excellent view of the Afghan night sky. In this part of the world, the lack of wide scale development reduced the mount of ambient light and subsequently increased the number of visible stars, and made it look more like something you'd expect to see from the Hubble Space telescope. Below, however, there was hardly a light to be seen for miles in any direction, and it was hard to imagine, in the solitude of this moment, the conflict that raged beneath me. Having a brief moment to myself also made me think about Lux and wonder what made her kiss me at that moment? Maybe it was just the stress of heading out on a dangerous mission. Combat could do strange things to people, make them appreciate life, and act a little more impulsively. Shit, I needed to stop thinking about her and get my head in the game. There was little or no room for romantic meanderings at the moment.

I suffered alone and in silence, my testicles the unintended victims in a tug of war between gravity and my body, and I had been floating so long on my trajectory that the ground was coming up a lot faster and sooner than I had expected. My night vision goggles were back on, and I was making last minute course corrections in hopes of finding a decent landing zone with as few obstacles as possible. A sprained ankle or broken foot wouldn't help anyone right now. I found my spot and managed to land perfectly in a nice little open patch of dirt that was fairly level, but a slight gust of wind hit my chute, and I had to take two more steps and ended up tripping over a rock and falling on my face. Thank God it was dark, because it meant there was much less of a chance of me ending up on Afghanistan's funniest home videos. With my luck, I'd probably end up between a hilarious stoning mishap and a mistaken case of bestiality.

Face down in the dirt, my professional pride slightly diminished, I rolled onto my back and brought up my weapon. I didn't hear a sound except perhaps for the exuberant cries of my testicles, which were now shouting out in joy at having been released from the pressure of the parachute harness. The blood was returning to my lower extremities, and I had a fleeting thought about Lux and whether or not long-term exposure to parachute harnesses might cause erectile dysfunction. Shit, I'd have to research that later, as right now I needed to focus and find the Senator's son. I got up and did a quick visual sweep of the area. The helicopter was several meters below me on a small plateau, and the bad guys were probably lurking behind every bush, tree, and rock. I called them bad guys, but, in reality, they were a hybrid of Taliban, Al Qaeda, and a whole mess of other random assholes from all over the world who had come together to fight the great Satan.

I stowed my chute into its bag and made my way down the rocky hillside towards the helicopter, pausing intermittently to listen for bad guys. I heard nothing but the quiet serenity of the Afghan mountains, so it was likely the fuckers had crawled into their caves for the night. I finally reached the crash site and saw that the helicopter was lying on its side and looking as battered as a teenager's first car. The closer I got, the more I realized the usually fresh mountain air reeked of burnt plastic, aviation fuel, and some kind of sickly sweet barbecue smell. It gave me a bad feeling that the initial reports were correct, and John was likely the only survivor. I came around the front of the downed bird and at last saw the carnage. It was obvious that a fire had spread through the interior, and anybody inside would have died horribly but, hopefully, quickly in the flames. I continued on to the other side and found the potential future president of the United States, and he looked like a bug trapped under an enormous boot. He was lying on his back, and his legs, from the knees down, were trapped under the fuselage of the helicopter—the only upside being that he had avoided the fire that killed his crew.

"You look like shit, John," I said.

He obviously wasn't expecting company and practically jumped out of his skin, which was saying a lot considering he was pinned under a helicopter. The quick movement, however, made him cry out in pain, and I realized I should have been a little more delicate with my greeting.

"Goddammit, Finn, is that seriously you?"

"It sure is."

"Jesus! You just scared the shit out of me!"

"Good, because now that I know you have proper bowel function, I can skip the prostate exam and focus on the rest of you. Now, lay back and relax, so I can determine just how fucked up you actually are."

I turned on my small LED flashlight and started with his head, checking his eyes for any signs of a concussion.

"I have some good news," I said.

"What?"

"I'm pretty sure your flight helmet spared you from a head injury, so any impaired brain function can safely be blamed on your overly privileged childhood and time in private schools."

"Lovely, but, now, I have a serious question. Why the hell are you the only one here?" he asked.

"Booty call, though it was supposed to be a threesome. Unfortunately, Corn's chute got fouled, and he missed the drop zone."

"Shit, is he OK?"

"Yeah, he cut it free and deployed his reserve, so he's probably better off than we are at the moment."

"So, it's just the two of us."

"Yep."

"Actually, that's pretty convenient, considering I only have one condom."

"Good to know, as I might need to borrow it. Lux kissed me today."

"Don't feel special. She kissed everyone today."

He still had his sense of humor, which was a good sign, as that was often the only thing that kept someone from going into shock at moments like this. I continued examining him, moving down his body, and was surprised that he didn't look that bad considering he had survived a helicopter crash that killed his entire crew. Thankfully, his spine seemed to be intact, but his legs would be another matter entirely.

"I take it no one else escaped the fire."

His mood turned serious, his eyes appearing to lose focus as an intense sadness overtook his features.

"I'm not even sure if they survived the crash. It's not fair that I lived. They were my responsibility."

He was feeling survivor's guilt, and it was more common than you'd think and didn't always get better over time.

"I know you did the best that you could, and now you're my responsibility, so, let's get you patched up and back to base," I said, as I moved from his torso down to his thighs.

"Hey, easy there, cowboy. I expect at least a kiss before I go to second base," he said.

"Since when?"

"Since now."

"Well, then it's a good thing I brought breath mints," I said, taking a second to inspect John's legs.

He laughed, but he had a pained expression, and that wasn't a good sign, as it meant that he might have internal injuries that couldn't be treated until he was back at the base. I checked his chest again, and he grunted when I felt around his fifth and sixth ribs. They were probably broken or bruised, but it was hard to be sure without an X-Ray. Actually, it was hard to tell with an X-Ray, but, either way, he wasn't going to be doing any jumping jacks or having vigorous sex in the near future. I moved back to his legs, specifically his shins, which were trapped just below the knee by the helicopter. It wasn't exactly encouraging, and I was surprised he was even awake let alone talking to me and giving me so much shit. It was probably a combination of adrenaline, corticosteroids, and my personality. People enjoyed giving me shit, but then I gave as much as I got—which was the natural order of the universe.

"OK, here's the deal. I don't know how to tell you this, but you have a helicopter on your legs."

"Now it all makes so much sense. Is that why I can't reach my beer?"

"Yeah, and the simple fact that your beer is over seventy miles away and none of your appendages, including your penis, are long enough to reach it. But you're lucky, because I drank a six-pack before parachuting in. I've got a whole bladder full of beer for you. I like to think of it as extra filtered."

"Your straw isn't big enough."

"It will be—it just needs a little coaxing."

"So, what about the helicopter on my legs? I have a feeling your dick can't do dick about that."

"Don't be so sure. I'm thinking our best option might be to drench you in piss. Get you nice and slippery and slide your ass right out from under there."

"Do you give all the pilots you rescue a golden shower?"

"Only the pretty ones."

"So, what's my prognosis here, Dr. Finn, medicine woman?"

"You're totally fucked. If you're lucky, the coyotes will finish you off quickly, but I'll do my best to make sure your wallet and personal items make it back to your family. Oh—speaking of which, I'll probably need your ATM pin code."

"Fuck you. What's the real story?"

"The real story is that I'm going to figure out a way to get you free, but first, I'm going to give you a shot of morphine for the pain," I said, as I inserted the needle into his arm.

"Don't you mean Rohypnol?" he asked.

"Since when have I ever needed you passed out and helpless to get a little loving?"

"Pretty much, never."

"Exactly, so now, I want you to think happy thoughts and stay where you are, princess."

"Why? Where the fuck are you going?"

"Obviously, to have a look around to see if I can find something that might help me get your ass out from under that fucking helicopter."

"Whatever, *Mary Poppins*, just hurry the fuck up."

"I don't remember you ever saying fuck this much back at the base."

"Then you clearly weren't fucking listening. Now, hurry the fuck up and figure out a fucking way to get me the fuck out of here and back the fuck to base—fucker."

"Wow, do you kiss your mother with that filthy mouth?"

"Yes, I do."

"So, you obviously know about that little thing she does with her tongue."

"Of course—who do you think taught it to her?"

"Alrighty then, Oedipus, I'm going to take that as my official cue to excuse myself from this conversation."

Using my night vision goggles, I searched around the wreck and found a long section of one of the rotor blades. Perfect! This was exactly what I needed. It was one of the strongest man made materials on earth and might just do the job. I went back to John and dug out the dirt around his shins as gingerly as possible then wedged a number of rocks underneath the edge of the fuselage to stabilize it and make sure it didn't roll back any farther over his legs. Now that I had created some space, it was time to see if I could use the piece of blade as a lever to nudge the helicopter. I slid the end under the side and lifted as hard as I could, but the fuselage only made the slightest metallic creaking sound and remained mostly unmoved.

I needed more leverage, and that meant combing the crash site for a decent sized boulder that would serve as a proper fulcrum point. I found one a short distance away then rolled it over and placed it under the blade. Now that I had a proper lever, I pushed down on the opposite end and felt a semblance of movement. I, therefore, decided to use my entire body, and hopped up onto the blade, the extra weight at last lifting the fuselage up just enough for John to slide free. Unfortunately, the asshole wasn't paying attention and neglected to move. I think the painkiller was kicking in and making him a little dopey which, in turn, wasn't making my job any easier. I told him he was going to have to pull himself out the next time I lifted the fuselage, or I really would leave him behind and take his wallet. I counted to three and hopped up onto the blade one more time, and he finally slid free. I could tell by his expression that moving had been extremely painful, and the morphine was just barely able to help. I would have happily given him more, but I needed to administer it sparingly so as to maintain his breathing and blood pressure in hopes of keeping him coherent and able to travel. I propped him up and made him comfortable, and finally was able to get a good look at his legs. The left one was bruised and bleeding with major abrasions but structurally appeared fine. The right one, judging by the discoloration, swelling, and John's whining, obviously had a break in the Tibia about two inches below the knee. I cleaned and bandaged the lacerations, then prepared to set the bone, so that I could put John's leg in a proper splint and make him ambulatory.

"This might be painful for a small child, but it will be agony for a pussy like you."

"Just make sure you get hold of the correct appendage. Many a person has mistaken my penis for my leg."

"Maybe we should put a shoe on it, so you can use it to walk."

He laughed, but his look turned grave when I told him it was time to deal with his leg. I wedged his foot in my left armpit, and used my right arm to set the bone—a horrible snapping sound signifying the procedure was complete. John was oddly stoic throughout the ordeal, and I had to give the big lug some credit. A lot of bigger, tougher men might have already passed out from the pain, but the Senator's son was showing some real fortitude. I strapped the splint in place and got him ready to move. It wasn't going to be pleasant, but at least it would immobilize the leg until he got proper medical attention.

"OK, here's the plan. We're going to move seven clicks west and rendezvous with the Rangers who will have established a secure landing zone."

"What about the SEALs I dropped off?"

"They're already on their way, and if we hope to join them, we better get moving. Pickup is at first light."

"Why can't we just hold tight and wait for a ride?"

"There are too many hostiles, and if we stay here, we'll end up as the two least popular wives of a Taliban goat farmer. I could handle that kind of rugged life, but you're way too delicate."

"Bullshit. Look at these hands. They've got farmer's mistress written all over them."

"They look a little dainty, so, at best you might be able to milk the male goats."

I queued my headset and called HQ.

"This is Little Bo Peep, I've got the sheep."

"Roger, proceed to LZ 1."

"Affirmative."

I clicked off and looked at my patient. I wish he had been a hobbit or ninety pound computer nerd, but, unfortunately, he was easily six foot two and a hundred and ninety pounds. He had a broken leg, and I had six hours to move him seven kilometers over difficult terrain. How hard could it be?

CHAPTER FIVE
The Flight of the Yeti

The trek down the mountain was pretty fucking hard as it turned out, and, even with the aid of my night vision goggles, I spent most of the time slipping on loose ground, tripping over shrubs, and scraping the two of us against the rough foliage that thrived in the harsh Afghan climate. After about forty-five minutes of arduously slow progress, the pain in John's leg made it too difficult for him to continue, and we stopped and sat below a large rock outcropping. It probably wasn't the best idea to waste precious time, but my patient was definitely needing to rest. Needless to say, I kept a watchful eye on our surroundings, as our noisy footfalls and John's moaning had made enough noise to wake the entire Taliban, and it would be a miracle if they were not already closing in on our position.

"Why do you have to be so fucking big? I feel like I'm trying to rescue a fucking Sasquatch here."

"In this part of the world they would call me a Yeti."

"Whatever. You're a big, hairy, heavy son of a bitch. I thought pilots had to be smaller, under six foot tall, or they wouldn't fit into the cockpit."

"You're thinking of those wimpy little Jet pilots. Helicopter pilots are generally taller, more robust, and have larger penises."

"And tiny little vestigial brains."

"Yeah, but it doesn't matter when you have a large penis."

"That's sad but probably true," I said, as I pulled out my canteen and handed it to John.

He took a drink of water then handed it back, so I could do the same.

"Now, look, John, we are in some pretty serious shit here and really need to keep going."

"I'm sorry, man, but I can't. My fucking good leg hurts as much as the bad one."

"Shit monkeys."

Maybe I had missed something back at the crash site. I told John to lie back, while I leaned down and re-examined his good leg and discovered a subtle bump about halfway down the tibia that I hadn't felt during my first examination. He cringed when I put any pressure on the spot, so it was likely a hairline fracture — something that was going to make walking any distance impossible. Fucking double shit monkeys. The only way we were getting the Senator's son off this mountain was if I carried him. I was already lugging an eighty-pound pack, and I wasn't too happy about that pack gaining an additional one hundred and ninety pounds.

"Any way to get you to lose some serious weight in the next few minutes?" I asked.

"Other than cutting off my dick, I doubt it."

"How about emptying your balls? That should be good for at least a few ounces."

"Is this your subtle way of offering me a handjob?"

"Who said anything about hands?"

There was nothing as effective as penis jokes to keep a man's spirits up in times of adversity, but it certainly didn't lighten the actual load. That made the next two hours particularly grueling, for I had John draped over my shoulder as I struggled down the hill, stumbling and trying desperately not to lose footing on the unstable ground. Most of the valley was conveniently covered in nature's version of Teflon: a combination of dirt, sand, gravel, pebbles, and boulders, and all of it was making it harder to travel. It wasn't easy hoofing it with a combined weight of four hundred and fifty pounds, and it made me wonder how those incredibly obese people you saw in the news managed to survive. I guess they didn't—which is why they always ended up in the news. Eventually, luck gave out, and I slipped, sending both of us falling to the ground. It was a needed break, but I knew we couldn't rest for long and had to keep going or lose the cover of darkness, and, worst case scenario, our ride home.

"Look, Finn, we can't keep going. It's too much for you to carry me. We'll never make it together."

"I don't know what lame-ass shit they put you through in flight school, but we actually work for a living in Pararescue. This is a Sunday morning stroll for me. Hell, I've been jerking off for the last ten minutes just to get a little more cardio."

"I wondered why you were shaking so much. It was like riding a washing machine during the spin cycle."

"Yeah, but now I bet you feel dirty."

"Seriously man, leave me here. Rendezvous with the Rangers and come back for me with a helicopter."

"We can't have such a high profile target like you falling into enemy hands. That's why I'm here. I'm your ticket out of this shithole, so don't worry your pretty little head, Sasquatch."

"Yeti."

"Whatever—by morning you'll be back at base and bitching as usual about all the money you've lost at poker."

"You promise?"

"I promise—especially the last part about you losing money."

We sat for a few more minutes, hydrating, and eating energy bars, before I once again heaved him over my shoulder, and set off, slowly and painfully, down the mountain.

"Senator's sons are heavy as fuck," I said, after stumbling and hitting my shin on a root.

"It's all that blue blood."

We managed to travel about a half a klick before coming upon a clearing where we could hear a strange buzzing sound. I stopped and listened more closely and realized it was snoring, apparently originating from a dense thicket of vegetation just off to our left. I wished it could have been some of our guys, but they would have been smart enough to post sentries to keep any yahoo's like Sasquatch and me from wandering into their midst. It was, therefore, most likely a camp full of bad guys, and that meant we needed to make a drastic detour. I walked to our right in a direction that would take us safely around the periphery, and, even at a distance, I could tell by the noise that there had to be at least a dozen or more hostiles snoozing away. I continued on for another fifty meters and thought we were safely past the camp, until we came into another clearing, and I discovered a guy squatting down taking a dump. He looked over in our direction, probably having heard my labored footfalls, but, fortunately, he couldn't see us in the darkness. He called out in one of the forty different languages native to Afghanistan, and could have gone so far as to try each and every one, but it wouldn't have made a difference, as neither Sasquatch nor I were particularly versed in any of them. He sounded a little put off and must have assumed we were one of his buddies and was probably telling us to leave him alone because he was taking a shit. I knew the feeling.

Looking at the guy, I couldn't help but wonder who would shit in the dark without a flashlight or reading material? Life in the third world was truly uncivilized. Why wasn't he making the most of his special time, and, more importantly, what would he use as toilet paper? These were all good questions, but, sadly, none of them were relevant at the moment, for the real problem was communication. I had learned some rudimentary phrases in the most common language, Persian Dari, but, unfortunately, never picked up the words for, sorry didn't know you were taking a shit, so I'll just head back to the sheep I was fucking. The more he talked, the more agitated he became and, at last, I remembered the words for, oh, so sorry, but, it didn't seem to help.

"What the hell's going on?" John asked.

I was carrying him over my shoulder with his upper body dangling down my back, so he couldn't see what was going on in front of us. Of course, his orientation wasn't even a factor considering his lack of night vision goggles literally left him in the dark.

"We've got a shitter at twelve o'clock, and he sounds pissed," I said.

"So, what do we do?"

"I'm working on it."

The guy wiped his ass with his left hand then rubbed it in the dirt before pulling up his pants and walking in our direction. Even in this darkness, he'd be able to figure out we weren't local when he got close enough, so I needed to think fast. I couldn't use a gun because it would wake his friends, and I couldn't fight him with John on my back. Most important of all was the simple fact that he just wiped his ass with one of his hands, so I had no intention of getting into a wrestling match. Why hadn't the Taliban heard of moist towelettes?

We were pretty much screwed, and drastic times called for drastic measures, and the following move would never enter my after-action report. I waited until the guy had crept to within five feet, before I lunged forward and threw John at him with all the strength I could muster. The Senator's son was now nothing more than a human projectile and currently my quietest weapon if the fucker managed to keep his big mouth shut. The shitter sensed the incoming object and instinctively reached out and caught John in his arms. He was overwhelmed by the weight and stumbled and fell backwards onto the ground with John splayed out across his chest. The force of the one hundred and ninety pound person knocked the wind out of him and, thankfully, left him unable to scream. I stepped over John and realized my best option would be to cut the guy's throat with my knife. It would be quick and quiet, but, unfortunately, deep in the back of my mind was a tiny vein of sympathy for a fellow dumper. It might have been different had he been holding an AK-47, but, in this case, I decided to let him live, which meant I would have to incapacitate him in order to keep him from alerting his friends.

The irony of being Pararescue was that, in order to save people, we sometimes had to hurt or kill the unlucky people who got in the way. I had countless hours of hand-to-hand combat training and spent a lifetime studying martial arts, but that didn't make it any easier. This was up close and personal, but my training took over, and I crossed my hands and slid them into the collar of his jacket then grabbed and twisted the material into my fists to create a textbook front choke. In technical terms, I was applying pressure to the baroreceptors in the carotid artery, and this would trigger the baroreflex and confuse the brain into misinterpreting the blood pressure and hopefully make him go night-night in a matter of seconds. He stared wide-eyed in terror, until he at last relaxed and went unconscious. I couldn't help but feel a little bad and hoped I'd never have a dump end up like this, as it truly went against the laws of the International Accord on Bathroom Etiquette, ratified in 1902 in Geneva Switzerland. It stated very clearly that no man should ever be disturbed and, least of all, knocked out during a number two, and I hoped that my actions hadn't broken some holy covenant that would leave my own dumps forever cursed.

"That's what you call working on it?" John whispered, angrily.

"I thought you were very brave the way you took that guy down."

"Fuck you."

He struggled off the unconscious dumper and looked at me with an expression that resided somewhere between resentment and horror—perhaps both. So what if I tossed him like an empty beer can. At least I had waited until the guy was done shitting. Sasquatch should understand that we had bigger things to worry about—namely securing the dumper and getting the hell out of here.

"What in God's name is that awful smell?" John asked, as he sniffed the air.

"You're lying in the middle of a *Tali-bano*."

"Oh, sweet Lord!" he said, as he proceeded to make a gagging sound.

I used duct tape to secure the dumper's hands and feet, then placed a final piece over his mouth to make sure he didn't go telling his bearded friends about the two American soldiers who interrupted his late night deuce. We were moving as slow as fuck and, therefore, needed adequate time to get beyond the camp and its dozing occupants. I heaved John over my shoulder for the third time of the night and headed northwest, and, as the land got flatter, the going got easier, but I was getting more fatigued. We had made it almost six kilometers when we came to a river. According to the digital map, it was supposed to be a stream, but it looked a lot deeper in real life than it did on my GPS screen. Dawn was approaching and time was running out, though none of that changed the fact that I needed to take a little break to figure out the easiest way to get us across this final obstacle. I lowered John to the ground and decided it was also a good time to hydrate and get some more calories into my body, as adrenaline could only take me so far. I had just finished eating another energy bar when my radio crackled, and I heard Corn's unmistakable voice.

"Where the fuck are you, Little Bo Peep?"

"About one click away from the LZ, Little Miss Muffet."

"I made it to the flock, but I have bad news. The pick-up's been moved up. They want to extract everyone before dawn."

"Shit. That's only minutes away."

"Do your best, and I'll do what I can on my end."

"Thanks."

"You and John—stay safe out there."

"I love you too," I said.

I heard him laugh on the other end, and it made me smile. Of course, while I was enjoying that brief reprieve from the hell that was our immediate situation, I let my attention slip, and it took a minute to register that I was hearing voices behind us, and they were getting closer. Who would have thought that terrorists were early risers? It's not like they had to get to McDonalds before 10 a.m. in order to get a goat McMuffin. I grabbed John and moved into a more covered position—about as covered as you could get on an exposed riverbank with no cover. Shit, they seemed to be coming straight towards us, but then it hit me. We were right next to the only source of water for miles, so, of course, they would come here. It was, therefore, time to move, but where? We needed to cross the river, but we'd be too exposed—plus I had no idea how deep it might be. I could swim like a fish, but getting John across would be like dragging an inebriated walrus across an ice cold Olympic sized pool while men with AK-47's used us for target practice. Our best option was to hide and wait for them to move on, so I buried a very unhappy John in twigs, sand, and river rocks, and tried to do the same to myself. For all my effort, we looked like two guys buried in twigs, sand, and river rocks, but I hoped the predawn darkness would help disguise our presence.

The un-friendlies came onto the bank about fifty meters north of us then knelt down at the river's edge and began to splash water on their faces in what I imagine was the third world's version of a shower. They were busy talking amongst each other, completely oblivious to us, and I was starting to believe we might have a chance. That is, until another group appeared on the opposite bank. What the hell? I didn't even know these guys bathed, let alone at five in the morning. I lay there as still as I could, hoping

John was doing the same. My finger was resting on the trigger of my M4, and I was thinking about *Dorothy* from the *Wizard of Oz* clapping her heels together in order to go home, and I wondered if it would work. There's no place like home. There's no place like home. Nope, still here, and despite the cold, sweat was starting to bead on my forehead and slip down my face. I tried to slow my heart, control my breathing, and blend into my surroundings the way my childhood karate sensei had taught me. I'd learned similar techniques in sniper school, but none of my training seemed to be helping at the moment, and my heart was feeling like it might pound out of my chest like the heart under the floor in Edgar Allen Poe's story, *The Tell-Tale Heart*. Oddly, all remained quiet, and no one seemed to notice the two perfectly man-sized lumps on the riverbank.

Then, the inevitability of time and space came into play when hints of sunlight started to fill the eastern skies off beyond the towering Afghan mountains. The sun itself wasn't visible, but its warm rays were creating enough ambient light to add shadow and depth to the two man-sized lumps on the riverbank. The guys on the opposite side started yelling to the guys on our side. They were pointing at us, not necessarily because we looked like enemy soldiers, but probably because we in no way resembled the ground around us. The human brain has an incredible ability to find discrepancies in its field of vision, and because of that, the assholes on the other side of the river just found two large discrepancies. Our only option was to take the initiative, and that meant shooting first. I'd have given anything for a SAW. That's an acronym for squad automatic weapon, and it was a good friend to have at a time like this. Special operations units like SEALs always carried at least one. Come to think of it, I wished I had an entire SEAL team to go with the SAW.

The guys on our side of the river finally understood what their friends were hollering about and started walking our way, probably to get them to stop hollering. The un-friendlies obviously had superior numbers, but we had the element of surprise. I cued my mic and spoke as quietly as I could.

"This is Little Bo Peep and his lost sheep. We are one click away from the extraction zone on the east side of the river and are about to engage enemy hostiles."

"Do not engage the hostiles. Repeat. Do not engage the hostiles. Hold out until we can get a bird inbound."

"That's a big fat negative. The hostiles are inbound and ugly and looking for a fight."

Then I heard Corn.

"You give them hell and stay alive until we get there! Don't make a widow out of Lux, because you know the two of us will get together and have sex right after your funeral."

"You'll be crying too much to enjoy it."

"I'll be crying, but I'll still enjoy it."

Our short banter gave me a brief respite from the severity of our situation, but, now, it was time to focus, as surviving moments like this came down to training and experience. The first rule of a gunfight was to have a gun. The second was to focus on your training, while the third was to obey the first two rules. The movies always showed the hero carefully aiming with one eye closed, letting out a half a breath and pulling the trigger, but it never actually happened that way. Adrenaline forces both eyes to go wide open, and the shooter rarely, if ever, actually sees his sights. Close quarters combat, therefore, is more about developing a feel for where your weapon is pointed. The technique I utilized was perfected by Japanese archers in ancient times, and was about making the weapon an extension of your arm and, in turn, your body. Your weapon comes up to fire, your cheek touches the side of the stock, and what you see is what you kill.

The first guy came into my field of view, and I fired a three round burst into his chest. The NATO 5.56mm round wasn't as big as an AK's, but it delivered a lot of kinetic energy that made succotash out of any living matter it hit. He dropped like the sack of mashed potatoes that his insides had just become. By shooting first and killing their friend, we had gained the tactical advantage of surprise, and anything that bought you time, bought you life. It also didn't hurt that we were camouflaged by the debris and still kind of looked like a couple of amorphous blobs with an assault rifle. Now they were playing mental catch up, and I used that small window to drop two more. The third guy got his weapon up, but his nerves caused him to shoot wild and high. He obviously forgot rule two, and I put him down next. The fifth guy was luckier and more experienced and managed to fire off a pretty good burst that ripped up ground all around us, sending rocks and debris into my face. During the next barrage, one of the bullets splintered off a rock, and a tiny fragment managed to graze my cheek. It kind of felt like that moment in a Bruce Lee movie where his enemy finally scores the hit that draws blood. At that point, Bruce would taste it, shake off the blow, and beat the guy senseless. It was time to be Bruce. As I prepared to fire back and enact a little retribution, I heard a single shot and saw the guy look at his chest. Weird, I hadn't even pulled the trigger yet, but, as I glanced over to check on John, I saw that he had just used his sidearm to shoot the guy. Not bad for a pilot, except he only fired once, and the guy was still alive and about to shoot at us again. I fired another three round burst and finished the job.

"Goddamn it, John! Double tap! Double tap," I yelled.

"I'm conserving ammo!"

"Don't be such a tight ass. Give it to them!"

No sooner had the words left my lips, that bullets started ripping up the earth around us. It was the guys on the other side of the river, and they didn't seem too happy that they had just lost five of their friends. We needed better cover, so I motioned for ol' One-Shot to crawl to a slight depression behind some of the nearby river rocks. I put down some suppressive fire to cover his retreat and noticed he was moving slowly, and I could tell the pain of his injuries was starting to take its toll on his body.

I delivered one more three round burst of fire then joined him, feeling only slightly safer in our new spot. What I wouldn't give for a boulder the size of a jeep with a wet bar, coffee maker, and a barbecue grill. It was a ridiculous fantasy, but if I was going to imagine a better place to be, then I might as well add some amenities. The shooting suddenly became more intense, and we sunk down and tried to meld our bodies into the earth. Our situation was rapidly deteriorating, so I decided I better get on the radio and check on our ride.

"This is Little Bo Peep! The Sheep and I are still pinned down and receiving heavy fire from about two hundred meters away on the western bank of the river."

"Choppers inbound. Maintain your position."

What position? We were maintaining a tiny indentation on the side of a river with barely enough cover for one of us, let alone two. We couldn't move up the bank, because we'd be more exposed, and moving the other direction would bring us closer to the pricks who were trying to kill us.

"John, I need you to lay down some suppressive fire."

"Fuck you. I'm not moving."

"Just point your pistol in their general direction and shoot—at least twice this time."

"Screw you. You have a bigger gun!"

"It's not about size."

"Keep telling yourself that!" he yelled.

John thankfully lifted his pistol above the berm and fired in the general direction of the bad guys, which allowed me to pop up and fire my own quick burst. Despite the greater distance, the shots rang true, and another guy went down. The victory was short-lived, however, as the others responded in kind with a brutal fusillade of return fire. I dropped back behind cover, and the area I had been only a second earlier was torn apart in a maelstrom of violent bullet impacts that sent dust, rocks, and lead fragments in all directions.

"I take it you didn't get all of them?" John asked.

"Afraid not, as I forgot to load my rifle with magic bullets."

The intensity of their firing suddenly increased as though they had heard my little quip and decided to punish us by sending hundreds of bullets to tear apart every square inch of earth around our mostly inadequate refuge. We attempted to shrink into our tiny cover and were cuddling closer together than a couple of virgins on their honeymoon. I popped out my magazine and loaded a fresh one as it was standard procedure to reload whenever possible. Where were those Goddamn helicopters?

Their aim seemed to be getting better, which meant our situation was growing more dire by the second. It was easy to discount a lot of these freedom fighters, because many of them were either poor brainwashed idealists or spoiled Middle Eastern college students who decided that driving their parents' Mercedes was boring compared to being an international terrorist. But, the Taliban was a mixed bunch and some of these guys had been out here fighting since before I was born and had gotten pretty good at it—which seemed to be the case with the fuckers on the opposite bank. Lovely. Why couldn't it be a bunch of dipshits like the guy who left America to join the Taliban? Until the Americans nabbed him, he was probably cleaning up goat shit and taking hormones, so he could grow a beard and blend in better with his hairy new friends. Suddenly, beyond the loud report of the AK-47's, I could hear the gloriously welcoming sound of approaching helicopters.

"Little Bo Peep, we are inbound. Can you clarify your position?"

I could have thrown out a smoke grenade, but, instead, used my GPS to give them our exact coordinates.

"Roger that, Little Bo Peep, and where are the hostiles?"

"Hostiles are angry as all hell and about two hundred meters northwest of our position on the opposite river bank."

"Affirmative. The cavalry is en route. Hold your position."

I listened to the radio chatter between the helicopters and heard that the first was going to clear the area and provide cover fire while the second would be making the pickup. Holy shit! The voice from the second helicopter was Lux.

"John, my girlfriend's coming! Time to go home!"

"Corn's here?"

"Lux, you asshole!"

"She's not your girlfriend. It's combat fatigue. Your mind is finally gone."

The first helicopter swept down like a bird of prey over the river, its front mounted 30mm chain gun going into action and sounding like a turbo charged popcorn maker. The people in its path were obliterated and on their way to heaven before their bodies even hit the ground. All enemy fire ceased, and the call came for the second helicopter to make the pickup. I lifted John up over my shoulder and carried him out and set him down closer to the water's edge where the ground was more open and would make a better landing spot. Lux's helicopter was still out of view, but I couldn't help imagining her beautiful smiling face, and it felt as though a lifetime had passed since that kiss out on the tarmac.

Then, everything went to hell—yet again. The sound of the helicopter was so deafening that I didn't hear the RPG that came sailing over our heads. It missed the chopper by inches and exploded on the far side of the river. I looked to see where it had come from, but the ground cover was too dense to see the shooter's position. Shit—it was very likely that the rest of the guys from the shitter's camp heard all the noise, and decided to come join the party. The helicopter rotated left and started firing at the bad guys, and it was looking as though they might have gotten the shooter until a second RPG came flying overhead. Fortunately, it missed its target and exploded on the ground, with only a few small fragments reaching the chopper, which bucked slightly but remained aloft. It wouldn't take much of a hit to damage one of the rotors and down the bird, so, with there already being too many losses in this operation, orders came over the radio that the landing zone was too hot, and they were calling for the air units to pull back. There goes our ride home. The lead helicopter abruptly pulled up and flew out of view, and, while part of me was glad that Lux was still safely out of range, the other part of me knew that we were totally fucked. It was, therefore, time to cross the river and put some distance between us and the guys from the camp, which meant I was going to have to pull the inebriated walrus across the ice cold Olympic sized swimming pool after all.

"We have to take a swim, walrus."

"Now it's walrus? Why don't you pick one fucking large hairy mammal and stick with it?"

"Fine, Sasquatch—we need to cross the river, as we are about to be overrun by the friends of the shitter you jumped on earlier."

"Fuck you! It's Yeti, and might I remind you that you threw me on him."

"There's no time to argue the details."

John groaned as I picked him up and waded into the river. What was he grousing about? Riding on my shoulder, he would hit the water long after my balls. Too bad he wouldn't shrivel up like my privates, as it would make him a hell of a lot easier to carry. With each step, the river got deeper and exponentially colder, because the water here came from snowpack farther up the mountain and didn't warm up much by the time it made its way down into this valley. We were about a third of the way across when it was finally deep enough that we had to swim. I moved John into a position where I could tow him then set to work, making definite, although arduous, progress. He couldn't kick his legs, but at least he used his arms in a half assed attempt at dog paddling. He was in pain and cold as hell, but he kept going, and I had to give it to the guy. He had survived a crash that broke both his legs and killed his entire crew, yet he still managed to give it the old college try.

"You might have made a good PJ," I said.

"No way. I'm afraid of needles," he said, through quivering lips.

"You're afraid of your own dick?"

"Of course, it's big enough to kill a horse."

"Maybe a pony, and only if it was already dying."

Only idiot guys could continue to make dick jokes at a time like this, but humor was one of humanity's great coping mechanisms. If you could still laugh, you could still live, and, as miserable as we were, we were both smiling—though it was hard to tell through the teeth chattering pained expressions on our faces. We crossed the halfway point, and the river eventually became shallow enough that I could put my feet on the bottom. We were still up to our shoulders, but it was a hell of a lot easier for me to pull John along behind me. We were also lucky that the river was flowing nice and slowly, and it looked as though we were going to reach the other side. That is, until the bullets started coming. When the helicopters pulled back, the Taliban moved in, and now they were on the opposite bank, firing like wild monkeys. I, therefore, decided I better get on my radio.

"Little Bo Peep and his Sheep are about to die in the middle of a freezing cold fucking river."

I wasn't exactly sure if anyone responded because the noise of the rifles and subsequent splashes from bullets landing everywhere around us made it impossible to hear. I pulled John underwater and exhaled half of my air to reduce my buoyancy then dove for the bottom, where we swam with the current, the goal being to gain as much distance as possible from our antagonists. The bullets would keep coming, but at least they would be farther away, and we'd be a lot harder to hit. We surfaced and took another breath then went down again. The third time we popped up, I assumed we would be downriver and have gained a little breathing room. Unfortunately, they had followed us down the riverbank and were pretty much the same distance away.

Fuck. I brought my rifle up and laid down more suppressive fire, possibly hitting one, though I didn't have any time to confirm, as I was preoccupied with trying to send out another message on the radio.

"Little Bo Peep and Sheep have moved downriver along with our new friends."

"Orders still stand for choppers to hold back. We'll see if we can divert the Ranger team to your location."

I was freezing, so I knew John was freezing as well, which meant we couldn't stay in the water much longer, or we'd be at risk of hypothermia. If that happened, our minds would go first, and we'd probably end up taking off all of our clothes and spending our last minutes of life skinny dipping and giggling like a couple of inebriated sorority sisters. The radio crackled.

"Asshole! Hold your position. Lux wants to come in for a pickup," Corn said.

"Are you fucking crazy? The orders to pull back were issued for a good reason."

Lux chimed in to the radio chatter at that point.

"Stop being a dick. I thought you wanted to see me again."

"I do. I really do, but not here. I can't let you see me like this. I have a man in my arms."

"Nothing I haven't seen before," she said.

Corn came back on the radio and told us to get to the riverbank, but, as much as I wanted them to come, I knew that it was too dangerous.

"Back off! There is no point in all of us dying here."

The helicopter swept into view and raked the opposite shoreline with machine gun fire, and, even from this distance, I could see the resolve in Lux's expression as she kept the bird steady for the side door gunner. When she was determined to do something, she did it, whether it was winning a poker game or flying into enemy fire to rescue a couple of water logged, freezing cold assholes.

"Goddamn it, Lux! Get your ass out of here!"

"I'm coming in. Be ready, or I'll take your frozen dick and leave you behind."

"Don't call John a dick."

"Very f—f—f—funny," John muttered, who was so cold that his mouth was barely able to form the words.

"I'm serious, Lux. You need to get the fuck out of here."

A number of shots suddenly rang out from the bad guys' position and struck the helicopter. I saw Lux grab her arm, and it was all I could do not to scream and make a glorious charge at the assholes on the opposite riverbank.

"Are you hit? Goddamn it Lux! I told you to get the fuck out of here!"

"I'm not leaving you behind!" she said.

"You have to!"

She ignored me and dropped down and landed on the opposite bank, and I could now see that Corn was standing in the open doorway, firing his M4 beside the side door gunner—the two of them doing their best to cover our asses as we approached the helicopter. A RPG came whistling through the air and landed a short distance away in the river, where it exploded below the surface and sent up a great deluge of water that rained down on everything in the immediate vicinity. That was more than enough motivation to get me to heave John over my shoulder for the last time of the day and make a glorious final sprint. Twenty feet from the chopper door, I felt a terrible shooting pain in my left hip, and it suddenly became harder to use my left side. Worse still, I could feel warmth flowing around my back, which meant I'd been hit. A few more steps, and the water was shallow enough that I could now see the blood stain spreading quickly through my wet fatigues. It was only a matter of time before I lost consciousness, so I struggled on with nothing but adrenaline and sheer force of will fueling my efforts until I reached the helicopter and tossed John bodily through the door.

"Not again," he yelled as he sailed across the floor and landed on the opposite side.

I collapsed with only my chest in the open door, and Corn reached down and pulled me the rest of the way into the chopper, and I was feeling a little light headed as we climbed steeply up and away from the riverbank. Bullets were pinging off of the fuselage, but Lux flew aggressively, performing a series of evasive maneuvers to make us less of an easy target. The shooting finally stopped, and she leveled off the helicopter and set a course for Bagram, allowing me to struggle up onto my knees and lean into the cockpit to check on her wound. She lifted her visor then turned to me and smiled as she brought her left arm around into view.

"See—it's just a scratch," she said.

I smiled back at her, feeling relieved that we had all miraculously survived.

"Thank you for coming for us."

"That's what girlfriends are for," she responded.

The dizziness from both blood loss and happiness took over, and I collapsed onto the floor.

"Corn! Better put a bandage on my girlfriend's arm."

"Girlfriend? You mean John?" Corn asked.

"No, he means you, Corn," John groaned, beside me.

"He obviously means me, you assholes," Lux said, looking back at the three of us.

I smiled and felt particularly good, considering I was exhausted, delirious, and had just been shot.

"I told you I'd get you home, Sasquatch," I said.

"Yeti, goddamn it," he groaned.

That was the last thing I heard before passing out. Corn stabilized my wound, and they got me back to base, where I spent the next twenty-four hours in the ICU. I awoke feeling somewhat better and discovered that the Senator's son was one bed over. We then spent our awake time arguing about whether or not Lux was actually my girlfriend. He contended that I was indeed still suffering from combat fatigue and had imagined the entire affair as a coping mechanism. He stubbornly professed this view until an hour later when Lux was finally allowed to visit. She crawled into my bed, and I gave John the finger as she slid the divider curtain closed, allowing us to spend some non-coital quality time just four feet from the mythical Sasquatch. Thankfully, he was quiet, keeping his moans and groans mostly to himself.

The next morning, news came that the bullet was lodged in my hip only millimeters from my spine and would have to be removed by a specialist in the States. I was being put on a plane within the hour, so Lux and I took advantage of the last moments we had together and made out like a couple of hormone fueled teenagers until my nurse came and told me it was almost time to board the plane. Lux got up and pulled back the curtain to reveal John quietly reading a magazine — the expression on his face being one that would have been more at home if he had a pipe dangling from his mouth and was sitting in an easy chair in front of a fireplace.

"Disgusting. About time you two came up for air," he said.

"We were just cuddling. You know Finn isn't in any kind of shape to do anything too strenuous."

"And how is that different from any other day of the week?"

"It's not," Corn said, as he walked in and joined us, sitting on my bed and frowning as he regarded me.

"It's sad that you had to shoot yourself just so you could get a quick trip home to States."

"It's sad that you probably shot me yourself just so you could get a stab at my girlfriend."

Corn put his arm around Lux.

"Me? Never, though I do promise to keep a close eye on her for you."

"I can take care of myself, thank you," Lux said, indignantly, as she shrugged off Corn's arm.

The orderly arrived, and an uncomfortable silence descended over the group. It was a relief surviving a combat tour, but you never wanted to leave your friends behind. Out here, in this foreign land a million miles from home, we had become each other's family, and combat was the unlikely glue that held us all together. Corn looked up at me, smiled, and I could see the beginning of tears forming in his eyes.

"Tag..." he said, before abruptly pausing as he became too emotional to continue.

"It's Ok, Corn. I know what you're going to say."

"No, I have to get this out."

He took a few breaths to calm down then started over.

"Tag, you have been, and always will be—my friend."

Everyone, including the orderly, laughed, which meant there were at least five legitimate Star Trek fans in Afghanistan.

"Obviously, you know that quoting Spock is the easiest way to make me cry, but do you also understand that you're inferring I'm Captain Kirk—and everyone knows Kirk gets the girl."

"Well, yeah, but only until he's shipped back to Starfleet."

We shared a little laugh at our silly Star Trek banter.

"Seriously now, Finn—we're going to miss you, so have that bullet removed and get your ass back here," Corn said.

"I will, and you stay safe, but, more importantly, really do keep an eye on Lux for me," I said, as he leaned down and hugged me.

"Just an eye?"

"Just an eye—or even both eyes if need be, but no penis, hands, or any other part of your body—other than your eyes."

"I've got it—just the eyes."

"No penis."

"You already said that."

"I know, but I just wanted to be extra clear."

"I'll give it my all," he said, as he released me and stepped back.

Now, we were on to John who was unable to move due to the apparatus keeping his legs elevated.

"Finn, I would hug the shit out of you if I could only get out of this damn bed," he said, as we, instead, shook hands.

"It's the thought that counts, Sasquatch."

"Goddammit. How many times do I have to tell you — it's Yeti. Sasquatch is only native to the Americas. Obviously, I'm his Eurasian cousin, more suited to the cold, and packing substantially larger appendages — my penis, for example."

"I'm glad you mentioned that, because I've put in a recommendation to your doctor that you need immediate penis reduction surgery. It's putting far too much stress on your heart."

"You mean your heart."

The orderly, who had been patiently waiting, looked at his watch and said it was time to load me onto the plane. John grew uncomfortable and cleared his throat as he started to speak.

"Finn, seriously — I can't thank you enough. What you did was..."

He started to get choked up and had to pause to regain his composure.

"I was just doing what any friend would have done," I said.

He wiped his eyes and cleared his throat.

"I'll never forget what you did for me — even when I'm rich and powerful and happier than all three of you put together."

Everyone shared another laugh, but now it was time to leave. The orderly transferred me to the travel gurney, and an uncomfortable silence descended upon the room.

"Finn, make sure you think of me when you dump," Corn said.

"That goes without saying."

"Good, then I'll just stay here and play cards with Sasquatch, and let you and Lux have some alone time," he said.

"How many times do I have to keep telling you people that it's Yeti, goddammit? Didn't any of you pay attention in school?"

Now, I was out in the aisle and had a final look at my friends.

"Well, then — until we meet again," I said, feeling my own eyes starting to tear up.

I was going to miss Corn and John, and I gave a final wave as I was rolled out of the room, savoring every last second of their banter. We exited the building, and Lux walked alongside, holding my hand all the way to the plane, not even breaking contact when they strapped my gurney into place. At that point, she leaned down and kissed me, and I could feel the wetness of her tears warm against my cheeks. I hated goodbyes and had to admit that leaving Lux was going to be the most difficult thing I'd ever done. We could hear the engines revving up and knew our last goodbye was finally here.

"I'm sorry, ma'am, but it's time to leave," a crewman said.

Lux looked down at me, her expression anxious and her heart visibly pounding.

"I like you a lot," she said.

"I like you a lot you, too."

She smiled, and I'm pretty sure she was thinking the other L word, but both of us were too chickenshit to say it.

"Lux, thanks for coming back for me out there. You know I owe you one now."

"I know."

She kissed me one last time before releasing my hand and wiping the tears from her eyes. She smiled sadly then turned and walked towards the exit ramp, pausing at the very end to look back. She started to say something but stopped, looking uncomfortable before turning back around and continuing on her way. I, however, never took my eyes off of her until the rear door closed, and she disappeared completely from view. That was the last time I saw Lux Vonde.

CHAPTER SIX
The Honey Pot

CURRENT DAY.

I sat there staring at the last sip of coffee in my cup, and, while I may have physically been sitting on my deck in my weather beaten chair, my mind was ten years, seven thousand, four hundred and eleven miles away. I had wanted to continue what we had started in Afghanistan, but life had a funny way of making its own plans. After I was transferred stateside, the surgeons removed the bullet, but I would never make it back to Pararescue. They gave me an Air Force Cross for saving the Senator's son and assigned me to a desk job in intelligence doing background investigations on civilian contractors. Lux, meanwhile, finished her tour and came back to the states six months later, but our paths would never cross.

I spent my remaining time in the Air Force in a cubicle, and it was, for me, like being the human equivalent a veal calf living in a feeding pen. Fortunately, my educational background, military service record, and time with the Joint Special Operations Command soon got me noticed by the guys from Langley—which is why I knew a thing or two about plausible deniability. They asked me to join the Special Activities Division or SAD, a fairly unknown, and highly elite faction of the CIA that did everything I used to do in Pararescue—and a whole lot more. I was practically James Bond, except for the fancy car, champagne, and endless parade of beautiful women. I suppose I was more like his distant American cousin who did all the same work but drove a beater Hyundai. There were a few beautiful women, but I rarely saved them, and our relationships never lasted any longer than my assignment at the time. It was crazy work and as close as I could get to the good old days of being a PJ, but that phase of my life eventually ended, however, when I went on a mission that directly conflicted with my personal ethics, and I decided it was time to get out and build a new life on my own terms as a civilian.

I moved back to Northern California, specifically the quaint little town of Sausalito, and hoped it would feel like home again, but, at that point, it felt as foreign as everywhere else I'd been in the world. In time, however, I put down roots, found some old friends, made new ones, and opened my own private investigation business. It paid well when it paid, but, with the cost of living in the Bay Area so high, I pretty much took every job that came my way, and that, of course, is how I ended up with a client like Steven Green.

I worked out of my houseboat, which I'd bought at a discount shortly after the market crashed, and, while an office might have been more professional, clients seemed to like it, and I think it added to my private investigator mystique. It was an interesting place to live and resided on the fine line between the haves on the hill and the have-nots on the water. This was the nether region of Sausalito, the unspoken no man's land between poverty and excess where the normal people lived—well, as normal as they got in Marin County.

My place sat at the end of the dock in one of the smaller, nicer marinas and had million dollar views without the necessity of actually having a million dollars. It had three levels, four bedrooms, and a cool bar I'd built to look like a miniature version of the one in *Star Wars* where Obi-Wan Kenobi and Luke Skywalker met Han

Solo. It also blended nicely with my minimalist Scandinavian furniture to give the place a modern open feel. More important than its interior design motif, however, was the fact that this was the first place I'd called home in my adult life, so I was determined to keep it, regardless of the economy's ups and downs. If worse came to worse, I might even end up moonlighting at Starbucks to pay my mortgage, but what was life without challenges?

So, there I sat, reliving the last ten years in a little over ten seconds. I drank the last sip of coffee and couldn't help wondering what the hell Lux was doing working for the Agency, least of all, in a place called Soft Taco Island. Nothing was ever as it appeared, however, and my gut was telling me to proceed with caution.

"Well?" Bridgette asked.

I let out a long sigh as I stared into my empty coffee mug that I suddenly wished was full of vodka. Of course, I was going to get Lux off Soft Taco Island. I owed her my life, but, more important than that or the million dollar bonus was the simple fact that she was a friend, and I would have gone to the ends of the earth to save her ass.

"Yeah, I'll do it."

Bridgette smiled, and her face lit up with relief as she leaned over and hugged me. Then, without removing her arms, she looked at me with those eyes so much like her sister's then proceeded to kiss me. It was nothing like the whopper Lux had landed on me all those years ago, but it still made me a little uncomfortable and brought back a flood of memories I'd spent ten years trying to forget. It was a hell of a way to get a new client, and I couldn't shake the nagging feeling that she wasn't telling me the entire story. Bad things always seemed to happen after someone or something ruined my morning dump, and I took those omens seriously.

"Thank you," she said.

"What's our time frame? How soon do we have to do this?"

"My uncle wants this done as soon as possible—preferably no

more than a week."

"That's not a lot of time."

"It's all we've got."

A week wasn't a lot of time when you were working alone. It wasn't like the good old days with the Special Activities Division where we'd go halfway around the world with only a moment's notice and very minimal planning to rescue a dignitary or snatch a terrorist. Of course, it was a hell of a lot easier when you had a team of trained professionals and the resources of the entire United States government at your disposal. We could get a submarine, plane, or even a trained pig if the mission called for it.

"OK, but there are some things I'm curious about," I said.

"Ask away."

"Lux's last name is Vonde not Vandenberg. What's the story behind that?"

"Vonde was our mother's maiden name. Lux refused to share the same name as our stepmother and had it changed."

"You didn't?"

"It's the name I was born with, so there was no way in hell I was going to let that wicked bitch of a stepmother take it away."

"Fair enough, but I find it strange that Lux never told me anything about her family."

"I suppose she wanted to get as far from the Vandenberg name as possible so that she could make it on her own merits."

I nodded, realizing that went along perfectly with the Lux I fell in love with back in Afghanistan. Now, I had only one more, rather unusual, question.

"Have you ever wondered what the hell made Lux decide to fly the very object that was the vehicle of her father's demise? It's a strange career choice, and I can only imagine it was an attempt to conquer her own demons."

Bridgette took a moment to ponder my words before answering.

"I never really thought about it, but that's an interesting theory,

Doctor Freud."

"Yeah, analyzing people's motivations is one of the hazards of having been a psychology major. Well, now that we have that out of the way, I suppose I'm going to need you to tell me everything you know about Soft Taco Island."

We decided we should talk over lunch, so I took a shower, put on some proper clothes, and we went to my usual local diner, where she spent the next two hours filling me in on everything she knew about the island. It sat just north of Martinique, and it was small compared to its neighbors—no more than ten miles across at its widest point. It was owned and governed by a French aristocrat named Adrien Babineux, and, on the surface, his island looked like a Club Med. It had five star accommodations and warm weather activities such as jet skiing, parasailing, and snorkeling, but its number one tourist destination was its highly renowned casino, which was, apparently, frequented by the famous and über-wealthy. Like every place with lots of money and important people running around, it had a lot of security—more than it needed, in my opinion. They had state-of-the art electronic surveillance systems and enough manpower and vehicles to protect a small country, which, I suppose, it was. Most of the security staff were former military in some form or another who had traded in their fatigues for a fat paycheck, swim trunks, and a Tommy Bahama shirt.

Lux was able to infiltrate Babineux's operation by working as a helicopter pilot, flying its exclusive guests to and from the Island of Martinique. Bridgette didn't know the specific details of her sister's mission, but she had noticed that Lux her spent her free time reconnoitering the island's various attractions—especially the casino, where she mingled with staff and guests alike. She had always been a good card player, so it made perfect sense that she would be drawn to that particular location. Interestingly, the employees were allowed to gamble, which meant the island often reclaimed what it paid out in wages, and the really unlucky ones incurred so much debt that they actually became indentured servants working for free until they paid off their marker. As a business model, it was particularly creative if not totally amoral. God only knew why the CIA was interested in Soft Taco Island, but my initial suspicion would be that they were thinking about investing. I took detailed notes and would get additional information from a source I still had at the Agency. Of course, my final stop would be the Internet where a shitload of useful information was often stored in plain view.

After lunch, we still needed to do a lot of planning, but she said she wanted to go to her hotel and pick up some things. It was located only a short distance away and seriously overpriced in my opinion, so, without thinking, I asked if she wanted to save her money and stay with me. She said yes, and suddenly I had a very beautiful houseguest. Lovely, I was going to have to get up at five in the morning if I wanted to take a decent uninterrupted dump. She headed off to her hotel to get her things, and I thought I would have at least a couple of hours to do a quick cleaning before she returned. I needed to put fresh sheets on the bed in the guest room and do a little laundry. Surprisingly, she made it back in twenty-five minutes flat and looked as happy as could be as she rolled her luggage into my living room.

"What should we do for dinner?" she asked.

"You're the client, so you get to make the call."

"I'm happy with whatever, but it might be nice to dine in and put some steaks on the grill. That way, we can talk more about the case."

"Sounds good, but we'll have to go to the grocery store."

She headed for the door, and, as I followed right behind her, I couldn't help but admire how well her tight fitting exercise pants fit her round, muscular little backside. It was hard not to stare, and I would even go so far as to say it was bewitching, not unlike the fabled eyes of Medusa. Unlike the monster of Greek Mythology's deadly stare which turned people into stone, Bridgette's ass only hardened one part of my body—namely, Tag Junior, who even now was starting to strain against the fabric of my pants. I must say, it was hard to look at Bridgette's backside and not think of Lux, who, like her sister, also had quite a lovely posterior. I never met Lux and Bridgette's parents, but I am absolutely certain that at least one or both of them had a really nice ass.

"You sure look a lot like your sister."

"Yeah, but I think I have a nicer ass."

"Oh really? I hadn't thought much about it."

She turned and smiled, giving me a look that told me she knew exactly where my eyes had just been. Bridgette obviously knew that no mortal man could keep his gaze off of her fine form, and I decided it would be a lot easier to avoid staring if I simply walked side by side with her from here on out. We reached the parking lot, and she paused.

"I turned in my rental car and got a ride here, so I hope you don't mind if we take your car," she said.

"No problem. Do you have a strong neck?"

"Why? What did you have in mind?" she asked, with a naughty smile that sent my imagination into overdrive.

"The Silver Hornet," I said, pointing at my car.

That was my nickname for my silver Subaru WRX STi, and was, of course, an homage to Inspector Clouseau's car in the movie *The Revenge of the Pink Panther*. His car, like mine, was silver and had a ridiculously large spoiler amongst other aerodynamic appendages. While his was a piece of shit, mine was a testament to automotive engineering with its all-wheel drive, three hundred horsepower and torque, and ability to rocket to sixty miles per hour in about four point two seconds—which wasn't bad for a car that cost around forty grand brand new. The downside, however, was that I took a lot of scorn from Marin County's elite, the majority of whom wouldn't be caught dead in anything less than a BMW, Audi, or Mercedes. I loved my car and knew that it had what mattered, where it mattered. Bridgette, however, looked a little skeptical.

"What's the wing for?"

"Sixty motherfucking pounds of down force at a hundred and twenty miles per hour," I said, proudly.

"Does it have heated seats?"

"No."

"Well there you go."

"How about you drive it to the store."

"Fine."

I hit the unlock-button on the key fob then threw her the keys. We climbed in, and she started the engine and looked at me apprehensively.

"I hope no one recognizes me," she said.

"They won't at a hundred and twenty miles per hour."

She pulled onto Gate Five Road, hit the gas, and the turbo charged engine roared to life and drilled both of us firmly back into our seats. She was caught off guard by the blazing performance of the Silver Hornet and screamed out loud as if she were in the throws of an earth shattering climax. She let off the gas then looked over at me, her expression one of bewilderment, as though she had just experienced a miracle.

"I take it all back," she said.

"I knew you would."

"Who needs heated seats?"

"Not you. Your ass is already hot enough."

We pulled into the parking lot, found a space, then made our way to the entrance of the store. It was crowded and there weren't many carts left, but I still managed to find one of those new compact models that made it a hell of a lot easier to navigate the busy aisles. We decided to start in the produce section and had just passed the overpriced organic tomatoes, when, only ten feet away, I noticed my ex-girlfriend Melanie. She was dressed in her usual business attire of high heels, tight black dress pants, and a body hugging white turtleneck sweater that she wore to accentuate her ample breasts. As usual, her makeup was perfect and her long brown hair was blown out and looking as though she had just come from the salon. She seemed a tad bit overdressed for casual shopping, but she was probably just on her way home from her office and had stopped here to do a little shopping. Still, it was a tad bit strange to see her here, as she wasn't much of a cook and generally preferred to dine out at fine restaurants whenever possible. Bridgette, sensing my unease, asked what was wrong, and I told her that the woman up ahead of us was my ex-girlfriend.

"So, whats the big deal?" she asked.

"I generally prefer to avoid her because she's kind of a bitch."

"I see that as all the more reason to go say hello."

Bridgette put her arm through mine then dragged me forward towards the hell that was my past, and we arrived to find Melanie rooting around for the perfect basket of strawberries.

"Hello, Melanie—are those strawberries for the Champagne that you're going to be drinking on the yacht later tonight?"

She looked surprised to see me but quickly composed herself before responding.

"Oh, hello, Tag, and yes, they are as a matter of fact. How did you guess?" she asked.

Before I could answer, Bridgette joined the conversation.

"Oh hi! I'm Bridgette. I take it you know Tag," she said, in a bubbly tone, playing it off as though she didn't know our real relationship history.

"Yeah, we used to—um—we're friends," Melanie responded.

"Ex-friends," I muttered, under my breath.

Melanie, apparently, heard my comment and gave me an annoyed look before turning her judgmental gaze back to Bridgette, whereupon she proceeded to scrutinize her from head to toe. Men often viewed women in a similar manner, but it was generally a product of our biological imperative and subsequent desire to procreate. Women, however, seemed to be compiling the competition's strengths and weakness—both physically and in terms of hair, makeup, and clothing. I suppose that too may have been a biological imperative, but it was generally done in the pursuit of hate rather than love. Whatever the reason, Melanie was not happy about how she compared to Bridgette, and, while she was beautiful, Bridgette was stunning, and that only served to make me feel that much better about our chance supermarket encounter.

"It's very nice to meet you, Melanie," Bridgette said.

"Yeah, you too, Bridgette," Melanie responded, without an ounce of conviction.

Bridgette glanced at her watch and feigned sadness.

"Oh, I'm sorry, but we should really get going, as we're celebrating our two month anniversary and still have a lot of things left on our to-do list."

I wanted to blurt out that anal was at the top of that list—purely for shock value, but I knew I'd probably be scorned by both parties.

"Oh—well then—um—congratulations," Melanie said.

"Thanks, and it was nice meeting you."

"You too," Melanie said, as she completely ignored me and turned to leave.

Feeling a little left out, I decided I should do the polite thing and make a point of saying goodbye.

"Goodbye, Melanie!" I said, loudly.

She stopped and turned around, smiling and giving me her *fuck you* face, a face I knew only too well.

"Oh, I'm sorry—goodbye, Tag. It was really nice running into you," she said, her snottiness and complete lack of sincerity inadvertently making me smile, as it reminded me of how lucky I was not to be with her anymore.

"Yeah—and you as well."

She proceeded to make a hasty retreat, and I had a moment to gloat as I thought about the fact that Bridgette had just said two months. That was, coincidentally, the exact amount of time

I had been broken up with Melanie! Sweet ramblings of revenge! That made it seem as though I'd moved on more quickly than she thought. I waited until I was sure we were out of earshot of Melanie before speaking.

"That—was—awesome!"

"What do you mean?"

"I've never seen her so uncomfortable."

"Not even when you broke up with her?"

"She broke up with me—for fucking Yacht Club Guy."

"What does that even mean?"

"Obviously, it means that the guy belongs to a yacht club."

"And what's wrong with that?"

"Nothing per se, as I, myself have been known to frequent the local Sausalito yacht club, but the yacht club guy I'm referring to belongs to the St. Francis, one of the most exclusive yacht clubs on the West Coast."

"Oh yeah, I know about it, because my uncle's a member."

"Then you know that it attracts a very exclusive clientele, a clientele which, unfortunately, includes one very smug stockbroker who enjoys bedding other men's girlfriends on his yacht."

"Well shit, if I had known that, I would have really played it up."

Played it up? Jesus, I thought she had. One could only wonder at the amazing cruelty women were capable of, but, in this instance, Melanie deserved it. She was one of those women who was attracted to men by the size of their bulge—and by that I mean wallet. She loved the money more than the man and went through both like a Boy Scout through beans. I told Bridgette about the night that Melanie had bedded Yacht Club Guy and then called me from his yacht to break up—right after they had sex.

"Fuck her, and I don't mean that in the literal sense," she said, as she made her way deeper into the produce section.

I followed along, unable to stop replaying our little exchange, my smile lasting all the way from the avocados to the onions. Bridgette eventually looked over at me with a puzzled expression on her face.

"I don't get it," She said.

"What?"

"You're out of her league."

"Seriously? Most guys think she's pretty hot."

"I think you're a little hotter. Maybe it's time for you to take a man pill and man the fuck up."

Man up? What the fuck was that supposed to mean? And what was that compliment all about? I don't think a woman had ever specifically used the word hot before, but maybe I was getting better with age—like a fine wine. Or, more likely, she was just blowing smoke up my ass to keep me happy so that I would rescue her sister. Either way, my self-esteem was approaching an all time high, or, at least it was until Bridgette saw me glowing with pride and perhaps thought I needed a little grounding.

"Don't get too excited hotshot, because her leaving you for Yacht Club Guy could mean you have a shitty personality," she said.

"Can't be that shitty if you moved out of your hotel to stay with me tonight."

"Excellent deduction, which means Melanie doesn't care about looks or brains."

She patted me on the arm and walked ahead, surveying the various fruits and vegetables, thus giving me the same amazing view I'd enjoyed earlier. Now that she was on her own, however, it was fun to watch the surrounding guys move in from all sides and circle like sharks as they tried to grab covert glances. It didn't take long before she had an entire entourage in tow that was watching her every move. I'm pretty sure she had caught on, because she made a very exciting show of licking her lips as she manhandled a giant cucumber. It's too bad that she didn't have the cruel awareness to see if her love struck lemmings would unknowingly follow her into the feminine hygiene aisle, as it would have been an excellent open field experiment to demonstrate the blind dumb lust of the average male. When I caught up to her, the guys all quickly averted their eyes and scattered like cockroaches as though they were trespassing on my private property. Men were strange. If she had been my girlfriend, it wouldn't have bothered me in the slightest that they found her attractive. Their stares only meant that I had chosen wisely, if not superficially.

I grabbed some asparagus, then we moved on to pick out some grass-fed, feel-good steaks before finishing up in the freezer section, where we hoped to find dessert. We both agreed on ice cream, but decided to go with gelato, as it had less fat and a richer texture. She opened the door and rummaged around for a good minute before finding two potential flavors. She turned to me to reveal a pint of Italian frozen heaven in each hand, though my eyes were drawn elsewhere—namely to the emergence of her very prominent and particularly hard nipples. I'd seen a very similar incident in the movie Kingpin, but seeing it in real life was exciting enough to make my penis start pitching a tent in my pants.

"Which of these do you prefer?" she asked.

"Honestly? I find myself equally drawn to both."

"Come on—Tahitian vanilla bean or sea salt caramel?"

"Well, if you're referring to the gelato, then my answer would still have to be—both."

She looked puzzled, until she glanced down and realized that her nipples were particularly protrusive and doing their best to bust through the fabric of her tight shirt. She made a brief, though exciting, show of unsuccessfully trying to get them to stand down, and I was happy to see that they were fighters and resisted her best efforts. The world could do with a few more nipples, and let's face it—they seemed like the point of having breasts.

"OK, I guess we'll just have to get both. Now, come on. We better get going before you start whacking it on the frozen vegetables," she said.

"Too cold. Doesn't do a lot for penis size. I'd rather rub one out on a nice warm rotisserie chicken—preferably free range as my semen has enough hormones as it is."

She responded with a mildly disapproving look, then we headed to the front of the store and went to the nearest check stand. The checker turned out to be a guy named Jonathan who I knew pretty well from shopping at the store, and he gave me the I approve look when he saw Bridgette. He too noticed the nipples and tried not to stare—a lot. I felt his pain. It was man's burden to admire the female form, and nipples were to breasts what exclamation points were to bold statements—and it wasn't an accident that a banana split had a cherry on top. Just as I was about to pay and end the highlight of Jonathan's day, Bridgette beat me to the draw and ran her card.

"Wait! Don't pay!" I said.

"Why—did we forget something?" she asked.

Melanie just happened to be one check stand over and was obviously listening in to our banter, so I decided to throw a little fuel on the fire of our faux anniversary.

"Yeah, what about the massage oil, bath beads, and candles?" I asked.

"Already in the cart, and you'll be happy to hear that I also grabbed some utility rope, because I don't think the silk sash you used to tie me to the bed will be strong enough if I keep having so many intense orgasms."

"Well, then we'll just have to hope the rope holds."

Melanie's checker finished bagging her items, and she was forced to walk past us on her way out.

"Well—um—have fun on your two month anniversary," she said, not even trying to sound sincere.

"You, too."

"Pardon?"

"I said, you too."

She looked confused but then realized that it was, more or less, her two month anniversary with Yacht Club Guy.

"Well, thank you, Tag, and might I say that we'll obviously be starting our celebration tonight at the St. Francis Yacht Club."

Leave it to Melanie to try and hurt my feelings by playing the fucking yacht club card.

"That sounds absolutely fabulous. Unfortunately, Bridgette and I will be spending our evening in, though I suppose I'll still be eating out—if you catch my drift."

That last comment was an intentional jab based on the fact that I had heard from a mutual friend that Yacht Club Guy was apparently a little stingy in the oral sex department.

"Childish as ever," Melanie said, giving me an icy glare before abruptly turning and heading towards the door, where her haste caused her to accidentally bowl over a toddler who was waiting to get a helium balloon.

The kid started crying and his mother was not pleased in spite of the fact that Melanie did her best to apologize.

"See you later, Mel! Oh, and say hello to Yacht Club Guy for me," I called out.

She proceeded to give me the finger then continued on her way, moving like a woman on a mission. All in all, her behavior seemed like a rather extreme reaction to the thought of me being with a new woman, but people often held on to the idea that they had some kind of proprietary hold over their exes and imagined them living in a kind of abstinent purgatory. Sadly, I had been unintentionally living in that place, which is why I took so much joy in making Melanie uncomfortable.

We picked up our bags and exited the store to discover that we had, coincidentally, parked right next to Yacht Club Guy. He was sitting in his Mercedes, obviously waiting for Melanie, and he was, as usual, wearing his silly looking captain's hat as he screwed around on his smart phone—most likely checking his stocks. He, therefore, didn't notice her until she tapped on his back fender, and, at that point, he pulled the trunk release and returned his attention back to his phone. What a gentleman. We were parked to his left, so Bridgette had to walk right past his open window to get to her door, and there was nothing like a beautiful woman in a pair of yoga pants to get a man's attention. Now, Yacht Club Guy was officially uninterested in his phone and had placed his full attention on Bridgette. To make matters even better, Melanie was now seated in the passenger seat and focused on her man—or more specifically, the fact that he was focused on another woman—the very same woman I was supposedly now dating. Bridgette, being the devious creature she was, obviously knew that she had a new admirer and decided to put on a show. Keeping her legs ramrod straight, she bent over at the waist to re-tie her shoelaces, the gesture making her backside a glorious ornament as it hovered mere inches from Yacht Club Guy's wanting gaze. She stayed there for a long moment before coming back up and transitioning into a quick stretch of her upper body. She locked her hands together behind her butt then lifted her arms, arching her back and thrusting her breasts out against the thin fabric of her shirt, allowing her particularly prominent nipples to poke through and say a heartfelt hello to all those around. It was quite a show, and, as I was already at half mast, it was fair to say that Yacht Club Guy was hiding a serious chub in his Dockers. Better still, this little exhibition would most likely be haunting him as he went to bed with Melanie on his yacht later tonight. Bridgette finished her stretch and sat down in the Silver Hornet, where she made a good show of appearing to be completely unaware of our immediate neighbors. Life didn't get any better than this!

"That was brutal," I said.

"What do you mean? I was just stretching. If I had truly wanted to be mean I would have done something more like this," she said, as she leaned over, kissed me passionately, then dropped her head down in my lap and began to bob it up and down over my manhood.

"What the..." were the only words I could get out before I realized she was pretending to deliver oral sex.

I played it cool, rolling my head back as though engulfed in sweet ecstasy, but a very large part of me was legitimately excited to receive faux felatio—as it was the closest thing to real felatio I'd experienced in quite a while. I continued my act for a bit longer then innocently turned my gaze over towards Melanie and Yacht Club Guy, and I pretended to be surprised and embarrassed when we locked eyes. The two of them were staring in rapt attention as I reached down and hit the button to lower the passenger window.

"Oh, shit. Hello Melanie—and Yacht Club Guy. I didn't see you two there," I said.

Bridgette popped her head up, doing an excellent job of looking embarrassed.

"Oh, wow. This is awkward," she said.

"Yeah, it sure is. Sorry about that, but sometimes I fear my manhood is like catnip for women."

"Meow!" Bridgette said.

Melanie didn't look very amused, and Yacht Club Guy just looked envious, obviously because of my current company and our supposed current activity—though I couldn't help but suspect my enormous spoiler was a contributing factor. We left the store parking lot, both of us laughing at our little encounter as I made the turn onto Gate Five Road. We drove along in the unusually warm afternoon sun, and, gazing over at my new client, I had to take a moment to catch my breath. My life was truly changing for the better, so all I could do was watch and wait to see what wonders the world brought next.

CHAPTER SEVEN
Warm Milk

The sun was slowly dipping down behind the coastal mountains, and the sky above was awash in brilliant hues of orange and pink as we ate dinner, sipped our cocktails, and watched the seabirds hunt for fish outside in the dying light of the day. We were having such a good time, it felt as though we should be lighting a fire and enjoying it from a faux bearskin rug rather than planning a rescue mission. We finished dinner and moved into the living room, where we could see the lights of Tiburon coming to life and reflecting off the dark calm waters of Richardson Bay. Of course, spending time with Bridgette and seeing how much she looked like her sister, I found it hard not to think about Lux, and wondered how she was doing at the moment and why in the hell she was in a place called Soft Taco Island. Still, Bridgette was fun to be around, and we talked so long that I lost all sense of time. Hours later, when I finally looked at my watch, I saw that it was getting close to midnight and realized it was probably a good idea to go to bed so that we could get an early start in the morning. We were flying out the next day at four o'clock on the Vandenberg private jet, which didn't give me a lot of time to pack and prepare for an impromptu rescue mission a half a world away. We went upstairs, and I showed Bridgette to the guest room. I hadn't had time to put on fresh sheets earlier in the day, so we worked together to make the bed. I was very meticulous about getting the top sheet properly centered while she was haphazard, not really caring if the same amount hung on her side.

"You're as bad as my sister," she said

"It's probably from being in the military. It's hard to break the habits."

"I never saw the point. It's just a bed, and I only do two things in bed."

"Only two? That's a little limiting."

"Not the way I do them," she said, with another of her wonderfully mischievous smiles.

I could only imagine.

"Good talk. I'll see you in the morning. There are towels in the bathroom and just knock if you need anything else."

She came forward and gave me a nice long hug, then I adjourned to my room to take a quick shower. Afterward, I put on some pajama bottoms and a T-shirt then slid into bed and opened up my laptop. I googled Soft Taco Island and clicked on the link for their official website. I went through the various pages and saw that the place looked exactly as Bridgette had described, which meant that she had a surprisingly good mind for details and would have made an excellent spy. My final task was to click on the map link and memorize the layout of the island—a habit I formed during my time in special operations and the Agency. It was always a good idea to know your surroundings in case the shit hit the fan. Finished, I decided I'd done enough for the evening and closed my laptop, set it on the bedside table, and was about to turn off the light when I heard a knock at the door.

"Come in," I said.

Bridgette popped her head inside a second later.

"Hey, do you have soap or body wash?"

"Oh yeah, shit! Sorry about that. I forgot to put some in that bathroom. Let me get you a bar."

She walked in the rest of the way, a towel the only thing covering her body from her breasts to her butt, and, if I had truly been thinking ahead, I would have made sure she only had a washcloth in that bathroom. Oh well, as they say, hindsight is always twenty-twenty. She followed me into my bathroom, and I opened a drawer and pulled out a bar of soap. She took hold of it, looked at the label, then gave me a questioning smile.

"What?" I asked.

"Pomegranate and lemon verbena scented Dove soap?"

"What? Too feminine for a guy? Are we back to the damaged or gay thing?"

"No, I'd say we've officially moved on to metrosexual."

"Maybe, but it takes a real man to pull off pomegranate and lemon verbena."

"I completely agree," she said, as she headed back to her room.

I turned off the lights and lay in my bed, listening to the sound of the water running through the pipes. This, of course, made me think about what was taking place on the other side of the wall and, more specifically, what part of Bridgette's body she was washing at that moment. It wasn't doing much to help me sleep, so I instead imagined Yacht Club Guy folding endless pairs of his khaki Dockers. I fell asleep at nineteen.

I had no idea how long I had been asleep when I felt a presence in my room and came awake to discover a figure standing at the foot of my bed. The room was mostly dark, but the ambient light from the half full moon shining through the skylight was enough for me to see my late night visitor was Bridgette. She was wearing only a pair of thong underwear and some kind of camisole top that was no better at concealing her breasts than a sheet of cellophane. Of course, seeing her in such a heavenly state of semi undress made me wonder if I might be dreaming—that is, until she spoke.

"Tag, are you awake?" she asked.

"I am now. What's up?"

"I can't sleep."

"Do you want me to go downstairs and make you some warm milk?" I asked, instantly regretting my words.

Sweet lord of unintended double entendres! When I was a youngster, my mother used to make me a glass of warm milk when I had trouble sleeping, but, at this very moment, it suddenly sounded like a colorful euphemism for taking hold of my man-handle and churning out a fresh batch of ball butter. Thankfully, Bridgette didn't have an equally dirty mind and took it the way it was intended.

"No, it's nothing like that. You see—with all that's going on, I just don't want to be alone right now. Is it all right if I sleep in here with you?"

Shit. I had been single for two months since Melanie left me for Yacht Club Guy, and I was definitely craving a woman's affection. It certainly didn't make it any easier that I had spent the last two weeks watching Jessica Green and Tarzan attempt every position imaginable on his living room couch, but, it was also a moral dilemma. I was attracted to Bridgette, as any sane man would be, but she was a client and the younger sister of the love of my life who was, at this very moment, being held prisoner on a ridiculously named island. Perhaps it was a perfectly innocent request, and I was just fooling myself into thinking that anything could happen. Guys always had a way of twisting the slightest communication from a woman into a full-blown come on, so, in reality, Bridgette probably wasn't the least bit attracted to me. We were just two adults sleeping together, and it did not in any way imply sex. Surely, it would be unfair to deny a fellow human being the comfort and emotional support she desired in a time of great need.

"Of course, come on in."

I did the gentlemanly thing and lifted the covers on her side of the bed, allowing her to slide in and snuggle up alongside me. She threw her arm over my chest and now her breasts were pressed firmly up against me and her head was resting on my shoulder, the scent of her freshly washed hair flooding my senses. I could feel the warmth of her body radiating through my thin cotton pajama bottoms, and I suddenly wished I had worn thick flannel, although it would do little to contain the hard-on that was most certainly going to come between us — so to speak.

She was moving the way a cat does as it tries to get comfortable, and all but purring as she shifted around and slid her leg up and down my thigh. Things suddenly got more interesting, however, when she moved her hand underneath my T-shirt and began caressing my chest. Instinctively, I did the same, as it seemed rude not to reciprocate, though I obviously steered clear of her breasts and stuck to the neutral areas of her side and the small of her back. With each pass, she reached a little lower, and I unconsciously followed her lead, moving my hands in perfect synchronicity with hers. A couple more swoops and my hand crossed the friend line, the theoretical border where the flesh of the back becomes the curvature of the buttocks. Oh shit.

My fingers danced ever so lightly over the terrain, and I was keenly aware that at any moment she would likely make a hasty retreat. Instead of pulling away, however, she pressed forward with her hips each time my hand slipped down a little farther across the top of her buttocks. Sweet siren of sexual tension! I was starting to sense this might be moving towards a more dynamic form of comforting. Of course, while I was busy focusing on what my hand was doing, she had moved hers down to my thigh, where it was dangerously close to my emerging hard-on. The consummate explorer, she continued on to my other leg and hit a very obvious obstacle in the middle. After giving it an exploratory squeeze, she moved her hand up and into the waistband of my pajama bottoms — the encounter leaving my head spinning and my penis fully erect. I was at a dangerous crossroad and knew that whatever I did next was going to have a major impact on my life in the coming days. Of course, the decision was taken out of my hands when the more powerful will of my penis overrode any reservations, and I reached down and took full hold of her buttocks—the move inspiring her to press her hips against mine and let out a little moan. I was finally able to put my hand upon what I'd seen in those pants, and it felt as good as it looked—firm and round, and I could tell this horse was built to run. Our faces were hovering only an inch apart, our lips practically touching, and I felt like a silly teenager as I lay there feeling her up without so much as a first kiss.

"Fuck. Second base," I said.

"What?"

I didn't respond, as I was thinking about how I had somehow made it to second base without even tagging first. If memory served me correctly, first base was kissing while, I think, fondling was clearly closer to second. Time to backtrack. Our lips were practically touching, so it was no surprise when she closed the distance and kissed me. It started with the simple touching of our lips, but quickly grew more passionate as our tongues came together and battled for supremacy in the once neutral ground between our mouths. We parted lips for a brief second, and I unconsciously blurted out another idiotic baseball reference.

"First base."

"What?"

"Shit. Nothing, sorry."

My two months of abstinence had obviously taken their toll on my mind, and I was blathering like an idiot. Thankfully, she kept going, and, as our lips came back together, her capable hands took firm hold of my manhood, and I realized the kid gloves were off, and it was time to run for third. I slid my hand under her shirt and kept going up until the topography changed from the hard muscle of her stomach to the soft curvature of her breasts. I traced the outlines of each one, starting at their farthest dimension and working my way to their centers, where I felt the areolae contract and the nipples harden at my touch.

"Wait—is this also second base?" I asked, as I momentarily broke free of her lips.

"Excuse me?"

"Nothing—fuck. Sorry."

I went back to enjoying the riches of her body only to be interrupted when she slid off my pajama bottoms with her foot. I decided to go along with her idea and rolled her onto her back and peeled her shirt off over her head. She did the same to me then reached around my neck and pulled me down, bringing our lips back together with a sense of urgency that only existed in a moment of hot, harried passion. We kissed and hungrily explored each other with our tongues, until I made a hasty retreat and moved south, kissing her neck and using it as an expressway down to her breasts. I reached her right nipple first and traced a path around it with my tongue before tickling its hard tip and moving on to its neighbor. She let out a soft moan and slipped her hands down towards my penis, which was uncomfortably hard and waging its own private battle with the fabric of her underwear. The prodding had gotten it the attention it wanted, and she began stroking it, paying special attention to the tip by encircling it with her fingers at the culmination of each pass. I was drunk with lust and what tiny shred of guilt remained was quickly dissipating. I didn't exactly initiate any of this, but I certainly wasn't doing anything to stop it either. Could this all fit under the umbrella of comforting another person? Perhaps guilt was an unnecessary bi-product of the puritanical roots of the early pilgrims, and a more enlightened approach would be to adopt a more international sensibility in these matters. The Europeans were famous for this kind of comforting, especially the French whose national pastimes were wine, cheese, and sex.

"Vive la France!"

Bridgette, thankfully, continued to ignore my outbursts and set upon my manhood, using her mouth and hands to conduct her own version of tug of war. Feeling the obvious winner was going to be me in only a matter of seconds, it was time to return the favor.

With the will it would take to reach the peak of Everest, I pulled away from the immense pleasure and shifted her onto her back, and took a moment to gaze at my beautiful guest. What divine twist of fate brought this woman into my bed to drag me from my long dark time of abstinence? I slid her underwear off then reached down and ran my fingers along her shapely legs, the only blemish to mar her perfect skin being a tiny crescent shaped birthmark on her left inner thigh. I moved my hands farther along and ever closer to her feminine essence only to feel her open her legs and invite me in. The time for contemplation was over and the moment for action was here. I leaned forward and kissed her breasts then dragged my lips ever so slowly down her stomach, taking my time to enjoy every inch of her tempting flesh. She wriggled in sweet delight as I dropped below her hips and approached her well-manicured grass-land, where I discovered that the summer monsoon season had already started. I pressed my tongue into her essence then made my way north to her clitoris, where my efforts elicited soft moans of pleasure. I gradually increased the pace and pressure and, soon, I felt her legs extend around my shoulders and pull me in like the pincers of a praying mantis. I reached around and took hold of her buttocks, pulling her pelvis to my mouth, the tension rising in her body until a great cry erupted from her lips, her back arching as she passed the point of no return and entered the sweet throws of cli-max. Her entire body was engulfed in spasms of pleasure, loud cries escaping her lips until I at last eased my efforts. She came to rest, her thighs still quivering as she lifted my head to hers and kissed me long and hard on the lips before breaking free to speak.

"I want you inside of me," she said.

"Fourth base?"

"Seriously now—don't say another word. Just lie down and be quiet."

I rolled over, and she slid on top and used her hands to guide my throbbing manhood into her vagina as skillfully as a gondolier uses an oar to navigate the canals of Venice. The docking completed, she began rocking up and down, making sure to maximize her clitoral stimulation by grinding her hips firmly against mine at the end of each pass. We worked our way into a robust rhythm, and, with her on top, my hands were free to explore the treasures of her body. I ran my hands down her back and took hold of her buttocks, feeling its firm curves as I helped to steer her hips into mine. Soon, my attention was drawn to the playful dance of flesh upstairs, and I felt like a kid in a candy store as I reached up and took hold of her breasts, which were moving up and down in a marvelous display of gravity versus inertia. I held one in each hand, a nipple between the thumb and forefinger as I fought to hold them steady against the stormy ride of our lovemaking. I was suddenly reminded of Jessica and Tarzan, and I smiled to myself as I increased my efforts, bringing my pelvis to hers in a great clash of flesh. Bridgette obviously sensed that I was nearing the finish line and leaned forward and braced her hands on my shoulders as she, too, quickened her pace—her sweet moans of pleasure growing gradually louder. I felt myself losing control as though I were tumbling over a waterfall, when, all of a sudden, her head flew back, and I could feel her body tense as we both reached that ultimate crescendo and set forth upon the magnificent reckoning of mutual climax. We continued moving in concert, completing a great sexual concerto until each orgasmic aftershock slowly faded in intensity, and we lay there motionless in the silence of the night. It was then, in the clarity that one only achieves after coitus that a terrible truth sunk in. I just had sex with the love of my life's little sister—and it was glorious.

She collapsed and lay on my chest, both of us covered in a lover's sweat that cooled our bodies now that the heat of our lovemaking had passed. I ran my fingers gently down her back and over her perfect backside which was glowing in the moonlight. I gazed up through the skylight at the heavenly body hundreds of thousands of miles away then down to the one beneath my fingertips—musing over the fact that it was a quarter moon up there, but a full moon right here in my bedroom. We stayed in that position for some time, before Bridgette broke from our quiet reverie and spoke.

"Home run," she said.

"What was that?" I asked, still floating in the absent minded giddiness of post coital euphoria.

"Fuck you, Mr. Baseball! You're lucky I kept going after you blurted out fourth base."

I thought for a moment then felt a little stupid, as I suddenly understood why she was giving me shit.

"Oh yeah, I get it. There is no fourth base because it's fucking home plate. Well, it's been awhile. I was out of practice."

"If that's practice, then I'd love to see you in the game."

We lay there and drifted off to sleep, Bridgette in my arms and the world at rest—at least until morning when the cold light of day might have other plans for my rapidly evolving life. Things sure could change quickly.

We awoke late, and Bridgette slinked out of bed, put on her underwear and top, then padded downstairs while I brushed my teeth and shaved. With two of my morning habits completed, I threw on some shorts and a T-shirt, and was about to go down and check on her when she came strolling into my room carrying two cups of coffee.

"Is it too early to propose?" I asked.

"Yeah, now, shit, shower, and shave, so we can eat breakfast and get the hell out of here."

"I already shaved."

"Good, then all you have to do is shit and shower, and, don't worry, I won't call you this time."

She headed to her bathroom to get ready, and I did the same, though I threw her a curve ball by shitting fast and showering faster, and I had already been sitting at the kitchen counter working on my laptop for ten minutes before she finally made it downstairs.

She was wearing more of that form fitting athletic clothing, and I found it hard to believe that I had intimate knowledge of what lay beneath. She took a seat, and I stood up and put on another pot of coffee then cooked up some eggs and chicken apple sausages. We enjoyed a lovely breakfast together, but then I needed to excuse myself, so that I could do a little more research on Soft Taco Island. I went into my office and called a friend who told people he worked for the State Department, which meant, in the case of this particular friend, that he actually worked for the CIA.

His name was Doug Griffith, and he was a good person to know if you needed information. I had met him back in the glory days with the SAD, though he worked on the intelligence and planning side along with another friend coincidentally named Justin Beeber—except that my Beeber spelled it with an ee and was in no way related to the Canadian pop menace. We formed a highly effective little group we called the Three Amigos, and, while Beeber and I had moved on, Doug stayed at the Agency and rose steadily through the ranks. Now, with his stellar security clearance, he had access to most, if not all, of the government databases. When he finally answered his phone, I asked him to tell me everything he knew about Soft Taco Island, and he told me to stop getting belligerently drunk and going to strip clubs.

"It's obviously an Island, dipshit, and, for the record, I don't believe in the whole strip club thing," I said.

"Bullshit."

"No, it's the God's honest truth. I've never been to one and don't ever plan on going to one."

"You're un-American."

"I don't believe in shoving money down someone's G-string for a few minutes of false affection."

He didn't seem to believe me, so I dropped the subject and focused on the main reason for the call—namely that an old friend, who also happened to be one of his fellow CIA agents, was being held there, and it was likely a matter of life or death. Unfortunately, it took five minutes of arguing and a visit to the island's official website to finally get him to stop laughing and take me seriously. At that point, I sat and patiently listened to the sound of him tapping away on his computer keyboard, while he apparently navigated through the various security screens. He was probably just closing out the windows of the porn sites he had been visiting before I called.

"OK, here's what the State Department has on Soft Taco Island. It is indeed a legitimate sovereign nation in the Caribbean."

"I told you it was real, you dick."

"Whatever, civilian."

He liked to call me civilian to remind me that I was no longer on the inside, but I think he just missed having me around.

"Whatever, government lackey. Get on with the story."

"The place was originally called Black Pearl Island and was a French territory with a small indigenous population and a run-down resort. In 2008, it was deeded over to a French industrialist named Adrien Babineux, and he declared himself president then changed the name to Soft Taco Island. At that point, he poured a shitload of money into developing the place, and now their thriving economy is based on tourism, gambling, and the distilling and export of premium rum."

"Premium rum? Shit! Why haven't I heard about this place before?"

"Because you gave up an exciting life as a secret agent to become a lame version of *Magnum P.I.*," he said.

Magnum P.I. was an extremely popular nineteen eighties television show that took place in Hawaii and starred Tom Selleck, John Hillerman, Roger E. Mosley, and Larry Manetti. While Doug, Beeber, and I had grown up separately, the one childhood experience we all shared was that we had spent our formative years watching the show on a daily basis after it had gone into syndication.

"Hardly, I'm his totally awesome mainland counterpart, the only major difference being that I don't have a formidable mustache or drive a Ferrari."

"Exactly."

"Well, if I'm lame *Magnum*, then you're lame *Rick*."

Rick, as well as his other best friend, *TC*, were two of *Magnum's* cohorts on the show, and the people he always went to when he needed help on a case.

"Why not *TC*?" he asked.

"You don't have the muscle tone, and, more importantly, you're afraid to fly."

TC was pretty ripped and also happened to be a helicopter pilot.

"Fine, but that means Beeber is lame *Higgins*."

Higgins was in charge of the beautiful ocean-front estate where *Magnum* lived, and he was a bit small in stature, which did kind of gel with Beeber in terms of his height.

"Good, and now that we've got that settled, why don't you do something useful and tell me about President Babineaux?"

I heard another series of clicks.

"He comes from an old aristocratic French family, but he crossed the channel and went to Oxford and studied business. Upon graduating, he returned to France and joined the French navy and became a Naval Commando."

"Not bad for a cheese eating French aristocrat."

"No shit, but then after he resigned his commission, he returned to the family business and expanded their holdings into technology, aerospace, mining, the hospitality industry, and, not surprisingly, the industrial military complex of Europe. For you civilians, that means the manufacture and sale of arms."

"He certainly knows where the money is. Sounds like a real prince."

"More like a king, and I have to say, Babineux and his island look mostly legit. I'll see what we have in our CIA databases."

"You've got to have something. One of your agents was arrested on his island for fuck's sake."

"We'll see."

After another series of taps, Doug spoke up with a little excitement in his voice.

"Weird."

"What?"

"Holy Shit. We've got a file on Soft Taco Island."

"Told you so."

"Yeah, but we generally only have files on people or places that pose some kind of security threat to the United States."

"So, Soft Taco Island is considered a threat to the free world? I don't understand? Are they making weapons grade rum?"

"It's certainly possible. You know, I got seriously fucked up on some of that in college, and it wasn't pretty."

"Oh, did you end up crying your eyes out and making sweet love to your roommate's pillow?"

"Pretty much."

"Well, don't feel bad, because that's how I often finish up my evenings these days—except it's with my own pillow."

We had a little laugh then Doug went back to work, tapping away on his keyboard.

"Wait a minute, I've got something interesting," he said.

"What?"

"The file is restricted."

"You can't access it?"

"No—which is pretty weird. The only clearance higher than mine would be the Deputy Director."

"Just my luck that my closest friend at the Agency is a peon."

"Fuck you. Whatever is happening on Soft Taco Island is apparently important to someone here, so my advice to you, civilian, is that you better watch your ass and be very careful while you're down there."

"Thanks. Now, you're free to get back to your porn."

"Very funny. My porn is a stack of paperwork a foot high on my desk."

"Magazines are out of date. Use the Internet."

He hung up, and I took a sip of coffee and thought about what I had just learned. Why in the hell would the CIA give a shit about a crappy little island? None of it made any sense, but I suppose I would find the answer to all those questions and more when I finally dug my little toes into the warm sand of Soft Taco Island. I went upstairs to pack to my things and started with the boring stuff like socks and underwear before moving downstairs for the fun stuff like knives and guns. Since we were flying privately, I could pack whatever I needed and didn't have to worry about airport security. Of course, I would miss the invasive TSA pat down, but I think I had gotten more than enough foreplay last night. I went to what I liked to call my man-room. It was only about ten feet by six feet, and was accessed via a shelving unit that served as a secret door. I didn't really need a secret room, but I had the space and thought it would be a cool project. Four trips to Home Depot and two weeks of work, and it was done.

Standing in front of the bookcase, all I had to do was push on my copy of Ian Fleming's Casino Royale to unlock the secret door and voila, the entire unit slid along the wall and revealed the opening to my man-room. I hit the light switch, and the entire place came ablaze in a bright bluish halogen glow that showed off the weapons and equipment that I'd collected during the course of my unusual career. Everything was neatly hung on the walls, and organized into separate sections allowing me to quickly decide on what I would need for Soft Taco Island. I chose my pistols first, going with the Glock 19 and Walther PPK, the former for firepower and magazine capacity, and the latter for its slimmer profile and concealability. Next, were the long guns which included my DSR-1 sniper rifle, my HK94, and my Colt M4—similar to the one I had used in the service. Some people packed too many pairs of underwear or T-shirts, but I usually packed too many guns. I was good at improvising in the field, but I couldn't improvise pistols, rifles, and submachine guns, and, since Soft Taco Island's security force was well armed, it only made sense to be a little over-prepared. Beyond weapons, I also grabbed my body armor, tactical vest, some climbing hardware, duct tape, underwater GPS, two syringes full of the sedative Ketamine, and some electronic doodads for defeating security systems and sensors. As I was about to leave, I decided to go back and grab four stun grenades—or, as we called them in the trades, flashbangs. I had just put them in the pack when Bridgette came up from behind and tapped me on the shoulder. I wasn't expecting her and was so startled that I screamed like a little girl.

"Jesus, you scared the living shit out of me!" I said.

"Sorry, I thought that the presence of that dangly thing between your legs meant you were a man."

"Hey, even a lion can be startled."

"Well then, Simba, you mind telling me what this room is for?" she asked.

"Do you want to guess?"

"Masturbating?"

"No, that's the guest bedroom."

"That would explain all the Kleenex."

"I'm not using it to blow my nose."

She laughed, but then the expression on her face began to look a wee bit uncomfortable the longer she gazed at the various items in the room.

"Seriously—what is this place?"

"This is my man-room, and every man has a version of it. Some are filled with tools. Some, porn. But, mine is full of weapons and equipment."

"That's a little scary."

"Not really. It's just modern man's last vestige of his manitude that he must hide from society in a sad little secret room."

"Tragic."

"Maybe, but you women can hide all your shit in a purse in plain sight. We men put it in a closet, garage, drawer, or a secret room if we're lucky."

"Jesus."

"He probably had one too. But his was full of carpentry tools and godliness."

She shook her head in dismay.

"Have you packed everything you need?"

"Everything but dive gear."

"Don't worry about that. We have everything you'll need down there on the yacht—in a secret place we call the dive room."

"In that case, I'm ready to go," I said, as I hit the light switch and closed the door to my secret man-room.

CHAPTER EIGHT
Where Eagles Dare

We walked up to the Silver Hornet, put our luggage in the trunk, and headed off to the San Francisco International Airport to catch the Vandenberg jet. Traffic was light, and we made surprisingly good time crossing the Golden Gate Bridge and getting through the city, and we were soon passing one of my favorite late night weaknesses in South San Francisco. Just off the freeway, and residing side by side, were an In-N-Out Burger and a Krispy Kreme donut shop. It was a great place for a late night snack, and I'd succumbed to its siren like call on more than a few occasions. Salt and sugar were the natural capper to alcohol, completing the most perfect yet least healthy triumvirate of a decent Friday night.

We reached the San Francisco Airport private terminal then parked and made our way out to the tarmac, where Bridgette pointed at a Boeing 777 business jet with a navy blue V on the tail—which obviously stood for Vandenberg. The company jet was bigger than I expected and was basically a large commercial airliner outfitted for private use. A rather fit looking guy in a pilot's uniform was waiting at the bottom of the boarding ramp, and he smiled when he saw Bridgette, revealing some of the whitest, most perfect teeth I had ever seen. He also had movie star good looks, blonde hair, and the kind of tan that hinted he probably lived in one of those warm and sunny places like Los Angeles or Phoenix, where everyone managed to spend ample time out in the sunshine. Sweet Lord! If he wasn't a pilot in real life, he could have played one on television. He turned to me, and the smile disappeared, but it returned once his gaze fell back on Bridgette. He kissed her on the lips then picked up her bags, and guided her up into the plane, leaving me to board alone.

"What? No kiss for me?" I asked, as they disappeared inside.

That was an interesting interaction, and gave me the distinct feeling that the glorious night of lovemaking I shared with Bridgette may have been a one-time affair now that the man with the tan was on the scene. It was probably a good thing, as I wasn't exactly sure how I would explain the entire affair to Lux. Still, it was quite a night and a welcome respite from my recent dry spell. I boarded the plane and continued aft, walking past the crew's quarters and galley to enter the main lounge, where I realized that I needed to make a lot more money. This was the way people were meant to travel! The center of the room was occupied by plush looking white leather sectional couches and a Noguchi coffee table, while just beyond it resided a large dining room table and, more importantly, the bar. I had everything I could ever want or need on an airplane, and if I had been flying around in jets this nice in the Air Force, I would have never jumped out of them. Mr. Tan and Teeth, who had ignored me thus far, finally decided to introduce himself.

"Hi, I'm Brett. I'll be one of your pilots," he said, as he held out his hand.

He looked and acted like the guy in the movies who had the girl in the beginning but always lost her at the end because he was an asshole.

"I'm Tag. I'll be one of your passengers," I said, as I reached out to complete the gesture.

As I expected, he tried to crush my hand as if it would somehow establish him as the alpha male in our little pecking order. Insecure guys always did that. Unfortunately for Brett, I worked out a lot more than he did and also knew a lot more about anatomy. The trick is to clamp the median nerve and deliver more pain than actual pressure. Brett's smile started to fade, and he looked as though he was clenching down on a flaming hemorrhoid until I finally released his hand. I smiled and enjoyed watching him rub the life back into his sore digits, and that was when I noticed he had a United States Naval Academy Ring. Now, it all made sense! He was a ring knocker.

"I see you were Navy."

"Yeah, and Mr. Vandenberg told me you were in the Air Force."

"Once upon a time."

"Yeah, so I don't quite understand why you're here. We don't need another pilot, and, unless you're going to fuel up the plane, I don't see how you can help."

"I'm a private investigator now, but I used to be a PJ, and we spent our quality time rescuing people who were in a shit tone of trouble."

"PJ? Never heard of them."

"It's short for Parajumper or, more specifically, Pararescue. You must be a decent pilot otherwise we might have met on the job."

"Still not following you."

"Had you crashed your F-18 Hornet out in the middle of nowhere and your teeth were starting to look a bit dull, I would have been the guy who parachuted in with whitening toothpaste to put the sparkle back in your smile."

"I think you're mistaking yourself for a Navy SEAL," he said.

"No, definitely not. I worked side by side with them many times, and I can say without a doubt that they don't carry any oral hygiene products."

He seemed to be done talking to me and turned his attention

back to Bridgette.

"I assume you'll be staying in the master suite, and we'll put Tag in the number two stateroom. Anything else you need, just ask Tiffany."

"Who's Tiffany?" I asked.

"The plane's steward and chef. She'll be back any minute with groceries for the flight," Brett said.

"You won't be cooking for us?" I asked.

Brett didn't answer and, instead, smiled blandly, turned, and walked back towards the cockpit, probably to go bleach his teeth and spend some quality time under a sun lamp. At least I knew there was actually a cock in the cockpit—cocksucker, that is.

"So, I take it that you and Brett are more than just friends?"

"Kind of. We have an on-again, off-again kind of thing. I date him when I'm single or bored. I know he dates other women, but he's still a little territorial."

"You think?"

Bridgette shrugged.

"So, what's Tiffany like?" I asked.

"She's pretty and has big tits. I doubt she's your type."

"Isn't that every man's type?"

"Well, my uncle certainly didn't hire her for her cooking."

"What about Brett and Tiffany? Were those two ever an item?"

"No idea. Why do you ask?"

"Just curious, as I get the impression that Mr. Tan and Teeth probably gets around."

I glanced at the coffee table and saw a news magazine with a picture of Bridgette's uncle on the cover, and I picked it up, hoping to learn a little more about my new employer. I thumbed to the article and skimmed the first page to find it contained pretty boring stuff about their market strategy and how they were still thriving in spite of the challenging economy. Just as I turned to the second page, I heard someone coming from the front of the plane and looked up in time to see that Bridgette's description of

Tiffany was accurate, if understated. She was beautiful and statuesque with honey blond hair pulled up into a bun, blue eyes, and a smile so bright that it made me wonder if perhaps she and Brett went to the same dentist. That same smile, however, became icy as she looked at Bridgette, but it warmed when we made eye contact, and I couldn't help but return the gesture as I took in the rest of the details of the woman standing before me. Her official Vandenberg uniform consisted of a short blue skirt, white thigh high stockings, and a white button-up shirt, and all of it was doing an excellent job of revealing her spectacular figure—especially her lightly tanned and ample cleavage, which was peering amiably over the straining buttons that were barely able to keep the tightly fitted garment from busting open. At long last, I broke from my stupor and realized it was about time to stand up and properly introduce myself, but she beat me to the punch and leaned down and held out her hand to greet me, the move sending her breasts falling forward and improving an already fantastic view.

"Hi, I'm Tiffany. It's nice to meet you," she said, as we shook hands.

"I'm Tag, and it's nice to meet you too."

"Well, Tag, I'm the official steward and chef on the Vandenberg jet, so please feel free to tell me if you need anything," she said, as she let go of my hand then reached down and secured my seatbelt.

Gulp. Now, I was facing double jeopardy, for not only were her breasts hovering directly before my eyes, but now her hands were precariously close to my manhood—the experience making my head swirl with lustful musings.

"Do you mind if I ask what you mean by anything?"

She smiled in spite of my mediocre attempt at a double entendre.

"Not at all, Tag, and to clarify—should anything come up during the flight and require my attention, please feel free to alert me immediately," she said.

Now that was a good double entendre and now something was,

indeed, already coming up, but luckily it was safely secured in my pants. We shared a laugh at our little exchange, and I had to admit that Tiffany's presence was going to be a welcomed respite from the menace of the man with the tan. Bridgette, however, wasn't feeling the same warm vibes and cleared her throat to interrupt our fun then proceeded to ask Tiffany to get her a mineral water over ice. Tiffany, unfazed, gave her a surprisingly sincere smile and headed for the galley, and I couldn't help but notice how her skirt hugged her hips and accentuated the dangerous curves of her backside. She stopped a few paces off, turned around, and didn't appear the least bit offended when she caught me enjoying the view.

"Oh, Tag, I'm sorry did you want anything."

"Oh, no thank you. I'm fine."

"You sure? It's no problem."

"I'll have whatever she's having."

"All right, and I'll throw in a slice of fresh lemon."

"Thank you. That would be lovely."

She left, and I pretended to read more of the article about the Vandenberg Corporation, while Bridgette continued to glare at me. After a moment, I finally looked over.

"What?" I asked.

"Fresh lemon," she said, in a mocking tone.

Tiffany returned with the beverages, and I thanked her, and she gave me another of her stunning smiles, before she turned and headed back towards the front of the plane. I took a sip of the sparkling water then looked over at Bridgette with a satisfied smirk on my face.

"Delicious. Who says she can't cook?"

Brett came over the intercom system and told us we'd be departing soon, and, shortly thereafter, I heard the gangplank pull away and felt the thump of the forward hatch as it closed. The big jet's engines fired up, and the scent of jet exhaust started coming in through the ventilation system as we began our slow crawl to the runway. We got into the ground traffic pattern and lined up just behind a Hawaiian Airlines jet that was obviously headed to Hawaii. It roared off into the friendly skies, and we took its place and prepared for takeoff. The Vandenberg jet's engines throttled up, and we could feel the vibration coming through the floor until the brakes were released, and the jet started accelerating down the runway. Seconds later we were climbing skyward, the g-forces pushing us back into our comfortable leather seats, and I could see the city below between tufts of fog. We heard the landing gear retract with a thump, and, ten minutes later, Brett came on and told us we were free to move about the plane. Still feeling a little tired from the fun of the previous night, I decided to find my cabin and take a little break from all the drama.

"So, I'm in the number two stateroom?" I asked Bridgette.

"Yeah, it's towards the back of the plane."

I ventured into the aft passageway and passed a number of staterooms before finding number two on the lefthand side at the very end. I opened the door and stood in mild shock, not unlike the previous day when I first saw Bridgette on my doorstep. Holy shit. The room was unbelievably luxurious and rivaled the best five star hotels, and made my modest accommodations back home seem so—common. The room had built-in furniture like a yacht, and all of it was covered with the same white leather as the main lounge. The bed was king size, and the bedspread was white with the navy blue Vandenberg V logo in the center. There was a coffee machine, mini fridge, and I had my own bathroom complete with a custom bathtub that was both a shower and a Jacuzzi. Could a plane carry that much water? What would happen if we hit turbulence? I suppose I would learn the answer to those questions when, and if, any of those things occurred. I lay down on the bed and stared at the ceiling, taking a moment to clear my mind and relax. Minutes passed, and I closed my eyes and felt the subtle movements of the plane gently lull me into a glorious afternoon nap.

A knock at the door brought me awake, and I had to take a second to remember where in the hell I was at the moment. Oh, yeah, that's right—I was on a private jet on my way to the Caribbean. Sweet lord, I must surely be dreaming. The door opened a crack, and Tiffany poked her head in and told me dinner would be ready in half an hour. In the meantime, there would be cocktails in the lounge. I could do with a cocktail, so I brushed my teeth and headed out of my cabin and forward to the main salon, where I could already smell dinner wafting from the galley. Bridgette and Brett were sitting at the bar, while Tiffany was behind it making what I was pretty sure was a pitcher of Dark and Stormies—probably in honor of our destination being the Caribbean. I walked over and took a seat on one of the empty stools.

"Who in the hell's flying the plane?" I asked, the tan menace.

"The other two pilots—Tatyana and Wendy. Jets this size usually carry at least two pilots in case of an emergency, and it also allows us to trade off on long flights."

"So, I take it you're free until we reach Martinique?"

"I sure am," he said, smiling as he held up his glass.

"How wonderful."

Tiffany handed me a Dark and Stormy with a fresh wedge of lime, and I held it up to honor the hostess.

"To Tiffany!" I said.

We clinked glasses, then I took a sip and let the flavors play out on my palette. A Dark and Stormy consisted of rum, ginger beer, and fresh lime, and was only as good as the quality of its ingredients. Apparently, Tiffany had used all the right stuff, because it was delicious and gave me that warm feeling and mild sense of euphoria you only got from a good cocktail. Now that we all had our drinks, it was time to move to the couches and get comfortable. Brett sat down next to Bridgette, and I settled onto the other couch next to Tiffany, who, at that moment, decided it was time to let her hair down—literally. She reached up and removed a single clip, and her long golden locks fell down past her shoulders, making her go from being temptingly sexy to a full on sexy temptress. It certainly didn't hurt that she was turned towards me, and I could see the supple flesh of her upper thighs over the tops of her white thigh-high stockings.

"So, what's your story?" she asked.

"Not much to tell really. I'm a private investigator. It can be boring a lot of the time, but it gets exciting every now and then."

"Like when you're rescuing a girl from an exotic Caribbean island?"

"Absolutely, though this is definitely the exception rather than the rule."

"Yeah, I imagine finding missing cats is probably more your speed," Brett said.

That was an interesting insight on Brett's part, and I decided to acknowledge his insult by cleverly shoving it back in his tan face.

"Funny you should mention that Brett, because finding lost cats is, indeed, one of my specialties, though that list would also include dogs, bunnies, birds, and pretty much anything anyone could love."

"So, you're like a real life Ace Ventura: Pet Detective," Brett said, in a condescending tone.

"I suppose I am at times, but pets aren't just animals Brett—they're family members. So, whenever someone comes to me looking for help in finding his or her lost family member, I do everything in my power to bring them back together. You're probably not sensitive enough to understand, but I derive a lot of joy from those cases."

That statement, while meant to fuck with Brett, was actually quite true and had the additional side effect of making

Tiffany gush as she regarded me.

"Oh my God. You must seriously be the sweetest guy in the world," she said, placing her hand on my thigh.

"No, I'm just a guy who likes to help people—one person or pet at a time."

"Bullshit," Brett muttered, under the guise of a muted cough.

Tiffany gave Brett an annoyed look to which he responded with an innocent smirk and a shrug of his shoulders.

"So, how did you get into this line of work?" Tiffany asked.

"Being a Social Psychology major in college certainly helped, as it's extremely useful to have an understanding of people and their motivations, though a lot of my practical investigative training was from the Air Force and government."

"I didn't know the Air Force did anything like that," she said.

"They don't," Brett interjected.

"As a matter of fact, they do, and I spent the remainder of my time in the service doing background investigations on civilian contractors."

"Oh, and what did you do before that?"

"Well, that part of my military career takes us back to the whole helping people theme. As I was telling Brett earlier, I was in Para-rescue. It's a fairly unknown branch of special operations that are similar to Navy SEALs in that we operated on sea, air, and land, though we also had extensive medical training, and our primary job was to rescue anyone who needed it, pretty much anywhere in the world. So, if a pilot, like our man with the tan here, crashed his plane, they would send in someone like me to get him safely back to base and into a tanning bed as quickly as possible."

Tiffany laughed.

"It's funny you mention Brett's obsession with maintaining his perfectly bronzed skin, because he really does go to the tanning salon at least twice a week," she said.

"You're exaggerating," Brett responded.

"No, it's true. He even has one of those frequent tanner cards where he gets a free session every fifth tan," she added.

"They give them to everyone!" he complained.

He had, inadvertently, admitted his obsession, and everyone laughed except Brett, of course, whose tan face had started to turn from bronze to red.

"Going to the tanning salon isn't a fucking crime," he said, sounding annoyed.

"Not literally, but it is a crime against nature, and leads to premature aging of your skin and makes you look like a tangerine," I said.

Brett didn't like being the butt of everyone's joke and decided to steer the conversation into an area he thought would restore some of his dignity and chip away at mine. He asked where I had gone to college. People generally only ask that question when they want to tell you what college they had attended, and I was pretty sure that everyone in the room already knew that Brett had gone to the Naval Academy. It was a good school without a doubt and hard as hell to get into, and Brett obviously believed that it would set him apart and, more importantly, above me.

"Stanford, but I did it on a drinking scholarship," I said.

"Excuse me?" Brett asked, looking confused.

Tiffany laughed, so she obviously understood that I was fucking with Brett.

"That was a joke, Brett. At least the drinking part, as I did go to Stanford, though I did it on a partial swimming scholarship."

"Oh."

He hadn't expected that and took a minute to quietly finish his drink before getting up and pouring himself another. I guess Stanford was a good enough school to keep the Naval Academy out of the conversation for the moment. Of course, I wasn't going to tell him that I saved my parents some serious money by doing my first two years at a junior college.

"Enough about me. What's your story, Tiffany?"

"Well, I went to UCLA and got my degree in hospitality management, then, only a month out of college, realized that my true love was cooking. So, I went to culinary school, and then started working as a chef at a little restaurant in Santa Monica. I had only been there for about a month when Mr. Vandenberg happened to come in for lunch, and he loved my cooking so much that he offered me a job. I decided to get out of the grind for a while, and, now, I make even more money and have the bonus of free travel."

"It certainly doesn't get any better than that."

Bridgette, uninterested in Tiffany's life story, rolled her eyes and sighed.

"Speaking of your cooking, Tiffany, is dinner ready yet?" Bridgette asked.

"I'll check," she said, ignoring Bridgette's aloof demeanor by mustering a cheerful voice.

I hated people who used their position to demean others. Sadly, you saw it all the time in the service industry, where high maintenance customers, usually without a lot of stature in their lives, loved to order their waiters and waitresses around as though they were their personal servants. Tiffany, unfazed, stood up and headed towards the galley at the front of the plane, while Brett smiled at me as he reached over and placed his hand on Bridgette's thigh.

"I notice that all that tanning is giving you some crow's feet around your eyes. Did you ever think about trying a little botox?" I asked, which made the smile disappear.

Tiffany came back a moment later and saw Brett's hand on Bridgette's thigh and gave him an angry glare. Bridgette saw their exchange and placed her hand on top of Brett's hand. I placed my hand on the pillow next to me, which bothered no one except perhaps the pillow next to it. With our brief round of strategic hand placement at an end, we all stood up and moved to the dining table, which was set for four but had room for more than eight. Clearly, Vandenberg occasionally traveled with quite an entourage. Brett and Bridgette sat on one side with Tiffany and me on the other, which would have been fine except that every time the tan menace opened his mouth, his teeth would reflect the cabin light and temporarily blind me. Tiffany headed back to the kitchen and returned carrying two plates, each loaded with a pork chop, purple colored whole grain rice, and some grilled asparagus. There were four of us dining, so I assumed she could use some help and followed her back to the galley to discover that it was a lot nicer than what you'd expect to find on a plane. There was every kind of appliance imaginable, and it certainly explained how she was able to cook such an elaborate meal.

"Dinner looks incredible!" I said.

"Thanks, I hope it tastes as good as it looks."

"If the chef is any indication, I'm sure it will."

She gave me a lovely smile then grabbed the two other plates while I carried the silverware and another pitcher of Dark and Stormies. I was happy to see that we were sticking to one kind of alcohol, as it was always the best way to avoid a hangover other than not drinking, of course. Wine might have gone better with dinner, but vomiting would have definitely gone worse with breakfast. As we approached the lounge, we could hear Bridgette and Brett talking heatedly, but they stopped the minute we arrived and tried their best to appear as though all was fine. I put the pitcher on the table, and Brett immediately picked it up and filled both his and Bridgette's glasses then set it down, unaware he had forgotten about the rest of us.

"Thanks, Brett," Tiffany said, looking annoyed as she pointed at her glass.

"Oh, sorry," he said.

I picked up the pitcher, filled Tiffany's glass, and was rewarded with a thankful nod. At that point, she turned her gaze back to Brett and delivered an expression that one might imagine a woman giving to a man just before she uses a garlic press to test the tensile strength of his testicles. I decided to try and ease her relationship suffering with a little praise and some subtle levity at

Brett's expense.

"A meal this good deserves a toast!" I said.

Everyone lifted their glasses.

"Alrighty then, here's to the most beautiful and talented chef to ever fly the friendly skies. May this wonderful meal she cooked bring sustenance to our bodies, warmth to our hearts, peace to our minds, and, more importantly, may the correlation between excessive UV exposure and irritable bowel syndrome not make our resident Naval Academy graduate all bloated and farty, because, let's face it, at least some of the air we're breathing is recirculated. Cheers!"

Tiffany let out a small giggle, but neither Brett or Bridgette were particularly amused.

"Seriously now, Tag, I think you've turned a corner. That toast was a little childish—even for you," Bridgette said.

"I didn't hear you calling me childish when we were running around the bases last night," I responded.

"What's he talking about?" Brett asked.

"Nothing," Bridgette said, as she delivered some corporal punishment by kicking me in the shin.

It was a solid hit, and, as I leaned down to rub the impact spot, my view inadvertently dropped below the table, and I was suddenly privy to an oft overlooked secret adult playground. Brett, to my surprise, had his hand between Bridgette's thighs, and he was tickling her lady taco. Bridgette, not one to be left out, was returning the favor by handling his ham over his neatly pressed pants. It was both a dick and bitch move to do it right under Tiffany's nose, and a real example of the cruelty that occurred during a lover's spat. Of course, this little display of secret affection piqued my inner psychology major and made me wonder how many illicit affairs had cruelly played out beneath the eyes of unsuspecting diners. This was certainly the omen of an interesting evening. I popped back up, took a medicinal sip of my cocktail to help dull the pain in my shin, then enthusiastically dug into dinner. It was delicious, and everything was cooked to perfection—the meat tender, the asparagus crisp, and the rice fluffy. Contrary to Bridgette's earlier statement, Tiffany was a fabulous cook, and there wasn't an item on my plate that couldn't have been served in the finest restaurant.

"Tiffany, this is absolutely amazing," I said.

"Thanks, Tag."

As I returned to enjoying dinner, I noticed Brett was looking at me curiously.

"What is it now, tan menace? Are you thinking I look a little pale or perhaps need to consider some whitening toothpaste?" I asked.

"Neither, as I was just wondering about the origin of your name? Did your parents perhaps work in retail?"

I feigned a deep over-exaggerated belly laugh before responding.

"Oh, I see! You're referring to tag, as in the kind you find on a piece of clothing. That's a very original interpretation, but, as it turns out, the real origin is Irish, and it means handsome," I said.

"Then your parents obviously named you properly," Tiffany interjected.

"Thank you, Tiffany."

"You're welcome, but now I'm curious about the origin of the name Brett," she said.

"You're in luck, as I know the answer. The name originates from the Old Testament, and was a term used to describe a person who had wandered too long in the desert and acquired an excessive tan and disagreeable demeanor."

"Fuck you. It means of Britain."

"See what I mean? Very disagreeable demeanor."

Bridgette was apparently tired of our subject matter and steered the conversation in a new and slightly more vindictive direction.

"So, Brett, you seeing anyone?" she asked.

Now, she was openly playing the bitch card against Tiffany, and everyone got quiet and looked at Brett, who, very slowly, turned his gaze from Bridgette to Tiffany and back again. I couldn't help but wonder if he was still fondling Bridgette under the table or quietly shitting his pants.

"Um—no. No one serious at the moment," he said, the discomfort obvious in his voice.

"That's interesting," Tiffany said.

Brett, unsure what to say at that point, asked if he could get a refill of his drink. Tiffany, cool as a cucumber, picked up the pitcher of Dark and Stormies and dumped the remainder in his lap. It was only about a half a glass, but it was more than enough to do the job.

"There you go," she said.

As much as I hated to give Brett any credit, he took it like a man.

"Thank you. That was very refreshing," he said, showing no sign of the true discomfort and humiliation he was probably feeling as he used his napkin to dry his lap.

"Should I go make another pitcher," I asked, trying my best not to laugh.

"No, I'll do it," Tiffany said, as she took the empty pitcher and headed to the bar.

She returned a moment later and smiled as she stood beside Brett with the full pitcher.

"Would you like some more?" she asked, innocently.

"No, thank you, I can get it myself," he said.

She set the pitcher on the table, took a seat, and Brett filled his own glass, allowing the rest of the meal to go by without incident. After dinner, Bridgette and Brett slithered over to the leather couches while I helped Tiffany clear the table and bring everything into the plane's galley.

"Thanks, Tag. But I can do the rest," she said, as we piled up all the dishes in the sink.

"Bullshit. You were nice enough to cook for me, so it's the least I can do to help you clean up."

I rinsed off the dishes while she placed them in the dishwasher, and, with the two of us working together, it only took a couple minutes to get the job done. At that point, she poured us each a cocktail and leaned back against the counter, looking a little melancholy as she let out a long sigh.

"Here's to a lovely dinner and an even more lovely chef," I said, as I clinked her glass.

"And a shitty boyfriend," she added.

"Hopefully a shitty ex-boyfriend."

"Yeah, I guess you've figured out that Brett and I are kind of going through a rough patch."

"Yeah, I picked up on the subtle signs of your rough patch when you dumped the rest of the pitcher of Dark and Stormies in his lap. It's almost a shame to waste such a good cocktail on that tan dick's cock."

"Yeah, but, believe it or not, there's a nice guy buried beneath that tan."

"Maybe, but I'd say that nice guy is buried pretty fucking deep at the moment. Clearly, Mr. Tan and Teeth is still holding a major torch for Bridgette, and doesn't appreciate a good thing when it's right in front of his eyes."

Tiffany smiled at me.

"Thanks for the sentiment, but it still hurts."

"I know. My last girlfriend cheated on me with a yacht club guy then called to break up—right after they had sex on his fucking yacht. It took a little over a month before I realized it was the best thing that could have ever happened to me."

"Clearly she also doesn't know a good thing when it's right in front of her. Well, either that or she's just a bitch."

"Maybe it's a little bit of both."

We shared a smile.

"Here's to exes," she said, clinking my glass yet again.

After a moment of quietly reflection, Tiffany got an annoyed look in her eye as she spoke.

"It's just so lame. Everything was great until Bridgette popped back into the picture two days ago. How the hell am I supposed to compete with that? She's beautiful and rich and can have any guy she wants."

I suddenly felt a little uncomfortable as I thought about the previous night and how easily I too had fallen under Bridgette's spell.

"Yeah, I guess so, but none of that takes away from the fact that you're also beautiful, and woman to woman, there is nothing Bridgette has that you don't."

"Bullshit."

"Bullshit? Do you own a mirror? Because if you do, you might want to take a good look at yourself. You're absolutely stunning!"

"I don't feel stunning at the moment."

"Only because you're hurting, but, trust me, you are."

"You really think so?"

"Of course, and if I were to be completely honest, I'd reveal that I've been having some pretty interesting fantasies about you since the moment we met, and not one of them involved clothing, the Naval Academy, or whitening toothpaste."

She seemed to perk up a little and almost smiled as she regarded me.

"You're just trying to make me feel better."

"Yeah, by being honest, and I didn't want to play the boob card, but let's face it, you've got a bit more going on in that department."

Tiffany's almost-smile transformed into a full fledged ear to ear smile.

"I suppose my boobs might be a little bigger than Bridgette's."

"A lot bigger, and you can trust me, as I'm a bit of an expert in this area."

"Well, thank you, Tag. It means even more coming from an

expert."

"Damn right, and there's no need to thank me. I get all the thanks I need just being in your company."

She smiled bashfully, and I had to smile back in return, as I always found it particularly charming when a beautiful woman was unaware of her beauty.

"Still, this whole situation is especially frustrating, because it goes beyond Bridgette's looks and right into her pocketbook. Back when she and Brett first started dating, she used to wine and dine him and take him all over the world—everywhere from Fiji to Monte Carlo, and, let's face it, that's a hard act to follow."

"All of that shit is meaningless if there isn't a real emotional connection. Without it, he's just a boy-toy and she's just his sugar momma."

"I suppose."

I had a moment to think about Tiffany's statement and was suddenly curious.

"Wait a minute. I thought Bridgette and Lux were kind of estranged from the Vandenberg money."

"Are you kidding? They get whatever they want—at least Bridgette does. I don't know much about Lux."

"Interesting," I said.

"Well, thanks again for the pep talk, Tag. You're a nice guy."

"You know what they say about nice guys."

"It's not true. They don't finish last."

"They do when it counts."

"And when is that?" she asked, curiously.

"In bed."

Tiffany raised an eyebrow and smiled as we left the kitchen. We walked back to the lounge, and it was like déjà vu—all over again. Brett and Bridgette stopped talking and looked up at us with the same innocent smiles. The evening was getting a little weird for my tastes, so I decided it was a good time to excuse myself and go back to my room to relax and unwind. I said goodnight, but, before I could leave, Tiffany walked over and gave me a wonderfully unexpected hug. She was holding me tightly, her ample bosoms pressed against my chest—the experience making my head once again swirl with lustful musings about my beautiful new friend. At the end, she abruptly kissed me right on the lips, and I was caught completely off guard but managed to pucker up just in time to complete the gesture. Sweet Lord! Between the hug and the kiss I had more than enough unexpected affection to fill my lonely moments before bed. I turned and, with a new spring in my step, headed for my cabin, sad to be leaving Tiffany behind, but relieved to be out of the glare of Brett's teeth, ever thankful that my presence did nothing to make him smile.

CHAPTER NINE
Bathing and Feeling Dirty

I sat on the bed, took a moment to reflect, and found it hard to believe that I was actually on an airplane and not in a five star hotel, considering the abundance of fine food, drink, high speed Wi-Fi, and beautiful women. I guess this was how billionaires lived, and I was pretty sure I would never again be satisfied flying coach. I looked at my watch and saw that it was ten-thirty Pacific time, and I couldn't help but smile as I thought about the fact that two nights ago at this same hour, I had been sitting in a freezing cold park watching two people get it on in a warm living room. The times they truly were a-changing, and this was a hell of a case to come up out of nowhere, but one very important question kept nagging at the back of my mind—namely, how in the hell was I going to take a decent dump on an airplane without getting interrupted?

I drank the last sip of my cocktail, then decided to head out to the main salon for a refill. All was quiet, so it would appear that everyone else had also decided to retire for the evening. I slipped behind the bar only to find it had run out of ice, which meant I needed to continue on to the galley. The plane's interior lights were dimmed, and there wasn't a sight or sound of the others until I entered the forward companionway and heard voices coming from one of the crew cabins. Planes were made to be light, so walls and doors weren't exactly soundproof, and I couldn't have heard Tiffany and Brett's argument more clearly had I been in the same room. I entered the galley, grabbed a glass shaped like a boot, then made myself a large, though slightly less alcoholic, Dark and Stormy, all the while trying my best not to eavesdrop. Unfortunately, in the absence of noise canceling headphones, I was privy to every word.

"Look, it's over with Bridgette, but, right now, I really need to talk to her," Brett said.

"What could you possibly have to talk to her about right now?"

"Tag. I don't trust him, and what the fuck is a PJ? I've never heard of them."

"Would it be different if he had gone to the Naval Academy?"

"Yes, as a matter of fact, it would."

"Do you realize how stupid you sound?"

"I don't care! I'm going to go talk to Bridgette."

"If you walk out right now, we're done."

I heard their cabin door open, so I slipped farther back into the shadows of the galley. Brett walked past in a huff, the heaviness of his footsteps telling the tale of his mood. I waited a second and followed behind him, trying to keep my drink steady so that the ice cubes didn't rattle against the glass. He continued on down the hall and knocked on Bridgette's door before entering and disappearing from view. Sweet Jiminy Cricket did life move fast with this crowd. It was like being back in high school except we were all adults.

I went into the peace of my cabin, and, remembering the Jacuzzi, decided that I might as well enjoy it while I could. I turned on the water and let the tub fill while I looked through the vast assortment of bath accessories. I decided on the scented bubble bath pellets and added a few to the mix, watching as a goodly amount of bubbles started to form and spread across the water. The tub would take a few minutes to fill, so, in the meantime, I got undressed then took a closer look at the accoutrements in the room. There was a stereo system with a connector for an outside device, so I plugged in my iPhone, navigated to the Radiohead album, The Bends, then headed back into the bathroom, where I dimmed the lights to complete the mood. I noticed there was a little touch screen beside the switch, and, upon closer inspection, realized it was a second set of controls for the stereo system. Oh, to be a billionaire.

The tub was now full, and wisps of steam were rising off its surface as I lowered my feet into its hot, wet embrace. I would have to take it slow and let my body adjust to the temperature, taking proper precautions not to scorch my privates. Interestingly, the Japanese actually had a form of birth control where they dipped a man's balls into hot water in the belief that it would kill all his sperm. My theory is that dipping a man's balls into burning hot water just might kill his sex drive before it kills his sperm. At last, I was down to my thighs and finally slid the rest of my body into the water with hardly a splash. The heat was soothing, and it helped empty my mind of the craziness of the last twenty-four hours. I decided to take it up a notch and hit the button for the jets and wondered, yet again, what would happen if we hit turbulence? Ah, fuck it. This was the most fun I'd had in years, so I decided to lean back, enjoy myself, and let the music carry me away.

The second song had just started when I heard a knock at my stateroom door. Shit. I tried to yell that I was in the bathroom, but, apparently, the person couldn't hear me. Just as I was about to get up and grab a towel, I heard the door to my room open, followed by the sound of footsteps as the intruder approached the bathroom. Who in the hell would be bothering me at this hour? Perhaps it was Brett coming to tell me that I was full of shit. That would be particularly awkward, as there was nothing more uncomfortable than arguing with someone when you were completely naked. The visitor drew closer, and, as I eyed the doorway, Tiffany came walking into view, the look of frustration obvious on her face. Without saying a word, she came in, picked up my cocktail, and took a long sip.

"Mind if I join you?" She asked.

"In the bath?"

"Obviously."

For some reason, I was reminded of the visitor I had the night before and wondered why my luck with women had changed so drastically in the last twenty-four hours. Perhaps I needed to hang out more often with heiresses on private jets. I looked up at the beautiful, though sad, woman standing above me, and couldn't help but feel her pain. She was facing the same misery I had endured only two months ago, and she probably just needed someone to talk to, and, more importantly, someone to listen. Obviously, things weren't going well with Brett, and there was a broken heart underneath those beautiful breasts. It was, therefore, my obligation as a fellow human being to look beyond such superficial trappings, and reach out and comfort her in her time of need. The fact that we would be naked and splashing around in a bubble bath was completely inconsequential.

"Come on in my sweet, sad, buxom, and ever so beautiful bath buddy."

She undid her shirt, and I could practically hear each button cry out in relief as its burden was lifted. The garment swung free and dropped to the floor, leaving her clothed in only a sheer bra and underwear—the view getting substantially better as the layers came off. With a quick snap, the bra dropped and joined the shirt, leaving her beautiful bosoms free to dance before my eager eyes. She certainly wasn't shy, but then she had no reason to be. Women across the world went to gyms and plastic surgeons in search of what Tiffany came by naturally, and, viewing her nude, was a visual treat I would probably never forget. She was down to the thigh high stockings and a fancy looking thong, all of which, she slid off and tossed on the pile, thus leaving her truly and completely naked. My gaze briefly fell upon the thong on the top of the stack of undergarments, and it occurred to me there was a great deal of irony in the unusual fact that the cost of underwear went up in direct proportion to the lack of material. Women literally paid for each inch of flesh they chose to expose rather than cover, and, though I was a strong proponent of the thong, I found the pricing structure particularly contradictory. But, such was the illogical paradox of the fashion industry. Now, Tiffany was unabashedly naked as she at last joined me in the tub, her presence causing the water level to rise just enough to send a little wave sloshing over the edge and onto the floor.

"Oh, I love this album," she said.

"Yeah, and I think it sounds even better when you're naked. Clothing just seems to get in the way of great music."

"I would have to agree."

The tub was larger than a standard bathtub but small enough that two people couldn't be in it without touching. She was directly across from me, her legs over mine, and her nipples were peering at me amiably just above the layer of bubbles. She moved her hands back and forth, playing with the water, and each time it created a brief window of her full nudity before the surface tension would bring the bubbles back together and block my view of her golden valley. It was becoming hard to focus and even harder with the smell of her perfume drifting across the tub—the sweet scent tickling my libido and making my loins swell. Sweet Lord! Sitting in a bathtub with a woman wasn't necessarily anything more than communal bathing, but being naked in the same tub as Tiffany was, in and of itself, a sexual act.

"Just so you know, I can't promise I won't get aroused," I said.

"I think I can promise you will."

She placed her hands on the sides of the tub, shifted onto her knees and slid closer. There was no point in even trying to disguise my erection, as my penis had already made its own decision to inflate like an emergency life raft and head for the surface. Soon, it became wedged between our bodies, and there was little I could do to hide my enthusiasm. Maybe the Japanese hot water ball dip wasn't so crazy after all.

"See, I told you, you'd get turned on," she said.

"I hope this doesn't *come* between us."

"I'm kind of planning on it."

My heart suddenly skipped a beat as she smiled then reached down and began gently caressing my manhood.

"Have you really been having fantasies about me since we first met?" she asked.

"Definitely, though I neglected to include a Jacuzzi in the scenario."

"Well, in that case let's make this fantasy a reality. Tag—you're it."

She brought up her other hand and wrapped it around the back of my neck then pulled me close and kissed me. Sweet mother of God. This would be two women, two times, in two days, and James Bond I was not. I considered myself a one woman man and didn't go trolling the bars for one night stands, yet, here I was aboard a private jet, flying along at thirty-five thousand feet, and sitting in a Jacuzzi tub with a beautiful woman I had known for less than a day. It was better than freezing my ass off on a cold jungle gym watching Tarzan and Jane play hide the banana, so it was time to stop thinking and start enjoying one of the few perks life had thrown at me in quite some time.

The kiss was just the starter on a menu of delicious sexual dishes to come, and, before you could say foreplay, I had lifted Tiffany onto the edge of the tub and was working my way down her neckline to her vast mountain region. Both breasts looked so good, I wasn't sure where to start. It was like choosing between a Lamborghini and a Ferrari. I decided on the left one, the Ferrari, and gently kissed the nipple, teasing it with my tongue until it became hard and proud. I did the same to the Lamborghini then pulled back to admire my work. Now, they were a perfectly matched set, or, as the Italians would say, perfettamente ab-binato. I decided not to stop there and continued down to the Bugatti Veyron which resided at my favorite intersection. After diamonds, the clitoris was a girl's best friend and nothing made that more apparent than the growing frequency of Tiffany's cries of pleasure as I used my tongue the way a Formula One driver used a steering wheel—each twist and turn bringing her closer to the finish line. Her moans started coming more frequently, her breasts rising and falling violently as each wave of pleasure grew stronger until the pinnacle moment when she braced herself with her hands on the edge of the tub, arched her back, and set into a powerful climax. I continued on, my mouth firmly upon her es-sence, my tongue moving about her clitoris until she could take no more, and I at last relented. She relaxed and opened her eyes, her face aglow and flushed with color as she returned from the selfish pleasure only an orgasm could provide.

"I guess you were right. Nice guys do finish last," she said.

"There's nothing wrong with last—as long as you finish."

In a hurry to continue what started in the Jacuzzi, we exited the bath and started anew on the luxurious five hundred count Egyptian cotton sheets that apparently were a standard courtesy on the Vandenberg Jet. I knew that little detail because I had already checked the tag, curious how deep wealth went into the objects of everyday life. She lay back and beckoned me onto her, whereupon I slid into her reaches and started into a slow purpose-ful rhythm that allowed me to relish every second of pleasure. I kissed her long and hard, all the while pressing my hips to hers, grinding at the apex of each thrust, slowly but firmly working to-wards the ultimate of crescendos. We soon achieved the synergy of a racehorse and its rider—the two of us pounding down the final stretch, our bodies slick with a lover's sweat as we at last crossed the finish line and climaxed together in a photo finish.

With our hips entwined and our lips pressed together in a heated kiss, we drifted in a haze of orgasmic bliss, our beating hearts the only sound beyond the low thrumming of the jet's engines. After a time, she slipped free, smiling as she got up and headed to the bathroom.

"I'll be right back," she said.

I sat there in post-coital bliss forgetting anything that existed beyond the walls of my stateroom. It was a moment of quiet reflection, and I jokingly imagined that if Tiffany were to reappear with a cold alcoholic beverage then I'd know I was dead and had surely gone to heaven. True to my unlikely prediction, she reappeared with my half full cocktail from earlier, and all I could wonder was when had I died? Was it before or after my orgasm? She took a sip then handed me the glass, the ice cold drink a welcomed respite from the heat of the room. I finished the last of the Dark and Stormy then set the empty boot glass on the nightstand. Tiffany kissed me then motioned at the bathroom.

"Come on, Mr. Nice Guy, let's get you cleaned up. Two orgasms is a lot of work for one night."

"Three, if you count mine."

We showered, then returned to the bed, where I wrapped my arms around the beautiful Tiffany and held her as we drifted off to sleep, my thoughts ever optimistic of the adventure that lay ahead.

Morning came, as it always did after a night of drinking and debauchery, a little too early. Tiffany was beside me, and her magnificent breasts and toned stomach were glowing in the warm rays of the morning sun that shone through the small aircraft window. She stirred and opened her eyes, smiling and looking a lot happier than when she had arrived the night before. She leaned over, and we shared one of those morning after *I really want to go brush my*

teeth kisses, then I got up and strolled into the bathroom. I put toothpaste on my brush and set to work, ever careful not to drip any on my manhood, for it had a tendency to burn and was the main reason I usually wore clothing for this particular activity. Of course, this kind of movement also came with the unintended consequences of sending my manhood flopping back and forth, making a slapping sound as it hit each leg. Tiffany came in at that very moment and laughed as she took in the sight and sound of my percussive extravaganza.

"Nice drum solo," she joked.

"It's *Moby Dick* by *Led Zeppelin*."

"Good one, though, I assume you know that song can go on as long as nineteen minutes?"

"Of course, but think how clean my teeth will be!"

"As clean as Brett's."

"Good point," I said, immediately putting down my toothbrush and rinsing out my mouth.

She picked it up and proceeded to brush her teeth, and I found it funny how much intimacy could be gained by a night of passion. After rinsing out her mouth, she stepped into the shower for a quick rinser then both of us departed the bathroom together, and she threw on her clothes and smiled at me.

"Tag, I can't thank you enough for last night. I really needed that, and now you've given me all the motivation I need to leave Brett behind."

"And find a nice guy this time."

"Yeah, though you certainly set the bar pretty high."

"Believe me—Mr. Right is out there somewhere, and when he finds you, he'll be the luckiest guy in the world."

"Well then, how about a final kiss—to remember each other by?" she suggested.

"Excellent idea."

She stepped forward and wrapped her arms around me, and, now that we were both fresh and minty, she kissed me with a real vigor, the experience bringing memories of the previous night flooding back into my mind. And with those memories came a different kind of flooding, namely the kind that fills a man's gentleman region and brings on the glory of morning wood. It was kind of strange to be completely naked and kissing a fully clothed woman, but neither of us apparently wanted to stop—least of all Tiffany, who was playfully caressing my member and working it into a fully fledged boner. This, in turn, sent subconscious signals to my brain to begin exploring, and, before you could say twin peaks, my hands were on her breasts, my fingers making deliberate circles around her areolae until her nipples were as hard as my penis. Our exchange was now more desperate, our tongues fully engaged as we enjoyed our final kiss—that is, until a voice came blaring over the plane's intercom system that forced us to stop and listen.

"Good morning, everyone. This is your pilot, Tatyana, speaking. We're about ready for a lovely late breakfast, so we'll be needing Tiffany up in the galley," she said, cheerfully before signing off.

"Fuck! I better get going. I need to change my clothes before I make breakfast."

"Oh well," I said, gazing down at my throbbing member.

"Sorry, but I did make you a cup of coffee. It's right over there beside the mini-fridge. I'll see you at breakfast," she said, smiling a little guiltily as she left.

I walked over and picked up the cup and took a sip.

"Sweet brewed heaven on earth," I said, aloud.

It tasted as good as it smelled, and I was lost in the caffeinated pleasure of the moment when I heard voices outside in the hallway and figured it was time to get ready. Before I could make it back into the bathroom, there was a knock on my cabin door.

"Who is it?" I asked.

The door opened and in walked Bridgette, and she looked a little startled to see me standing there buck naked with a cup of coffee in my hand and my manhood at full capacity. I held up my mug then took a sip and smiled at her.

"What's up?" I asked.

"You, apparently," she said, casting a quick glance down at my gentleman breakfast sausage.

"This? It's more of a semi," I said.

She wasn't amused and, instead, took a moment to scrutinize the room, and I got the impression she could see the subtle signs that I hadn't slept alone. Tiffany hadn't left any of her frilly under-garments scattered about, but it was obvious by the indentations in the pillows that more than one person had been in the bed.

"You're being paid to rescue my sister—not fuck around with the help," she said.

"You seem a little cranky. Did Brett's snoring keep you up?"

I heard footsteps approaching in the hall, and, a moment later, Brett walked through the door.

"Did I hear my name?" he asked, his teeth glowing so brightly I had to squint.

He looked startled when he realized I was naked and sporting a boner. I tried to appear as casual as I could, considering the fact that I was the only naked and openly aroused person in the room.

"Yeah, I was just asking if you snore," I said.

"I don't."

Tiffany walked back in at that moment.

"Yeah, actually you do snore," she said, to Brett.

I took another sip of coffee and everyone stood there quietly, not sure what to say. Thankfully, Tiffany spoke and broke the ten-sion.

"Breakfast will be ready in thirty minutes. I hope you like scrambled eggs, French toast, and bacon."

"I do."

"Good, and you'll be happy to know the dress code is casual," she said, gazing at my obvious state of undress.

"Already there," I responded.

Tiffany smiled and headed for the galley, leaving Bridgette and

Brett standing there looking uncomfortable. I raised my cup, smiled, and nodded.

"Great fucking coffee!"

"I can see that," Bridgette responded, casting another glance at my manly goodies.

With nothing more to say, they at last left the room, and I walked over and closed the door, locking it this time. I felt my stomach grumble and realized the coffee was doing its job, and I began my preparations for the bathroom the way a pilot did a pre-flight check. My list was a little shorter, however, and consisted of refilling my mug, grabbing my book, and hitting the porcelain, happy to at last be alone in my special time.

CHAPTER TEN
Paradise Found

Having shit, showered, and shaved, I was more than ready for a new day as I joined the others in the main salon. Breakfast went a bit like dinner, though Tiffany refrained from throwing any beverage on Brett's lap, which was lucky for him since the only thing on the table was a pot of hot coffee. Tiffany proved, yet again, that she was, contrary to Bridgette's opinion, an excellent chef, and, while breakfast may not be considered fine dining, her French toast was world class. It wasn't too soft in the middle and had some secret spices and just the right amount of vanilla. Combine that with the scrambled eggs, bacon, and real Canadian maple syrup, and I felt as though I was dining in a little bed-and-breakfast in Vermont rather than flying over the Gulf of Mexico at five hundred miles per hour.

With breakfast at an end, Tatyana told us to buckle in for landing, as we were on final approach and would be arriving in Martinique in fifteen minutes. I was definitely going to miss the jet, but it would be nice to have a break from the soap opera in which I had unwittingly become a main character. Or so I thought until Bridgette announced that the entire ensemble cast would be continuing on with us to the Vandenberg family yacht. I had no problem with the idea of spending more time with Tiffany, but having Mr. Tan and Teeth along would certainly cut into the fun. I turned my gaze out the window of the plane and saw the Island of Martinique in the distance and realized how glorious it would be to breathe in some fresh island air. Exactly fifteen minutes later, we landed with hardly a bump and taxied to the private terminal, so it would appear that Brett was a decent pilot after all, or, more likely, one of the other pilots had landed the plane. I grabbed my bags and headed out of my room to find Bridgette was already waiting in the lounge. She was fiddling with her phone, probably texting or fucking around on Facebook, but she stopped and put it away as I arrived.

"We have a van and driver at the airport, and the yacht has already been provisioned, so we can get underway immediately."

"Sounds good. God only knows what a relief it will be to get off this horribly luxurious jet and move onto a yacht, so I can finally get a little rest," I joked.

"Oh—tough night on the bases?"

"Well, technically it was a double header, and I think I might have strained my penis, but it should be fine after I rub it out."

"What'll be fine?" Brett asked, as he joined us.

"My penis," I said.

He eyed me suspiciously as he stepped past and opened the plane's side door. I gave him a thankful nod then stepped out onto the boarding stairs, only to be instantly bombarded by the thickly sweet scent of fresh flowers and ocean air. It was that magical moment when your olfactory senses told you that you were on a tropical island, and it was time to relax, unwind, and have a good time. Or at least try—considering that it was a work trip. The van Bridgette had mentioned was parked just beyond the wing, and a young, good-looking man with dark skin and mischievous eyes was eagerly awaiting our arrival. We walked over, and he helped us load our stuff in the rear, then we all climbed into the van. I took the seat in the front next to our driver in hopes that I could ask questions and learn more about the Caribbean on the way to the yacht. The driver's name was Samuel, and he had lived here his entire life, only having left to go to study marine biology at the University of Miami. He was currently back on Martinique in order to finish his PhD dissertation and, in the meantime, paid his bills by moonlighting as a tour guide and driver. He was a nice guy from the moment he opened his mouth and had a distinctive gift for improperly telling jokes, which was kind of funny in and of itself. Within two minutes of shaking hands he delivered his first one.

"Two cannibals are eating a clown and one looks over at the other and says, does this taste strange to you?" he said, before breaking into laughter.

"I thought the punch line was, does this taste funny to you?" I said.

Samuel thought for a moment then laughed.

"Well, that is also good, but, honestly, I always found clowns to be more strange than funny."

He had a valid point, if not a particularly funny joke. We left the airport and headed south along a two-lane highway that would eventually take us to the yacht, which was moored down in Le Marin. I leaned forward and looked in the side mirror to check our six, or, in civilian speak, see if anyone was following us. It seemed unlikely, but old habits were hard to break, and, as I scanned the highway behind us, the only vehicle in view was a white Suzuki Jeep driven by a comely young island girl. The only thing she appeared to be interested in was the music blaring from her stereo, so I decided it was time to sit back and enjoy the ride.

As we approached the highway that would take us down to Le Marin, Bridgette told Samuel that she wanted to swing by her favorite shopping area, which conveniently resided only a short distance away on Rue Victor Hugo. Tiffany chimed in, also happy about this detour, and it was an unusual surprise to see them actually agreeing on something. I guess shopping was the universal neutral ground where even the most bitter of female rivals could come together in the hope of finding that perfect piece of clothing or pair of shoes. Either way, it sounded fun to me, as I'd get to see more of the island and have extra time to spend with my new best friend, Brett. Perhaps the two of us could browse the local market, and he could point out all his favorite dental hygiene and tanning products.

A few turns later, Samuel had us on the street, and it was crowded with hundreds of people dining, shopping, and enjoying the sights. We pulled over and parked in a loading zone, and everyone agreed to meet back up in about forty-five minutes—a time frame that no woman on this earth engaged in the act of shopping could adhere to in my mind, but, what the hell, we were in Martinique. I took a look around to get the lay of the land and saw a small white Renault sedan that looked vaguely familiar. It was hard to know for sure since we had passed at least a hundred of them on the drive over. Being in a sunny place meant that people favored light colored cars, as they tended to absorb less of the sun's rays. This car was different, however, because it was occupied by a couple of guys wearing light colored suits, and it was way too hot to sit in a car dressed like that, least of all, on an island where people rarely wore anything other than shorts and T-shirts. Only someone working in an official capacity would be stupid enough to dress that way in the heat and humidity, so it stood to reason they were just a couple of island bureaucrats taking lunch. I decided to ignore them for the moment, as I had my own agenda—namely, finding a caffeinated beverage. I gazed across the street and saw a cool looking café that had outdoor seating which stretched right out to the sidewalk. Perfect! I would have coffee and a view.

"Hey, guys, what say the three of us go get a coffee and hear more of Samuel's jokes?"

"I would love to come along, but I have to stay with the van," Samuel said.

"In that case, I'll bring you one. Brett, are you in, or would you be too worried the coffee might stain your teeth?"

"I'll go. I can order a mineral water."

The two of us left the van and headed for the café, luckily snagging an empty table a couple had just vacated. We sat down, and a tall sandy haired waiter with more muscle tone than you got from delivering coffee arrived at our table to take our order. He might be a waiter now, but I'd be willing to bet a large sum of money that he was ex-military or some kind of former college athlete. He smiled then proceeded to speak with a bad French accent.

"*Bonjour.*"

"*Parlez vous anglais?*" I asked.

"*Oui*, I'm Australian."

"*G'day*, the name's Finn, Tag Finn," I said, doing my best to pull off an Australian accent.

"Nice to meet you, Tag. My name's Dundee, Mike Dundee."

"Wait—your're from Australia and your name is seriously, Mike Dundee? That's awfully similar to *Mick Dundee* from the movie *Crocodile Dundee*."

"Yeah, well my name's actually Mick Dundee. My bloody parents loved that fucking movie so much, they decided to torture the living shit out of me by naming me, Mick. So, to avoid all the obvious comments that usually follow, I generally tell people my name is Mike."

"Honestly, it's not the worst movie character to be named after."

"Yeah, but how many times do you think some asshole has told me to throw another shrimp on the barbie?"

"Enough times that you call yourself Mike."

"Exactly, now, what'll it be, mates?"

"Well then, Mick, we can skip the fucking shrimp, because I'd like a café au lait," I said.

"And I'll take a sparkling mineral water," Brett added.

"All right then—café au lait for the gentleman and a sparkling mineral water for the lady," Mick said, as he turned and headed for the kitchen.

I couldn't help but laugh as I thought about Mick's quip and decided right then and there that he had just earned one hell of a tip. Anyone who gave Brett shit of their own accord was clearly an intuitive person and OK in my book. And seriously, who in the hell flies to an exotic French Caribbean island to order mineral water? It seemed like a pretty boring fucking move on Brett's part, but at least the outdoor café, unlike my companion, was interesting and rife with activity. To make things even better, our table location provided a perfect front row view of the throngs of people walking along the sidewalk. I turned my gaze towards the street and saw two pretty brunettes and one cute redhead walk past, leaving a gap in the crowd, where I noticed that the white sedan parked across the street was now empty. Maybe the heat had finally gotten to the two jackasses who'd been inside, and they were out enjoying a mineral water. That was doubtful, however, as the French would be smart enough to at least enjoy a good cup of coffee at this hour of the day. Mick returned with our beverages as well as two slices of a delicious looking *tropezienne*. The *tropezienne* was basically a cream-filled brioche with a dusting of powdered sugar, and it had enough calories to sustain a family of five for a week.

"A café' au lait for the gentleman, a mineral water for the lady, and a *tropezienne* for both."

"A pastry as well?" I asked.

"Yep, you gotta try it, it's the best you'll find outside France. My treat."

"Thanks, Mick."

"What can I say? It's nice to hear English, even if it is funny sounding American."

Just as he was about to leave, I held up my knife.

"Oh, sorry—do you need more silverware?" he asked.

"No, it was just a stupid ploy to try and get you to say the famous line from the movie."

Mick shook his head and smiled.

"Fine, you bloody fucker," Mick said.

At that point he decided the make the reenactment more authentic, and reached into his pocket and pulled out a folding knife then expertly snapped open the blade.

"That's not a knife. This is a knife," he said.

I realized I recognized the specific make and model of Mick's knife.

"Holy shit, you're not kidding! That's a classic Benchmade SPECWAR model, guaranteed to go through a human body or a car door with equal ease," I said.

"You know your knives."

"I dabble a wee bit. Mind if I check it out?"

"Not at all," he said, as he closed the blade and handed it over.

I snapped the blade open, then flipped the knife into reverse grip and gave it a quick inspection.

The blade was rust-free in spite of the salt air, and the hinge had obviously been oiled to allow for silent and efficient open-ing—which gave me the distinct impression that Mick was more than just your typical waiter.

"Lovely piece of weaponry. Does it get much use out here in the Caribbean?" I asked.

Mick got a conspiratorial smile on his face.

"Every bloody day when I cut up limes for my beer."

"A better use I can't imagine."

I folded the blade closed then handed the knife back to Mick, and he slipped it back into his pocket.

"Alrighty then, mates, I'm off to check on my other tables," he said, as he left.

Brett and I were officially alone and I used the time to engage in some small talk as we dined and drank.

"You been to the Caribbean before?" I asked.

"Plenty of times with the Vandenbergs."

"This is my first time, and, I must say, it's pretty amazing."

"Yeah, you should have been a pilot, as you'd have seen a lot more of the world."

"Saw a lot of the world, but there just aren't that many conflicts in places like this. I mostly got to see the shitholes."

"Sadly, I'd have to agree with you there."

I enjoyed my coffee so much that it kept emptying, and Mick kept continually refilling it each time he passed by with the pot. After a good twenty minutes of this pattern, and what could have easily been six cups if I were counting, I desperately needed to pee. I rose from the table and headed towards the bathrooms, which were located around the right side of the building near the back parking lot. On the way I passed a table with two guys who looked a lot like the suits from the white Renault. I smiled and nodded and was surprised that they both looked at me with recognition. It was exactly the way people looked at celebrities when they ran into them in person, but I wasn't a celebrity, which meant that our meeting wasn't likely a coincidence. I continued on to the bathrooms and discovered the women's had three uncomfortable looking ladies waiting in line while the men's had nary a man in sight.

I ducked in to drain my six cups of coffee and was happy to see a sliding bolt lock on the door, which I found to be very civilized and meant that I could have snuck out a deuce had it been necessary. With only a number one on the itinerary, I peed, washed my hands, then opened the door, and voila—there, to my surprise, stood the two Frenchmen from the table, and they were purposefully blocking my path. Now that we were up close and personal, I realized that both men smelled of sickly sweet cologne and body odor, and, judging by the rumpled suits and dour expressions, I'd guess they had spent the better part of the morning roasting in their little car—the two of them looking like a couple of slightly overcooked chicken cordon bleus.

"*Pardonnez-moi, monsieur*. Could we talk for a moment?" said the bigger of the two, his breath reeking of cigarettes and coffee.

He had the confidence that made me pretty sure he and his subordinate were either policemen or worked for some kind of government agency.

"Sorry, gentleman, but I'm on a rather tight travel itinerary."

The two men ignored my response and grabbed hold of my arms and roughly led me out behind the café. I played along with my new French friends for the moment, because they were taking me exactly where I wanted to go—namely a nice quiet place without any witnesses to call the authorities should things get a little ugly. We reached the back parking lot, and I saw that it was deserted except for a particularly mellow black lab sleeping in the shade of an old service truck.

"*Mes amis*, I'm flattered by all your attention, but, to be perfectly honest, I'm not into dudes and, least of all, threesomes. So, as exciting as a *ménage à trois* may sound, I'm afraid I'm not interested, and, for your future reference, studies show that at least one of the three participants will invariably feel disenfranchised at some point in the exchange."

The big guy smiled.

"Fucking Americans all think you are so funny, but you're not."

"Really? So, what is your opinion of Jerry Lewis?"

The French were notorious for having an almost pathological love of Jerry Lewis and his many movies.

"He is actually funny."

"Well, then some Americans are funny, which means your previous hypothesis is false."

"Yes, one American is funny—but not you. So, listen up asshole, because I have a message to relay."

"Really? Who is it from?"

"That's not important."

"I don't know. It might take away from the message and lessen the impact. How can I know the context if I don't know the sender?"

He was starting to get annoyed but managed to maintain his composure.

"Enough talking! Now, it is time for you to listen. You, my

friend, are officially not welcome here on Martinique."

"That's interesting, because I'm pretty sure this island's economy is based on tourism."

"I'm serious, which means you need to shut your mouth. We're not fucking around here, asshole!"

"Yeah, we're not fucking around," the little one said, in his slightly higher pitched voice as he poked me with his stubby little finger.

The feisty Frenchmen were obviously used to being respected on their home turf, and making light of their threats was making them a little testy. Of course, I was doing my best to antagonize them, the purpose being to get a better idea of just how determined they actually were to get me off the island.

"I don't really care if you are fucking around or not, because I'm on vacation, and I've had just about enough of you two," I said.

The big guy wiped his brow and took a moment to try and simmer down, which was an obvious sign that he was starting to lose his cool.

"Listen here, monsieur. It's time for you to leave Martinique and go back to America, so you can stuff your stupid face with hotdogs and hamburgers."

"Well, that shouldn't be a problem, as I happen to be leaving today."

"Forget about the yacht in Le Marin. Instead, you're going back to the airport, where we have already booked you a one way ticket back to San Francisco"

"What about my friend with the tan? I just can't leave him all alone. He's very sensitive under all that sun damage."

"No need to worry about that asshole," the big guy said.

"Well, at least we can agree that he's an asshole. I'd say that's a good start to a more amicable relationship."

"We're fucking serious here, asshole!" the little one added, as he once again poked me in the chest with his finger.

"Look guys, you're not doing very much for tourism with all this poking and threatening, which leads me to believe that you obviously don't work for the tourism board. So, the question is— who do you work for?"

They looked at each other then the bigger one answered.

"You don't get to ask the questions."

"That's not the answer I was looking for specifically, so, let me help. Does the name Adrien Babineux ring any bells?"

I decided to throw out the name of the president of Soft Taco Island, as he was a major part of the reason I was here, and the only person who might give a flying fuck about my presence. I patiently waited for a reaction, and was rewarded for my efforts when I saw the little guy look nervously at the bigger guy—his response giving me a big, fat, and obvious yes answer to my question.

"But, judging by the cheap suits and attitude, I'm guessing that you also work for the police or perhaps the government."

The little guy looked at his bigger friend again, which confirmed yet another yes. Ten more minutes like this, and I'd know their birthdays, favorite pet, and preferred sexual position.

"So, all this begs the bigger question, which is how in the hell does Adrien Babineux know about me?"

"Enough of your bullshit questions! Either you come with us right now, or we stop being nice, and, trust me, it'll be a lot harder for you to get on the plane in a wheel chair," the big guy said, his face reddening as his anger finally got the best of him.

"I'm not so sure I agree, as the wheelchair would most certainly qualify me for preferential early boarding."

The big Frenchman had, apparently, heard enough of my jokes and tried to slam me against the old service truck. I was ready, however, and remained unmoved by stepping back into a karate stance called a kenpo. It entailed extending the back leg and bending the front one, the goal being to brace your body and lower your center of gravity. It worked perfectly, and my French friend ended up looking a tad bit silly, which seemed to make him even more angry.

"I guess we are done talking, which means we're going to be making a stop at the hospital on the way to the airport," he said, as he drew his arm back and prepared to fire off an undercut punch towards my stomach.

Taking the initiative in a confrontation is all about swift, decisive action—namely, hitting your opponent with such speed and ferocity that he has no chance of forming any kind of reasonable defense. I hadn't thrown the first punch in this altercation, but I was definitely going to throw the last one. As his fist came rushing in, I swung my right hand down in an arc, hitting his forearm with enough force to knock it off course before using the same hand to deliver a back-fist to the side of his head. He was stunned, and it allowed me to slip my hand around the back of his neck and pull him down into a knee strike. As he buckled over, I stepped back and combined his momentum with my body weight to pull him off balance and ram him headlong into the door of the service truck behind me. It knocked him out cold, and he dropped limply to the ground.

"Since we're done talking, I don't suppose you have anything to say, do you, *porcelet?*" I asked, as I turned my attention to his little friend.

The term, *porcelet,* translated as piglet, and it obviously made him angry, because the little fucker immediately drew his Beretta 9mm pistol.

"Definitely not," he responded.

Fortunately for me, the piglet, in his haste, had left the safety on, so it was nothing more than a paperweight in its current state. Still, with a flick of his thumb, it would be ready to fire, and I had no desire to be on the business end of it any longer than was necessary. I, therefore, needed to take it away and that meant employing a little deception as well as some swift handiwork. I looked towards the street and pointed.

"Holy shit! It's Jerry Lewis!" I said.

"Nice try, but your stupid ploy is not going to work."

He suspected that I wanted him to be stupid enough to look, but I only needed to fill his mind with a thought—any thought. It's the same principle as saying don't think about the color green, which, of course, instantly makes you think about the color green. So, as he processed the thought that I was trying to trick him, I had created my opening for action. I moved to the right, inside the arc of the weapon, then took hold of the gun before twisting it back towards his center and out of his hand—potentially breaking his trigger finger if I were lucky. It turned out that he was the lucky one and survived with his finger intact, but not so lucky that he managed to keep hold of his pistol. Now, that I held the trump card, I proceeded to drop the magazine and pull back the slide, ejecting the round from the chamber.

"Now, we can settle this *mano a mano* without either of us getting seriously hurt," I said, as I tossed the gun onto the ground.

"Except, perhaps, you. I was my unit boxing champion in the army," he said, as he squared off, raising both fists up into a classic fighter's pose as he started moving smoothly back and forth, shifting his weight from one leg to the other.

Of course he was a boxer. Any man that short would face a lifetime of shit and, therefore, at some point, decide to learn martial arts or, in his case, boxing. He moved around me in a slow circle, apparently trying to feel me out and find his opening. He threw two quick fakes followed by a right cross that he managed to land on my jaw.

"Not bad," I said.

"I'm just warming up."

He threw another punch, which I parried then followed up with an undercut to his ribs, causing him to buckle over and step back to catch his breath.

"Me too," I said.

"Fuck you!" he uttered, still recovering from the punch—a tiny droplet of spittle flying from his angry little mouth.

He came forward again throwing several wild swings, but only landed the last one, the majority of the force lost to poor footwork. He certainly had lots of energy and wasn't a bad fighter, but he was heavily influenced by an obvious Napoleon complex, a term which was, in truth, quite ironic and fairly inaccurate. As it turns out, the great ruler of France had actually been slightly taller than the average person of his day, and the error that would seal his place in history as a little man occurred when his physical measurements were inaccurately translated from French feet into English feet—thus causing him to falsely lose four and a half inches of height due to a translation error. So, in truth, the real Napoleon could have eaten French onion soup off the *porcelet's* head.

Now, the little man's ego was bruised, and he was losing his cool as he moved in throwing several wild punches, believing that his anger would be enough to drive one home. It wasn't, but his next round was a little better, and he managed to get a solid undercut punch in to my stomach. Thankfully, I was ready and exhaled, tightening up my abdominal muscles to lessen the impact.

"Not bad for a little guy," I said.

That was apparently the final straw to break the petit camel's back, and he was ready to make one great final attempt to take down his rude American opponent. Hunkering low and forsaking his boxing skills, he dashed in for a tackle, reaching out with both hands as he closed the distance. It was an angry, desperate move, and one I would counter by opening up my arms, keeping the left high and the right low, all the while waiting until he was just within range. As he arrived, I stepped off to my right and rotated both arms in a counterclockwise motion reminiscent of a two bladed windmill. The goal was to deflect his grab and divert all his energy safely past me, and I sent the little bastard head first into the hard steel door of the old service truck behind me, thereby allowing him to knock himself out cold in the process.

"*C'est la vie mon petit cochon*," I said, which basically translated as that's life my little piglet.

With the situation mostly resolved, I looked around and saw that we were still alone except for the dog, who ambled over and smelled me, curious what all the excitement had been about. I petted my new friend then squatted down and searched the Frenchmen's pockets, hopeful I'd figure out their actual job titles. It turned out they both apparently worked for the French General Directorate for External Security, or, in layman's terms, the DGSE—though it was hard to tell whether or not their ID's were legitimate, as authentic looking documentation was only a click away with the advent of Photoshop, photo printers, and the Internet. Considering the two men's attitudes, however, it was fair to assume they were most likely the real deal, though I was pretty damn sure they also worked for Babineux. The big question, then, was how in the hell could Babineux possibly know about me when I'd only agreed to come here two days ago and had only been on Martinique for a little over an hour.

As I leaned down to return their wallets, the dog moved in and licked my face, which was about the friendliest welcome I had gotten since reaching the island. You can always count on man's best friend for a little unconditional love and acceptance. I stood up and was taking a minute to pet my new canine friend when Mick came around the corner, looking a little concerned as he took in the scene.

"I had a bad feeling when I saw those two follow you back."

"Sadly, you missed all the fun."

"I can see that. Jesus mate, you might want to drink a little less coffee. I think it might make you a wee bit irritable."

"It wasn't the coffee. These two fuckers were trying to change my travel itinerary."

"Not very successfully, apparently."

"Thankfully not. Can you help me with something?"

"Does it affect my tip?"

"Absolutely."

Mick came over and helped me drag the two Frenchmen into the shade, where we repositioned them to look as though they were spooning. The final touch was to place the *porcelet's* arm around the other man's body so that his hand was resting on his friend's package.

"Reach-around—it's only fair," I said.

"They make a nice couple."

"They do, don't they. I'd sure love to be here to see their expressions when they wake up," I said, admiring my work.

Mick took a moment to scrutinize the two men.

"So, who are these two fuckers? They look like government types."

"Correct—they're DGSE agents."

"Any idea why they were giving you shit?"

"I'm pretty sure it probably has something to do with my latest case."

"What are you? An attorney? Because you definitely don't look like one."

"No, I'm just a lowly private investigator at the moment."

"Well you certainly handled yourself pretty well for a lowly private investigator."

"I used to have a more exciting job, once upon a time."

"If I had to guess, I'd say military, probably a special operations unit, considering you also happen to know a thing or two about knives."

"Good guess, I was in Pararescue. Ever heard of it?"

"Of course, I worked with you guys a few times while I was in the SASR."

The SASR, or Australia's Special Air Service Regiment was a seriously badass unit modeled after Britain's SAS.

"Well done. Where did you serve?"

"All sorts of shitholes, but Afghanistan was my last deployment."

"Me, too. Small world."

"Yeah, too small at times, but I got out four years ago and have been here ever since. Needed a good break—some fun and sun after all that shit."

"No doubt."

We both stood there and quietly ruminated on that thought until I had an idea.

"Hey, any chance I could get your number?" I asked.

"Sorry, I don't date customers."

"It won't be a date. We'll just talk, though I might be calling to offer you a potential job."

"Sounds like you'll be asking for a *wristy*."

"*Wristy?*"

"It's Australian for handjob."

I laughed as I acknowledged the fact that the Australians were some of the most colorful slang crafters in the world.

"No *wristys*—or *gobbys* for that matter," I responded.

I might not know the Australian slang for a handjob, but I did know the term for a blowjob, as I'd learned it from one of his fellow SASR team members back in Afghanistan. Now, it was Mick's turn to laugh.

"I see you speak some Australian."

"Just enough to get by—if you know what I mean."

"So, why would you possibly need the skills of an ex SASR man turned waiter?"

"Well, the reason I'm here is that I have an old friend who's gotten herself into some trouble on Soft Taco Island."

"I've heard of that place, but I thought it was some kind of silly vacation island."

"Apparently, people can still get into trouble on silly vacation islands."

Mick thought for a moment.

"Oh, what the hell! These days all I ever do is make latte's and surf, so it might be fun to get up to a little mischief."

"Excellent. I might just give you a call at some point."

I didn't have my iPhone on me, so Mick gave me his number on a card I'm sure he usually preferred giving to attractive female tourists. I returned to the front of the café to find Brett chatting up a couple of beautiful German women who were seated at the adjacent table. He seemed to be making good time and did his best to ignore me when I tried to interrupt. Say what you will about the tan wonder, he was a smooth operator with the ladies, but, sadly, his sex life would have to wait. I said his name three more times before finally resorting to pouring a dash of his mineral water on his crotch in a re-imagining of his humiliating episode from the previous night. He looked up at me angrily, red color appearing on his normally tan face while his new German friends laughed thinking it was some kind of prank. Unfortunately, he missed the humor and looked as though he wanted to punch me.

"*Guten abend meine damen,*" I said, as I turned my attention to the German ladies.

"Ahhh—you're also American!" the one to my right said, with a smile.

"*Ja,*" I said, slightly dejected that my German didn't pass muster.

Brett's new friends were lovely, and I can't say I wasn't a little tempted to stay and chat, as it would have been fun to try out more of my German language skills. Unfortunately, we had French security agents who might wake up at any moment and call in reinforcements. I, therefore, paid Mick, said *auf wiedersehen* to Brett's new friends, and took an extra coffee to go for Samuel before leaving the café. As expected, the tan wonder complained incessantly until I explained to him the reason for the hasty exit.

"So, how in the hell did they find you? We've only been in Martinique for an hour," he said.

"No fucking idea."

"Well, it was pretty shitty timing. I was making some real progress with those *fräuleins*."

"*Ja*, but had we ended up in jail it would be unlikely they'd allow conjugal visits."

"Are you kidding? We're on French soil. They're probably mandatory."

"I hate to admit it, but you might actually be right."

We continued on to the van to discover that the girls, of course, still hadn't returned. I handed Samuel his coffee then took a moment to look for our missing flock.

"Any idea where the girls are?" I asked, Samuel.

"Right there, in the boutique where that couple just walked out."

I zigzagged through a bevy of tourists to enter the store and found the girls at the counter. Tiffany was looking in my direction and waved, but Bridgette was facing the person at the register.

"Hello, girls!" I said, loudly.

Bridgette abruptly turned around, looking mildly startled as she regarded me.

"Oh—hey Tag," she said.

"I must say, I'm more than a little surprised to see you're actually done shopping."

"We did say forty-five minutes," Bridgette responded, looking at her watch.

"And, it's only been forty," Tiffany added.

"Well, OK then," I said, surprised to see the two of them almost bonding.

I guess shopping really was the great unifying force in the universe when it came to women. We left the store and joined the throngs of people on the crowded sidewalk, but, before we could reach the van, Bridgette paused to fiddle around with her phone. I used the moment to gaze at the display in the front window of the men's clothing shop next door and found myself smiling in wonder. Sweet Cary Grant's ghost! I couldn't resist and went inside only to be immediately pounced upon by a salesman. I told him I'd buy the entire outfit on the mannequin if the shop could do the alterations in under ten minutes. He agreed, and it required going in the back for my quickie fitting. When it was done, I walked back out to the front counter and irresponsibly charged a little over four thousand dollars to my Visa. I couldn't afford to pay the bill at the moment, but I was optimistic I would rescue Lux and get the million dollar bonus. The man placed my items in a garment bag, then I exited to the street to find Brett looking particularly anxious as he stood beside the van.

"I thought you said that we didn't have much time and needed to get the hell out of town," he said.

"I did, but good style is timeless, my friend."

Once again, we loaded into the van and headed south towards Le Marin. The drive would take about forty minutes, but I was more than happy to spend the time enjoying the beautiful scenery and talking to Samuel. About halfway into our journey, we passed a bakery in one of the towns, and the van filled with the glorious scent of freshly baked pastries. I felt a grumbling in my stomach, and looked at my watch and realized it was well after lunch, and, having only eaten the tropezienne, I was sorely needing some food. I asked the others if they were hungry, and, thankfully, I received a unanimous round of approval. Samuel, being the world's best driver and tour guide, said that he would take us to one of his favorite lunch spots, and we could grab some sandwiches for the road. It was conveniently located in the next town, and, soon thereafter, we pulled over in front of a busy looking restaurant and could already smell the savory scent of grilled meat and bread. My stomach was grumbling as we walked inside and went to the counter to put in our order. The girl at the register said it would be a few minutes before it was ready, so I decided to use the time to empty my bladder.

I left the others and followed the signs to the hallway that led to the bathrooms, but had a fleeting thought about my little incident at the café, and decided I should take a look around to see if I was attracting any undue attention from anyone in the restaurant. The people were all definitely more interested in their food than me, but, as I was about to continue on my way, a man standing near the front door looked over in my direction. Shit. He was rather clean cut and happened to be wearing a light colored suit that was similar looking to the one the porcelet and his friend had been wearing, and it instantly made me wonder if Babineux had more of his people out looking for me? The man soon lost interest in me, however, and pulled out his phone and began fiddling with it, so perhaps I was just being paranoid. I entered the hallway and passed the women's room first then stepped inside the men's to find it wonderfully deserted. That meant I was free to choose either the standard toilet or the urinal, and I went with the latter, as I wouldn't have to take the time to lift the seat. I began emptying my body of the remainder of my earlier coffee binge and was lucky enough to have the musical accompaniment of a long dry fart making its way out of my ass on it's journey to freedom. Finished, I used my elbow to flush the toilet then headed over to the sink to wash my hands. There, I couldn't help but smile, for I had finally managed to spend a little quality time in my holy sanctuary without being interrupted. Sure, it was only a pee stop, but I still saw this as a sign of smooth sailing ahead. With warm feelings of optimism swirling in my mind, I exited only to be startled by the presence of the man who had been watching me from the front door. Goddammit! The fucking French menace was back, but, this time, however, I was going to take the initiative, and, before he could react, I grabbed him by the lapels of his suit jacket and slammed him against the wall.

"Look, asshole, I've already dealt with your other two friends at the café, so there's no way in hell you're going to get me on that plane!"

"Excuse me, but..."

"Oh, how convenient—you speak excellent English. Well that's good because you'll understand when I tell you that, if you don't march your ass out of here right now and go tell your boss Babineux to fuck off, I'm going to go full-on Jim Henson on your ass. Comprende?"

"Um—not really."

"Well, then listen up, Kermit, because it means that I'm going to take my fist and shove it so far up your ass that I..."

At that moment the women's room door opened, and I stopped talking as I turned to see a rather attractive though stern faced woman come out and proceed to stand directly beside me.

"Excuse me, but do you mind telling me why you just threatened to shove your fist up my husband's ass?" she asked, her voice belying the obvious bourgeoise accent of someone from the northeastern United States.

Shit, it would appear that my unwelcome stranger wasn't a French agent but rather an overdressed fellow American waiting for his wife to come out of the bathroom. That certainly explained why he spoke such excellent English, but it also meant that I needed to think fast and hopefully diffuse the situation I had inadvertently created.

"You mean other than because he's devilishly handsome?" I responded, as I let go of him and stepped back.

"Yeah, other than that."

"Well—um—to be perfectly honest, I mistook him for a French DGSE agent."

"Really? In Seersucker?"

I looked more closely at his clothing and realized that he was indeed wearing a blue striped seersucker suit, but even more unusual was the fact that his wife was wearing a matching seersucker dress. The two agents I'd tussled with earlier were definitely not wearing seersucker, but, in the heat of the moment of finding this guy ominously looming outside the bathroom just now, I hadn't had time to take a closer look. Needless to say, I was feeling a tad bit stupid as I tried to come up with an adequate response to her question.

"Obviously, you don't know the formal dress code of the French

General Directorate for External Security," I said.

"Nice try, asshole. Now, if you don't mind stepping aside, we need to get going."

"Yeah, apparently to a J.Crew catalog photo shoot."

The woman gave me a disapproving sneer then took her husband by the arm and left, and I realized it was true what they say—you can take a person out of the Hamptons, but you can't take the Hamptons out of the person. I, therefore, made sure they were long gone before walking out and joining the others at the front counter. We soon had our order and returned to the van, whereupon I set about eating my hot ham and cheese sandwich. It turned out to be a bit on the French side of the sandwich spectrum, meaning it had lesser amounts of meat than you would expect in America, but it was still delicious. A full stomach made the rest of the trip even more pleasant, and it wasn't long before we reached the southern end of the island and began heading east along the scenic shoreline. About a mile later, we went around a long sweeping left turn and could now see the town of Le Marin and the adjacent bay.

"That's where we're headed," Bridgette said, pointing at a massive yacht anchored several hundred meters off the shore.

I looked over to see a truly magnificent vessel, far larger and more elegant than any of its peers, and I found it hard to believe that it was going to be our ride to Soft Taco Island. We entered the town of Le Marin and drove along the picturesque waterfront where rustic and colorfully painted buildings bordered the clear blue waters of the bay. Just ahead was the Le Marin Marina, and Samuel pulled in and brought us right up to the main pier. We unloaded our things then I took a moment to say goodbye to my new friend.

"It was nice to meet you, Samuel, and I hate to admit it, but I'll be missing your jokes," I said, as we shook hands.

"Good, then, I'll send you on your way with this final one. Why did the chicken go to the séance?"

"No idea."

"To get to the other side."

"Now, that is funny," I said, as I turned and headed down the dock.

As expected, the tender was nearly as nice looking as its bigger sister, though, in a sleek, sexy, and Italian kind of way. It was dark blue, about fifty feet in length, and had a long sloping bow that made it look as though it was built more for speed than pleasure. To balance out its aggressive styling, however, it had a large luxurious looking cockpit with seating for at least ten people. We climbed aboard with the help of a crewman dressed in a starched white sailor suit, then settled into the comfortable white leather seats. The crewman manning the helm, started up the throaty engines, and, soon thereafter, we were idling slowly out of the harbor and towards the yacht. Twenty-four hours ago, I had been in the cold and windy Bay Area fog belt, and, now, as I looked around at the clear blue water and cloudless skies of the Caribbean, I couldn't help but smile, for I was truly in Paradise.

"So, that's the family yacht," I said, to Bridgette.

"Yeah, my uncle's pride and joy."

"Does he use it much?"

"Mostly to wine and dine his business associates or wealthy friends."

"Then I obviously need to get seriously chummy with your uncle."

"Rescuing Lux will certainly be a good start."

I looked across the bay at the stern of the yacht and read the name *Sozo* and was curious about its origin.

"Does the name have any particular meaning?" I asked.

"*Sozo* is Greek, and means to save from harm."

I smiled.

"Then I'd say it's a perfect name considering what we're about to do."

We cleared the harbor and the helmsman throttled up the big

engines, sending a wonderful deep rumble up through our feet as the boat powered forward and moved gently up onto a plane. We were doing at least thirty knots as we passed a number of other mega yachts, and the closer we got to the *Sozo*, the larger it loomed, until the tender looked no bigger than a bath toy next to the long, sleek dark blue hull of its larger sibling. We slowed and came around to the starboard side, where the rear section opened up into a launch and docking area. Another crewman tied off the boat and, gazing at his starched white uniform and thick mop of dark brown hair, I couldn't help but think of the character *Gopher* from the old television show *The Love Boat*. The show was a silly, if not extremely successful, comedy drama that ran from 1977 to 1987, and, after going into syndication, filled many of my early childhood television hours. I suppose it was mean to compare the *Sozo's* crew to the show's cast, as it wasn't their fault that their wealthy employer liked to dress his employees in nerdy sailor suits. Perhaps if they were all beautiful women and their uniforms were mini skirts made of thin white cotton, I might feel differently.

"Welcome aboard, Miss Vandenberg," the crewman said.

"Hello Kip, it's nice to see you again."

As Kip stepped closer, I had a better look at him, and could see that his hair was the only similar trait he shared with his Love Boat counterpart. Unlike *Gopher*, Kip was built more like a gymnast, and had the jawline of a male model, proving that all of the Vandenberg employees were unusually comely.

"It's nice to see you, too. Now, everyone, please follow me," Kip said.

Kip led us up a stairwell onto the aft section of the main deck, and I had to say that I was truly impressed. I'd seen plenty of yachts living on the water in Sausalito, but never anything quite like this. It was well over three hundred feet long and appeared to have all the amenities of a luxury cruise ship but without the crowd. It was a testament to marine engineering and design with its beautiful blend of modern and classic esthetics. The hull was sleek, its dark blue color contrasting nicely with the white super-structure—the two areas married together by the polished teak deck—a deck I hoped to be standing on while having a cocktail later tonight. We entered the main salon to find it was enormous, plush, and could comfortably hold fifty of your closest friends and, like the jet, was adorned with blue trimmed white leather furniture that was apparently customary of all things Vandenberg.

At the far end was a massive dinner table, and in the middle along the port side was, in my opinion, the most important fea-ture—the bar. It had a teak paneled front facade and a smoothly polished black marble top, and was easily thirty feet long from end to end. On the wall beyond it resided a very ornate collec-tion of top shelf alcohols that included everything from Ketel One vodka and Patron tequila to, believe it or not, Soft Taco Island Rum, which I'd have to sample at some point—purely for research.

Standing on a stool behind the bar was a brown haired woman trying to reach a bottle on the upper shelf. She was wearing the same geeky uniform as the rest of the crew, but she made the plain white shorts and top look a lot better than her male coun-terparts. Of course, I was making that judgement after my eyes unconsciously traveled up her long muscular legs and happened upon her lovely backside. It was round and firm and hinted at some serious gym time. She abruptly turned around, and I did my best to swiftly shift my gaze up to her face, where I discovered she was, in the tradition of every Vandenberg female employee who I'd met thus far, utterly beautiful. She had delicate, almost elfin features and green eyes—her overall look a bit exotic, perhaps from having some Eastern European heritage. Better still, her athletic figure hadn't caused her to lose her soft feminine curves, and a rather lovely bosom lay beneath her starched white shirt. I was, therefore, instantly smitten, and could't help but ponder the idea that people often said they felt a spark when they met someone for the first time. In this instance, I would have to say that it felt as though I had just been struck by lightening.

"Hello," I said.

"Hello, I'm Estelle Connor, the official activities director on this yacht, and you must be our special guest. It's nice to meet you, Mr. Finn," she responded, her full lips parting to form a smile that made my heart flutter like a schoolboy.

"Please, call me Tag or Finn, no Mr. is necessary."

"Well then, Tag it is."

I had a brief moment to look around the room and take in the sights before bringing my gaze back to Estelle.

"So, what do you think?" she asked.

"Absolutely beautiful."

"Thank you—and how about the yacht?"

It took a second to realize she was fucking with me.

"Not quite as beautiful, but she'll turn a head or two," I said, receiving a smile for my efforts.

Sweet mother of boners! My penis was practically at full mast, and my balls were dancing around it like it was a maypole. This girl was all kinds of sexy before she even opened her mouth, but, now that I knew there was some serious sassiness and intelligence behind those sparkling green eyes, I was ready to propose. Brett came up beside me and her expression instantly cooled, and I realized that she too might be another of Mr. Tan and Teeth's romantic conquests. He sure made his rounds of the Vandenberg employees, but then who could blame him?

"Hello, Estelle," Brett said.

"Hello, Brett. You're looking very—tan. Have you been out in the sun?" she asked, in a sarcastic tone.

"No, but he has been at the tanning salon," I said.

"Not recently."

"Bullshit," Tiffany said, as she arrived at that moment.

"This is my natural coloring."

"You're Swedish," Tiffany said.

"On my mom's side, but my dad was..."

"A baked potato? It makes sense. Golden brown outside and starchy white on the inside," I said.

"Fuck off."

Kip cleared his throat to get our attention.

"How about I show you all to your rooms, so you can unpack and get comfortable."

We continued through the main salon towards the front of the boat to the guest cabins, where Bridgette, of course, got the master suite, which must have been amazing if my guest room was any indication. Just like the jet, I had a king size bed, my own coffee maker, and, more importantly, a full bathroom that included a Jacuzzi tub and a glass enclosed shower. I stowed my gear and took a moment to peer out my oval shaped porthole at the harbor and gently sloping hills of southern Martinique. It was hard to believe that I was a world away in the fabled land of pirates. I had spent much of my life and career near the ocean, though mostly the Pacific and Mediterranean, and never got closer to the Caribbean than Florida, where I had done my underwater combat and dive training to become a PJ. So far, I had to say, this was a lot nicer. Hell, this might just be the nicest place on earth. I brushed my teeth and headed back to the main salon to find Estelle and Kip organizing the various liquors behind the bar.

"Quite a boat you've got here."

"It's technically a yacht, and yeah, she's amazing," Kip said.

"I'm Tag, by the way," I said, holding out my hand.

"And, I'm Kip," he responded, as he took hold of it.

We shook hands and his grip was neutral, not too hard, not too soft, and we were about the same height, making us eye to eye as he leaned in uncomfortably close and sized me up from head to toe. This wasn't a typical handshake and seemed to be going on forever, feeling more like the prelude to a duel than a polite exchange between gentleman. At long last he released my hand and regarded me.

"This should be an interesting voyage, Tag," he said, with the unmistakable hint of a challenge in his voice.

Shit, I already had the tan menace to contend with, and now I had gymnast Gopher. Oh well, it was still early in our relationship, so I decided to try and take the path of least resistance and did my best to be friendly.

"Must be a pretty fun job getting to travel around on this yacht," I said.

"Sometimes, though not all the guests are what you'd call—fun," he answered.

"Well, I'll try my best to bring the fun."

"You do that," Estelle said.

"So, how about the Vandenbergs? What are they like? Fun?"

Estelle thought for a moment before responding.

"I don't think I would call Mr. Vandenberg fun, but he's always nice to us. Some of his friends are pricks, but that's how the haves treat the have-nots."

"How about Bridgette and Lux?"

"They have their moments. Lux has always been nice, but Bridgette can be a little—difficult—at times."

"Difficult—I can see that, and I must say, I find it oddly refreshing how candidly you talk about her—considering she's the owners niece and all."

"I wouldn't say this to everyone who comes aboard, but you don't exactly strike me as one of her mindless playthings."

I cleared my throat uncomfortably.

"I certainly hope not, but any man can quickly descend into stupidity in the presence of a beautiful woman."

"Oh, really?"

"You betcha, and I happen to be feeling a little stupid right now as a matter of fact."

"So, is someone making you feel stupid, or were you already stupid to begin with?"

"Someone is definitely making me feel stupid—so stupid, in

fact, that it's imperative that I get a guided tour of the *Sozo* to make sure I don't get lost."

"I'll do it," Kip said.

Shit, that wasn't exactly the outcome I was hoping for.

"It's OK, Kip, I've got this one," Estelle said, as she came around from behind the bar and joined me.

"Are you sure it's not too much of an inconvenience?" I asked.

"Not at all. Besides, we wouldn't want to lose you on your first day aboard. Now, come on and follow me, stupid," she said, leading me out of the main salon.

Estelle was beautiful, intelligent, and now—funny, which meant I might just be falling in love. We stepped onto the rear deck, and, while I had ventured this way earlier, I had neglected to take a closer look at the more important details such as the pool, outdoor bar, Jacuzzi, and abundance of comfortable looking seating that was probably common to most multi-million-dollar yachts. We continued on and went down a rear stairwell, and she led me onto the aft boat deck which housed the launch, a rigid inflatable, and another boat they probably used for water skiing or quick trips ashore. There were also smaller toys such as jet skis, kayaks, and even a parasailing rig. On the far side of the room, she opened a door and took me into the dive room, and I was shocked to discover it had more diving gear and underwater toys than a SEAL team. Bridgette really wasn't kidding when she said that I didn't need to bring my own stuff.

"We have all the latest dive gear, and that includes, tanks, regulators, and even aqua scooters."

"Shit, this is state of the art," I said, looking more closely at the air tanks.

"Yeah, those Draeger bubble-less re-breathers were just flown in this morning, as Mr. Vandenberg wanted to make sure that you had everything you needed for the job."

"That was pretty damn nice of him."

"It was, and he also said that we were to extend you every courtesy."

"Every courtesy?" I asked, raising an eyebrow.

"Almost every courtesy," she said, with a smile.

"Almost is better than nothing."

We headed towards the bow, passing the ship's gym, before using the front stairs to arrive in the crew's quarters, which resided just forward of the guest cabins.

"Want to see how the other half lives?" Estelle asked.

"Sure."

She opened the door to her cabin, and I was surprised to see that it was not that much different from my own. It had all the same amenities, but the real difference was the addition of knick-knacks, souvenirs, and photos—the personal touch that everyone gave their space when they lived in it long enough.

"This is nice," I said.

"Home away from home."

"And where's your original home?"

"Berkeley. Born, raised, and educated."

"Educated, as in UC Berkeley?"

"Yep."

"So, you're a hippy?"

"Not really, though I minored in environmental science."

"And majored in?"

"Archaeology, and believe it or not, I wasn't far from completing my PhD."

"Most impressive, but how do you use all that out here?"

"Which part? The environmental science or the archaeology?"

"Both."

"Well, I use the former by enjoying the environment, and the latter by getting to explore the Caribbean's many historical landmarks. There's a lot of history and culture in these islands, so I see my work on the *Sozo* as a kind of research sabbatical."

"Then you'll be going back to complete it eventually?"

"Yeah, once I've recharged my batteries—so to speak."

"Well, I can't argue with that, but, there is something I should have already told you. I went to your rival school."

"Stanford?"

"Afraid so."

"You Cardinal scum!" she said, in a low ominous voice.

There was something in her words and the way she spoke them that made my gentleman sausage want to point north, and when realization sunk in, it all but leapt from my pants.

"Was that a subtle Star Wars reference?" I asked.

"Well, more specifically, Return of the Jedi."

"Would it be awkward if I were to tell you that you just went from a ten to an eleven?"

"Yeah, because any man who uses a numbering system for women is a piece of shit. Of course, I would be even more offended because it should be obvious I was already a twelve."

"How about we let bygones be bygones and face the fact that you left twelve behind about the time you graduated from high school, and are now a full blown fifteen."

"I can live with fifteen, and just so you know, I don't give a flying fuck where you or anyone else went to college — and that goes double for Brett and his precious Naval Academy."

I had to smile as I regarded the ever beautiful and complex woman before my eyes. Sweet mother of God, I had met some pretty damn amazing women in the last twenty-four hours, but this one was turning my world upside down and inside out.

"I totally and completely agree," I responded.

"Do you know that tan asshole spent our first two dates talking about his fucking alma mater."

"Two dates? And not a word about dental hygiene?"

"Not a word."

"I bet you know a shitload about the United States Naval Academy."

"By the end of that last date, I pretty much felt as though I'd gone there myself."

"I just spent twelve hours on a plane with him, so, believe me, I know the feeling."

"Well, now that you've seen the main and lower deck, I might as well take you up to the bridge and introduce you to Captain Billings."

We left her cabin and headed aft to the main salon, and, from there, took the stairs to the top level, which housed the captain's quarters and another lounge a bit smaller than the one on the main deck. Also on this level was the obligatory helicopter on the aft landing pad, as well as our final and most important stop on the tour—the bridge. We stepped through the door, and I was surprised to see it was as sophisticated as any military ship that I'd ever been aboard and had all the latest and greatest navigation equipment spread out around the room. Residing front and center was the helm station while beside it was additional seating, probably for the first mate or navigator. On the other side of the room, wearing a starched white uniform and staring intently at a computer screen, stood the captain. Estelle politely announced our presence, and he looked over and smiled before coming to introduce himself. He had to be in his late forties and had light blue eyes, dark hair, and the sun and wind weathered skin of someone who had spent a life at sea. He was also an imposing figure, as he stood at least six feet tall, was in good shape, and had the kind of bearing that hinted he was very likely a former navy man.

"Welcome aboard. You must be Mr. Finn."

"Please, call me Tag or Finn, no Mr. is necessary."

"Well then, it's nice to meet you, Tag."

"Nice to meet you too, Captain Billings."

"Call me Pete," he said, as we shook hands, and I noticed that he, too, had a Naval Academy ring.

Shit, another ring knocker, but at least his grip was firm and purposeful though not crushing, which I took as a sign that he was a secure and well-adjusted person.

"I hope I'm not inconveniencing you too much."

"Absolutely not. It'll be a hell of a lot more fun than ferrying around a bunch of Vandenberg's pompous business buddies."

"I hope so."

"I know so."

"Well, thank you, Pete. I appreciate your help."

"Since you're up here, you might as well hang around while we leave port. It's the best view on the boat."

Estelle and I walked out onto the bridge deck, and the first mate joined us but stood on the opposite side, where he kept an eye on boat traffic. This allowed Billings to focus on easing the *Sozo* forward as they weighed anchor and prepared to get underway. Soon, the big yacht was free and moving, and the breeze was a welcome respite from the heat and humidity. I felt eyes on me and looked over to find Estelle looking at me appraisingly.

"What?" I asked.

"You're lucky. He doesn't let many people hang out up here."

"What can I say? I'm a people person."

"I can see that."

"Yeah, but you must be one too—to be in this line of work."

"I suppose, but I'm only a people person with the people I like."

"So, you're like a brutally honest version of *Julie McCoy*."

Julie McCoy was the activities director on *The Love Boat*, and it was her job to make sure all the guests had a good time. Of course, Estelle neither acted or looked anything like the real *Julie McCoy*.

"Absolutely not, and I definitely wouldn't refer to the *Sozo* as *The Love Boat*," she said.

"Well, not yet, anyway."

She smiled at my comment.

"Seriously now, that fucking show has been off the air for at least thirty years, yet, somehow, every one of these trips has at least one asshole who thinks he's the first one to make a *Julie Mc-Coy* joke about me."

"So, technically that makes me the asshole on this trip."

"It sure does."

"Well, then perhaps you could be the edgy *Julie McCoy* in the new darker *Christopher Nolan* re-boot called *Love Boat Begins*. Instead of perky, you're a brooding, though insanely hot, activities director whose unlikely activities includes seducing the male guests and collecting kinky sexual encounters the way other women collect China dolls."

She gave me a disapproving look.

"What? Too much?" I asked.

"Only the brooding part."

We shared a little laugh and there seemed to be a subtle inkling of sexual tension between us, though it was probably just wishful thinking on my part. We cast our gaze out towards the horizon for a moment before Estelle turned back to me with a curious smile on her face.

"So, do you really think I'm insanely hot?" she asked.

I looked into her eyes and considered my answer very carefully.

"A lesser man might run like a frightened deer from such a loaded question, but I'm going to be perfectly honest and give you the real answer which is—yes, you are insanely hot."

"Good to know."

"Is there anything you want to tell me?" I asked, hopeful for even a semblance of a reciprocal compliment.

"Nope."

"Nothing at all?"

"Nada, though I have a feeling this is going to be a very interesting voyage," she said.

Kip had, more or less, said the same thing only minutes ago, but, for obvious reasons, I found Estelle's words more enticing.

"Interesting, indeed," I responded, as I turned my attention towards the spectacular view of Le Marin, which was fading into the distance as we moved farther out into deeper water.

My attention was drawn towards the lower deck when a figure suddenly appeared. It was Brett, and he looked particularly annoyed that I was up in Captain Billing's private domain with Estelle. I, therefore, decided to give him a nice friendly little wave, but he returned the gesture by very deliberately holding up the middle finger on his right hand.

"If you're trying to inform me that you need to go potty, then you better be sure it's just a number one, because I'm not going to be the one to clean up your shorts if it's a number two again," I yelled, down to him.

He smirked and lowered his finger before walking back inside. Meanwhile, I stood with Estelle and enjoyed the view as we headed west into open water and left the island of Martinique well behind. The *Sozo* proceeded to make a long gentle turn towards the north then, a minute later, Billings came out and joined us.

"Cocktails and dinner on the aft deck this evening?"

"Sounds good to me."

"I'm afraid I can't. I'm on duty until eight," Estelle said.

"This cruise is off the books, so you're officially invited. In fact, it's an order. Oh, and remember to bring swimsuits. I'll see you all at dinner," he said, before disappearing back inside the bridge.

It was a perfect moment with clear skies, calm seas, and a beautiful woman at my side. I felt truly lucky to be alive and decided right then and there that I liked the Caribbean.

CHAPTER ELEVEN
The Sea Makes Men Hard

Estelle and I hung out on the bridge for another hour before eventually heading downstairs and parting company in the main salon. She said she'd meet me after she told the others about dinner, so I went to my cabin and put on my swimming shorts. They were the nylon surfing kind that dried quickly and were perfect for the constant eighty-degree weather and humidity and, more importantly, gave Willy Wonka and the Oompa Loompas plenty of breathing room. Speaking of which, I couldn't help but wonder if Brett would show up in a Speedo, as he seemed like the type. I brushed my teeth and headed back to the lounge to discover Estelle in a fairly skimpy, black two-piece bathing suit, and I realized that I had greatly underestimated her figure. As a professional investigator it was my job to notice important details about people, and, as a man, it was my job to notice important details about women in particular—and I certainly noticed Estelle's details. My earlier comparison to *Julie McCoy* had grossly underestimated her physique, and, now, I understood why she found it so annoying. Beneath the nerdy white sailor suit, she had indeed been hiding some very nicely sized breasts, likely a sporty C cup, as well as a backside that was formidable—round and muscular, and everything you wanted in a butt, so to speak. She was indeed a stunner, though, unlike Bridgette and Tiffany, had that wholesome girl next door kind of vibe that made her the perfect person to proudly bring home to meet your parents. Of course, the minute dinner was over you would want to take her back to your place and hump the stuffing out of her. Where did Vandenberg find these women? He was a man among men and slowly becoming my hero. We walked out to the back deck, and Estelle headed for the bar, but Billings cut her off and motioned her towards a seat.

"I got this round. Any requests?" he asked, as he grabbed a pitcher and some ice.

"How about Dark and Stormies in honor of the Caribbean," I suggested, as I took a seat on one of the outdoor sofas.

"Sounds good, and we've even got Soft Taco Island Rum."

"Excellent, might be good to get a little acquainted with the place."

"That's probably the best thing you'll find on Soft Taco Island."

"Interesting—as I found that their website painted a rather nice picture and made it look a bit like a Club Med."

"On the exterior it looks pretty nice, and, personally, I didn't have any problems while I was there, but I've heard some stories about people running into trouble after losing big in the casino. Apparently, they take their debts very seriously. One bad hand and you could end up working for the island until you pay off your marker."

"In that case, I should probably see what kinds of openings they have on the Soft Taco Island job board before I make any serious bets at the casino."

We shared a little laugh, then Billings went on to tell me that he'd heard gossip from other captains. Sailors liked to talk, and there was an abundance of tales about unfortunate souls who'd ventured into the casino on Soft Taco Island hoping to make a windfall, but ended up losing their shirts and, supposedly, in some cases, their lives. It wasn't exactly the pretty picture their website painted, but neither Vegas nor Atlantic City were the most innocent places in the world.

Billings poured us another round, and, just as we clinked glasses, Bridgette appeared from the main salon. She had donned a rather small, white, two-piece bikini and looked annoyed that we had started without her. She walked over to join us and might as well have been on a catwalk with the way she placed one foot directly in front of the other. It was that runway stroll that models did to emphasize the motion of their hips, and it had the added benefit of making Bridgette's breasts jiggle seductively at the impact of each step. It was impossible to look away, and all the men around stared in rapt attention. Estelle, not quite so enthusiastic about the show, let out a long sigh as Bridgette made her timely entrance, and I realized that it couldn't be very easy running in these circles.

"So, where have you been, Tag? I haven't seen you since we came aboard. Oh, Estelle, could you get me one of whatever you're drinking?"

"I'll get it," I said.

Estelle nodded a silent thank you as I went to the bar, poured another glass from the pitcher, and brought it to Bridgette. She smiled and gave me a quick kiss on the lips then sat down beside me. Where the hell did that come from? She'd been giving me the cold shoulder ever since the jet. Too bad the human potato had missed it, but he was probably off whitening his teeth. Then, as if on cue, my favorite starch appeared, his teeth whiter than a dollop of sour cream, and he was wearing nothing but a red Speedo. Classic. Now he looked like a eurotrash Ken Doll, but at least his blindingly bright smile disappeared when he saw that Bridgette was sitting next to me. He proceeded to pour himself a drink then tried his best to squeeze between Bridgette and me but slipped and ended up in my lap. It was pretty unsettling to have a large, tan

Speedo-clad man smelling of cocoa butter nesting on my crotch, so I tried to coax him off me by patting his behind and telling him to run along. He jumped up in a panic and looked mortified as he tried to regain his composure. I decided to be nice and gave him the space next to Bridgette, as it allowed me to move to the other sofa and join Estelle. No sooner had I sat down, that the party got more interesting as Tiffany, the final member of this ensemble cast, made her entrance. She had changed and was now wearing a sexy new red bikini—the scant amount of material drastically emphasizing the amount of flesh it was barely covering. She saw that Brett was next to Bridgette and sat next to Estelle and me on the other sofa. There was plenty of room, but she squeezed as close to me as she could, which appeared to annoy Brett, even though he was clearly still pining for Bridgette. Billings, a new-comer to this soap opera, tried to be polite and maintain proper eye contact, but his gaze kept shifting between Tiffany's beautiful face and her generous curves. He jumped up and got her a drink, which in turn got him a smile, and I thought I detected a potential new love connection.

"I don't believe we've met. I'm Pete," he said, as he clinked her glass.

"I'm Tiffany. It's nice to meet you, Pete."

You could always tell when people had chemistry, and, as I watched the two of them look at each other, it was as though someone had set fire to their loins with a Bunsen burner.

"She works for the family," Bridgette said, attempting to quash the potential romance in the air.

"We all work for the family," Billings responded.

That comment got Pete a lovely smile from Tiffany.

"Well, Pete, I must say—I'm really looking forward to spending some time aboard your vessel here."

"And I'm looking forward to doing everything I can to make sure your stay is as enjoyable as possible."

Tiffany's cheeks turned a bit red, and she smiled abashedly.

"Oh—well—um—thank you. I appreciate that, Pete."

"Believe me, it's my pleasure."

One romance point for Captain Smooth! I turned to Tiffany, and we shared a brief smile, as my prediction of her finding a nice guy might actually be coming to fruition. We finished our first round of drinks and, fortunately, only endured one Naval Academy story from Brett. It had something to do with him and a fellow classmate dunking a plebe's feet in a couple of urinals and calling it water skiing. I guess it was a Naval Academy tradition, but only Brett thought it was funny. The rest of us thought it was mean and stared blankly when he tried to explain the humor. Thankfully, he gave up and decided to silently sip his cocktail. I could see he thought that Billings, as a fellow ring knocker, would join him in talking about their beloved alma mater, but Billings preferred to talk about his active time in the Navy, where he had served as the captain of a Cyclone Class Patrol Boat. It was smaller than *Sozo* by at least a hundred feet and was primarily used to support SEAL team operations. In an unusual twist of fate, I just happened to be familiar with his vessel, because I had served on one with SEAL TEAM SIX during a Joint Special Operations task force in the South China Sea. It was yet another bonding moment with Billings, but it left Brett feeling left out and a little low on the man ladder, so he decided the best way to move up a rung was to take another swing at the Air Force.

"So, why would someone from the Air Force be working with the SEALs? I can only assume you were there on a fact finding mission to see what real men did for a living," Brett said, looking pretty pleased with himself at having come up with such a clever insult.

"You know, I could acknowledge your little comment by saying yeah, I was there to see what real men did for a living, but I'd probably put a little spin on it by saying I was there because the SEALs were obviously the only real men in the Navy. Of course, I wouldn't do that, because it wouldn't be fair to group Pete or the rest of the Navy in with a bunch of overly tan, tooth whitened jet jockeys, and, more importantly, I'm not the kind of person to hurl insults at anyone who has bravely served their country."

Turning someone else's insult against them was often the best defense, and my long winded response to Brett thankfully made him once again go back to quietly sipping his drink.

"Mr. Vandenberg told me you were in Pararescue. That's not an easy job," Billings said.

"I don't think any job in the military is necessarily easy, but, I can say without a doubt, it wasn't boring."

"What's Pararescue?" Estelle asked.

"They're kind of like Navy SEALs, except their primary mission is rescue operations," Billings said.

"So, you were like a SEAL with a big heart."

"Yeah, and you know what they say about men with big hearts?"

"What? Big feelings?" Estelle asked with a sassy smile.

"Exactly," I said, tapping my chest.

"How sweet," she responded.

"Sweet may not be the right word. PJ's go through some of the most difficult and lengthy training of any of the special operations forces," Billings said.

"Oh—come on! We're talking about the Air Force here! Everyone knows they have some of the easiest training regimens in the entire United States military. If you want a real challenge, then try being a Navy pilot," Brett blurted out, clearly unable to keep his annoyance to himself any longer.

"You know, Brett, all this macho rivalry stuff makes me realize you're kind of like Iceman to my Maverick."

Iceman and Maverick were the two rival jet jockeys in the nineteen eighties blockbuster movie Top Gun. It starred Tom Cruise, Val Kilmer, and Kelly McGillis, and made every guy in the world want to become a fighter pilot.

"You seriously think calling me Iceman is supposed to be insulting? Honestly, I take it as a compliment."

"Of course you do—because you're missing the subtle homo-erotic subtext of the movie. You probably saw the romance as being between the lead male and female characters, but, in my opinion, the real love story was between Iceman and Maverick."

"Meaning?"

"Meaning, all of these insults about the Air Force are just a clever form of verbal foreplay that you're hoping will lure me into your cockpit."

Brett wasn't very amused and stood up from the sofa.

"You know what? I've got a real problem with that mouth of yours," he said, as he moved towards me, his body language show-ing that he was about ready to throw down.

"And here comes our first kiss," I said.

Billings stood up and intercepted Brett by placing a hand on his chest.

"Easy there, sailor. You've got to be willing to take a little shit if you're going to give it," he said, in a soothing tone.

Brett acquiesced and sat back down, thankfully bringing our silly battle of man-ness to an end for the moment. This just left the battle of the breasts, which was slowly developing on the playing field that was the *Sozo's* aft deck. The casual observer might have missed it, but, as a student of psychology, I enjoyed the subtlety of human behavior and interaction that was playing out before everyone's eyes. Bridgette was quietly appraising Tiffany, possibly feeling a little outdone by the attention her new bikini was get-ting from the men, while Tiffany, probably still mad about Brett, was giving Bridgette an intermittently icy glare whenever their eyes crossed paths. Estelle, basically an innocent, but still a player by nature of her gender, did her best to ignore all of it. Madness. Each of them were uniquely capable and beautiful, yet each still found something to envy and abhor about the others. It was kind of sad, but at least it was entertaining.

The first official salvo began when Bridgette got up and walked to the pool, taking a rather circuitous route that passed all the nearby men. She reached the deep end, adjusted her bikini top, then did a perfect dive and swam an obligatory lap before pulling herself up onto the edge of the pool. At that point, she leaned back on her elbows, and the wet bathing suit clung like a second skin—thus making her nipples particularly visible as they pointed prominently through the thin fabric. All of us menfolk stared in rapt attention, certain parts of our own anatomy probably becoming visible, and I was, therefore, happy not to be wearing Brett's Speedo, for it wasn't nearly enough coverage for this good of a show. Bridgette had officially just taken the lead in the race for the men's attention.

Tiffany, literally not willing to take this sitting down, stood up and walked to the far side of the pool, whereupon she executed an equally perfect dive. Instead of swimming a lap, however, she popped up and stood in the shallow end, where she, purposefully or not, gave us the show of our lives. The cups of her top had slid off to each side, and both of her ample breasts lay bare and glistening, each nipple gazing playfully at the crowd of gawkers. Time seemed to slow down as we all stared, and, not too surprisingly, no one managed to tell her about her wardrobe malfunction and the very obvious fact that her breasts were out for all to see. It finally fell on Bridgette to put an end to the show.

"Tiffany, your breasts seem to have fallen out."

"Oh my goodness—I am so embarrassed. Thanks, Bridgette."

She slipped her breasts back into her top, then carefully adjusted each one until it was resting properly within its inadequately sized cup. I turned and realized that Kip was standing behind me, though he seemed unfazed, as I suppose he saw this kind of thing all the time on the Vandenberg yacht. He cleared his throat to get our attention then told us dinner was about to be served. No less than a minute later, crewmembers appeared with trays of food, the delectable scent wafting towards us on the warm trade winds. Everyone moved to the table and took seats, practically drooling as they stared at the amazing meal. There was beef Wellington, fresh spinach salad, and broccoli florets in a hollandaise sauce. Billings waited until everyone had a plate then gathered our attention by standing up and raising his glass to toast.

"Here's to new friends, and all of us getting to know each other better," he said, directing his gaze specifically to Tiffany, who acknowledged his subtle innuendo with a smile.

We all dug in to our delicious dinner, and hardly a word was spoken until everyone was done eating. Billings, upon popping his last bite of broccoli into his mouth, got a conspiratorial smile on his face as he spoke.

"We won't reach the island until tomorrow, so we might as well have a little fun tonight," he said, as he walked over to the bar and turned on the stereo, thus filling the air with the groovy sound of reggae music.

"I'm going for a dip in the Jacuzzi. Who wants to join me?" Brett asked.

He stood up, and an attractive female crewmember I hadn't yet met was the only one willing to brave his scantily dressed state and follow him to the bubbling inferno. As she walked past me, I could see that she was beautiful and had long brown hair, blue eyes, and a supple figure, and all I could wonder was why she wasn't put off by the Speedo. I suppose it was possible that she was European or perhaps too blinded by the glare from his teeth to notice.

I stripped off my shirt, grabbed my drink, and headed over to the shallow end of the pool, inadvertently catching Estelle watching me from the other side of the deck. I was probably misreading the signals, but it sure as hell seemed as though she was checking me out. Of course, guys checked out girls all the time, as it was in our DNA, but it was rare, if not impossible, to catch girls doing it. Either they were above such superficial viewing of the opposite sex, or they were a lot better at not getting caught—probably the latter. I set my drink on the edge and slid into the cool water, feeling the welcome respite from the heat of the tropics as I relaxed and took in the scene. First on my personal radar was Brett who was simmering away in the Jacuzzi and seemed to be having a good time with his very attractive new friend. I sincerely hoped they didn't get too excited in the next few minutes, as I planned to go there next and didn't relish the thought of finding any of Brett's creamy goodness making laps around the Jacuzzi.

The rest of the crew, meanwhile, had spread out around the pool area, and the deck was awash in party chatter. Billings refilled his drink at the bar then stripped off his shirt and headed over to the pool, where I could see that he was in even better shape than I previously thought and apparently carried his military discipline into how well he took care of himself. He set his drink on the edge, swam a few laps, then grabbed it and joined me in the shallow end.

"So, Tag, as you already know, I spent the majority of my military career supporting special operations, so any help you need, just ask," he said.

"Thanks, it's nice to know I have a fellow professional along."

A series of ripples disturbed the surface of the pool, and I looked up to see Estelle and Tiffany joining us, and Estelle, like an angel of mercy, was carrying a fresh pitcher of Dark and Stormies. She refilled our glasses, then we all toasted and took generous sips of our delicious cocktails, and I realized that it was a perfect moment. The sun was just setting off to the west, and directly in front of me were two of the most beautiful women and four of the most fabulous breasts that I'd ever seen in one place. It was just too bad that it was a working trip, but so far it was working out pretty well.

The alcohol and the atmosphere were doing an excellent job of promoting the party mood, and it was feeling less like reality and more like a scene from some wacky romantic comedy movie. This one would be called Caribbean Vacation, and it would include lots of dudes, boobs, and booze, and the obligatory annoying guy would be unnaturally tan, have blindingly white teeth, and call himself the Brettster. Ready to move on to the next scene in our live-action movie, we took our foursome into the Jacuzzi. There, we joined Speedo Boy and his new friend, and I was happy to find the water was free of foreign liquids that had the color and consistency of tapioca pudding. Bridgette and a couple other crewmembers joined us, and, shortly thereafter, the swirling water became a veritable pot of sweetly scented boob stew.

"So, Brett. What's your story—and I'm talking about after the Naval Academy, or, more specifically, when and why you left the Navy?" I asked.

He was quiet for a moment as he regarded me, probably thinking that I was baiting him into some kind of insult. At long last, he took a sip of his drink then spoke.

"I served in Gulf Two's air campaign, but the stress started to get to me by the end, so I figured that it was about time to resign my commission and get a job with an airline and start enjoying the good life. I did two years with United Airlines then was offered this job with Mr. Vandenberg and I've been here ever since."

"I see you cleverly left out the part about opening a chain of the worlds first all-in-one dental and tanning clinics called Plaque and Tan," I said.

"Obviously, I don't want to give away my secret retirement plan."

"Obviously," I responded.

I had to smile, as Brett was finally understanding that accepting his foibles was the best way to combat teasing.

"Well, now that you know my story, why don't you explain when and why you gave up your exciting life as a PJ," Brett said.

"The official *when* was at the beginning of 2006, though the event that facilitated it occurred in 2005 during my last active deployment in Afghanistan."

"What happened?" Estelle asked.

"I got shot while rescuing a helicopter pilot."

"Can we see the scar?" she asked.

I stood up and turned around.

"Ouch, that doesn't look fun. Care to tell us the details?"

"Nah, it's kind of a long story."

"We have plenty of time."

"And it's boring."

"I seriously doubt that, so, come on, spill it."

"OK, fine, but don't blame me if you end up falling asleep."

Brett rolled his head back and made a snoring sound, which prompted Tiffany to punch him in the arm. He pretended to jerk awake, and, now that I had everyone's attention, I began the story.

"Alrighty then, as you already know, the person was a pilot, but it was his location that was the real problem. He was trapped in the wreckage of his helicopter on the top of a mountain that was surrounded by Al Qaeda and Taliban forces. That meant I had to parachute in under the cover of darkness and exfiltrate the fucker about seven kilometers to where the Army Rangers had established a secure landing zone."

"And what exactly do you mean by exfiltrate?" Tiffany asked.

That was an excellent question as the word exfiltrate was mainly a military term that wasn't very meaningful in the civilian world.

"In that particular case, it meant I had to personally carry that one hundred and ninety pound pilot to the extraction point."

"That alone sounds terrible enough," Estelle said

"It was."

"So, when did you get shot?" she asked.

"Twenty fucking feet from the door of the pickup helicopter. It turns out the Taliban were early risers, and we ended up in a bit of a gun battle—and, believe it or not, the only reason that the pilot and I survived is because Lux disobeyed a direct order and came in under heavy enemy fire to get our asses out of there."

"That's our girl," Billings said.

"So, that's when you ended up with a desk job doing background investigations?" Brett asked.

"Yeah, then I mustered out and worked for a different branch of the government, where I continued doing more boring investigation shit."

"Boring investigation shit? I would think a person with your expertise would be more likely to go into the CIA," Estelle said.

"No—nothing so exciting."

"Nice try, but you're a shitty liar."

I shrugged, as I was a shitty liar, and it was, therefore, probably a good thing that I had gotten out of the CIA, considering lying was their modus operandi.

"Do you miss it? Being a Parajumper, I mean," Tiffany asked.

"I do. There's nothing like living life on the edge and going all over the world to help those in need."

"But, I imagine that kind of job stress must eventually wear you down," Estelle said.

"It did, but it was worth it. I know this will probably sound a little cheesy, but every time I reached an injured person, the look on their face was something that I'll never forget. I'm not exaggerating when I say that they saw me as an angel of mercy sent directly from heaven to save their ass from certain death."

"That must have been pretty amazing," Tiffany said, with a sigh.

"Yeah," Estelle added, as she gazed into my eyes.

Brett groaned, and I was getting the feeling that he'd had more than his fill of my storied past, and our temporary truce might be coming to an end.

"OK, enough about Mother Teresa here. Let's move on to a new subject," Brett said.

Tiffany glared at Brett, but he responded with a shrug as he took a sip of his drink. His interruption, however, brought a momentary end to the conversation in the Jacuzzi, and now the only sound filling the air was the music and the bubbling of the jets. War stories could certainly be a conversation stopper, and I'd have to remember in the future that it might be prudent to keep my unusual past to myself. Now, however, it was probably a good time to heed the tan menace's advice and change the subject to something a little more upbeat. I smiled and held up my glass for a toast.

"I hate to say it, but Brett might actually have a point, so, let's take a moment to raise our glasses in celebration of this moment and how lucky we all are to have met and made it into this Jacuzzi on this sweet ass fucking yacht! To rum, fun, and sun!" I said.

Everyone clinked glasses and enjoyed the beautiful Caribbean night, and even Brett's glowing white teeth and Speedo couldn't detract from the food, folks, and fun that surrounded me in the Jacuzzi. The drinks were flowing and feet, hands, and other more exotic body parts were mingling in the turbulent waters. Billings, riding high on a healthy rum buzz, seemed to be hitting it off with Tiffany and decided to send a ship-wide invitation to any of the crew not otherwise engaged, to come join the party on the aft deck. More people showed up, and the party spread throughout the usually forbidden spaces generally reserved for their employer and his exclusive guests. It was a good time for all, and, after a solid hour of boiling away, Estelle and I climbed out and headed for the bar. I was only a few steps behind her and couldn't help but enjoy the view of her lovely backside in her skimpy bikini. Each step made it seductively sway back and forth, and it was all I could do not to give it a friendly bite, as a butt that good deserved one. We reached the bar, refilled our drinks, then took a seat, and my gaze inadvertently fell upon her bosom, where I happened to notice that the sea breeze was cooling her skin and bringing her nipples to their full exciting potential. Unfortunately, my reflexes, dulled by the vast quantities of rum, were slow as hell, and she laughed when she caught me staring.

"Oh my God—they're just nipples," she said.

"And the Sistine Chapel is just a church."

Estelle shook her head in dismay.

"Men—it's almost sad."

"I hardly think appreciating the opposite sex's anatomy is solely a male thing, least of all, considering I caught you checking me out earlier."

"Oh, well, that was more scientific curiosity. The way one might observe a primate at the zoo."

"Well then, Jane Goodall—was Brett a scientific curiosity?" I asked.

"Do you really want to know about Brett? Because I'd love to hear about Bridgette and Tiffany."

"What about them?" I asked, innocently.

"Gossip travels fast on a ship. Two girls in two days is a little sleazy."

"I wouldn't call it sleazy. I would call it coincidence."

"Care to elaborate on that?"

"I could, but I'd rather not."

"Give it a try. It certainly couldn't hurt your reputation."

"OK, in the case of Bridgette, I was, coincidentally, sleeping in the room next door when she basically seduced me."

"All the way from her room? I didn't know she was that good."

"To clarify—she strolled into my room half naked in the middle of the night and ran me around the bases."

"Bullshit."

"No, I'm afraid it's true."

"Why the hell would she seduce you?"

"She knew I was vulnerable and hadn't had sex in two months, and it was her way of sweetening the deal to make sure I took the job. The minute we were on the plane, nookie time was over."

"Well, except for that little kiss earlier tonight."

"Oh, did you see that?"

"It was hard to miss."

"That was obviously an anomaly, and is unlikely to be repeated."

"Let's hope so. Now, how did you coincidentally end up boning Tiffany?"

"I was coincidentally on the same airplane with her when she found out that Brett was cheating on her with Bridgette. She needed a shoulder to cry on."

"And instead, you gave her your penis."

"It seemed to help."

"I hope you understand that you didn't really have to sleep with either of them. You could have said no."

"Maybe to Bridgette, but Tiffany legitimately needed me. You see, the two months of abstinence I experienced were because I had also been dumped, so I understood how shitty she was feeling and how important it was to restore her self-esteem by making her realize that she was still beautiful and desirable."

Estelle gazed discerningly into my eyes as she took a moment to consider my words.

"I suppose at some level you were actually trying to be noble, but I'm afraid you're still a man-whore."

"Well, how was I supposed to know I was about to meet the girl of my dreams working as the activities director on a yacht in the Caribbean?"

"Good answer—for a man-whore."

"I may seem like a man-whore right now, but it's not really who I am. I'm guessing it's this place."

"The Caribbean?"

"Yeah, normal guys come down here and miraculously turn into James Bond."

"You're not normal."

"I used to be."

"I seriously doubt that."

We sat there enjoying the balmy evening, and it was nice to have a moment to just sit and sip my drink as I took in all the activity across the deck. Billings and Tiffany had moved to one of the sofas, and they were talking animatedly and gazing into each other's eyes, which meant that they were obviously hitting it off. Bridgette and Brett, however, were quietly arguing in a back corner near the pool, and I would bet good money that she was voicing her displeasure about his new friend in the Jacuzzi. Play with the bull and you got the horns. It certainly made me pretty darn happy to be well out of that little social circle. Kip, meanwhile, was talking with a fellow crewmember, but seemed to be watching Estelle and me very closely, so perhaps he had a thing for her. I suppose it was hard not to step on somebody's toes, even on a yacht this size. I decided to direct my gaze astern and noticed the partial moon was just rising, casting the sea behind us aglow and making the Caribbean night even more beautiful. Unfortunately, it was well after midnight and, therefore, probably a good time to head off to bed, so I would be fresh for tomorrow.

"Well, this man-whore is ready to call it quits for the night."

"I better escort you. God only knows how many women might try to seduce you or need comforting between here and your cabin."

We left the aft deck via the main salon and arrived at the guest cabins, only to hear Brett and Bridgette arguing as they came up the passageway behind us.

"Fuck you, Brett! I'll just go find Tag if you're going to waste your time trying to bed the chef," Bridgette said, angrily.

Apparently, Brett's new squeeze is the *Sozo's* chef, and, like Tiffany, is both beautiful and gifted in the culinary arts.

"Fine, go fuck that fucker!" he said.

I felt legitimate panic as I looked at Estelle.

"You gotta hide this man-whore. I don't want to be seduced again," I whispered.

"Come on, you can hide in my cabin until she's gone."

We were only a short distance ahead of Bridgette as we raced past my cabin and towards the crew's quarters. Estelle threw open her door, and we stepped inside, and I was surprised to find her room aglow in an eerie blue light. I looked for the source and discovered it to be a little blue lava lamp sitting beside her bed. I would have called her a fucking hippy except it would be redundant having already established the fact that she grew up in

Berkeley. We remained vigilantly quiet, our attention focused on the passageway, where we listened as Bridgette knocked on my cabin door and called out my name. Eventually she gave up and stormed off, probably to find a new victim.

"Thanks for hiding me. If there's anything I can do to return the favor, just ask."

"I think there is something you can do," she said, as she moved closer.

"Oh really? What might that be?"

"Well, I've been at sea for quite a while now, and, sometimes, I get these uncontrollable cravings for a man's affection, so I was hoping you might be able to help."

"What a coincidence. It just so happens that I am an easily seduced man-whore with a penchant for helping women in need."

"I believe the proper term is now ex-man-whore. After tonight you're never going to need to be a man-whore ever again."

It didn't exactly feel like I was giving up that title, but I wasn't about to argue—especially after she shoved me up against the door and kissed me hard on the lips. She wasn't gentle, but I didn't care, as there was just something particularly sexy about the hot harried passion of a woman who knew what she wanted. Her tongue arrived a moment later, tasting of sweet rum as it slipped between my lips and made itself right at home. Our mouths were now fully engaged, our hands around each other's bodies as we made out with wild abandon. Things were progressing quite rapidly, and I found my hands slipping down over her buttocks where I learned that it felt as good as it looked, and I gave it a purposeful squeeze. That seemed to have been an unspoken declaration to move things along, for she slipped her nimble fingers into my waistband and proceeded to slide off my shorts. She had the hand-eye coordination of a world class magician and before you could say abracadabra, my shirt had magically joined my shorts on the floor, and I was standing there buck naked with my manhood at full mast. It wasn't very fun being the only unclothed person in the room, so I had to pull free of her lips for a moment to do a little magic of my own on her bikini top. Fortunately, its slinky straps gave me no more resistance than a shoelace, and, soon, her beautiful breasts were laid bare before my eyes, her large hard nipples standing out in stern contrast to the surrounding flesh. Her heart was pounding as I returned to her mouth and kissed her, our tongues coming together yet again in the playground that was our lips.

Unfortunately, her entire body was such a physical and visual aphrodisiac, that every second of contact was making my desire grow, until I had to move on and partake of the rest of the treasures of her flesh. I slipped down and kissed her neck before making a pass at her earlobe, biding my time, while I reached down and took hold of her breasts. With one resting firmly in each of my hands, I took a second to admire their form before bringing my mouth to her formidable nipples. They were like insolent children in need of swift discipline, and I gave them a thorough tongue-lashing that set them straight and hard. She moaned in delight as I tickled their tips, finishing off with a playful nibble before pulling my head back to take stock of my pointy friends.

"So, you still think they're just nipples?" I asked.

"Maybe you should kiss them again, so I can make a more accurate judgement."

"There's really no need to feel obligated to appease my male obsession with breasts."

"Shut up, man-whore and put your lips back on my nips!"

"All in good time, m'lady. All in good time."

I raised up and kissed her lips once more then returned to her breasts, this time teasing them more gently by running my tongue around each areola until she let out a soft moan and arched her back in anticipation. That was when I decided to take another moment to pause and gaze up into her eyes with the evil intent of rubbing in my little victory of the flesh.

"Is there a reason you stopped?" she asked, sounding annoyed.

"Well?"

"Fine, fucker. You were right about my nipples, so quit your gloating and get back to work."

"Work? The day this counts as work is the day I have my balls bronzed and mounted above the fireplace."

I gave each nipple another kiss then knelt before her and slipped my fingers into her bikini bottom.

"Don't tell me you're already moving on," she said.

"I'll definitely be back, but I'm afraid I have another stop on my travel itinerary."

I began sliding her bikini bottom slowly down her thighs, and, with each passing second, her heart began to beat visibly faster. With her last article of clothing lying at her ankles, I ran my hands up her calves, over her thighs, then reached around and took hold of her buttocks. I leaned in and kissed her stomach then pulled back to gaze down upon her feminine magnificence, and I found myself more than a bit surprised to discover that someone had been keeping up with her landscaping.

"I see you've chosen to deviate from the accepted Berkeley grooming standard," I said.

"Brave members of the resistance smuggled in razors and bikini wax once a month."

"Then I owe them my gratitude."

The time for talking was apparently over, for she took firm hold of my head and steered it between her legs, where, for the third time in as many days, I approached my favorite intersection and set to blows against my favorite opponent: the clitoris. With my lips pressed firmly against her essence, I used my tongue the way a fencer uses a foil, every move intended to probe her defenses and unlock her secrets of arousal. I circled it, varying the speed and pressure, intermittently slipping down inside her essence before starting anew. Her world opened up like thunderclouds on a dry desert plain, and the thin veil that held her back from the final edge of ecstasy was pierced as she arched her back against the door and began running headlong towards an impending climax. With each successive wave of building pleasure, she began to bang on the door and cry out.

"Yes, yes, yes, oh fuck, yes!" she screamed, her cries growing to an ear shattering crescendo as she at last climaxed.

Estelle came to rest and stared dreamily into my eyes as I held her steady upon her legs, which were still shaking in the aftermath of her orgasm. Our reverie was rudely interrupted, however, when we heard Kip outside the door.

"Seriously now, there are other people on this boat—so, if you're going to scream like that, then it might just be time to consider pulling out the ol' ball gag," he said, in a snarky tone, before continuing on his way.

"Was he joking, or do you actually have a ball gag?" I asked.

"Oh yeah, I've got one. Do you want to wear it?"

"No—as I wasn't the one screaming."

"You will be. You—will—be," she said, in a low froggy voice.

"I must admit that your Yoda impression has me pretty turned on, but it's late, and the coast is clear, so, as a man-whore in recovery, I should probably get dressed and go," I said.

"Yeah—go over there to the bed, lay back, and shut the fuck up, or I really will pull out the ball gag."

She pushed me backwards across the floor towards her bed, where I tripped over a stuffed Cal Berkeley bear and fell onto her mattress.

"Be gentle, I'm but a delicate flower of a man-whore."

"I figure if you can carry a one hundred and ninety pound pilot seven kilometers, you might just survive the night."

"Might?"

That was the last word I uttered as she slithered atop my legs, pinning me in place and signifying that it was time to be quiet. She leaned down and her mouth fell upon my manhood leaving me suspended in ecstasy and charmed into a state a stupefaction at the sheer pleasure she could elicit between the teamwork of her mouth and hands. She cruelly paused for a moment to gaze up at me, a devilish smile playing on her lips as she ran her tongue around the tip. After several passes she was back to work, making my heart race and my head spin as I approached the inevitable.

"Um..."

She kept going.

"Um, you really might want to..."

She finally looked up and realized, by my almost pained expression, that I was merely a twist of her tongue away from ending the evening early.

"Oh sorry, I got a little carried away," she said.

"It's OK. I generally like that kind of carried away."

"I can see that," she said, as she took hold of my manhood, moved forward, and guided it unto her warm, wet reaches.

I felt euphoria overtake my mind and the breath escape from my lungs as we reached full mount. She began to rock her hips fore and aft, maintaining a luxurious pace that allowed us to join our lips and entwine our tongues. Desire eventually overcame restraint, and we were forced to part mouthes as we accelerated into a breakneck pace. I slid my hands up to steady her breasts, using the moment to play my fingertips over her sizable nipples. The gesture elicited soft moans of pleasure that grew in intensity until she abruptly dug her fingers into my chest and climaxed, her body spasming as she continued to grind her hips against mine. She came to rest and took a moment to catch her breath, all the while smiling dreamily.

"Well, now that the score is officially two to zero, it's probably about time you got your turn," she said.

"Oh, there's no need to worry about me. As a fully qualified man-whore, I can honestly say that I'm just warming up."

"We'll see about that," she said, in a challenging tone.

She began moving her hips against mine, staring wickedly into my eyes, all but daring me to climax. She ever so gradually quickened her pace, and, as hard as I tried to hold back sweet release,

I knew the inevitable was coming. Fortunately, I could feel that Estelle was also close, and, when she arched her back and threw back her head, I took hold of her hips and unleashed every last ounce of my strength. With a final cry of pleasure erupting from our lips, we climaxed, coming together in the glorious moment where two souls can exist as one. There, we floated in the doldrums of a lover's abyss, our bodies looking ethereal in the light of the little blue lava lamp—the dancing globules the only evidence of the passage of time. We came to rest and took a moment to gaze into each other's eyes.

"Shit, would that technically count as being seduced?" I asked.

"Oh yeah—and now I realize I'm going to have to work extremely hard to break you of your man-whorish ways."

"What do you think that will entail, doctor?"

"Lots of repetitive therapy, and I don't care if I have spend endless hours pounding it out of you."

"Well, let me just say that I'm totally onboard with this treatment regimen."

We lay back and relaxed on the bed, and, all of a sudden, the theme song from The Love Boat inexplicably entered my mind, and I began to sing.

"*The Love Boat*—soon will be making another run. *The Love Boat*—promises something for—every—one. Set a course for adventure, your mind on a new ro—mance."

Before I could start the next verse, Estelle place her hand over my mouth.

"OK, fine. The *Sozo* just might be *The Love Boat*, so, I'm conceding the point. Now, it's time for bed, man-whore."

The song continued in my head, though it was accompanied by my own visual re-creation of the opening Love Boat credits. Instead of the original actors, however, it starred the *Sozo's* crew, and the last to appear was Estelle, smiling at me and looking ever beautiful as I drifted off to sleep, bidding a fond farewell to a perfect Caribbean night.

CHAPTER TWELVE
The Island

Dawn came early in paradise, but you didn't really care, because it meant yet another day—in paradise. Estelle's window was open, and I could hear seabirds and smell land, which meant we must be getting close to Soft Taco Island. We climbed out of bed and made our way into the shower to wash off the previous night's festivities. It felt good to get under the stream of hot water, and it was a hell of a lot more fun showering with a partner, as it made it a lot easier when you had someone to wash those hard to reach places like your penis. We dried off, dressed, and headed for the bridge and came upon Brett and Bridgette as they talked outside her cabin. They didn't appear to be all that happy, so I was guessing they were officially moving their relationship status from on-again to off-again. We muttered a few awkward hellos and continued on our way until coming upon a sour looking Kip, who grumbled some indiscernible morning greeting as he went about the yacht's business. It had been such a wonderful night, however, that I hoped my new antagonist had scored in some form—whether it be with another crewmember, or even one of his hands. We arrived on the bridge to find Billings looking particularly happy, and the reason became obvious a moment later when I noticed Tiffany sitting out on the flybridge still wearing her bikini from the previous night. Apparently, she hadn't been back to her cabin, which meant yet another romance point for Captain Smooth.

"Grab a cup of coffee, guys. We're almost to the island."

Estelle and I ambled over to the silver service tray, poured ourselves a cup of fine French coffee, then added some cream and partook of the most heavenly beverage on earth. I let out a long sigh of pleasure, as there was nothing like the first sip of the day to open up your mind and part the clouds of a night of excess. It also helped if your view happened to be the crystal clear blue waters of the Caribbean. Kip appeared a few minutes later with a tray of French pastries and fresh tropical fruit, and everyone hungrily dug in to our unexpected breakfast. This was the life, and I wondered if perhaps I might be able to get a job on the yacht when this was all over.

"Come on out to the bridge deck. We'll be clearing the point in just a few minutes, and you can see the Presidential Palace. It's quite a sight," Billings said.

We moved out onto the deck, coffee in hand, and took in the spectacular view that was Soft Taco Island's southern tip. It was lush and green, and the smell of tropical flowers carried out over the water. No more than a couple hundred meters away and looming above us on the rocky bluff was the presidential palace. It was four stories tall, cream colored, and every level had enormous floor to ceiling windows with white silken curtains that billowed in the sea breeze. The architectural style was reminiscent of something you would expect to find in Cannes or Nice, though its most unique feature was the lowest level. It appeared to have been carved directly from the cliff, and it had a large patio that was currently occupied by a dark haired man in a white linen suit. He gave us a little wave, so I waved back. That must be the lord of the manner, President Babineux, and his gesture made me wonder if he made a habit of personally greeting all the mega yachts that arrived at his island.

"Quite a piece of real estate," I said.

"It's magnificent," Bridgette responded.

"Would you be referring to the house or the island?" I asked.

"Both, but mostly the latter."

"Yeah, I would have to agree, but what self-respecting French-man could name such a beautiful place, Soft Taco Island?" I asked.

"Supposedly it's named after his ex-wife. According to the ru-mors, she was a bit prone to infidelity, and it was his own private joke about her," she said.

"Fabulous! Adultery immortalized in the name of an island."

"We'll be anchoring up in the main harbor on the northwest side, so, in the meantime, you might want to take in all the sights and get a feel for the general topography of the island," Billings said.

"Excellent idea, Pete."

We stayed on the bridge as the good ship *Sozo* traveled north up the island's west side, and just beyond and below the presidential palace was a beautiful cove with a little matching beach house. It would be a lovely place to bring a date, and I bet Babineux brought all his soft tacos here when he wanted to get lucky. He was French, after all, and they lived on wine, cheese, and fornication. On the outer edge of the cove, a massive yacht called the *Sarsarun* drifted lazily at anchor, and I suspected that parking this close to the Presidential Palace must mean the owner was a special guest.

"Does everybody here have a mega yacht?" I asked.

"Not everyone, but most. Welcome to the playground of the rich and famous," Billings said.

"I wanna play," I responded.

"Don't we all."

The *Sozo* continued on up the coast, and next on the tour was the casino, which was quite a building and appeared to be a re-creation of Monte Carlo's famous gambling mecca. It was such a majestic structure, however, that it was strange to imagine how many people had probably destroyed their lives behind those gilded walls. My reverie was interrupted a moment later when Billings pointed out the rum distillery.

"Now that's a landmark I need to know more about," I said.

"That shouldn't be a problem, as they have daily tours and a tasting room!" he added.

"Strategically, I think it's probably a good idea to focus most of our efforts on that facility first. You can learn a lot about a place from its vices."

"I like your thinking, Tag," Billings said.

We both laughed and clinked our coffee cups together, the moment perfectly coinciding with Brett's arrival. He scowled, and I suspected that it must be killing him that I was bonding with one of his fellow ring knockers. The tour officially came to an end when we reached the northern bay, and Billings turned serious as he took hold of the helm, expertly choosing his spot using the *Sozo's* sounder and computerized GPS chart system. Finally finding a suitable place, he dropped the anchor and backed the big yacht off until it had enough scope to keep the *Sozo* from drifting. The hard coral of the sea floor should give us plenty of hold, but he told the first mate to monitor our position on the GPS to make sure that we weren't getting any drag. A good captain always put his ship's welfare first and foremost.

"Welcome to Soft Taco Island, folks. I suggest we meet again in the main salon for lunch at 1:00 p.m. to figure out our plans for this evening. I'll have Kip set up the conference system, so feel free to bring your laptop or any other materials that you think will be useful."

Billings and Tiffany disappeared into his private quarters, and everyone else dispersed to their own nooks and crannies on the ship. I was feeling the coffee and pastry bringing forth an inevitable bathroom stop and wondered how I would swing a moment alone. Fate, for once, finally made a timely and useful entrance when Estelle spoke.

"I imagine you probably want to go back to your cabin to do

your man stuff while I go back to mine to freshen up," Estelle said.

"So, men do man stuff and women freshen up?" I asked.

"Yep."

"And what activities might you be referring to?"

"Oh, you know—taking a shit."

"I always assumed women were doing their makeup when they said they were freshening up."

"Nope, we're keeping the romance alive by making you believe that lie, while in reality we're taking a shit."

"Aren't you killing the romance right now by telling me this little secret."

"No, because you're a man-whore, and I know you'll still want to have sex with me."

"True. So, what will you do after freshening up with a lovely morning shit?"

"I'll be heading down to the gym."

"Good to know. Maybe I'll join you there."

We walked downstairs together but parted ways at the door to my cabin, where I headed inside and found it exactly as I had left it—since I had spent no more than ten minutes in it since boarding the boat. Like the jet, I had my own personal coffee machine, so I made another cup, grabbed my laptop, then headed for the head where it was nice to have a moment to myself and, best of all, no phone service to interrupt my dump. Dropping my shorts to the floor and using a basic rear squat mount technique, I gingerly sat down to spend some quality time with my old friend, Monsieur toilet. Peace at last! I looked at the wall to my left and noticed there was a little table that folded out, and I'm pretty sure that it was intended for a laptop. These people obviously knew how to live and, more importantly, how to dump! I set my MacBook Pro on the little table, opened my screen, then checked for any new emails from my friend Doug at the Agency. I had nothing in my inbox except for the usual spam about male enhancement, as well as one legitimate one from my mother asking me why her email wasn't working. How could she have emailed me that question if it wasn't working? I closed my email, opened my web browser, and looked at the news, quickly discovering that the world had not changed in any significant way since the day before. I took another sip of coffee and decided that my business was done here. My watch read 10:45 a.m., which meant that it was early enough that I might as well join Estelle for a quick workout before the lunchtime meeting.

I left the bathroom, threw on shorts and a T-shirt, then headed off for a run around the ship. Considering all the cardio I'd gotten the night before, I figured two laps were more than enough and decided to make my way to the gym. As I crossed the aft deck, I was temporarily blinded by what I thought was a signal mirror from a distressed boater, except it turned out to be Brett smiling at a female crewmember. As I looked closer, I realized that the girl in question was the same one he had been frolicking with in the Jacuzzi last night. At the moment, they were standing together over by the railing, and Brett appeared to be doing most of the talking, which meant that he was very likely telling her about the Naval Academy, as that was his favorite subject and always seemed to make him smile. Unfortunately, he didn't understand that most women probably cared very little about his precious Naval Academy, and he would get a lot more interest if he said he went to the fashion institute and now designed shoes. I also happened to notice that he had on a different Speedo from the night before. Why would he own more than one? Better yet, why did he own one at all? He was American for fuck's sake and part of our national pride was based on the fact that we didn't wear those things outside of swimming competitions.

I left Speedo Boy and his dazzlingly white teeth, and headed down the aft stairs to the gym. It was smaller than my place back home but not lacking in equipment, and appeared to be a hot spot for the ship's crew. Billings was on the bench press, while Kip spotted Estelle on the squat rack. The other crewmembers, most of whom I hadn't met yet, were on elliptical trainers and various other weight machines and equipment that filled the space. Billings smiled and waved before pressing a solid 280 pounds for twelve reps. Not bad, and I certainly wouldn't be challenging him to an arm wrestling match anytime soon. I headed to the free weights but used a Physio Ball as my weight bench, as it would destabilize my body and emphasize my core. The term core was very hip these days and was the fitness buzzword of the current generation. It really was an important component of any effective workout, but it didn't do much for your masculinity around classic gym rats who expected men to lift big weights rather than do planks. I finished up the less-manly stuff and went over and hit the leg press for three sets then hit the bench press for three more. Between sets, I couldn't help but steal quick glances at Estelle, who had moved on to the adductor leg spreader machine that, when occupied by a woman, always attracted attention from the guys at the gym. It was alluring, whether they were pressing out or pulling in. Estelle was currently pulling in, and she caught me watching and smiled at me as I marveled at her substantial thigh strength.

"Do you feel lucky you survived last night?" she asked.

"I do, and I can't shake the feeling that my ears are a just a little closer together."

Kip, who was only a bunny hop away, heard our exchange and angrily moved to the weight rack, whereupon he picked up a couple of forty pound barbells and started aggressively doing curls while staring at me menacingly. It kind of made me feel a little bad, so I did my best to ignore him while I finished up my workout with some ab exercises. After three sets, including legs lifts, bicycles, and crunches, I went to say goodbye to Estelle, who had moved to the floor to stretch and do some yoga. I found myself staring in rapt attention, completely entranced by the combination of the poses and her extremely tight fitting exercise clothing—all of it working together to bring back fresh memories of last night's sexual festivities. This, in turn, brought a healthy flow of blood unto my gentleman region, where a very happy Tag Junior was just dying to come out and say hello.

"Oh, were you coming to join me for some partners yoga?" she asked.

"It's probably not a good idea."

"Why is that?"

"Health purposes. There's a known correlation between women in yoga pants and increased heart rate and excessive swelling in the male genitalia."

"Interesting. I guess I know what I'll be wearing to bed tonight," she said, with a devious little smile as she assumed the cat and cow pose, the second part entailing her arching her back down towards the floor, the move conveniently bringing her lovely backside up into prominence.

Sweet Aphrodite's hindquarters! No wonder yoga didn't attract a lot of men! Spending a full hour in the company of women in tight athletic clothing doing these poses would do nothing to help a man relax and the only stretching would occur in the seams around the front of his shorts.

"Well, I'm going to go freshen up before lunch, and by that I mean take a shower, not a shit," I said.

"OK, but feel free to think of me," she said, as she dropped her butt down to the floor and opened up her legs into a full split.

"Now, you're just being mean," I said, as I turned and left the gym.

I jogged back to my cabin, stripped, and stepped into the shower with nothing to keep me company except thoughts of Estelle and the vast assortment of bath products. There was bar soap, body wash, bath gel, shampoo, conditioner, and even an exfoliating bath scrubber, which meant they definitely got their fare share of female guests aboard the *Sozo*. As a man, I tended to stick with just the soap and shampoo, but I guess all this other shit explained why women spent so much time in the shower. Men were equally capable of that kind of water wasting, but usually only did so if they were masturbating in response to being tormented by a beautiful woman in exercise clothing. I kept my shower short and to the point, however, and, after lathering up, I closed my eyes and slipped under the torrent of hot water to enjoy the soothing massage action of the showerhead. Too bad it didn't have an additional nozzle at groin level, but then I'd never have a reason to leave the bathroom.

I turned off the water, grabbed one of the plush cotton towels, and dried off, the experience leaving me feeling completely refreshed. I applied deodorant, face cream, and cologne then walked out to my room to find something to wear. All I had brought were shorts and T-shirts so it came down to color. Black—or black. I chose, not surprisingly, black shorts and a black T-shirt, and couldn't help but wonder if this was what Goths looked like when they visited the tropics. Probably, but at least I would soon have a healthy tan to distinguish myself from any of my darkly clad pale counterparts. I looked at my watch and saw that it was 12:45 p.m., and I left my cabin feeling like a new man, more than ready to face whatever life threw my way.

I arrived at the main salon and was amazed at how completely it converted into a conference room. On the forward wall were a series of three large flat screen monitors instead of the artworks that had been there before. The two outer monitors had the Vandenberg logo bouncing around as a screen saver, while the center monitor had what I assumed was a Google Maps satellite view of Soft Taco Island. Groovy! I set my laptop down and took a seat to the left of the main keyboard console then leaned over and decided to check out the system while I waited for the others. Using the track pad, I zoomed in on the view of the main beach on the western shore until I located some people, or, more specifically, two topless women, a brunette and a blond, lying on their stomachs. I was surprised at the resolution and zoomed in until the blonde's entire back filled the screen, and the detail was so incredible that I could actually see freckles. Suddenly, she rolled over to reveal two ample breasts that were easily as large as Tiffany's. Sweet mother of finely freckled bosoms! The *Sozo* had a real-time satellite feed, though that was an unusually advanced feature for a pleasure craft. I stared at the screen, entranced by the incredible view, and I couldn't help but think of her breasts as looking a bit like giant eyes—kindly staring back at me. Just then, the others came in, but I didn't have time to zoom out, and I felt like a kid who had been caught looking at porn on the Internet. Estelle shook her head in dismay as she regarded me.

"Alone in an empty room, you still find a way to be a man-whore," she said, quietly under her breath.

"I guess I'm special that way."

"What do you think of the real-time satellite feed?" Billings asked, smiling as he stood there gazing at the woman on the screen.

"Amazingly real!" I responded, enthusiastically.

"I highly doubt those are real," Estelle said, as she sat to my immediate right and took control of the keyboard by nudging me aside with a purposeful bump.

Estelle used the track pad to zoom out until the entire island took up the screen, thus bringing the show to an abrupt conclusion. With everyone seated, a waiter I recognized from the party the night before brought out a pitcher of ice water and glasses while another delivered a large bowl of salad and a tray of delicious looking little sandwiches. I didn't like to talk with food in my mouth, but I always thought better with a full stomach, so I grabbed a sandwich and put some salad on my plate then set about enjoying lunch. Interestingly, studies had shown that digestion released chemicals that stimulated memory—a fact which explained why meals were such a perfect time to reflect and talk.

Once everyone else had their plates filled with food, Bridgette asked Estelle to bring up the casino on the main monitor, thus setting our lunchtime planning session into motion.

"We can assume Lux is being held in the island's holding cells located in the basement of the casino," Bridgette said.

"Can we verify that?" I asked.

"Yeah, we have someone on the inside. His name is John Parker, and he works at the casino and, coincidentally, delivers the meals to the prisoners in the holding cells. Just a second—I'll upload his picture?"

Bridgette pulled out her phone and, shortly thereafter, the monitor on the left went out of sleep mode, and a picture came up of a smiling man with his arm around Bridgette. He was a good-looking guy and probably local judging by his dark skin and short, well maintained dreads that were common to the people of the Caribbean. I studied the guy's face and put it to memory.

"Can we trust him?" I asked.

"He owes a big chunk of cash to the casino, so he's no friend of the establishment."

"How do we get into the holding area?" I asked.

"Through the casino, but there's a lot of security and every inch is covered by cameras. You'll obviously want to check it out for yourself."

"Obviously, and I should probably start at the bar."

"Obviously, you should start with John Parker."

"That's what I meant. What's his story? How do I meet him? Any chance he's a Bartender?"

"No such luck. He'll be working in the casino restaurant tonight, so you'll need to move fast and make contact with him during his shift."

"Sounds easy enough, but I think it'll look less suspicious if I have a date."

"I'll go," Estelle said.

"Perfect. Where do we go ashore—the harbor on the southern

end of the bay?"

"Yeah, that's the official port of entry."

"How official is it?"

"Armed guards and a kiosk where all the guests must check in when entering and exiting the island."

"That might be a problem for me."

"Why?" Bridgette asked.

"I had a little run-in back on Martinique with a couple of French DGSE agents while you girls were shopping, and they made it pretty clear that they wanted me to get the hell out of the Caribbean."

"How would that effect you here?" Estelle asked.

"They knew my name and face, and it turned out that they also worked for a certain president named Adrien Babineux."

"Shit! If he knows who you are, then it's going to be a hell of a lot harder getting you past security and onto the island," Bridgette said.

"Isn't this place just a glorified Club Med?"

"In appearance, but Babineux runs it like a military base."

"Then, I'll just skip the port of entry and swim ashore near the main beach."

"That would be fine except that the security there is equally tight. As you can see on the satellite feed, there's a breakwater, and they patrol it with boats until around nine in the evening. Assuming you get past that, you'll be in full view of all of the beach security cameras."

"So, I'll swim ashore after nine and then it'll be too dark for the cameras."

"Unfortunately, John Parker only works until nine, then he leaves to make the meal deliveries to the holding cells."

"Do you know what the area of coverage is for the cameras?"

"I believe it stretches from the beach to the breakwater."

"Well, then I'll just swim ashore somewhere else."

"No chance. The rest of the coastline on this part of the island is mostly jagged rocks and cliffs, and, even if you did manage to get past any of them, you wouldn't have enough time to get to John Parker before his shift ended."

"Then it sounds as though the only way to infiltrate the island would entail fast roping down from the *Sozo's* helicopter."

"Not a bad thought, except they have very sophisticated radar that covers any approaching aircraft above five hundred feet, and anything flying below that would likely be picked up by the acoustic sensor array or the lookouts that are strategically placed around the island's perimeter."

"An acoustic sensor array and lookouts on a fucking tropical resort island? What the hell is Babineux so worried about?"

"No idea, but I can only assume it has something to do with Lux's mission here."

"So, you're telling me that I need to somehow breach the island in a way other than swimming that avoids the beach security cameras, sensor arrays, and lookouts—all the while staying above the water but below five hundred feet and without the aid of a boat or helicopter?"

"Pretty much."

"Well, that's going to require an extremely creative plan, formed and perpetrated in a very small envelope of time and space."

"Which is why you get such a big bonus if you're successful."

"Yeah—if."

"At least Estelle can go through the official port of entry, but if you hope to join her, you're going to have to get pretty creative," Bridgette said.

"Estelle, can you zoom in a little bit on the main beach and resort area?" I asked.

She adjusted the view, and I gazed at the various landmarks on the screen, letting my mind wander until I suddenly had the beginnings of an idea forming in my mind. I then remembered something I had seen on the boat deck of the *Sozo*, and that idea became a full fledged plan, possibly even a good one. Well, it seemed good at the moment, but anything could happen once you took it out into the real world.

"Pete, what are the wind conditions going to be like this evening?" I asked.

"Winds out of the west about five knots. Maybe a little lighter by sunset."

"Perfect! I'll rendezvous with Estelle on that little bridge on the walking path," I said, pointing at the screen.

"I'm serious when I say that they have this island pretty locked down. You really can't just swim ashore," Bridgette said.

"I don't plan to swim," I said, with a smile.

"What are you going to do — fly?" Brett asked, sarcastically.

"In a manner of speaking."

I finished lunch and went back to my cabin to look through my gear. I always brought an assortment of various climbing hardware like carabiners and similar doodads, and, finding what I needed, I headed down to the aft hold to build my improvised infiltration device — or, in military speak, the IID. After an hour of tinkering, I had the whole thing pretty much ready to go. Unfortunately, I had no way to test it out, so it could fail miserably and I'd look like an incompetent jackass, or it would work gloriously and I'd look like a low-rent James Bond. At least it would be dark, so the chances of some tourist capturing it on his phone and posting it to the Internet would be unlikely. I went upstairs and, on the aft deck, saw Kip restocking the outdoor bar with fresh bottles of alcohol. I said hello, but he only nodded and went back about his business. Perhaps I would buy him a T-shirt on the island tonight in hopes of mending his angry heart. I continued through the main salon and up the stairs to the next level, and spied Billings and Tiffany relaxing in the sun on his private deck. It was nice to see that the two of them were hitting it off, as he seemed like a nice guy, and she could certainly use one after Brett. I continued on to the open doorway and could now see that she was wearing a different bikini, and this one was bright pink and had barely enough fabric to cover one of her breasts, let alone two—though I suppose that was probably the point. It was a veritable mantrap and certainly caught my attention. I knocked on the edge of the doorframe, and the two of them turned in my direction.

"What's up?" Billings asked.

"Me, now that I've seen your lovely companion in that bikini."

He turned his gaze to her and smiled.

"Yeah, she's painfully beautiful isn't she?" he said.

She smiled back then leaned over and kissed him, and I was suddenly feeling like a third wheel.

"Maybe I'll come back later."

"Nonsense! Come on out and join us," he said.

I was reminded once again of just how amazing the view was from the *Sozo's* bridge as I gazed out in awe at the harbor and various landmarks. It was a commanding view, and one that a captain would want in order to take quick stock of his ship and surroundings. Speaking of which, I could see Bridgette down on the bow talking on her cell phone. She waved when she saw me, so I waved back, wondering how in the hell she got reception out here. Oh well, it was time for a more important question, so I turned my attention back to Billings.

"Pete, I have a question for you about this evening."

"Fire away."

"I'm going to need a good helmsman tonight for an unusual insertion."

I explained what I had in mind, and he laughed out loud.

"You have a flare for the dramatic, my friend. You really think it'll work?"

"It's worth a try, and you know what they say—play hard or go home."

"Well, most of the crew is more than qualified, but I'd be happy to do it."

"I was hoping you'd say that."

"Sounds like it might even be fun."

"We'll see about that, but, in the interest of preserving my dignity, no taking any videos. If I fail and end up dangling from a fucking palm tree, I'd rather suffer in anonymity."

"Still pictures?"

"Only if my face isn't visible and give me a twenty-four hour advanced warning before you upload to any social media."

"Agreed."

I left the bridge and headed back downstairs, once again passing Kip, who had moved inside to the main salon's bar, where he was now making sure there were enough cocktail napkins. I suppose this was the unglamorous side of working on a mega yacht. While he performed mandatory, but unexciting boat chores, I was drinking, fornicating, and plotting a daring rescue mission. No wonder he hated me. He was like a towel boy, while I was the quarterback who got to play in the big game. I gave him a polite nod then headed to Estelle's cabin, where two knocks brought her to the other side of the door.

"Who is it?" she asked.

"Room service, I believe someone ordered a man-whore."

"That would be me," she said, as she opened the door wearing only a white fluffy cotton robe.

"Would you like him right here or on the bed?"

"Neither. I'm afraid I'm going to have to send you back. I ordered my man-whore without dressing."

"Not a problem," I said, pretending that I was going to take off my shorts.

We shared a brief laugh, then Estelle's look turned serious.

"So, what's up?" she asked.

"Can't I just stop by to say hello?"

"No, you obviously need something. What is it?"

"I wanted to stop by and see if you had something particularly elegant for tonight."

"Oh really? Because I assumed that the fact we were going to a glamorous casino frequented by the rich and famous meant that

I could wear jeans, a T-shirt, and my Birkenstocks."

"Wait—do you seriously own Birkenstocks?"

"Of course not you fucking jackass! Nor am I going to wear jeans and a T-shirt."

"So, my original question was particularly stupid."

"Yeah, and then some," she said, sounding annoyed.

"Well, then I suppose I'll get going and let you do your thing."

"Good. Now fuck off and go get ready," she said, as she leaned forward and gave me a quick kiss before retreating back into her cabin and abruptly closing the door.

So much for trying to be helpful. I headed back to my room and decided to take a quick nap to make sure I had plenty of energy for tonight. In the service you learned to sleep when you could, so I lay back on the bed and tried to relax by thinking of soothing images. I thought about Estelle in her bikini, frolicking on a beach and playing in the waves. I imagined her running in slow motion until a large wave hits her from behind and strips off her bikini top, leaving her breasts bare and glistening in the warm sun. She's smiling and—wait a minute. This was definitely not helping and certainly not making me relax. New visualization. Instead, I imagined Brett brushing his teeth. He was using a whitening toothpaste and started with his molars before carefully working his way forward making little circles. I was asleep by the time he reached his canines.

CHAPTER THIRTEEN
Dressed for Success

I awoke just after five o'clock and got out of bed, brushed my teeth, and walked over to Estelle's cabin. I knocked, and it took her an unusually long time to come to the door, and, when she appeared, she was wearing two towels, one around her head and the other around her body.

"What's up now?" she asked, impatiently.

"This won't do at all. Maybe you really should go with jeans and a T-shirt."

"Fuck you. What do you want?"

"To wish you luck. I won't see you until we meet on the island."

"You're the one who's going to need luck. All I have to do is go ashore."

She gave me a quick kiss, and what I suspect was meant to be a simple peck, grew out of control like a wildfire on a dry summer meadow. Our tongues were entwined and blood was flowing into my happy place, whereupon I found myself instinctively peeling away her lower towel as I would an orange's skin to reveal the lovely fruit underneath. I took hold of her breasts, instantly forgetting about the fact that we were in a very public and busy passageway on the boat. That is, until Kip appeared, sporting a casually caustic expression on his face as he proceeded to stand so close that I could smell his mint flavored mouthwash. Estelle and I awkwardly tried to pretend that nothing was going on, though it was a futile effort considering she was buck naked, and my penis was angrily straining against the fabric of my shorts.

"Hello, Tag—Estelle. I hope I'm not interrupting, but I have the latest inventory sheets here," he said, giving us the once over.

"Thanks, Kip. Now, if you would excuse us, we were just about to..."

"Fuck?" he asked, as he turned his gaze my way, giving me a long intimidating look, before grunting his disapproval and continuing on his way.

Shit. That fucker is going to try and kill me in my sleep. I reached down, grabbed the towel, then handed it to Estelle before saying goodbye and heading back to my cabin to get ready. I took the clothing items I had bought in Martinique and laid them out on the bed before adjourning to the bathroom to take a shower. Fresh, clean, and smelling like a true gentleman, I came out and put on everything but my sport coat then went to my equipment bag and grabbed my smallest pistol. It was the Walther PPK, but mine, unlike James Bond's, carried seven rather than six rounds. I slipped on my shoulder holster, then my jacket, and made sure everything fit perfectly. My Glock 19 might have been more useful with it's larger magazine capacity, but I was going for stealth rather than all out firepower. I stepped out into the passageway but paused in front of an ornate alcove that had a mirror and a little table with a vase full of flowers. I picked a single red carnation, stuck it in my lapel, then drew my pistol and posed like an idiot.

"The name's Finn, Tag Finn, now, please feel free to remove your bra," I said, as I slipped my pistol back in my shoulder holster and set off for the boat deck, all the while humming the James Bond theme song.

I arrived to find the main tender had already left, so Estelle was on her way to the island, and our plan for the evening was officially set in motion. Billings and Tiffany were waiting patiently in the ski boat and both looked up and smiled at me.

"Nice outfit, but I believe you forgot the vodka martini," Billings said.

"It's OK, I'll get one on the island."

"You are looking seriously good, Tag," Tiffany said.

"Thanks. I think it's important to dress for success."

"Then there's no way in hell you could fail."

I stepped down into the boat, and Billings started the engine, which roared to life with a throaty growl. He let it idle and warm up for a minute, then Kip undid the lines, and we eased away from the *Sozo's* side. It was a perfect Caribbean evening, the temperature around eighty degrees as we cleared the moored yachts and hit the open water. I slipped into the parasailing harness and felt a familiar pinch in my gentleman region. Why did tourists actually pay to do this? It seemed kind of crazy, as there was no way that the view was worth the discomfort, but it would be a hell of a way to get me onto the island—assuming it worked. I checked my handiwork one more time, giving each connector a quick pull to make sure it held. Everything looked and felt good, except, of course, for my testicles.

"Assuming you make it ashore, you'll eventually want to leave the island, so here's a waterproof radio to contact us when you're ready for your pickup."

"Good thinking, Pete. I was so concerned with getting ashore that I forgot about coming back."

"Understandable. Now, for the important part. Once we get up to speed, Tiffany's going to reel you out, then I'm going to get us as close to the breakwater as possible. Then, when you're in position, just signal that you're going to cut loose."

"Got it."

"Oh—one last piece of advice. The higher you go, the more

likely you might catch some wind coming over the point."

"Roger that, Pete. Higher means more wind. Let's do this!"

It was perfect conditions for parasailing with the wind no more than a whisper, and the water as flat as a pancake. Billings hit the throttles, and the ski boat quickly shot up onto a plane, and we released the parachute and let it fill with air until it popped open, abruptly lifting me up off the back deck. Billings throttled up a few more knots, and Tiffany started to reel me out like a large overdressed man-kite. In less than a minute, I was well over a hundred feet in the air, but it looked like a mile from my vantage point. It was a spectacular view of the island, and I could see the three main hotels as well as the distillery and the casino. With another pass, I was up around four hundred feet and even the *Sozo* looked like a toy as it bobbed at anchor in the harbor below. I looked towards the beach, and there, slowly idling along the breakwater, was one of the patrol boats Bridgette had mentioned. There were two crewmen, one at the helm while the other stood in the cockpit keeping a vigilant eye on the surrounding area. Thankfully, he was completely oblivious to me as I soared well above him, so it would appear that everything was going according to plan.

The sun dropped down over the horizon and day gave way to night as lights appeared in the boats in the bay and the buildings on shore. Now that we had the altitude and a dark sky, Billings worked us closer to the breakwater, and I decided we were in range and signaled I was ready to go. He gave me a wave, and I whispered a silent prayer as I unclipped myself from the towrope. I decelerated quickly, steering the parachute hard to the right to direct my flight path towards the shore, and, though it wasn't as maneuverable as what I was used to in the military, the wind and the modifications I had made to it were making up the difference.

My primary objective was to clear the water and the part of the beach under the most security camera coverage then land on the soft sand just in front of the main hotel. Of course, I had to contend with basic physics. The air over the water was cooler and, therefore, tended to increase the rate of descent, which meant I would have less flight time. In spite of all the variables, everything was going smoothly, allowing me to take a moment to scan the dark beach for my landing spot. Sadly, the topless women were long gone, likely having changed into some slinky evening wear and headed off to dinner. Too bad, they seemed like such nice girls in the satellite feed.

I was nearing the breakwater, and I could see the lights of the patrol boat beneath me as it made its final pass. I continued floating along on the air currents, and it looked as though I would have no problem reaching the beach. As I flew over the sand, however, the warmer air was keeping me aloft, and I was a little higher than I had anticipated. I sailed over my intended landing spot and was rapidly approaching the hotel's crowded beachfront restaurant and bar. I tried my best to pull back and slow my forward motion, but the parachute had developed a mind of its own. I saw a nice open spot in between the tables and used every ounce of my strength and willpower to steer for it, but a small puff of wind came from my right and pushed me left and over my target. I was only about five feet off the ground when a waiter carrying a tray full of cocktails passed in front of me, and I had to lift up my legs in order to miss his head by mere inches.

At last, the luck of the Irish came to bear, and I dropped down and got my feet firmly planted on the ground. Unfortunately, my attention was immediately drawn to the sound of two security vehicles approaching from down the beach. They were moving fast and must have spotted me when I flew into the bright lights of the outdoor restaurant. Shit—I guess Bridgette had been correct when she said they kept a close eye on the beach. I quickly disconnected the parachute harness, rolled up the shoot, and stowed both of them under the nearest lounge chair then decided it would be best to blend into the crowd and hide out until the security men had passed. As I gazed around at the sea of diners, I spied two beautiful women, a blond and a brunette, sitting at the table directly in front of me. They were dressed rather elegantly in frilly evening dresses and both were staring, obviously wondering why in the hell the stranger in the tuxedo had just fallen from the sky and landed at their feet. The waiter I had missed only seconds ago was passing by, and I managed to snag a martini from his tray before taking a seat with my lovely new companions.

"Good evening, ladies. The name's Finn, Tag Finn," I said, holding up my glass to toast.

They both clinked their glasses to mine, but the blonde was the first to speak.

"I'm Isabella, and this is Monique, and I must say, Tag—you certainly know how to make an entrance. Any chance of you dropping into room one-twenty-nine later this evening," she asked.

As I looked more closely at my female companions, I came to the surprising revelation that they were very likely the two topless woman I'd seen in the satellite feed earlier in the day, though I'd of course have to see their breasts in the flesh, especially Isabella's, and conduct a thorough examination to be absolutely certain. Needless to say, I saw this as a subtle sign that fate might just be on my side tonight, and that theory was about to be put to the test, for at that moment the two Soft Taco Island security vehicles rolled up and stopped just beyond the beachfront tables. The man in the passenger seat gazed at the crowd of diners for a moment then shrugged and spoke something to the men in the other vehicle, and they continued on up the beach. Hot damn! I had successfully infiltrated the island.

"I'd love to, but I'm afraid I'm here on official business this evening," I said, as I finished my drink and stood up from the table.

"But wait! Where in God's name did you come from?" Isabella asked.

"Up there," I said, pointing at the sky.

"Heaven?" Monique asked, batting her eyelashes.

"Definitely not, though if I stay here much longer, I'll most certainly be going to hell."

"At least you'd have some company," she responded.

"True, and might I say that is extremely tempting," I said, as I pondered her words.

Isabella used the time to take a sip of her drink, but turned her full attention back to me once she set her glass back on the table.

"So, Tag, you still haven't answered my question."

"Oh, yeah—about that," I said, as I took a moment to consider my response.

Technically, I was on a covert mission and being paid handsomely for my discretion, so I decided to do the right thing—and lie—albeit creatively.

"I came from an airplane."

"I didn't see skydiving on the list of Soft Taco Island activities," Isabella said.

"Correct, and let this be a lesson to you not to book your flights online," I said, as I started to leave.

"Will we see you again?" Monique asked.

"I certainly hope so, and perhaps we might even be able to meet up for a little topless sunbathing."

Isabella and Monique shared a surprised look before turning back to me with curious smiles on their faces, obviously wondering how I knew about their rather bold beach habits.

"Don't worry, girls, I'm the master of applying sunblock and making sure that every inch of your lovely exposed skin is properly covered."

I left the two of them to their imaginations and made my way past the bevy of bustling diners and into the hotel. The lobby was nicely appointed with a well-thought-out decor that was a blend of classical European style and tropical island chic. The floor was bamboo, the furniture stately, and all the fabrics were patterned with plant and flower prints in bold shades of green, yellow, and blue. It was a kaleidoscope of color and class, and, combined with the crowd, was enough to make my head spin. I made my way through the maelstrom to see that all the guests were tan, wealthy, and self obsessed, which made it feel a lot like home except for the tan part—as that would have been Southern California. If only Brett were here, he'd feel so comfortable to at last be among his people. Of course, they might not accept his artificial glow, as these lucky folks had lifestyles that afforded them ample time out in real sunshine.

I came out the opposite side of the hotel, squeezing between a tall Swedish couple and their tall Swedish children, and headed south towards my meeting place with Estelle. The cobblestone path, lit by faux tiki style torches, snaked around lush island greenery, flowers, and a man-made river. Up ahead, standing on an ornate little bridge, was a beautiful woman leaning against the railing, and she was wearing a devilishly red silky dress that clung to her curves in a way that made my pants fit a little snug in the crotch. The closer I got, the better the view became, and I could now make out the supple lines of her shapely backside, long legs, and pert breasts. Unfortunately, her face was still unknown, because she had turned her head to gaze off towards the ocean. When I stepped onto the bridge, she felt my presence and turned towards me, and my heart skipped a beat when I realized it was my date for the evening. Now, I could understand why she had been so irked when I told her to dress up—though it was by no means unusual for a man to unintentionally say something stupid or behave like a jackass. It was, apparently, hard wired into our brains, part of our basic operating software and included most of our root functions such as masturbating and laughing at farts.

"Hello, stranger. I see you managed to get onto the island unscathed," she said, as she smiled at me.

"I did, but after seeing you in that dress, I was afraid I might have gone to heaven instead."

"Oh, did I do OK picking out my outfit for tonight?"

All I could do was gaze in awe at Estelle. Sweet mother of all that is right and just in this cruel world! In the wettest of my wet dreams I could have never imagined the combination of a beautiful woman and a piece of clothing being able to elicit such deep feelings of desire. A breeze came blowing from the bay at that moment, and it was as if the world could feel my painful longing, for the wind caused the slit of her dress to billow open and reveal tempting expanses of her shapely upper thighs. My heart was now racing as my eyes continued moving up, traveling north towards her breasts where her nipples were looking particularly prominent as they pressed through the thin silken fabric of her dress. But why stop there when the face of an angel was residing only inches above. I already knew Estelle was beautiful, but tonight, she had thrown in some dark lustrous red lipstick and some sultry eye shadow that combined with the dress to truly bring out her deep inner temptress.

"Well?" she asked.

"Oh, sorry about that, I couldn't form any words because all the blood in my body was rushing to my penis."

She reached down and gave my gentlemanly goodies a healthy squeeze.

"You weren't kidding."

"Definitely not, and, I must say—if I had any idea you were going to look so completely stunning, I would have dressed a bit nicer," I said.

"Yeah, that dashing tuxedo of yours is a little lowbrow."

"Apparently, you just can't get anything decent for four thousand dollars these days."

She smiled and stepped closer.

"Well then, Prince Charming, Cinderella is feeling a little thirsty and would love a drink."

"Right this way m'lady."

I took Estelle's arm in mine, and we headed south towards an outdoor restaurant and bar that resided beside a giant swimming pool with stone paved edges and quaint waterfalls that made it look like an authentic tropical lagoon. A reggae band was playing on an artificial island in the middle, and the entire place smelled of fresh flowers and booze as people in shorts and bikinis happily danced to the mellow island groove. Estelle and I moved into a gap between two people at the end of the bar, and the bartender, a tall man with dark skin and a welcoming smile, came over and asked what we wanted. Estelle ordered a Mai Tai, and I ordered the same. He left to get our drinks and Estelle turned and smiled at me, her green eyes sparkling in the ambient lighting.

"It's too bad we're working right now and not actually here for fun," she said.

"What are you talking about? I think this is about as fun as it gets."

"You know what I mean."

"Yeah, I do, and face it—this is fucking fun."

The bartender returned with our drinks, and I went to pull out my wallet, but he stopped me.

"Don't worry man, the first drinks are always free," he said, the word man sounding more like *mon*.

"Thank you," Estelle said, nodding at the bartender.

I left him a generous tip, and we took a couple minutes to finish our drinks before leaving the bar and heading south. We were at the northern end of the resort area, so the casino was about a ten-minute walk to the south. We set off on the path, its ambient lighting and purposeful landscaping making it feel as though we were walking through an interactive postcard. People, mostly in pairs, meandered along, stopping at various points to take pictures and enjoy the view. Along the way, I spied several distinguished looking older men with much younger women on their arms, and I honestly couldn't tell if they were wives, mistresses, or even daughters. They might even be paid escorts supplied by the island considering the fact that gambling and prostitution went together like peanut butter and jelly.

Just up ahead, I could finally see the lights of the rum distillery, and before that, they had an outdoor tasting bar right on the path. A beautiful girl with red hair and even redder lips, walked out to greet us with a tray of rum samples. She was wearing a low-cut shirt, similar to the kind that the German girls wore at Oktoberfest, and it was doing a fine job of amplifying her impressive cleavage. She certainly knew how to work a crowd, and had her breasts strategically resting on the tray directly behind the two glasses of rum—their placement guaranteeing that she would have the attention of any and all men who stood before her. She certainly had mine.

"Would you like to try a sample?" she asked, her voice belying the subtle hint of a German accent.

"Does that offer include everything on the tray?"

"For you, absolutely."

"Well then, if given the choice, I'd have to start with the two in the back."

My silly joke was immediately understood, and she broke into laughter, her breasts jiggling, and the movement, of course, drawing my gaze to her ample bosom like a moth to the flame. As a man, I had enough self-discipline to keep my eyes off of stationary breasts, but moving ones were impossible to ignore, and, now, I was as engrossed as a cat watching two deliciously plump mice bouncing about before its eager eyes. Warm jolts of electricity started traveling from my brain to my penis, which was now smiling bashfully in my pants. I suspect, my busty fräulein was aware of this little fact, because she continued to laugh for a bit longer than my mediocre quip deserved. Estelle, not too surprisingly, didn't find it funny at all and pinched my arm just hard enough to elicit a pained yelp.

"Are you OK?" the girl asked, looking concerned.

"Apparently, you have some rather large and vicious mosquitos on this island," I said, rubbing my arm.

"Well, I have just the thing for the pain," she said, handing each of us a glass of spiced rum.

"*Auf uns,*" I said, as I held up my glass to my fräulein.

It meant to us in German, a language I sincerely hoped Estelle didn't speak.

"*Auf dich arschloch,*" Estelle said, looking at me with a hint of annoyance.

I believe that translated as to you, asshole, which meant she did indeed speak German. Oh well, live and learn, for now, it was time to move boldly forward and try the rum. I rolled the amber liquid around in the glass then smelled it as though it were a fine wine before taking a sip. As the rum hit my palette, bolts of gastronomical pleasure spread throughout my body, filling me with warm feelings of universal contentment. It was alive with subtle hints of cinnamon, vanilla, cardamom, and just a touch of brown sugar, the combination of flavors feeling as though my taste buds were experiencing an orgasm. It was as smooth as butter and went down as easily as hot chocolate on a cold winter evening. I'd tasted plenty of exotic alcohols but never anything quite like this. Estelle looked equally happy, and, in a perfect world, we would have stayed there and sipped rum all night. Sadly, we had places to be and people to meet, so we finished off our samples and placed the empty glasses back on the tray. The girl smiled and nodded at the rum bottle in her hand, ready and waiting to pour us a refill.

"Another?"

"*Nein, danke.*"

She gave me a pouty smile as though I had just broken her heart, then she moved on to her next victim. She was a hell of a salesgirl and would have plenty of customers fall prey to her charms before the night was done. Fortunately, or unfortunately, depending on how you looked at it, we had just avoided falling into Soft Taco Island's first trap. This was just like every other place in the world with gambling—they preferred you drunk and, therefore, more likely to drop a buck or two, which was obviously the reason for that little rum speed bump. Still, it was Goddamn delicious, and I was going to have to figure out a way to smuggle out a few bottles before this was over.

The taste still on my lips, we rounded the last bend in the path, and there, just ahead, was the casino. It was glowing like a jewel of light in the darkness of the surrounding jungle—its sinister existence cleverly concealed beneath its cream colored facade. I'd already seen it from the *Sozo*, but, now that I was merely a stone's throw away, I could see it was, indeed, a perfect replica of it's eighteenth century Baroque brethren in Monte Carlo. It was as wide as a city block, two stories tall, and its entryway stood between two massive rectangular pillars that stretched all the way up past the second story to the roofline. There, finely carved statuary stretched from one end of the building to the other, and in the very top center resided a seashell pediment and clock that was bordered on each side by bronze sculptures of fairies. One story below that, and just above the entrance, was a white handblown stained glass and wrought iron awning, which was obviously there to complete the look of the building as well as shield guests from the occasional rain squall. Clearly, no expense seemed to have been spared in the casino's construction, for it was built to attract everyone from royalty to those trying to live like royalty. Unlike Vegas and Atlantic City, which were coated in cheap painted plaster, this was the real deal, a touch of the old world right here in the heart of the Caribbean.

Between us and the casino, however, was a beautifully mani-cured garden with fountains, strategically placed shrubbery, and a lighted tile walkway which we used to reach the entrance. There, we joined the throngs of people entering the casino and passed two beautiful women in revealing evening dresses—the two of them serving as greeters to personally welcome each and every visitor to *La Maîtresse*. In English, that meant *The Mistress*, which wasn't a bad name for a casino considering how many men prob-ably spent time here away from their wives. We walked through the lobby, and the quiet idyllic sounds of the island were replaced by those of every casino the world over: the din of human greed.

Roulette wheels, slot machines, card tables, and the sounds of fortunes being made and lost filled the air. I took a good look around and noticed the ceilings were dotted with the usual cameras, while security men sporting dress suits and radio earpieces stood quietly watchful on the periphery. We continued moving deeper into the chaos until our progress became slow as we neared the middle where the congestion grew as guests and cocktail waitresses converged in a navigational nightmare. It was quite a crowd and hardly a man we passed, regardless of the woman on his arm, could avoid giving Estelle a thorough once over. Stranger still, even I felt the eyes of the women we passed, but I suppose there was nothing like a tuxedo and the appearance of wealth to drive up a man's status—which meant I just might have to consider giving up the board shorts for some fancier clothing when I got back home. We were almost through the worst of the traffic when an opening allowed Estelle to gain a slight lead, and it afforded me yet another excellent view of her figure in that red dress. The way it adhered to her body, brought a distinct tingling to my man parts, and I wondered if I could get ejected from the casino for sporting wood. If so, then I was already halfway out the door.

The crowd finally started to thin as we reached the stairs and headed up to the restaurant, which was located on the second floor on the ocean side of the casino. We walked past a horribly sunburned Russian couple arguing at the entrance, and I could practically feel the heat coming off their pink skin. I'm pretty sure that it wouldn't be a stretch to assume their argument was over who forgot to pack the sunblock. We gave them a wide berth and found the hostess in the anteroom. She was a lovely woman with her coco brown skin, glowing white teeth, and jaw dropping figure. Unfortunately, she was up to her perfect jaw line in hassle thanks to a group of pushy American tourists. She smiled to let us know she had seen us, so we waited patiently until she was free. Sometimes it was embarrassing to be an American, but it was a big country, and foreigners often judged us all by the few assholes they met. It was very similar to disliking the French just because of the Parisians. At last, she was able to usher our fellow Americans off to the bar and returned, looking relieved to be free of their presence.

"Welcome to *La Maîtresse*. How can I help you?" she asked, with a charming Jamaican accent.

"How can you help us? How can we help you? Those people were terrible. Clearly they were Canadian."

She laughed and appeared to enjoy having a moment to recover with some less pushy customers.

"Now, I assume you will be dining with us this evening?" she asked.

"Yeah, it's our anniversary, and we came here on our honeymoon a year ago, so we were wondering if it's possible to get our same waiter—a really nice guy named John Parker."

"John is working, but he has the most popular section, and it's very crowded tonight."

"Oh, that's too bad, we were really hoping to see him again," Estelle said, putting on an excellent show as she gazed sadly into my eyes.

"It's OK, we're just happy to have any table," I said.

The hostess thought for a moment, her gaze traveling from the Russian couple to the pushy Americans before returning back to us.

"To hell with it! You're the nicest people I've met all night, so I'm going to do you a favor and squeeze you in. Come this way."

We followed the hostess through the crowd and past a series of tables laden with freshly served meals. Each one was a culinary landmine of amazing looking food and exotic smells, and it was all I could do to keep going. This part of the Caribbean had its own unique mixture of French, Creole, and Indian cuisine, and every dish was an olfactory overload that made my stomach ache with hunger. We stepped through a wide double door and into John Parker's section, which was out on the deck. No wonder it was the most popular, as it provided a fabulous view of the resort and bay, and had the added ambiance of a Reggae band playing in the corner. She seated us at a table right at the edge of the deck, and I held Estelle's chair then sat down and joined her as the hostess handed us our menus. She asked if we'd like to start with a drink, so I asked if she had any suggestions, and she recommended the house specialty.

"It's named, *La Maîtresse*, in honor of the casino, and is a blend of Soft Taco Island Rum, fresh coconut milk, pineapple juice, and a splash of lime."

"Sounds delicious!"

"Yes, but she's so good it's easy to over do it, and she might sneak up and bite you in the morning," she said.

"In that case, we'll take two, please."

She left us, and we sat there enjoying the moment, smiling at each other as though we were actually celebrating our one year anniversary. The moon was about three quarters full and just coming up over the horizon, and the sound of the band's music was filling the air and drifting out over the water. I was pretty sure this was officially the best job that I'd ever had or ever would have, and, had I been independently wealthy, I would have retired on this very spot for fear that it would never be this good again. Clearly, I needed to market to a different clientele. No more lost pets unless their owners were beautiful heiresses, and their furry little loved ones were lost in places like this. A waitress delivered our drinks, and we held them up to toast.

"To the Vandenbergs," Estelle said.

"For without them, we wouldn't be here tonight," I added.

We clinked glasses and sampled our decidedly delicious drinks, and I realized we'd have to stay strong to resist the urge to order too many. A few sips later, Estelle leaned over and kissed me, making her cleavage an inviting view across the dull void of the table. Just as we parted lips, John Parker, who I recognized from the photo, appeared on the patio and came to our table, smiling amiably though looking a little confused.

"The hostess told me I'd been your server on your honeymoon, but I'm sorry if I don't remember you—in spite of the fact you are certainly memorable," he said.

"Actually, you don't know us. My name is Tag, and this is Estelle. We were referred by our friend, Bridgette Vandenberg."

John Parker got an uncomfortable look in his eyes.

"I'm afraid I don't know anyone by that name."

"Oh, I'm sure you do. No man could forget her," I said, only to feel Estelle kick me in the shin.

Sweet Lord! There was just something about me that made women feel the need to kick me in the shins. First, it was Bridgette on the jet and now Estelle. If this kept up, I might have to find a soccer supply store and get some fucking shin guards.

"Sorry, but I don't," John Parker said, with a shrug.

"Look, Bridgette hired me because I'm an old friend of Lux's, and, more importantly, she said you could help us."

He looked around nervously before returning his gaze to me.

"Can you give me any kind of details to prove what you say is true?"

I took a moment to think about the night on my houseboat with Bridgette and suddenly remembered a tiny little detail that brought on a smile, though I doubted Estelle would have the same reaction.

"Assuming you know Bridgette, then you might know that she has a little crescent moon shaped birthmark on her left inner thigh."

Estelle kicked me in the shin again, this time a lot harder, but the upside was that John Parker relaxed and smiled.

"Yes, I have seen it," he said, getting a faraway, though distinctly pleasant, look in his eyes.

"I never thought I'd use a woman's birthmark to verify my credibility."

"The Caribbean is a magical place my friend, though I must say it's a good thing you established it when you did, because I fear your lady friend was only a kick away from breaking your leg," he said, with a laugh.

"Yes, I believe she was."

Estelle was tired of our man banter and interjected.

"Do you know if Lux is still in the holding cells beneath the casino?"

"Yes, she is, sadly. Cell nine. It's not a nice place for such a woman."

"Any chance they would move her?" I asked.

"Doubtful, as they rarely move anybody unless it's out for good or into a body bag."

"So, what's the best way to get down there?"

"Just do something to get in trouble, and you'll be down there before you know it," John Parker said.

He was a funny guy, and we all shared a little laugh at his joke.

"So, John, any chance I can get past casino security to reach the holding cells?"

"No chance in hell. There are too many cameras and too many guards. They barely let me in with the food, and it's my bloody job."

"Well, that certainly doesn't make things any easier," I said.

"There might be another way."

"Sleep with President Babineux?"

"Yeah, maybe if you looked like her," he said, motioning at Estelle, who smiled at his compliment.

"No shit, and since that's not the case, then what's the other way?"

"I believe there may be a secret entrance—a tunnel," he said.

"That sounds like an old pirate's tale."

"It's no tale, but it is not easy to find, as it's supposedly underwater. I don't have time to tell you everything right now. You're my last table, and then I have to deliver dinner to the cells. I'll be done about nine fifteen, and then I can meet you in Old Town around nine thirty."

"Old Town?"

"Yes, it's on the other side of the island. It's where all the locals live, and there's a bar called *Le Cochon Ivre*. It's on the main street, and you can't miss it, as it's the only bar in the town."

"Why can't we meet on this side of the island?"

"Too many eyes and ears here, and trust me, it'll be worth it. My friend who knows about the tunnel will be there as well, and he can tell you the specific details."

It looked as though we had another stop on our sightseeing tour tonight. Of course, it could just be a clever trap, but I had a good feeling about our new friend John Parker.

"We'll see you there at nine thirty."

"Excellent, but don't go in until I arrive, as it's a local's only kind of place."

"No problem, we'll wait for you outside."

"So, my friends, now that we have business out of the way, what would you like to order for dinner?"

"What do you recommend?"

"I'd go with the *poulet boucané*. It's chicken smoked over sugar cane, and it comes with wild rice and fresh vegetables. It's delicious, and your dinner and cocktails are, of course, on the house, as I think President Babineux can afford it."

John Parker disappeared inside, and Estelle took hold of my hand and looked at me, her expression a combination of concern and excitement.

"Do you get nervous doing this kind of thing?"

"Eating and drinking? Only in Mexico."

She smiled at my silly joke.

"You know what I mean," she said.

"I do, and to be perfectly honest—I'm more excited than nervous at the moment."

"That's such a guy thing to say."

"Well, yeah, that's because I'm a guy."

John Parker returned about seven minutes later with our food and two more of those same cocktails.

"I'm going to be closing out my tables, then I'll be making the food deliveries to the prisoners. That means I'll be seeing Lux in about ten minutes. Any message you want me to give her?" John Parker asked.

"Tell her I'm coming for her."

He nodded and went to finish up with another table before heading inside the casino. Estelle and I dug in to our plates, and I was happy to discover that John Parker's recommendation was spot on, and we enjoyed a spectacular dinner under the stars. The moon was now practically over the beach, and the entire bay was bathed in soft lunar light, and we could see the *Sozo* and all the other boats as they sat quietly at anchor. It couldn't have been a more beautiful night, and, suddenly, I felt a twinge of guilt knowing that Lux was locked away in a cell below our very feet. Hopefully, John Parker will bring her the *poulet boucané* for dinner. It was definitely good enough to brighten up even the most dismal of accommodations. We finished our fabulous meal, and I leaned back in my chair to ease the tension of a full stomach.

"I guess we should get going," Estelle said.

"Yeah, but we have some time to kill before we have to be in Old Town."

"So, what are you thinking?"

"I'm thinking it's a shame to waste that dress," I said, gesturing at the band.

"And it's a shame to waste that Tux."

"How about a dance? I hear hippies like reggae."

"I'd like that, man-whore."

CHAPTER FOURTEEN
The Drunken Pig

The band was playing a damn good cover of *Bob Marley's* song *Coming in from the Cold* as Estelle and I squeezed onto the crowded dance floor and joined in with the drunkenly undulating crowd. We were carving out a space between a sunburned Danish couple and a pair of British sisters, and I wasn't sure if it was the magic of the Caribbean or Estelle grinding against my groin, but I felt a real happiness settling over my private parts. I was back to wondering about whether or not a boner was a party foul in a casino, when Estelle felt it pressing against her lady-bits and gave me a naughty little smile. I took that as a signal that it was time to go, realizing that the sooner we met John Parker, the sooner we could return to the ship and finish what my penis was trying to start.

"Ready to go?" I asked.

"Yeah—and I can tell you are too."

"Oh, did you feel my *Lone Ranger* riding roughshod over your *Lady Tonto?*" I asked.

"It would be hard to miss."

"Good one."

We turned and started heading through the crowd, and Estelle was unceremoniously bumped by an enormous middle aged man with drooping jowls and the red eyes and complexion of someone who had been out drinking in the sun all day.

"Oh, excuse me," Estelle said.

"Yes, excuse you, my darling," he said, in heavily accented English.

Clearly, he was as French as a big oozing hunk of brie cheese.

"I'm sorry, but I need to get by you," she said.

The man was belligerently drunk, and, as Estelle tried to slip past him, he reached down and put his arms around her waist and attempted to force her to dance. She tried to break free, but he outweighed her by several hundred pounds, and he used his excessive girth to envelope her body like a giant fleshy jellyfish.

"You are a feisty little American minx," he said, licking his lips as he eyed her from head to toe, soon settling his gaze upon her lovely bosoms.

He, apparently, liked what he saw, because he proceeded to reach up with his right hand and grope her left breast. She looked shocked and, before I could intercede, slapped him hard across the face, sending the rolls of his fat cheeks flying sideways in a visual spectacle reminiscent of an old Bugs Bunny cartoon. He released his grip and stepped back, an angry sneer forming on his lips. The prick absolutely deserved it, but I needed to calm Estelle down before we attracted too much attention. Just as I reached her side, two guys with very strong grip suddenly grabbed hold of each of my arms, and it didn't take long to realize they were casino security. I never even saw them coming and, voila, they were on me in an instant, which was some pretty efficient work for a couple of mercenaries turned beach bum.

"Excuse me, but that guy just assaulted her," I protested.

"I don't give a shit. Monsieur Flavion is a valued guest—and you are obviously American," he said, with a shitty smirk on his face.

"Oh, is that a crime on Soft Taco Island?"

"It is now."

"Well then, judging by your lovely attitude and obvious disdain for personal hygiene products, I'm guessing you must be Parisian."

"How did you guess?" he asked, before punching me in the stomach.

I exhaled at the point of impact, but it still didn't feel good—nor did it look too good, which prompted Estelle to get in the faces of the security men.

"Let him go right now you assholes! That prick right there is the one you should be taking away!"

The guy on my right used his free hand to reach up and activate his lapel mic to call for some backup, obviously, to deal with Estelle.

"Now, you will be coming with us as well, madame."

Monsieur Flavion overheard his words and decided to intercede.

"No, bring the American bitch to my room, and I will personally teach her some manners," he said.

Now, Estelle was downright livid.

"Clearly, you would be more at home molesting a ham instead of me, because, let's face it, the ham probably won't throw up on you when you try to have sex with it," she said.

I thought that was a pretty funny retort, but the security man on my right didn't agree.

"She's yours, Mr. Flavion, and this piece of shit will be taken into custody immediately," he said.

We really couldn't afford to get pinched by the Soft Taco security force, as our rescue mission would be over before it even began. That meant I needed to do something drastic, though it wouldn't be easy with a security goon on each arm.

"You're seriously going to let that fat French fuck get away with this?" Estelle asked the security guy, her face red with anger.

"But, of course," he said, with that same shitty smirk—a smirk I'd like to wipe off his face with my fist.

Shit monkeys. We needed a distraction, and, fortunately for us, Estelle provided it at that moment when she grabbed the drink out of the hand of a nearby person and threw it in the face of the security guy on my right. It stung his eyes, and he cringed in pain, thereby giving me my opening. I slammed my right heel into his instep, and he released my right arm, allowing me to elbow him in the face, the blow knocking him backwards onto the ground. Continuing from there, I swung the same arm around and delivered a punch to the throat of the guy on my left. He let go and stepped back, both hands going to his injured neck as he labored to breath. I threw a left back kick to his groin, and he buckled over, allowing me to slam my left elbow down onto his neck. It knocked him out cold, and his body went slack as he collapsed onto the ground. With French asshole security guy number two out of the way, I returned my attention to French security asshole number one, who was looking dazed as he tried to stand up.

"*Vive l'Amérique!*" I said, as I kicked him square in the face, putting him back onto the ground, where he went night-night like his friend.

The drunken Monsieur Flavion watched the whole thing in horror and started shaking when I turned my attention towards his drooping face.

"Ah, my sweet *cochon*—perhaps I should take you back to your room and teach you some manners," I said.

"No! Please! I was only joking."

He hadn't been joking and, therefore, deserved to face some kind of justice. I thought for a moment and smiled as his punishment came to mind.

"Tit for tat, Monsieur Flavion."

"But, what do you mean by that?" he asked, looking panicked.

"This," I said, reaching over and giving him a nice, hard titty twister.

He gave out a pained yelp then proceeded to massage his beleaguered man-teet.

He'd grabbed Estelle's tit, so I thought it only fitting to return the favor—with an ironic twist, of course. With justice officially served, I took a second to appraise our situation and was relieved to see only John Parker running over to join us.

"More security men will be here soon, but there's only one way you're going to get out of the casino. Follow me!" he said.

We followed him, and he led us over to the railing, where he stopped and pointed over the side.

"You'll have to jump for it," he said.

"Jump for it—as in off the deck? Are you fucking kidding me?" I asked.

"No, look! There's a pool below us. You'll be fine."

We looked over the balcony and directly below us was, indeed, a swimming pool, though the area around it was crowded with people dancing and enjoying the band. It wouldn't be the quietest exit, but I suppose it was our only option.

"OK, but then how in the hell do we get to Old Town after that?" I asked.

At that moment, fate threw us a bone when, just beyond the pool area, two men in a tiny pickup truck pulled up to the side entrance of the casino. John Parker regarded them for a minute before turning to us with a big smile on his handsome face.

"Those men over there are making a rum delivery to the restaurant, but they also happen to be good friends. I'll have them take you to Old Town. Now, jump down into the pool then go over and wait for them in the truck."

Estelle looked at me nervously.

"You have to go now! More security men will be here any second!" John Parker said.

"Thanks, John. We'll see you later," I said, as Estelle and I climbed over the edge of the deck and stood on the other side of the railing.

It was probably about a twenty foot drop to the pool below, but it looked more like fifty, and anyone who's been at the top of a high dive knows the feeling. It doesn't seem very intimidating until you get up there and, suddenly, it feels as though you're about to jump off the top of the Eiffel Tower.

"Wait, I don't want to ruin my dress!" she said.

"Why, is it dry clean only?"

"It's made of fucking delicate silk, you asshole!"

"So, it might tear, or perhaps get a bit clingy? I see that as all the more reason to get it wet."

"Fuck y..."

I didn't wait for Estelle to finish her statement, and, instead, grabbed her hand and jumped. It was probably closer to thirty feet, and we hit the water hard, going down a lot deeper than either of us expected. It wasn't easy swimming while encumbered by all of our fancy clothes, and, when we were finally able to surface, Estelle looked a bit annoyed.

"I'm sorry, I didn't catch that last word," I said.

"It was *you* as in *fuck you*," she said, a smile soon forming on her lips.

"Admit it—that was fun."

"Maybe a little."

The crowd around the pool gave us a round of applause, which meant we weren't doing much to maintain a low profile. Oh well—shit happened when you were out in the field, and all you could do was adapt and overcome.

"Next show is at eleven," I called out, which inspired yet another round of cheering and clapping.

We swam to the edge, climbed out, and made our way through the crowd of people and towards the little truck. We arrived to find it had three wooden cases in the flatbed, and Estelle and I sat beside them while we waited for our impromptu getaway driver and his friend to return from their delivery. A minute later, the two men appeared, the closest one smiling as he put out his hand. We shook and I could see that he was in good shape, about my height, and had dark skin and the unstressed demeanor of a person who lived on a beautiful tropical island. His most distinguishing feature, however, was his set of perfectly straight, blindingly white teeth, which would have made even Brett jealous. I was getting the feeling that Soft Taco Island had an excellent dental plan, and, while I never considered my teeth to be the least bit dull, I was seriously considering getting them whitened when I got back home.

"I'm John Stanton, and this is Johnny Ray—nice to meet you."

"Nice to meet you, too. I'm Tag, and this is Estelle."

He raised an eyebrow as he regarded us, probably wondering why we were soaking wet from head to toe.

"Might I say that you two are wearing some pretty formal looking swimwear."

Estelle and I looked at each other and smiled.

"Yeah, as you can see, we took an unplanned dip in the pool."

"Well, it's certainly a lovely night for it. Now, John Parker said you needed to get to Old Town, so just sit back and enjoy the ride, my friends."

"I hope it's not too much of an inconvenience."

"None whatsoever! We were going there anyway to drop off some of Soft Taco Island's finest," he said, reaching back and patting one of the cases.

I had a closer look and saw that they were full of the same premium rum that we'd sampled earlier, which meant we were truly riding in style. They climbed into the little truck, and we pulled out of the casino and headed north on the access road and into the quiet star filled island night. About a hundred meters later, we made a right turn and headed east along a road that was covered on each side by a dense thicket of vegetation, the result being that the occasional branch went bouncing off the side of the truck. We didn't have the most comfortable seating in the world, but the sweet scent of wild flowers and the view of the night sky were more than enough to make it a truly magical moment. Estelle was obviously feeling the same way for her face was aglow with a radiant smile, visible even in the scant amount of light emitted by the little truck's instrument panel.

"Don't you get nervous doing stuff like this?" I asked.

"You mean riding in the back of a truck with a trio of strange men? Only in Mexico."

The road turned south, and the dense vegetation gave way to the beginnings of a town. Lights were on in most of the windows, and people milled about in the streets. We went past a residential area, and the small downtown came into view. There was a market, hardware store, bank, restaurant, and, up on the right, was the bar, *Le Cochon Ivre*. A number of patrons sat on the bench out front, smoking and talking, and, as we drove past, I could see that the place looked crowded and had the familiar sound of reggae music spilling from inside. We turned right on the next block and right at the one after that, putting us onto the back alley that ran parallel to the main drag. We pulled in behind the bar and parked in relative darkness, the only light coming from a flickering bulb hanging from a rusted fixture attached to the back of the building. John Stanton and Johnny Ray stepped out and each grabbed a case of rum.

"Feel free to grab a few bottles when you go. Compliments of the island," he said.

"Thank you, I certainly will," I said, appreciatively.

"You're welcome, now, I suggest you wait here until you meet John Parker. He'll be along any minute."

They opened the back door and took their two cases inside the bar, allowing the sound of music to temporarily spill out into the night. The old spring-loaded door creaked as it swung shut and thumped against the frame, causing the flickering light above to at last fizzle out for good, leaving us in complete darkness. We sat there in the eerie stillness of the night, the only sound being insects and the occasional distant bark of a dog. Estelle shivered and put her arm around me, and held me close.

"This alley is a little spooky in the dark," she said.

"Maybe we should bust into the remaining case and drink a little liquid courage"

"Excellent idea."

Before I could grab a bottle, I heard a whistle, and looked over to see John Parker standing at the corner—his pearly white smile a beacon in the night. He waved for us to join him, and Estelle and I jumped down off the truck bed and walked over to the corner.

"Let's go get a drink and talk," he said.

Just then, John Stanton appeared from the back door. He grabbed the last case from the little truck then looked our way and called out.

"Don't forget your rum!" he said.

"I won't," I responded, as I turned and followed John Parker around towards the front of the bar.

"Why not just go in through the back?" I asked.

"I figured you should have the grand tour since Le Cochon Ivre is a bit of a historical landmark. You see, this bar has been here since the mid sixteen hundreds and famous pirates such as Sir Henry Morgan and Charles Vane were known to come here for a glass or two of rum before getting a little loving at the brothel that used to be upstairs."

"What a coincidence, as I pretty much have the exact same two items on my evening itinerary, though I was hoping to be getting my nookie on a yacht in the bay," I said, receiving a laugh from John Parker and a smile and a little pinch from Estelle.

We continued around the next corner and encountered the patrons sitting on the bench out front, and all of them gave us curious looks as we passed—probably because Estelle and I were both a little overdressed and still soaking wet from head to toe. We reached the font door, and I looked up at the sign above it and laughed as I saw the old faded image of a pig holding a cocktail. The French name now made sense—Le Cochon Ivre: The Drunken Pig. John Parker led us inside, and I could instantly smell marijuana as I did a quick visual recon of the room. There was a reggae band on a little stage in the back left corner, and every other inch of floor space was crowded with people dancing, drinking, and appearing to be having a genuinely good time. We were no more than a few steps through the door when everyone turned to see the latest arrivals, and then, as if on cue, the band suddenly stopped playing and the entire place went deathly quiet. Everyone's attention was focused on us, and a quiet and uncomfortably long moment passed before the crowd burst out laughing. Shortly thereafter, the band continued playing their song, and all activity resumed as if it had never stopped. John Parker turned to us and smiled.

"Not a lot of tourists come to this side of the island, so we like to make a big show of freaking them the fuck out when they first arrive—which is obviously why I wanted you to wait for me."

I looked around and saw that he was mostly correct about the locals only thing, as the majority of the patrons were likely from the Caribbean, although there were also quite a few fair skinned folks amongst the crowd. All of the people here obviously worked at the resort and probably enjoyed time away from their spoiled clientele. He led us to a table near the back where a tall, dark, muscular, and handsome man in a sleeveless Bob Marley T-shirt stood up to greet us.

"This is the man who knows about the tunnel," John Parker said.

"How do you do—I'm John Livingston."

"Nice to meet you, John. I'm Tag, and this is Estelle."

He kissed Estelle's hand, shook mine, then offered us a seat at his table. We sat down and a waitress came to take our drink orders. She was beautiful and had perfectly smooth dark skin and strong features, pretty much like everyone else I'd seen on the island, and I was starting to think that they might deport all the ugly people. Perhaps Soft Taco Island had a dirty little secret and somewhere nearby was Ugly Island where all the ugly people lived and worked. I turned to the waitress and ordered a Dark and Stormy, and Estelle had the same. John Parker said to make it a pitcher, and she left to fill our order.

"So, you need to get someone out of the island's holding cells,"

John Livingston said.

"That's right, though John Parker says it would be impossible to get in through the casino."

"Correct, but, fortunately for you, I believe there is another way."

"Yeah, and John Parker says it's a tunnel."

"Yes indeed, though it's underwater, and, coincidentally, is in the cove directly below the presidential palace."

"No shit?"

"No shit. I discovered it one day when I was taking a group of tourists diving. Two of them, a couple of troublesome young newlyweds wandered off following a sea turtle. They swam past the warning buoys and came upon the opening of the tunnel and decided to explore it. I followed and found them forty feet inside, and thank God I got them back out without anyone seeing us or their honeymoon might very well have turned into their funeral."

"So, you think the tunnel actually connects to the casino?"

"Absolutely. You see, I got curious and did some research in the island's historical library and found an old geological report that documented an unusually long lava tube that stretches from the cove to the exact spot where the casino was built."

"And you don't think it's a coincidence."

"Absolutely not. I have been diving in these waters for all of my life, and I can tell you if a lava tube is natural or not. That tunnel has been altered, squared off and widened. It definitely has a purpose."

"Why in the hell would Babineux need such an elaborate back door?"

"Perhaps he moves the money from the casino out that way. God only knows what craziness wealthy white men get up to. No offense."

"None taken, I totally agree."

I thought about what my friend at the Agency had told me about the illustrious President Babineux. He had his fingers in a lot of pies, least of all the military industrial complex of Europe, so, now we had weapons, money, a French arms dealer, and a mysterious underwater tunnel. No wonder the Agency was interested in this place.

"Shit, I think you're on to something here, John."

At that moment, the waitress arrived with our pitcher of Dark and Stormies, and she took the time to fill the glasses and pass them around.

"Thank you, Chantel," John Livingston said.

"You're welcome. Now, will you be needing anything else?" she asked.

"Oh yeah, would you mind getting us another glass? My friend will be joining us shortly," John Livingston said.

"No problem, darling," she said, with a smile that made me think they were more than friends.

"Who's joining us?" I asked.

"A good friend and fellow diver by the name of..."

"John?" I asked, stifling a laugh.

"No, it's Michael, Michael Brennan."

"Oh," I said, feeling a little deflated that my joke had failed.

I obviously should have said it before they ran out of Johns.

"So, Tag, you'll be pleased to know that Michael has also seen the tunnel and might have something to add."

"Good, because I've always believed in the saying, the more the merrier, and that goes for people, alcohol, boobs, and especially information," I said.

"Oh, that reminds me, I stopped by my place on the way here and put everything I know about the detention facility on this flash drive," John Parker said, as he handed it over.

"Seriously now, guys, I can't thank you enough for all your help," I said.

"Well, let's just hope you get our girl out of there. Oh, and Tag, I think you should know that the men who work for the Island's security service are not nice. They are all ex-soldiers—some of them cold blooded killers, so you best be careful down there. People who make trouble here have a tendency to disappear."

"I appreciate the warning, but I'm not exactly a stranger to this kind of thing."

"I'm sure you can handle yourself, my friend, but you have heart behind those eyes. You're not like Babineux's men."

We took a moment to sip our cocktails, and I could taste the premium Soft Taco Island Rum standing out from the other ingredients. It was smooth as silk, and it made the world seem just a little bit brighter. At least, it did until I thought about the fact that the pitcher was half empty, and I had to wonder if that made me a pessimist. We soon finished our drinks and John Livingston refilled everyone's glass then held up the pitcher to Chantel to show her that we needed another. John was clearly an excellent host and quickly becoming my new best friend.

Chantel arrived a few moments later with a fresh pitcher, and I decided to acknowledge that as the sign that our official business was mostly concluded, and Estelle and I were free to enjoy ourselves like a couple on a legitimate holiday. Of course, it was nearly impossible not to be drawn into the fun, as everyone around us was drinking, dancing, and smoking the reefer. This was real Island life, and it was amazing how it coexisted in such close proximity to the homogenized world of the resort. I had to wonder if the people who worked at those giant corporate theme parks had a local bar they'd go to after work where they could take off their costumes and do the same thing.

Estelle abruptly stood up and dragged me over to the dance floor, where we squeezed in just in time for a cover of *Bob Marley's* song *Jamming*. She took hold of my hips, and we started moving in time with the music, the two of us grinding on each other with the tenacity of badgers. I'm not sure if it was the alcohol, the marijuana in the air, or Estelle's very intimate dancing style, but I was feeling particularly good at the moment. Three songs later we returned to the table and partook of another ice cold Dark and Stormy. It was yet another perfect moment in paradise, but it would be short-lived, for a fair-skinned man with a concerned expression on his face came rushing over to join us.

"What's up, Michael? You look a bit worried," John Livingston said.

"There are Island security men in town, and they're looking for a man and a woman who were involved in some kind of altercation at the casino," he said, with an obvious Irish accent.

"Unfortunately, that would be us," I said.

"Then you should know that they'll be here any minute."

"Well, shit. I guess the party's over."

"Not a problem—we'll take you two out through the back and send you on your way. In the meantime, we'll keep the Island security men busy while you get back to your boat," John Parker said.

"Come on, Estelle. It's about time we explored the ol' back door," I said, with a wink.

CHAPTER FIFTEEN
Vanishing Point

It was time to get the hell out of Old Town, so we stood up and made our way through the crowd, past the bathrooms, and into the dark hallway that led to the back door of the bar. Up ahead of us on the left, soft yellow light was spilling out from a door that was partly ajar. As we passed the room, I noticed that it was used for storage, and there, in the middle, were the three cases of rum that we had carpooled with to the bar. I remembered our driver, John Stanton's generous offer, and I decided to make a quick detour into the room to grab a couple bottles. Estelle followed close behind, and it only took three steps to realize we weren't alone. There were two good-looking twenty-somethings having surprisingly vigorous sex on a couch that sat against the adjacent wall. The girl was straddling the young man, and they were both so completely engrossed in the moment that they were oblivious to our presence. I had to admire their focus, though it certainly helped that they were young, probably in love, and were enjoying the kind of wild sex where they didn't even have time to properly undress. The girl's shirt was pulled up over her breasts, obviously to give the young man something to hold onto, while his shorts were down around his ankles. I had no idea where her underwear were hiding, but her skirt was still on, thus covering their primary naughty bits and, subsequently, providing a modicum of modesty.

All in all, it made me a tad bit nostalgic for the wild sexual experiences of my youth, where it was not uncommon to get busy in cars, bars, gardens, storage closets, or even on the occasional kitchen counter.

"It stinks like sex in here," I whispered, to Estelle.

"Yeah, I think it's coming from those two people—having sex. Come on, skip the rum, we should go."

"No."

"What do you mean no?"

"John Stanton gave us something special, and I won't let him down. I don't care if I have to cockblock the entire island—I'm getting us some rum."

"I think you might have a serious alcohol problem."

"I don't have a problem as long as I have plenty of alcohol."

"Fine. Get your fucking rum. After we get back to the *Sozo*, I'll book you a nice room at the Betty Ford Clinic."

I ignored Estelle's little remark and crept into the room, trying my best not to disturb the humpers. It might have been my imagination or a matter of proximity, but every step that brought me closer to the rum seemed to increase both the pace and noise of their lovemaking. I looked back at Estelle and gestured with my hands, slapping the back of my fist into the open palm of the other hand to try and relate how hard the couple was going at it, but she seemed uninterested and angrily shooed me on. Whatever, she might be a little testy now, but she certainly wouldn't be when we opened up a bottle on the boat later tonight.

I finally reached the stack and grabbed four bottles from one of the open cases and couldn't help but cringe at the increase in noise from the couple. It had become downright deafening, and I kind of wished I had some of those ear protectors that airport workers wore when they were down on the tarmac. I was taking a quick look at the labels to make sure I had the right bottles when I detected a distinct vibration coming through the floor. It felt like a minor earthquake or possibly stampeding animals, but it turned out to be something even more primal. The girl was putting on a final burst of orgasmic speed, and she was moving up and down like a jackhammer as she cried out and pounded away at the young man beneath her. Thank God he was young and strong, as it was his best chance of surviving this sexual encounter. She started to tense, her back arching until she emitted one final ear wrenching scream as she and the young man at last climaxed. The room was now mostly quiet, the only noise being the muted sounds of the band playing on the other side of the wall.

"Well done," I said, delivering a brief round of applause.

It startled the girl and she used her left arm to cover her breasts, while the guy just leaned to the side and looked over at me, the weariness in his eyes like that of a prizefighter who had just heard the bell at the end of the twelfth round.

"Sorry for the interruption, but I needed to get some rum," I said.

"No, I'm sorry. We probably shouldn't be in here," she responded.

"Nonsense, there's nothing wrong with making a little love as long as no one gets hurt."

I reached back into the case and pulled out another bottle of rum and walked over and handed it to the girl.

"Here, you two must be thirsty."

"Shit! This is the good stuff! Thank you!" she said, as she opened the bottle.

I clinked one of my bottles with her bottle.

"Cheers," I said.

She took a sip then handed it to her boyfriend who probably needed it more than she did. Ah, young love. I turned and left to join Estelle back in the hallway.

"Satisfied?" she asked.

"Yeah, but not quite as satisfied as those two," I said, gesturing with my thumb towards the couple.

"The night is still young," she said, with a coy smile.

John Parker, who was waiting at the back door, held it open for Estelle and me, which was nice, considering my hands were now full of bottles of rum. The light above the door was still out, and we could barely see the little truck in the darkness of the back alley.

"Take the truck and head back to the resort. Whatever you do, don't leave via the official port of entry, as they'll surely be waiting for you there."

"Thanks, John Parker. You won't get into any trouble will you?"

"No way, my friend. I'll just tell them I have no idea what man and woman they are talking about, because all you white people look the same," he said, with a smile and a wink.

He gave the hood of the truck a friendly slap then headed back inside the bar. I stashed the bottles of rum in the open compartment on the dashboard then backed out into the alley, put it in forward, and headed north towards the far end of town. The street eventually dead ended, and I turned right and reached the main drag, where I looked back and saw a police jeep parked in front of the Drunken Pig. We had made it out just in time, and I hoped the bacon would take as long as possible searching the place. If we were lucky they'd even have a drink—except it might be too ironic to have a couple of drunken pigs in the Drunken Pig. I turned left onto the main street and headed out of Old Town, passing the last of the outlying dwellings before the road turned west and entered the dense jungle. I drove the little truck as fast as I could while Estelle kept vigilant watch to see if anyone was following us.

"I think I see headlights back there," she said, nervously.

I looked in the rearview mirror and saw that she was correct. Shit! We needed to disappear, so I turned off our headlights and drove by the light of the moon, whereupon I inadvertently drifted to one side or the other a few times and trimmed the foliage that grew right up to the road. Up ahead, I could finally see a light, which meant that we had finally reached the main access road, but the car behind was still there and slowly gaining on us. Of course, it was a lot easier to drive fast when you had the luxury of using your headlights. I made a hard right onto the access road, the back end skidding out as I put the pedal to the medal and headed north towards the main hotels.

"So, how are we getting off the island?" Estelle asked.

"The same way I arrived."

I pulled out the radio Billings had given me and pressed the call button.

"Pete! We need a pickup. Hot and fast. Same place you dropped me off."

"On my way."

We sped along the mini highway that ran parallel to the path we had walked earlier. It was probably a maintenance road that was meant to keep the help away from the guests, and it would hopefully be deserted at this hour. We came around a blind turn and discovered my theory was wrong, as there, just a short distance ahead, was a delivery vehicle coming from the opposite direction. I swerved hard to the right, then left, the abrupt motion making the tiny truck raise up on two wheels for a brief moment as we veered off the road and bumped past the oncoming truck with only inches to spare. I cut back onto the pavement, and we continued along on our merry way until I looked in the rearview mirror and saw lights appear in the distance behind us.

"I think our island security friends made the right turn back there—literally and figuratively," I said.

Estelle looked back to confirm my suspicion.

"Yeah, that's definitely them. Any ideas on how you're going to lose them?" Estelle asked.

"Not yet, but I'm pretty sure it's going to entail getting pretty fucking creative."

About a hundred meters ahead, I spied an open area with a manicured garden and lawn that appeared to access the beach.

"Problem solved! We're going to take the beach route!"

When we reached the area, I cut left and drove across the walking path and onto the grass only to see that there was a seawall coming up.

"Tag! I assume you see the drop-off?"

"I do, so you better hold on tight!" I said, hitting the accelerator.

Extreme circumstances called for extreme measures, and if we wanted to reach the sand, we were going to have to go full-on *Dukes of Hazzard*. That was a reference to the abundantly silly, yet totally awesome, early eighties television show of the same name. Each week, I tuned in for four reasons, the first three being related to one key element—namely the super hot female lead character Daisy Duke. Reason one was to see her beautiful glowing face, while reason two was to see her boobs in her usually tight tank top. Reason three was to see her long legs and backside in her short cut-off jean shorts—which is the origin of the Daisy Dukes short-shorts phenomena. The fourth, and final, reason was to see Bo and Luke Duke jump their 1969 Dodge Charger over a ravine—usually accompanied by the sound of a very loud yeehaw. In a bold tribute to the show, I drove off the edge of the seawall, the little lip helping to send us completely airborne, and I decided to make my re-enactment more accurate by letting loose my own mighty yeehaw. Estelle also screamed but hers was from legitimate fear, and it sounded more like something you'd expect to hear in a horror movie. We landed on the sand, the impact rocking us violently forward and backward as the little truck's suspension struggled to recover. I glanced over at my copilot and saw that she didn't look too happy about my little stunt, but I think she'd be even less happy in a Soft Taco Island cell.

"Are you and the rum bottles OK?" I asked.

"We're all fine, thank you, but count yourself lucky that you included me in that statement, otherwise you'd be finishing off this date with your hand."

I put the pedal to the metal, and the little truck took off, its engine screaming as we raced up the beach, swerving and skidding around numerous obstacles including a snack shack and an inadvertent slalom course made up of strategically placed lounge chairs. At long last, I could see the lights of the beachfront bar and restaurant, which meant we were almost home.

We stashed the truck around the back of a cabana, then grabbed the rum and ran over to the outdoor patio area. The majority of the diners were long gone and had probably moved inside to the dance club, leaving the tables mostly empty. This made it hard to orient myself, but I soon found where I'd stowed the parachute. I slipped on the harness, unrolled the chute, then stuck a bottle of rum in three of my jacket pockets, strategically keeping the forth bottle out so I could take a swig before handing it to Estelle. She also took a swig, and, as she was handing me back the bottle, we heard people approaching, and I was worried that someone might have reported us to hotel security. I was relieved, however, to see that it was the two women from earlier, Isabella and Monique, though Estelle, not too surprisingly, didn't look quite as pleased to see them.

"Hello, girls!"

"Hello, Tag, are you leaving us already?" Isabella asked, feigning sadness.

"I'm afraid I must, as a gentleman's work is never done."

"Well, then I hope you manage to *drop in* again sometime," Isabella said.

"Yeah, and next time, hopefully I won't have to *pull out* so early."

Estelle elbowed me in the ribs and pointed at the headlights racing towards us along the beachfront road. Assuming it was the island security, they were only a minute away, which meant that we were out of time. I bid farewell to Isabella and Monique, then Estelle and I headed across the beach and down to the water, where I could hear the rumble of the ski boat's engine as it idled just beyond the breakwater. I called Billings up on the radio and told him we were heading out, and, soon thereafter, the towline came sailing over the moonlit waters. It landed with a splash just a few feet away, and I picked it up and clicked it to my harness.

"Estelle, you have to hop up and wrap your legs around my waist, and put one of your arms around my neck, but, most important of all, hold onto the fourth bottle with your free hand," I said, handing it over.

"Can't we just swim out to the boat?"

"No, we can't risk getting the flash drive wet."

She nodded her understanding then hopped up and took to me the way a baby koala bear took to its mother—our arrangement conveniently leaving her right hand free to cradle the bottle of rum between our bodies. I looked south down the beach and saw that the Soft Taco Island security men had driven their jeep onto the sand and were getting close. Shit! They were probably following our tire tracks and would be on us any second. We didn't have a moment to spare, so I yelled out to Billings.

"Hit it!"

The ski boat's powerful engine came to life, and the hull roared up out of the water, dragging us violently off the beach. I had to run a good twenty feet through the shallows before the parachute filled and lifted us just high enough that my legs were skimming the surface, sending up a spray like a water skier. Unfortunately, the breakwater was looming ever closer, and it appeared as though we still weren't going to clear it. Billings, keenly aware of our predicament, throttled up, but, as I feared it wouldn't be enough, I stepped up onto the barrier at the last moment and leapt with all my might. The combination of the extra speed and my efforts made us shoot skyward, Estelle screaming out loud as we climbed steeply up into the moonlit night. She opened the bottle and took a swig of rum then leaned in and kissed me, her mouth tasting spicy and sweet. She handed me the bottle, and I took a swig then kissed her. Then we both took a swig and kissed each other. And so it went as we floated along in our private little world in the sky, drifting over the calm waters of the bay, completely lost to the unlikely intimacy of the moment. The excitement was, of course, causing blood to flow to my privates, but the parachute harness was pinching my balls and doing little to enhance the romance. Apparently, these harnesses weren't designed to be used with erections, which was something I might have to email to the manufacturer when this was all over.

I saw the *Sozo* coming up, and, soon thereafter, Tiffany started reeling us in, sadly bringing an end to our little flying make-out session. With each second, we lost altitude and dropped ever closer to the boat until my feet finally touched down on the padded back deck. Estelle climbed off, and we pulled in the parachute, and I was at last able to slip out of the ball choking harness. I shook my legs and rubbed my inner thighs hoping to lure some feeling back into my groin. It didn't make it any easier that I had a semi, but at least it was dark, and I faced my indignity alone. I dropped down into the back seat beside Estelle and enjoyed the ride as Billings steered us expertly alongside the *Sozo*, where Kip took hold of the lines and tied off the boat.

"Perfect timing, Pete."

"Happy to be of help, and I must say—it felt like being back in the good old days."

"That goes for both of us."

"Oh, by the way, I managed to get you two a little present."

I pulled out one of the bottles of rum and handed it over to the lovebirds.

"Holy shit, this is the good stuff! Thanks!" Billings said.

"You're welcome. It's the least I could do considering all your help."

"Well then, what say we call it a night and debrief in the morning and take it from there," he suggested, excitedly.

"Sounds good to me."

Billings and Tiffany climbed aboard the *Sozo* then everyone left, while Estelle and I sat there alone in the ski boat, enjoying the quiet of the night. She reached for the open bottle of rum and took a swig then handed it back. I took a pull as well, then looked over at Estelle and could see, even in the pale light of the moon, that she was bubbling with excitement.

"That was fucking amazing! No wonder you do this shit," she said.

"Oh, I like to think it's all about the job, helping people, and making a positive difference in the world."

"Bullshit. It's all about the rush! That was the best night I've ever had."

Adrenaline could be quite an effective aphrodisiac and Estelle had just suffered an overdose—the result being that she was like a fire dragon set loose upon a field of dry kindling. She climbed on top of me, and I could feel every inch of her body coursing with energy as we locked lips, entangled our tongues, and kissed with frantic urgency. Her heart was pounding, and her chest was heaving as I slid my hands up her stomach and over her breasts, where I discovered her nipples were hard and pressing out through the thin fabric of her dress. I was eager to free them from their confinement but couldn't find the zipper. Estelle, sensing my frustration, broke free of my lips to deliver some rather unexpected advice.

"Just tear it off," she muttered, plaintively.

"But..."

"But, nothing. You've been a man all night, so don't start being a pussy now."

I felt bad to ruin such a beautiful dress, but sometimes a man had to make hard choices—and hard choices demanded swift action. The soft silk gave way easily, and in one rip she was down to a pair of red silk underwear as she lay back on the seat, the moon giving off just enough light to see her dark, hard nipples standing out in stern contrast to the pale flesh of her breasts. I felt like a sailor lost in the fog, her body the channel showing me the path to safe harbor, as I kissed her breasts then worked my way back to her lips, where I could still taste the sweet essence of rum as we resumed our great clash of flesh. Our tongues were like soldiers on an ancient battlefront, pushing, pulling, gaining the advantage, and losing it just as quickly. Without missing a beat, she undid my shirt, pulled off my jacket, and somehow removed my pants—thus stripping me of both my clothing and my innocence in one fell swoop. Now, that she had gained the access she craved, she took hold of my manhood, first with her hands, and then with her mouth. I had been more than halfway there before she even got my pants off, so it was paramount that I slow her Herculean effort. Her grip was vice-like and taking back control of my penis was like wrestling a banana from the hands of a hungry silver back gorilla. I eventually broke Kong's mighty grip, and, once free, I removed her underwear and slipped down her body until I was eye to eye with her sweet lady fruit. I kissed her thighs and used them as guides to make my way towards the intersection where east meets west. A few slips of the tongue and soon she was the one getting too close. She wiggled free and pushed me back onto the seat then mounted me and began moving up and down, slowly and purposefully, her breathing heavy as she looked at me with eyes lost to the madness of lust. She was a woman on a mission, her muscles taught, every movement quick and powerful as she picked up her pace and approached climax. I too was feeling the glorious end of the chase coming, so I grabbed hold of her hips and matched her powerful strides until she began crying out.

"Not yet! Not yet! Not yet! Oh God—now!"

That was all I needed to hear to join her in the divine moment of climax, where together, we achieved the ultimate reckoning of heaven and earth that could only occur between two lovers. Pounding on until our bodies were spent, we at last stopped to regain our breath and held each other tightly, the gentle lapping of the water against the hull the only sound other than our pounding hearts. We kissed yet again, softly and slowly, soaking in the beauty of the moment until Kip's voice rudely broke us from our moment of post coital euphoria.

"Um—if you guys are finally done, I would really like to put the boat away now."

He was like a bad penny that just kept turning up every time

I thought that we had seen the last of him. We gathered up our clothes, Estelle throwing on my Tuxedo jacket as we left poor Kip to his task. Without another word, we took the forward stairs and made our way to her cabin, where we stepped inside and closed the door before finally speaking.

"Awkward," she said.

"Indeed."

"Hell of a night, though."

"Yeah, hell of a fucking night, and that boat hump session totally put those two youngsters in the bar to shame."

"It did, and what we may have lacked in youthfulness, we made up for with experience and enthusiasm."

"Fuck yeah," I said, holding up my hand for a high five.

She reached over and gave my hand a solid smack, and had she had the foresight to have installed a Clapper, the lights would have gone perfectly out at that moment. Instead, she had to reach over and manually flip the switch, thus letting the dark bring refuge from the day and guide us gently unto the world of dreams."

CHAPTER SIXTEEN
Into the Blue

I awoke to another day in paradise and lay there listening to the sound of seagulls cawing and boats cruising in the bay, all the while thinking about the night before and the day ahead. The easier part was behind us, while the more difficult part where people might get hurt was about to begin. Estelle stirred and saw that I was awake and smiled before getting up and heading to the bathroom. I heard the water running and figured that she was brushing her teeth, so I got dressed and popped my head in to tell her that I was going to go to my cabin to get ready and take a shower.

"Oh, you're sneaking off to take a shit, aren't you?" she asked.

"No, I'm sneaking off to take a shower."

"Yeah—after you take a shit."

"Well, yeah. Obviously, I can't shit in the shower."

"See, that wasn't so hard—telling the truth and admitting your human frailties."

"I don't want to talk about it anymore."

She squeezed my cheek like I was a child and told me to go take a potty like a big boy. And she wonders why I didn't tell her in the first place. I left her cabin and headed for my own, grateful not to run into Kip for once though, of course, it might mean that he was waiting inside my room. I opened the door carefully before doing a quick recon to make sure that Kip wasn't pulling a Kato. A Kato was obviously a reference to the character Kato from the *Pink Panther* movies, and he, as Inspector Clouseau's manservant, was also given the unusual task of surprise attacking him—the goal being to keep his boss's martial arts reflexes sharp. My Kato's motivation might be a bit different, but his tactics could be similar, so I wouldn't put it past my nemesis to be hiding in the closet just waiting to jump out and surprise me with a baseball bat to the head. Thankfully, I found it all clear and, therefore, headed straight for the coffee machine to make a quick pot. The brewing finished, and I filled a cup and took a moment to savor its lovely aroma. At last, I took my magical first sip, and, the minute the warm liquid crossed my lips, I could feel my entire body come alive, my mind clearing as my digestive system signaled that it was time to hit the porcelain. I didn't feel like messing around with any visual entertainment, so I went for a solo utilitarian dump, the kind the ancients must have taken before the invention of books, magazines, tablets, and smart phones. No frills—get in, let out, and get out. It wasn't great, but it was better than being interrupted by a phone call or knock on the door.

Finished, I shaved and hopped into the shower and picked a random shampoo from the myriad of choices on the shelf. It smelled nice, and I realized that it was the scent I smelled on Estelle the day before, and it instantly made me wish she were here in the shower—that is, until I thought about her little teasing session. Maybe later I'd find her weakness and tease her back. Ten to one it was shoes, as all women seemed to have that particular weakness. I toweled off, put on shorts and a T-shirt, and headed out into the passageway, where I saw Brett leaving his cabin with the *Sozo's* extremely attractive chef. She went in the opposite direction while he joined me en route to the main salon, and he was looking particularly happy, his dazzlingly white teeth blinding me as he smiled from ear to ear. It was a little early for anything that bright, so I slid my sunglasses off my forehead and down over my eyes.

"How did it go with Estelle on the island last night?" he asked.

I thought about dinner at the casino, drinking and dancing at the Drunken Pig in old town, and the wild hump session in the back of the ski boat.

"Excellent. We made a good team and really came together in the end."

"Good to hear," he said.

Wow, Brett was a lot nicer with this new woman, so, hopefully, things would continue to go well, and he'd remain this amiable. Of course, this also made me wonder what was going on with Bridgette. I said it before and I'll say it again. These people lived in a world that I'd only read about in sordid tabloid magazines—a world where people changed sexual partners as readily as I changed my socks. Still, I had been playing some pretty good catch up lately having gotten together with three women in four days, and I had to wonder if all man-whores got their start in the Caribbean. We reached the main salon, and everyone was waiting for me as I took the open chair next to Estelle, who smiled innocently as she reached over and gave my thigh a playful squeeze. I poured myself a cup of coffee, and looked up just in time to see a crewman bringing out a tray of scrambled eggs, chicken apple sausages, and waffles with fresh strawberries. I shoveled a bit of everything onto my plate, as I was hungry as hell. Gallivanting around an island all night was an activity that burned a shitload of calories, and I desperately needed to replenish my body. Unfortunately, the breakfast was so good that I crossed the replenishment line after my second helping and quickly moved into gluttony territory, but at least it would mean a formidable dump the following morning. Billings waited until we were all done eating before asking about how everything had gone on the island. Estelle was brimming with excitement, so I left it up to her to tell the story, and she gave a damn good summary that included all the necessary details but, thankfully, left out all the dancing, drinking, and sex, even though it was, in my opinion, the best part of the night.

"So, going in through the casino is out," Billings said.

"Yeah, it looks as though the underwater tunnel is our best bet."

"Do you trust John Livingston?"

"Absolutely, but I'd still like to see it for myself today by doing a little pre-mission reconnaissance of the cove."

"That place is a popular snorkeling spot, so you should have no problem blending in with the tourists and finding the entrance," Bridgette said.

"Just tell me when you want to leave, and we'll head out," Billings said.

"I have to grab something from my room, so how about in fifteen minutes?"

"Perfect."

"Oh, and I almost forgot. We have more good news. Assuming I make it inside, John Parker gave me detailed plans of the detention facility."

"You two kicked ass last night."

"It's all about teamwork," I said, as I smiled at Estelle.

I finished my last sip of coffee, then Estelle and I left the table and walked back to my cabin, so that I could pick up my underwater GPS. I rifled around through my bag of goodies and eventually found it, but, as I turned around, I noticed that Estelle was looking me with a rather peculiar expression on her face.

"Jesus. Do you always travel with this much shit?" she asked.

"No, I usually travel light, but this job called for a lot of specialized equipment, especially this little beauty," I said, as I held up my wrist mounted *Navimate* underwater GPS."

"Believe it or not, I have the same one."

"Seriously? An actual *Navimate*?"

"Yeah—didn't you know that right after we women gained the right to vote, we were also finally allowed to purchase electronics and sporting goods?"

"Hardy-har-har—my angry little aquatic feminist. The reason I'm surprised is because the company is fairly new, and the units are extremely hard to find."

"Yes they are, which is why it's more surprising that a landlubber like you would have one."

"Well, I have friends in low, wet places. How'd you get yours?"

"Friends in high, dry places. My boss is a billionaire."

"As you're the proud owner of a state of the art underwater GPS unit, can I assume that you scuba dive?"

"Of course. I work on a boat in the Caribbean for God's sake, and I'll have you know I'm a certified open water instructor and the lucky girl who gets to teach scuba diving to all of Mr. Vandenberg's lame-ass guests."

"Good, then perhaps you'll join me today."

"I'll have to check my schedule."

"Schedule? Maybe I should ask the girl that went with me to the island last night. I doubt that girl has to check her schedule."

"Fine, I'll come along with you on your little reconnaissance mission."

Fifteen minutes later we were back in the ski boat, heading south towards the cove, and, once again, it was a double date with Billings and Tiffany. Not too surprisingly, Tiffany was wearing yet another new and exciting bikini that was unable to provide adequate coverage for her sizable breasts—not that I was complaining. She and Billings were in the front seat, looking like a couple on holiday, while Estelle and I were sitting in the exact same spot where we had made mad passionate love the night before. We looked at each other and shared a knowing smile, and I realized it was yet another magical day in the Caribbean.

With plenty of sunshine and the water as smooth as glass, we rocketed down the Island's west coast and reached the cove in a little over ten minutes. It turned out to be exactly as Bridgette had said, and the area was rife with snorkelers, the majority brought in by boats run by the island. There was also a diving group, and I wondered if my new friend John Livingston was here taking out a fresh group of tourists. Billings expertly anchored us just beyond the cove and not far from the Mega Yacht *Sarsarun*, which was drifting lazily at anchor with no sunbathers or frolickers visible on her decks. What a waste of a perfectly good yacht. I turned my attention back to our little boat and was surprised to see that we had enough diving gear for all of us, which meant Billings and Tiffany would both be coming along. Of course, this begged the question of whether Tiffany, with her abundance of natural flotation in her bosoms, could actually achieve negative buoyancy.

Before we could hit the water, however, we needed to address our first concern, which was the sun. Tiffany reached into her bag and pulled out tubes of SPF seventy waterproof sunblock then passed them around. I set to work covering all my exposed skin, and had just gotten to my calves, when Billings tapped me on the shoulder and pointed at the girls. They were applying sunblock to all the interesting areas of their bodies—namely their chests, thighs, and buttocks. Sweet mother of aquatic erotica! It suddenly felt as though we were watching a cheesy softcore movie, the only thing missing being the bad keyboard music—at least that's how it appeared through our man-filters. Billings and I were mesmerized as we continued to watch and were, therefore, caught completely unawares when the girls looked over and noticed us staring.

"What's up with you two? Why aren't you getting ready?" Estelle asked.

"Oh—well—um," I mumbled, stupidly.

"Yeah what's up? Are you two OK? You look a little zoned out," Tiffany said.

"We're fine," Billings responded.

"Yeah, we're fine," I added.

Its funny, given the right outfit, a man could probably watch a woman shovel horseshit and still get aroused, as the male brain was like a sexual super computer that could turn even the most innocent act into something alluring. I tried to clear my mental hard drive then set about putting on my dive gear, while Billings hit a button on the console which lowered a swim platform off the back of the little boat. In my day we dropped over the side like discarded beer cans and had to get back aboard by getting scooped out of the water at high speed. If we were lucky enough for that same boat to be stationary then we shimmied over the side or climbed up the motor, ever hopeful we didn't cut our feet on the propeller. Apparently, everything was easier when you were a billionaire.

"Our new friend John Livingston mentioned there were warning buoys near the entrance."

Billings took out a pair of binoculars from a cubbyhole beside the helm and scanned the cove.

"There they are on the northeast end about fifty meters off the shore," he said, before handing me the binoculars.

I took a quick look and confirmed his observation before turning the binoculars on the *Sarsarun*. I had half heartedly hoped to catch a glimpse of a scantily clad sunbather, but my earlier observation had been correct, and no one stirred on the yacht. I handed the binoculars back to Billings then stood up.

"Big red warning buoys. No better way to keep tourists away from the entrance to your secret tunnel—or attract assholes like us. Who's up for some spelunking?"

Everyone raised their hands.

"Alrighty then, team—let's do this."

We ambled over to the swim platform and lined up to drop into the water. Estelle and Billings went first, then me, and, after submerging, I turned to watch Tiffany and was surprised to see that she could indeed, with the help of a weight belt, counteract her breast's positive buoyancy and dive below the surface. Still, her magnificent mammaries floated up and were only barely able to stay within the tight confines of her bikini top, and if we ran into any other divers along the way, they would certainly have something more interesting than the fish to hold their attention. We swam down to the bottom to join the others and the show only got better when I saw that Estelle's breasts, like Tiffany's, looked particularly exciting as their buoyancy fought the confines of her bikini top. Now, we had two beautiful women in bikinis making our little section of the underwater landscape go from a G rating to a solid PG-13, maybe even an R if we were lucky.

Boobs aside, I had gone diving in a lot of places around the world, but I would definitely put this in my top ten. The water clarity was phenomenal, and there was an abundance of rich coral growth that made the area rife with all manner of tropical fish. I programmed a waypoint into my GPS, then gave the others a thumbs up, and we headed off into the cove. In order to look more like tourists, we stayed in a loose formation and took it slow and enjoyed the scenery, pointing out the exotic and brightly colored sea life along the way. Soon, we were encountering other snorkelers and divers, and the last person we passed was a boy, probably around fourteen, who stopped looking at the fish and stared wide-eyed in awe at Tiffany and Estelle as they kicked past. He aimed his waterproof camera at the girls then snapped a quick photo. That would be the picture he'd show his friends when he got home from vacation, as pretty girls in bikinis generally outweighed tropical fish as a point of interest for males of the species.

We finally reached the series of chains that anchored the little red buoys, and saw that there were warning signs both above and below the water. They were somewhat overgrown with barnacles, but the wording was still clear enough: *Warning: Dangerous Currents! Keep away!* The area was free of other divers and snorkelers as we continued on past the signs, and I hoped that they didn't have any kind of underwater security system or listening devices, but, either way, it was better to find out now.

The depth held at around twenty-five feet and, judging by the topography of the bottom, had obviously been dredged at some point. About forty feet away, I finally spied the tunnel entrance, and it looked exactly as John Livingston had described. We all stopped and exchanged a thumbs up then swam towards the opening. It may have originally been a lava tube, but now it clearly showed human influence, as it was at least thirty feet across and had been widened enough to easily accommodate a small submarine. I plugged in another waypoint into my GPS, and we swam into the tunnel and continued until it got dark. I plugged in my final waypoint and was satisfied that I could find my way back to the exact same spot at night. Our recon was done for the moment, so I signaled that we could turn around and head back. So far, everything looked good, and there were no signs of any bad guys dashing out of the tunnel with spear guns, ready to make impromptu fish-kabobs out of the nosey tourists. As long as the tunnel actually reached the casino, I had found my back door.

On the return trip, the ladies led the way, and Billings and I swam behind them, enjoying a view that was as good as anything below us in the coral. I'm not sure if it was the angle of view or magnification of the water, but both Estelle and Tiffany's backsides looked particularly amazing as the two girls kicked along ahead of us, and I probably could have continued swimming behind them for all eternity. Billings tapped me on the shoulder and pointed towards the girls, and I realized he had been thinking the same thing. It made me laugh, which broke the seal of my mask and allowed it to fill with water, thus forcing me to stop and clear it while the others waited. Finally ready to go, we continued on and followed my GPS coordinates back to the boat and surfaced at the stern by the swim platform. I waited for the others to get out first. The girls thought I was being a gentleman but, mainly, it was so I could enjoy the view of Estelle's wet bathing suit as it clung to her body the same way her red dress had the previous evening. With everyone aboard, I pulled myself onto the platform, took off my gear, and grabbed a towel and dried off before taking a seat beside Estelle on the back bench.

"Looks like we found your secret entrance," she said.

"Yeah, though tonight will be a wee bit more challenging, since I'll be lugging an extra set of dive gear."

"The aqua scooter will make all the difference. You'll be in and back in no time," Billings said.

"I certainly hope so."

"Won't it be kind of freaky doing that dive at night all by yourself?" Tiffany asked.

"Yeah—but, technically, I won't be alone. There will be plenty of sharks and barracudas to keep me company."

Billings fired up the engine and idled slowly forward, while I went to the bow and brought up the anchor. I came back to the cockpit, and he put the throttle wide open, and we roared up onto a plane, heading north back to the *Sozo*. The trade winds had come up, so it wasn't as smooth as the ride down, but the powerful boat dug through the waves, and we made the trip quickly, arriving to find the same crewman greeting us to tie off the bow and stern lines. Why the hell hadn't he been there last night instead of Kip? Perhaps I might be able to get a look at the ship's crew schedule, so that I could keep track of my nemesis and thus plan my late night excursions a little better. We left the boat deck and headed upstairs to clean up, pausing at the door to my cabin.

"Want some company in the shower? I'll let you wash my boobies," Estelle said.

"I didn't want to say anything, but I was thinking they were looking a little dirty."

I turned my attention to the door and opened it slowly, making sure that Kip, or should I say, Kato, wasn't lying in wait. Thankfully, the coast was all clear, and we were completely alone. Estelle stripped off her bathing suit and headed for the bathroom, while I followed closely behind, thoroughly enjoying the view of *her* behind. We stepped into the shower, soaped each other up, and I couldn't help but gaze down in wonder as her soft slippery breasts pressed against my chest. It wasn't long before my manhood sprang to life and slipped up between her thighs to snuggle playfully up against her lady fruit. She smiled and took hold of it with her soapy hands, one tickling the stepchildren the other tenaciously sliding up and down the shaft. Of course, the more she scrubbed, the dirtier I felt.

"You might want to be careful as you're on the verge of bringing forth sack lunch—or what the elders call God-seed."

"Clearly, you're referring to the male elders, for I'm pretty sure the female elders call it ball-snot."

"I prefer God-seed, but, either way, it was known by all the elders to be highly nutritious when consumed orally, and medicinal when applied topically to your skin, making it look healthy, radiant, and youthful."

"So, it's like Oil of Olay?"

"More like oil of—*Olé*!"

"Oh really?"

"Yeah, really."

"So, I might want to shoot some on my skin and see how it feels?"

"Definitely."

"Well, after being out in the sun and saltwater, I was thinking I could use some on my neck and chest."

She knelt down, and my heart started to race as I watched my favorite appendage being double teamed by two of my other favorite appendages. Sweet Lord of ham sandwiches! This was turning into the best shower of all time. I was transfixed as I gazed down at Estelle who was looking up at me with a lustful twinkle in her eyes as she pressed her bosoms together and slid them up and down my manhood.

"Are you turned on right now?" she asked, in a sultry voice.

"I've been turned on since the day we met."

"No, I mean, really turned on, like you're about to blow your load all over me," she said, as she seductively licked her lips.

My mind was engulfed in the full stupidity of lust as I answered.

"Oh God, yes," I said, breathlessly.

"Good, because, now, you're all clean and ready for your mission," she said, as she abruptly stopped, stood up, and began rinsing me off with the handheld shower attachment.

"But..."

"But nothing. Everyone knows a fighter shouldn't blow his mojo before the big fight," she responded.

"Yeah, I'm sure that the discomfort of blue balls will increase my ability to perform complex and dangerous tasks."

"Well, I don't know about that, but I am pretty certain it'll help motivate you to get this rescue mission done as fast as possible, so you can come back and let me finish what I just started."

"I'm thinking archaeology majors shouldn't practice psychology. In fact, I would go so far as to call your little performance a cruel and unusual form of sexual bullying."

"Whatever gets the job done."

Estelle was cruel though clever, and I would hopefully find a similar way to return the favor at a later time. Of course, being a man, I could never have stopped where she did, so it was probably prudent to accept her victory and move on. We exited the shower, dried off, and adjourned to the bed, where we lay there happily cuddling until falling asleep for a well deserved nap after our exciting day of underwater espionage.

CHAPTER SEVENTEEN
Back Door Man

We awoke just in time to see yet another perfect sunset playing out through the porthole in my room. We climbed out of bed and decided it was about time to get dressed and ready for the evening, which meant Estelle needed to go to her cabin for fresh clothes. She wrapped up in a towel, and I followed her and kissed her goodbye in the open doorway, only to see that Kip just happened to be walking up the passageway.

"Oh, I'm sorry—am I interrupting a little afternoon delight?" he asked.

"Not this time, I'm afraid," I said.

"Oh, is Estelle being a little stingy with her loving? That never happened with me," he said, continuing on his way.

"What was that supposed to mean?" I asked, curious if perhaps those two had more history than Estelle was letting on.

"No idea," she responded.

Either way, that shit-burger Kip had an almost superhuman ability to interrupt us in moments of intimacy, which was making me think he needed to wear a little bell. At least that way, we'd have some advance warning when he was approaching. Kip continued on his way, and Estelle looked at me as though she felt sorry for him as she headed off to her cabin. I closed the door and went to my clothes bag and picked out yet another pair of shorts and a T-shirt. Dressing in the tropics was easy enough, but I also had to think about equipment for tonight. Things might get rough, but I was hoping I wouldn't have to kill anyone, as I'd done more than enough of that in my previous life. Regardless, I was up against an army of ruthless wine swilling French mercenaries, so I'd need some serious firepower and equipment if things went to hell. I felt a bit like Noah, except I wasn't packing my arc for a flood, but rather for my own personal armageddon. I grabbed two pistols, two knives, and two stun grenades following the old special operations adage that two was one, and one was none. Next, were my specialty items which included an assortment of devices for countering everything from electronic security and old-fashioned key locks to enemy personnel. For the latter, I packed one of the syringes of Ketamine, as it would put any unfortunate victim to sleep for several hours. It could be prickly delivering a shot to an enemy combatant, but it lessened the need for inflicting deadly harm. The last and most important item was the duct tape, the most versatile tool in the special operations arsenal. I placed it, the syringe, and everything else into my watertight gear bag and set it on the bed.

Now, it was time to look at the info on John Parker's flash drive. I slipped it into the USB port on my laptop and discovered that he had conveniently organized all the information into a PDF file. I double clicked the document and went page by page, memorizing the map he'd created of the layout, as well as reading all the notes he added regarding any relevant employee schedules. Satisfied, I closed my laptop and headed to the main salon for dinner and our final planning session before tonight's exciting festivities. Everyone was there when I arrived except for Brett who showed up about five minutes later smiling like a cat that had just swallowed a canary—a five foot eight canary with brown hair, blue eyes, and very lovely breasts—not that I'd noticed.

He sat down, and, soon thereafter, crewmen brought in roast pork tenderloin with broccoli, red potatoes, and a buttery California chardonnay. I didn't usually drink before a mission, but the wine was so good that I had to have at least a sip or two. It might be my last meal if the mission went to hell, so I might as well enjoy it. Billings held up his glass for a toast.

"To a successful mission and the return of one of our own."

We all clinked our glasses and took a sip of wine, and I noticed Bridgette looking unusually nervous and making little eye contact with the rest of us as she ate. It was understandable, as she was obviously just worried about getting her sister back. I turned my attention to my plate and dug into dinner which, as usual, was excellent, so excellent, in fact, that my fellow diners and I were mostly quiet until our plates were empty. Once the dishes were cleared off the table, coffee was served, and we decided to go over the plan.

"Pete, do you want to anchor, or should I deploy while we're underway?"

"If we anchor, you'll at least have an exact point to navigate back to in the dark."

"True, but we have to be far enough away that we don't arouse any suspicion."

"I'll bring Tiffany and some wine and cheese to make it look like a date in case any patrol boat comes by."

"If you bring Tiffany and some wine and cheese, it will be a date," I said.

"Exactly."

Everyone laughed.

"Anchoring it is. Now, according to the information in John Parker's PDF, our best time is around ten, as they will have just picked up the dinner trays. That means we should be on site by nine to give me plenty of time to navigate the tunnel and hopefully find my way to the holding cells."

"No problem, sunset will be around six, so we'll leave at eight and have plenty of darkness to cover our arrival."

"It's a plan," I said.

Everyone stood up and left the table, and Estelle and I headed for my cabin. In the main passageway, we came upon Bridgette who was chatting away on her phone in hushed tones. When she saw us, she hit the mute button then looked up and smiled.

"Tag, I have complete faith that you're going to get my sister off of that island tonight," she said, as she placed a reassuring hand on my shoulder.

"Thank you, Bridgette," I responded, pleased to receive a little positive reinforcement for a change.

She nodded then returned to her call, while Estelle and I continued on to my cabin to pick up my gear. I grabbed the waterproof bag that was packed with all my goodies, then we continued on down to the dive room to get everything ready for the mission. First, and foremost, I pulled out two of the Draeger bubble-less re-breathers. Unlike traditional scuba tanks, they didn't release the exhaled air and, not having a bunch of bubbles rising to the surface, would make my arrival on the other end of the tunnel a hell of a lot stealthier. This was some pretty unusual equipment to have around for recreational diving and was, in fact, standard issue for every special operations unit across the world. This meant someone, perhaps Mr. Vandenberg himself, had properly outfitted the *Sozo* for this mission and, consequently, made my job a shitload easier. I strapped the extra air tank to the aqua scooter then picked out dive gear and wetsuits for Lux and myself. I hoped she hadn't put on a lot of weight since I'd last seen her, or her wetsuit might be a little snug. It certainly wouldn't help that her meals came from the restaurant in the casino. If I had been eating that food every day for a week, they wouldn't even need a door on my cell, as my girth alone would have been more than enough to keep me from escaping.

With everything shipshape, we loaded my gear into the boat

then took a seat on the edge of the deck, where I had a little time to mentally walk through the various stages of the mission. Performing such a task was something I hadn't done in about five years, and it had the unusual effect of making me feel as though I had been transported back to my previous life as a spy. Confident that I had all the details firmly locked in my mind, I broke from my intro-retropspective and went into the dive room and changed into my wetsuit. By the time I emerged, Billings and Tiffany had arrived, and they were loading their picnic basket into the boat.

"I've got our cover all ready to go," Billings said, with a smile.

"Covert ops just aren't what they used to be."

"Yeah, they're way better now."

"Well, certainly for the support team, so let's hope that holds true for me when I'm all alone in that dark ocean tonight."

I stepped down and joined them in the boat, and Billings fired up the engine, letting it warm up for a few minutes until he checked the gauges and signaled to Estelle that we were ready to go. She leaned down and kissed me goodbye then untied the bowline as I went and undid the stern.

"Good Luck and hurry back, man-whore," she said, taking hold of her breasts and squishing them together to remind me of her cruel little shower prank.

"Thank you, I will, *Julie*-cocktease-*McCoy*."

Estelle and I shared a little laugh, then I took a seat and noticed Tiffany was smiling at me.

"Ahhh—you two have already given each other cute nicknames!" she joked.

"Well, if you wanted to talk about what's actually cute, we'd be discussing that picnic basket you fuckers brought along."

They laughed then Billings steered us away from the *Sozo* and out into the bay. The air was still and the water smooth as we made our way through the endless procession of tenders ferrying people to and from the island. We had to take it slow until reaching open water, but once we were clear, Billings opened up the throttles, and we headed south, experiencing the end of another beautiful day and the beginning of another beautiful night in paradise.

We passed the distillery, and next came the casino, whose outdoor deck was full of diners, and I could imagine John Parker tending to his section and recommending the Pollo Lauren. We continued on and reached the southern end of the island and were relieved to see the massive *Sarsarun* and some charter yachts still anchored in the cove. Having other vessels would provide natural cover and make us look a hell of a lot less suspicious. We still stayed a ways out, but at least the two lovebirds could have their picnic without any interruptions. Billings expertly set the anchor while I lowered the aqua scooter into the water then took a second to program the boat's current coordinates into my GPS.

"Enjoy your picnic, I'll hopefully be back with our girl in an hour or so."

Billings filled two wineglasses and handed one to Tiffany.

"We'll be here—holding down the fort," he said, clinking glasses with her before taking a sip of his wine.

"Now, you two be careful. I wouldn't want either of you to get a cramp in your tongue—or any other appendage for that matter."

"Don't worry, we'll be very careful."

"Good luck and stay safe, Tag," Tiffany said.

I nodded, slid my mask down over my face, then gave them a thumbs up before dropping backwards over the side of the boat. I'd bypassed the decadence of the retractable swim platform, because I liked doing it the old fashioned way, and it helped get me in the mindset of the good old days of SPECWAR. I took a moment to orient myself then grabbed hold of the aqua scooter and descended down into the dark depths. I'd done a shitload of night dives during my time in special operations and the Agency, but I'd never been able to completely shake the feeling that there was just something a little spooky about swimming in the ocean after dark. It was the time, after all, that a lot of the large predators like sharks hunted and, therefore, wasn't a good time to be in their domain. Of course, most of my missions took place at night or before dawn, but I usually had an entire team of armed people and, least of all, a dive buddy at my side. Tonight, however, I was gliding all alone through the darkness with only my GPS and a depth gauge to keep me company.

The aqua scooter was making the trip a lot easier, and I was doing a little over five knots and hoped that I didn't bump into anything large or hungry. I would have loved to use the dive lights, but I couldn't risk giving away my position in the clear waters of the cove, and that meant I had to fly blind until I entered the tunnel. I passed the buoy chains, and, soon thereafter, was at the entrance. I slowed down a little and turned on the dive lights, and practically crapped in my wetsuit when I realized I was face to face with a fairly large grouper—his giant mouth continually opening and closing as he stared at me with his massive, bulging eyes. His interest finally piqued after a moment, and he moved out of view and disappeared into the darkness. My heart was still pounding from the encounter as I continued on into the tunnel and followed my preprogrammed GPS coordinates. Even at half speed, the aqua scooter allowed me to make excellent time, and I quickly reached the spot where we had stopped earlier in the day. From here on out, I was in new territory, so I took it slow. Unfortunately, the lights didn't shine very far ahead, and it made it feel as though I was driving through fog, where details only came into view at the last second. Luckily, the tunnel was clear of debris or potential obstacles, though that meant it was probably used fairly often, and I was, therefore, more likely to run into some unexpected company between here and the casino.

I continued on through the darkness until at last seeing the proverbial light at the end of the tunnel. I shut off the lights, throttled down the aqua scooter to a slow crawl, then gazed ahead to see the water coming aglow as I entered some kind of large room. I ascended slowly, careful to make as little noise as possible as my head broke through the surface. I had a look around and saw that I was in a large subterranean chamber that appeared to have been dug from the rock. It might have started as a lava tube, but its current dimensions were clearly man-made. The room was easily twice the size of the average high school gymnasium, and its ceiling was over twenty meters high and well-lit by tracks of halogen lights. Down at the water's edge there was a pier and two docks, the longer one sitting below a loading crane, while the shorter one had two small identical grey submarines moored to it. Obviously, some pretty extensive work and money had gone into building this place, making me suspect that Babineux was using it to move something very expensive or very illegal.

I ditched the aqua scooter underneath the dock and separated the extra dive gear and did the ol' combat sidestroke to a ladder on the far side near the submarines. I had a little open water to cover and that particular swimming technique minimized splashing and was faster and more dignified than dog paddling. I climbed up onto the pier, lugging the extra wetsuit and my bag of goodies with me, then paused and took a quick look around the ceiling and walls for security cameras. As far as I could tell, there wasn't a single one, which meant that President Babineux was pretty confident that there was little or no chance of someone wandering into his secret lair. I started jogging over to the crane in hopes of finding a nice hiding place to stow the extra wetsuit and my watertight gear bag, but I paused when I heard voices echoing from somewhere in the chamber.

I turned and ran back to the side, slithering into the water just in time to avoid two security guards who came walking into view. The closest guy was thin and wiry while the other was stout and had a bushy little mustache—their combined appearance making me think that they kind of looked like contemporary versions of the old-time movie actors *Laurel* and *Hardy*. They were speaking French and had earpieces and outfits identical to the casino security, so it was obvious I was in the right place. The skinny one, or *Laurel*, laughed and pulled out a pack of cigarettes and offered one to *Hardy*. *Hardy* took it and they both lit up and stood there smoking and talking. I only understood a smattering of what they were gabbing about but the phrase *la belle jeune fille avait de gros seins* rang a bell. I believe it translated roughly as the beautiful woman with the large breasts. Of course, a couple of random guys working on a remote island in a secret underground chamber would be talking about boobs. It's just what guys do. And what else would you talk about on Soft Taco Island? The weather? Hell no, as that never changed. Beautiful women in bikinis, however, would be a constantly evolving topic as new and exciting guests came and went from the island every day.

They finally got to the end of their cigarettes and threw the butts into the water, where they landed only a few feet away from me. I hated litterbugs and always did my part to make the oceans a cleaner place, so I scooped them up and threw them onto the dock. The men turned and walked out the way they had come, and I climbed up the ladder and went back to the crane, whereupon I opened my watertight gear bag and pulled out a pistol and my assault vest—the latter item being the most important because it conveniently held all my various goodies. I hid the bag and extra wetsuit then headed up the stairs and made a beeline for the mini submarines. Obviously, Lux wasn't in either of them but my curiosity and deep inner manchild were absolutely dying to get a closer look.

I'd had the pleasure of going on several different submarines during my time in the military and CIA, and was curious what use Babineux might have for these little fuckers. I worked my way around to the other side of the chamber then headed down the ramp and climbed aboard the closer of the two. I had only just stepped aboard when I heard a vehicle, and turned to see a forklift with a pallet full of crates entering the chamber. Shit! It was heading in my direction, and the operator would soon be able to see me. The mini sub was the closest hiding place, so I shimmied down the open hatch and dropped into the cockpit to discover seats for a driver and copilot residing in front of a large viewing port. I sat down and took a minute to look at the controls and various instruments. There was a GPS, fathometer, knotmeter, and, more importantly, a battery level gauge that showed the range of the sub according to the current charge. The batteries were at their max levels, and, according to the readout, it could do a little over five nautical miles, which wasn't bad for a sub this size.

I stood up and decided to continue the tour. Just behind the pilot and copilot seats were two benches that were obviously intended for any extra passengers, and I moved past them and stepped through a watertight hatch in the bulkhead. The next compartment was a large open bay with doors on the ceiling that opened like the ones on the Space Shuttle. Clearly, these subs were designed for moving cargo rather than ferrying tourists around the island. Down below me there were hatches in the floor, and I opened one to see that it allowed access to its bank of batteries. They were the similar to the kind they put in golf carts and yachts and would power all the sub's engines and electrical systems. I closed the hatch and then made my way out of the sub to find that I was alone yet again except for the pallet of crates that the forklift operator had deposited beside the crane on the pier.

I stepped off the sub and went up to examine the crates and saw that they had Cyrillic writing on the outside. I'd bet good money that they were some kind of Russian weapons, probably surplus AK-47's. Too bad I didn't speak Russian, as I could have just read what they contained, but, sadly, my primary foreign languages were French, Italian and German, and I'd hardly spoken a word of any of them in years. I opened the nearest crate and found something with a bit more power than an AK. I was, in fact, staring at a shitload of Strela 2's, Russia's version of the shoulder-fired missile and not a good toy in the wrong hands. Between the twenty-five crates, there had to be more than two hundred and fifty launchers which was more than enough to start a small war—if not end one.

I closed up the crate and decided to check out the rest of the chamber, first and foremost being the two nearby doors. The first accessed a bathroom and locker room, while the second opened up into a small room with a computer workstation. I moved back the way I had come and out into the main chamber and spied an enormous set of double doors at the far end of the room. It was the same direction the forklift had come from and, therefore, the only likely exit. I approached the doors cautiously, desperately hoping that Laurel, Hardy, or any of their friends wouldn't be on their way back anytime soon.

Only a few feet from the doors, they opened automatically, just like the kind at supermarkets, and I found myself at the beginning of a giant hallway about a hundred feet long and twenty feet wide with four large doors on each side. The place was devoid of cameras as far as I could tell, so they obviously focused all their security on the casino end. That was good for me because defeating security camera surveillance was always a bitch. Either you destroyed the camera and gained a small window of time or fed it a bogus video feed, and neither of those options would have been particularly convenient at the moment.

I made my way down the massive corridor but stuck to one side so that it would be easier to hide if any of the French menace made another appearance. About halfway through, my fears came to fruition when I saw the doors at the end start to open, and I could hear what sounded like another forklift. I ducked into the closest door, and it turned out to be a large storage room filled with French FAMAS assault rifles and Beretta pistols. Once the forklift had passed, I went out and checked the other rooms and found that they had grenades, explosives, flak jackets, and all manner of ammunition. This place was a veritable supermarket for soldiers, so it was, indeed, clear that President Babineux was supplementing his income in the arms dealing business. It would certainly explain why he had a secret underwater tunnel and miniature submarines, as men generally only had those things if they were an arms dealer or were going through a particularly severe midlife crisis.

I moved on to the end of the corridor and the double doors opened automatically, revealing a giant warehouse that was filled with endless stacks of crates and row after row of military vehicles. At the other end of the room was a large freight elevator that probably allowed them to move vehicles and equipment to and from the other levels as well as the surface of the island. Babineux obviously had one hell of an operation here and more than enough arms to keep the third world busy fighting itself for years to come.

I worked my way around the left side of the room until finding a stairwell which led up to a catwalk, and I followed it to a short hallway that ended at an electronic security door. It opened without any problem from this side but required punching in a code when coming from the other direction. These locks could be tricky and time consuming to defeat, but this one called for a rather simple solution. With the door still open, I pulled the duct tape out of my tactical vest, and placed several pieces over the hole on the frame side to keep the bolt from engaging. It was simple, stupid, and totally effective.

Now, I was in a fairly large, nice looking lobby with an elevator that presumably accessed the casino above. I recalled the map from John Parker's flash drive and realized that I was at last in familiar territory, and my destination was the last door on the right. I walked over the fine Persian rug and across a small patch of marble floor to the far side of the room, where I stopped below a sign that read Sécurité. I had reached the holding cells! I hovered just outside the window in the door, hazarding a quick glance inside to see that the inner room had a series of cell doors on either side. John Parker had said that the guards sometimes took short smoking breaks, leaving the cells unguarded, but that wasn't the case at the moment. I had the luck of finding the only Frenchman on the island who apparently didn't smoke. Instead, he was sitting at a futuristic looking desk and casually watching a soccer game on a flat screen television mounted on the far wall. He sported a short military style haircut and looked to be in his late twenties and had plenty of muscle on his sturdy frame. Wonderful. I had also just found the only Frenchman on the island who apparently worked out, and I wondered why in the hell he couldn't have been an unhealthy smoker like his work mates *Laurel* and *Hardy*? At least I could hear the game through the door, which meant that the sound was turned up loud enough that it would hopefully cover the noise of my entrance. All of this would, of course, go down a hell of a lot easier if I could just slip into the room and take him out with the syringe full of ketamine. He was young and strong, and I didn't want to waste precious energy or time in any kind of prolonged confrontation.

I took a last quick look around the lobby to make sure I was alone before easing open the door, praying to God that it was properly hung and wouldn't squeak or make a noise. It was less than halfway open when the high pitch squeal of a tight hinge made me freeze, but the guard, fortunately, didn't react, as he was deep in the trance-like state that men often achieved while watching a sporting event on television. I slithered the rest of the way through the door, closed it, then moved towards my target, using the time to pull out one of the syringes. I removed the safety cap, squeezed out the remaining air bubbles, then took a second to focus on my breathing and keeping my adrenaline under control. It had been awhile since I'd done anything like this, and I was suddenly feeling a little nostalgic for those boring lost cat cases. Sure, it was mildly demeaning and you might get a few scratches, but, outside of the Pickles case, I rarely ended up in a physical confrontation or on the business end of a forty-five.

I reached striking distance and tried my best to stay calm as I realized that my earlier summation had been correct, and the guy before me was in good shape, physically my equal in all respects. Success would, therefore, come down to training and experience, and failure could literally carry with it the possibility of death. But, if all went well, he'd be out cold and dreaming of Brie cheese and French bread, while Lux and I would be long gone and swimming our way to freedom.

I moved my right foot one step closer and was just about to insert the syringe into his neck, when he jumped up and screamed after his team made a goal. Fucking soccer. Games could go hours or days without someone making a goal, but, of course, his team just happened to make one at this very moment. The guy was so excited that he clapped his hands, did a little dance, and spun around, stopping dead in his tracks when he saw me. He looked confused and I'm sure that it didn't make it any less strange that I was wearing a wetsuit and holding a syringe in my hand. Time to initiate Plan B: subterfuge and confusion. I decided to add to his uncertainty by asking him a silly question in French.

"Bonjour, où se trouvent les toilettes? J'ai la diarrhée terribles," I said.

This gave him a lot more to process, namely, who was the jackass in the wetsuit, and why in hell was he asking him where he could find the bathroom. Before he could answer, however, I used his moment of indecision to try and drive the needle into his neck. It appeared as though my little stunt was going to be successful, but he quickly shot out his hand to block, and the impact to my wrist sent the syringe flying across the room. Nothing is ever easy.

I smiled, the gesture intended to give him pause for thought, but it merely inspired him to throw a pretty decent left hook into my ribs that knocked me back a few steps. Shit, my opponent was indeed formidable, and he immediately followed up his punch with a right front kick to my stomach. He should have gone for the knee or groin, but since he didn't, it was easy to move right, catch his leg, and deliver a hard dragon punch to the saphenous nerve. It sounded like a fancy pants technique, but it just meant that I had extended the center knuckle of my fist to increase the amount of force into a smaller point as I hit him just above the knee on the inside of his thigh. He cried out and reacted by lurching forward and punching me in the jaw, thus forcing me to release his leg. Now, back on both feet, he prepared for another attack, this time foregoing any kicks, probably out of fear that I'd do the same. He threw a right cross, but I was ready and deflected his punch with a right inward block before grabbing his arm with my left hand and slamming a right hammer fist into his ribs. The blow stunned him enough that I was able to shoot my right hand up into the crux of his elbow and take hold of his forearm with the intent of leveraging it against his shoulder joint. Now, success would come down to footwork and intent. I stepped forward, maintaining the advantage as I slammed him backwards onto the ground. He landed hard on his back but broke free and rolled quickly onto his stomach as he tried to get to his feet. It was a bad move for him to turn his back to his opponent, and I used the moment to move in and try to apply a rear choke.

This technique, like the front choke I had used on the shitter in Afghanistan oh so many years ago, worked on the same principles, and it would usually only need to be applied for several seconds to cause the average person to lose consciousness. My burly French opponent was dazed from the takedown but far from average, and, therefore, aware enough to know what was happening, and he set about utilizing his formidable strength and agility to try and knock me off. I had never been in a rodeo, but I suddenly felt as though I was riding a big, angry French bull. The guy twisted and slammed me into everything within a ten foot radius, but, after colliding with the desk, he spun and lost his footing, and we both went down hard onto the marble floor. I rolled off to the right and happened to glance underneath the desk and discovered my syringe full of Ketamine. Bingo! Plan A was officially back on the table.

I snatched up the syringe with my right hand, but kept it hidden behind my back as my opponent and I stood and faced off yet again. He began circling menacingly, looking angry and ready to exact some revenge for my rude intrusion into his otherwise peaceful night in the Soft Taco Island detention center. His eyes suddenly went wide, an obvious giveaway of an impending attack, and he threw a left jab to my head. It turned out to be a feint, for he immediately followed up with another right front kick, this time keeping it low. I moved right, but his foot still caught me, thankfully landing just to the left of my testicles. It hurt, but it wasn't devastating and, subsequently, gave me the break I needed. I trapped his ankle with my left arm then kicked out his standing leg, sending him onto the floor, where he landed on his back and let out a pained grunt. With his right foot still firmly locked against my side, I jammed the syringe into his thigh and released the entire quantity of ketamine. He made a last ditch effort to break free, twisting his body and throwing several punches, but I held on tight until he was finally overcome by the drug and went unconscious.

I dropped his leg and took a few seconds to catch my breath then turned my attention to the next task at hand—namely, finding cell nine. It turned out to be conveniently located about twenty feet down on the left between cells seven and eleven. Odds were on the left and evens were on the right. I went to the door and realized that the lock was electronically controlled and returned to the guard's desk to find that it had a large touchscreen monitor built into its surface. I hit the button that said *ouverte* below the cell nine icon and felt my heart skip a beat as I heard the door click and unlock.

CHAPTER EIGHTEEN
Déjà Vu

As I pondered seeing the long lost love of my life for the first time in almost ten years, I realized I was more nervous now than I had been a minute ago facing off against the burly French guard. What was Lux going to say? Better still, what the hell was I going to say? We'd never really finished what we'd started back in Afghanistan, so God only knew what it would be like to see each other after all this time. Fuck it. I opened the door and walked in, my heart practically leaping out of my chest as our eyes met, and I saw that she was still as beautiful as I remembered. Her hair was now long, but everything else looked the same, the only real surprise being her clothing. For some reason, I'd imagined that she would be dressed in tattered striped prison garb, the shirt hopefully having a conspicuous tear that showed a hint of nipple, but I would have no such luck. Contrary to the musings of my vivid imagination, she was dressed rather elegantly in a tight grey short skirt and a fitted black shirt, and looked as though she was heading out for an evening on the town instead of rotting away in a French holding cell. Leave it to the French to turn prison uniforms into high fashion. We continued to stare at each other, lost for words, until I at last mustered up the courage to speak.

"Hello, Jugs," I said.

"Hello, Finn. John Parker gave me your message, but he didn't have to—I knew you'd come."

"Of course, I owed you one."

"Yeah, but you'd have come either way."

"True."

We shared a moment of uncomfortable silence until Lux spoke.

"This is really awkward," she said

"Yeah, I probably should have brought you flowers considering this is about as close as we've ever gotten to a proper date."

She smiled.

"You're still a jackass," she said.

"You're still beautiful."

She came forward and put her arms around me, the years melting away and taking me back to our last kiss on that airfield in Afghanistan. It was intoxicating to hold her again, and, when she pulled her head back and gazed into my eyes, she looked as though she was going to kiss me. Instead, she abruptly broke eye contact and looked particularly uncomfortable as she took a step back.

"I don't know what to say. I've wanted to get in touch and see how you're doing," she said.

"I know—me too, but life just goes by so fast and then suddenly it's been ten years."

She took hold of my hands and looked at me, a little sadness obvious behind her eyes.

"You look really good," she said.

"I've been getting a lot of exercise lately."

"I can see it. You're practically glowing."

Shit. I hope she didn't look too closely, as I doubted that she would be as happy to see me if she knew that her sister was partially responsible for that glow.

"You really haven't changed," I said, looking at her from head to toe, suddenly noticing that she had a wedding ring.

She saw that I was looking at her hand and started fidgeting with the ring.

"As you've probably already guessed, I'm married, and I don't think you're going to be too happy about the details," she said.

"It's OK. You have a life. So do I."

"It's more complicated than that," she said, her discomfort growing with each passing second.

"What's the big deal?"

She took a deep breath and let it out slowly.

"Corn and I are—um—married."

"Excuse me? Married?"

"After you left, we got together and it sort of—continued."

"Married is a hell of a lot more than sort of continued."

"Yeah—I know. I'm just sorry you had to find out like this."

"Goddammit. I knew it. That son of a bitch even joked about it the day I left."

"It just happened. I missed you so much that..."

"That you decided to dull the pain by getting together with Corn. Oh I understand—it makes perfect sense."

"It wasn't that simple. I was heartbroken and empty after you left, and Corn was there to fill the void."

"The void being your vagina, apparently."

"The void being my heart, you asshole."

I stood there, suddenly feeling a little numb as I wondered how the hell they could have done this to me, but then I realized I was probably being a little unreasonable. I was technically the one who left first and also hadn't made much of an effort to stay in touch. And to make matters worse, I wasn't exactly easy to reach while I worked for the Agency, as I was in a different time zone every other week. I suppose that we were just two people that fate had decided weren't meant to be together, but at least I had the consolation that I actually liked the asshole she married. Still, this was a lot of shit to process and all very confusing though not nearly as confusing as the burning question that now lingered.

"Why did you send for me? Why not Corn? I'd heard rumors that he worked for the Agency."

"Because he's not you, and I knew that you were the only person in the world who could pull this off."

"But, he's your husband."

"And now he's also the Deputy Director of the CIA for God's sake."

I suddenly felt like Han Solo waking up from the carbonite freeze only to learn that his best friend Luke Skywalker had gone on to a life of grandeur as a Jedi Knight.

"All the more reason for Corn to be here instead of me. He has the entirety of the Agency's resources at his disposal."

"Yeah, but he can't show favoritism by using them to rescue his wife. This was my mess, so I needed to clean it up."

"Which makes me the unlikely janitor while your highbrow hubby sits safely back at his desk at Langley."

"That's not fair."

"Life isn't fair."

"Look, if it makes you feel any better, I'm legitimately sorry that we never got in touch and told you before now."

"Considering we all worked at the Agency, I'm more than a bit surprised that we never crossed paths—though I suppose you two were purposefully avoiding me."

"Don't be ridiculous. The Agency is a big place, and you of all people should understand that they like to compartmentalize their assets."

I did understand, and she was correct. An entity as large as the CIA liked to keep its secrets, and that was a lot easier if the right hand didn't know what the left was doing. That feat was best accomplished by having a lot of independent cells all working on their own specific assignments. If an agent or asset was captured or compromised, then he or she could only divulge the knowledge specific to that person's individual operation. It was basic spy logic and made damage control a lot easier. Unfortunately, this last exchange brought on yet another uncomfortable silence, and I decided it was time to steer the conversation in a new direction.

"So, did the Agency send you here to infiltrate Babineux's arms dealing business or to learn how to make world class rum? I'm fairly certain it's the former, but deep in my heart of hearts I'm holding out hope for the latter."

"Unfortunately, it's the former and..."

The sound of people talking in the outer hallway abruptly brought Lux's response to an end, as we took a moment to listen. Their voices were growing louder which meant they might be coming into our area. Shit! I ran out and grabbed the unconscious guard and dragged him into the cell, quietly closing the door just as some men entered the detention center. I stood by the window and kept an eye on the room outside and saw, to my surprise, that it was my two smokers from earlier—*Laurel* and *Hardy*. Apparently, they were looking for their friend, who, coincidentally, happened to be the guy that I had just knocked out. His name was Joel, which I learned because they kept yelling it over and over. Hearing no response, *Hardy* turned his attention up to the television, which finally revealed to me the reason for their visit. They wanted to know the final score of the big game. He clapped his hands and said something to *Laurel* and they both left looking particularly excited. Maybe soccer wasn't so bad after all.

"Do you still want to hear about my mission?"

"Yeah, but you'll have to tell me later. Right now, we better get the hell out of here. Speaking of which—are you a good swimmer?"

"Yeah—why do you ask?"

"You'll see."

We left the detention center and saw no sign of the two Frenchman as we made our way through the well appointed lobby and back to the electronic security door.

"I assume you have the key code?" Lux asked.

"Don't need it. I have something better."

I simply grabbed the handle and pulled the door open. Lux looked mildly confused, until I reached out and pulled off the tape I'd put over the locking mechanism.

"Duct Tape. It's faster and easier," I said.

"Maybe James Bond had it wrong all those years going to Q when he could have just gone to a hardware store."

"Make your jokes, but duct tape is the reason that you're free to leave here at the moment."

"Too bad you don't have any chewing gum—you could be the next *MacGyver*."

I reached into my tactical vest and pulled out a pack of gum.

"You want a piece?"

"No thanks. Far be it from me to jeopardize our escape by depleting your precious resources," Lux said, shaking her head.

She still had a pretty good sense of humor considering where she'd just spent the last week. I put the gum back in my vest, and we went through the door and into the hallway that lead to the massive warehouse.

"Holy shit!" Lux said, as we emerged out onto the catwalk.

"I take it you haven't been in here yet?"

"Nope, and I had no idea that Babineux's operation was this big."

"There's more if you can believe it."

We continued down the stairs to the main floor and wound our way through the endless stacks of crates, the space feeling more like a maze than a warehouse, and it was a relief to finally see the doors up ahead. They began to open long before we were in range of the sensor, which meant that someone must be coming from the other side.

"Oh, shit. We're about to have company and need to find a decent hiding spot."

I grabbed Lux's hand and we raced across the room to the rows of military vehicles and climbed into the back seat of an olive green Humvee. I peered out the window and watched as a group of several guards walked down the center of the warehouse. Laurel and Hardy were amongst the crowd and they were all walking slow, talking, and had the relaxed body language of people who had just gotten off of work. It must be time for their shift change. That was good news, as once they were gone, it meant that we should be able to reach the underwater chamber without running into many more of Babineux's people.

"Now what?" Lux asked.

"Well—we have a minute to kill, and we are in a back seat."

Lux smiled.

"Can you last a full minute?" she asked.

"Probably not after ten years of fantasizing."

"Well, then I suppose we should abstain in hopes of maintaining your male prowess."

Oh well, better to have tried and failed than never to have tried at all. We waited until the men were long gone then climbed out of the Humvee and went through the automatic doors and into the massive corridor.

"What's in the side rooms?" Lux asked.

"Enough weapons to start World War III, IV, and V combined."

She opened each door and quickly peered inside.

"Jesus, he's got quite an arsenal down here."

"Yeah, it kind of puts my man-room to shame."

"What?"

"Nothing."

We continued through the last set of automatic doors, and I could already smell the seawater as we approached our destination. The chamber was empty and quiet as could be as we walked out to the main pier, where Lux immediately noticed the stack of crates and proceeded to open the exact same one that I had examined only fifteen minutes earlier.

"Shit, these are the missile launchers," she said.

"Yeah, I saw them on the way in. How do you know about them?"

"It's part of the reason that I'm here, but I'll tell you more when we get the hell out of here," she said, as she left the crates behind and joined me at the crane.

She paused and looked around the room, her eyes wide in awe.

"Jesus, would you look at this place?" she said.

"Yeah, pretty amazing piece of engineering. Babineux has gone to a lot of trouble and expense to build this chamber."

"Yeah, so, how exactly are we getting out of here?" she asked.

"You said you're a good swimmer," I said, as I handed her the extra wetsuit.

"Are you kidding?"

"Nope."

I tried to be a gentleman and avert my gaze as she stripped down to her black bra and frilly little thong underwear, but ten years of longing combined with a male brain had a funny way of overriding any kind of impulse control. I therefore couldn't help but stare at Lux, though seeing her in such a glorious state of undress, made it abundantly clear how much she resembled her sister. There was no mistaking the obvious similarity of their hair color, eyes, facial features, and, most of all, their curvaceous figures, though Lux's boobs were a tad bit bigger. Sweet Lord! How could one family have the genetic wherewithal to produce not one but two daughters as stunningly beautiful as Lux and Bridgette? I continued to watch as she slid one long leg and then the other into the wetsuit before wriggling into the top half. Her final step was the zipper, but she couldn't manage to get it past her substantial chest.

"A little help would be nice," she said.

"Clearly, the company that designed this wetsuit didn't have the Vandenberg sisters in mind," I said, as I reached over and zipped her up.

Lux immediately looked at me questioningly.

"What the hell is that supposed to mean?" she asked.

Shit, I realized I had stupidly forgotten that Lux was one of the sharpest people I had ever known, and absentmindedly using the word sisters in my comment might very well become the catalyst to inspire her to unearth my little sexual interlude with Bridgette.

I, therefore, needed to lock this conversation down before it evolved into a full-on inquisition.

"Nothing—now, we don't have time to stand around and chit-chat, so let's get the fuck out of here," I said.

"We're not going anywhere until you answer the question."

"There's nothing to answer, because it was a completely innocent comment about how your wetsuit fits."

"Oh, really? Because I find it a strange that your innocent little comment conspicuously occurred while you were helping me get the zipper up past my tits."

"Honestly, I think tits is a vulgar word."

"OK, then we'll call them boobs. Now, answer the fucking question."

I let a long pained sigh as I realized that Lux wasn't going to drop the subject, so I decided to keep my answer simple and to the point.

"Fine—my comment was obviously a compliment about your boobs."

"Yeah, and that would have been fine except that you just said Vandenberg sisters, plural, which means you were also referring to Bridgette. So, Tag, do you mind explaining to me when the hell you managed to get such a thorough look at my sister's boobs?"

Sweet siren of deductive reasoning! It was as though I'd struck up an argument with an especially fucking tenacious and fiery Sherlock Holmes.

"Excuse me, but we're in the Caribbean, so I've obviously seen her in a bikini."

"Yeah—and?"

"And what? A bikini tends to be fairly revealing. End of story."

I was quiet for a moment, as I hoped that was an adequate response, but Lux clearly knew I was hiding something.

"Bikini, my ass! Now, Tag, why don't you man-up and tell me the real story!"

I tried my best to think of a clever way out of this mess, but nothing clever came to mind.

"Well?" she asked, testily.

That's when the damn broke, and, with nothing else to say, I spoke the unthinkable.

"Well—honestly—it's—um—complicated?"

Fuck. I had just said the magic words—it's complicated. What a hypocrite I had become, and perhaps from now on I would have a little more sympathy when people spoke those words to me. Meanwhile, Lux didn't give a shit about how complicated my story might be, and she proceeded to glare at me as she stood there with her hands on her hips. Oh shit—here it comes.

"Did you have sex with my sister?"

"Why in the hell would you ask me that?"

"Because she tries to have sex with all of my boyfriends, and now that I know you have such thorough knowledge of her boobs, it's a fairly obvious conclusion."

"OK, I'll admit that I admired her boobs in her bikini, but that's what men do. We look at boobs, but it in no way implies that I had sex with her."

"Nice try, asshole, but I can see in your eyes that you're guilty."

I thought about closing them but knew that it would just be a dead giveaway. Unfortunately, I could tell by the tone of Lux's voice that she wasn't going to drop the subject, so I decided there was no reason to delay the inevitable any longer.

"OK fine, it happened, but I would like to clarify that she strolled into my room in the middle of the night and seduced me."

"Bullshit!"

"I'm absolutely serious, and what do you really have to complain about? I came halfway around the world to save your ass, only to find out that you married Corn."

"Oh, spare me, Finn! I thought that you of all people would be stronger. You're one of the good guys."

Now, that was mean. I was one of the good guys—or I used to be. Fuck. I didn't know what to think anymore.

"Look—it was a one-time thing. I was weak, and she took advantage of me, but, technically, this is all your fault anyway for sending her to my fucking doorstep!"

"I never thought in a million years that..."

I heard the main doors open, and I cut Lux off in mid sentence, pressing my finger to my lips in an effort to get her to stop talking. She glared angrily, but, thankfully, her practicality overruled my promiscuity, and she followed me off the dock and into the water.

"We're going to talk more about this later," she whispered, angrily.

Just then, I looked over Lux's shoulder and saw the new arrivals walking straight towards us, which meant the next shift had arrived. I had no time to warn her and, instead, pushed her head underwater, following her down an instant later. She must have thought I was pulling some kind of stunt, because she punched me in the ribs and almost knocked the wind out of me. I pointed up towards the men on the dock, and she thankfully understood. We swam around the pier, surfacing for air once we were well out of their view, and Lux looked as though she was about to continue our discussion, but, thankfully, we heard footsteps directly above us. That meant we needed to stay quiet—which was actually kind of a relief because it forced a temporary end to our rather uncomfortable argument. I'd forgotten about Lux's fiery temper, and sleeping with her sister was obviously a major point of contention. Still, it wasn't exactly all that fair and seemed like a textbook case of the kettle calling the pot black.

Meanwhile, my unlikely saviors were apparently having a cigarette, so I decided that it was as good a time as any to get the hell out of Dodge. I swam down and grabbed the remaining dive equipment that I had stowed below the pier, then we both donned our tanks and finns. Properly outfitted, we slipped silently below the surface, and I had her hold onto me as I hit the throttle on the aqua scooter. The thing took off quickly, but she held on tight, digging her hands into the flesh of my waist, perhaps a little harder than was necessary. Leave it to her to find such a creative way to relay her angry feelings. I hadn't even thought about how I was going to tell her about the night with Bridgette, and couldn't believe that I had stupidly blundered into it with that idiotic comment. So much had happened since that night, I had kind of forgotten about Bridgette. I was two girls removed after all and basically dating Estelle. Life was rarely simple—and always got complicated quickly when it involved the opposite sex.

The light from the chamber slowly faded as we entered the tunnel, and I turned my attention to the GPS screen, following the waypoints that I had entered on the way in. This allowed us to go a lot faster and make better time on the trip out, which must have been a little disorienting for Lux who had just traded a French holding cell for an undersea thrill ride through the dark. Every time a strange fish popped into the limited view of the lights, I could feel her body tense and her fingers dig deeper into my flesh. If we ran into anything as big as a shark, I was afraid that she might actually draw blood. It was hard to believe that this was the same woman who didn't think twice about flying into a maelstrom of enemy fire to save my ass, but I suppose everyone had their weaknesses—mine obviously being public restrooms.

We were almost out of the tunnel when we literally ran into that same Grouper, and, I could hear Lux's muffled scream as she dug her fingers into my flesh. I suspect that the large fish must live around here and find us an unwelcome nuisance to the peace of his aquatic home. He soon lost interest in us and swam off into the darkness, his departure making Lux relax her grip, though I was pretty sure I'd have bruises, if not scars, from the experience. We left the tunnel, and I killed the lights and navigated using the GPS. As we neared our final waypoint, I angled up, and we surfaced about ten feet from the ski boat to discover the two lovebirds casually drinking wine by candlelight.

"I sure hope there's still enough left over for us," I said.

Billings stood up and came to the rail.

"Don't worry—we've saved you the second bottle," he said, smiling as he reached down and hauled the aqua scooter aboard the boat.

We climbed out of the water and Billings came over and hugged Lux.

"How are you feeling?" he asked.

"Good, now that I'm out of there," she said.

"Nice job, Tag, I can't believe that you're already back!" Tiffany said, excitedly.

"It wasn't actually that difficult. They put all of their attention on the front of the Casino and forgot about the back door. Of course, all hell might break loose when they figure out that their security has been breached," I said.

"Hopefully we'll be long gone by then," Billings responded.

"We have to go back to the island," Lux said.

The ski boat became uncomfortably quiet as everyone looked at her.

"Um, excuse me?" I asked, desperately hoping I had heard her wrong.

"We have to go back."

"Why?" I asked.

"I hid something on the island before they captured me, and it can't fall back into their hands."

"What could possibly be that important?"

"Remember the missile launchers back in the chamber?"

"Yeah."

"Well, it's directly related to them and my mission here, and it was the thing I was going to tell you more about later."

"I'm all ears," I said.

"Well, as you already know, President Babineux makes the real money here by supplying arms, but he only came up on our radar about two years ago when it was rumored he was selling to some particularly unsavory clients. Then, about eight months back, the Agency received intel that he had a hundred million dollar deal in place to sell Russian shoulder-fired missiles to a number of terrorist groups, the most prevalent being ISIS and Al Qaeda. Apparently, they plan to simultaneously take out hundreds of targets in every major city across the world in what would be the single largest coordinated terrorist attack since September 11. So, the Agency sent me here six months ago with two objectives. The first was to infiltrate Babineux's organization and find out how it operated, while the second was to uncover the details of the upcoming arms deal, with the hope that we could learn who all the key players were and take them down long before the attack even occurred. As it stands now, all I've managed to do is delay the arms deal."

"Which is better than nothing."

"Yeah, but it doesn't do much for my spy self-esteem to have completed so little of my mission. Unfortunately, Babineux is a sneaky fucker and keeps everything tightly under wraps, so I still don't know much about his operation, who the buyers are, or even how the exchange is supposed to take place."

"So, what the hell went wrong?"

"Well, the deal got moved up, and I had to improvise a new plan. The money was thankfully arriving separately from the buyers, and I made sure I was the lucky pilot who flew it in from Martinique. Instead of delivering it directly to Babineux, I was just going to take it and leave the island, or so I thought, until I went back to my hotel to grab my things and discovered that Babineux's men were already waiting for me."

"Then, I'm guessing you must have had a major leak in your operation."

"Perhaps, but I have no idea who it might have been or how it occurred, so all I had time to do before they captured me was hide the money and send Bridgette to find you."

"At least I know you're still the same self-sacrificing badass who flew into overwhelming enemy fire to save John and me."

"I definitely don't feel badass. In fact, I feel more like a lame-ass."

"That's definitely not the case, but I am curious about something. Assuming we manage to get the money and keep it out of Babineux's hands, I don't see jihadists going home empty handed."

"That's probably true, but I know Babineux. He's a shrewd businessman, and as long as he doesn't get hold of the money, there won't be any kind of exchange—at least not in the short term, anyway. So, at this point, I suppose it's all about damage control."

In my opinion, damage control was pretty much the same as eating a shit sandwich, and nobody liked eating a shit sandwich. I, therefore, took a minute to think about Lux's mission and our resulting situation. I didn't have a lot of sympathetic feelings for the Agency, but this wasn't about my feelings. This was about terrorism and the safety of the free world. If lives were at stake, then it was my duty to help, and that help would be a lot more meaningful if it also facilitated completing Lux's mission—hopefully in its entirety. I sat there ruminating for a moment, and my gaze unintentionally fell upon the *Sarsarun*. It was lit up like a Christmas tree, and a lone man was standing on the deck smoking a cigarette. It was about time someone stirred on that fucking yacht. Suddenly, there was a little itch of a thought forming in my mind, and to scratch it, I gazed towards shore then back to the *Sarsarun*. At that moment, I felt instant relief for that itch had been scratched and in its place was an epiphany. We already had all we needed to know about Babineux, his operation, and the fucking arms deal.

"Fuck the shit sandwich!" I said, aloud.

"Excuse me?" Lux asked, taken aback by my outburst.

"I said, fuck the shit sandwich!"

"I know what you said, but what the hell does it mean?"

"Resorting to damage control is like taking a big old bite of a shit sandwich, but we're not going to eat that fucking sandwich, because once we have the money back in our hot little hands, we will have completed your mission—in its entirety."

"That sounds great, but I'm still not exactly sure how we're avoiding the shit sandwich."

"Everything we need to know is right here in front of our eyes. Now, let me start by asking you how long the *Sarsarun* has been here?"

"It came to the island last week, two days before they caught me, and, before you say what I know you're going to say, let me tell you that the boat is owned by a close and loyal friend of the Saudi Royal Family."

"Saudi? Well, then it makes even more sense. Trust me, that's your missile buyer."

"It's racial profiling."

"It's common sense. You wanted to know how Babineux is conducting business with his clients here, well, hello—we just swam out his supply route. And while I was in the chamber, I also happened to check out those little submarines. They're essentially underwater cargo ships, and, based on the battery level gauge, they only have a range of about five nautical miles, which means the buyers have to get close—basically this cove."

"But, I'm telling you—we already checked out the yacht's owner. He's squeaky clean, has absolutely no terrorist ties, and, beyond that, the guy is completely pro America."

"I don't care if he has an American flag tattooed across both butt cheeks and shoots out anti-microbial soap when he yanks his doodle dandy. We're sitting at a Goddamn drive through window. Babineux's clients just pull up, anchor, and out comes their order of shoulder-fired missile launchers with a side of authentically French fries. They do the whole thing under the cover of darkness, and no one's the wiser. Of course, the icing on this cake of intrigue is the timing. You said the deal got moved ahead of schedule, which means your buyers had already arrived, coincidentally, about the same time as the *Sarsarun*—and what better way is there to transport your missile launchers off the island than on a yacht owned by a guy who can pass CIA muster?"

Lux's gaze went from me to the yacht and back, at which point she stood up and slapped the side of the boat.

"Goddammit, Finn! It's so obvious, it's embarrassing, and even more so because it's been right in front of us the whole time."

"Well, to be fair, you hadn't yet seen his underground weapons storage facility and delivery tunnel."

"Yeah, but someone at Langley should have looked more closely at the yacht's owner."

"Unfortunately, that's one of the major problems the Agency has with intelligence gathering—context. The analyst who looked at the yacht's owner was back at Langley staring at data on a screen, while we were out here floating between the yacht in question and an arms dealer's secret delivery tunnel. It's not all that surprising they missed the connection, and this is why, back in my Agency days, I worked with my two close friends and fellow agents, Doug and Justin, to circumvent this very problem by combining intelligence gathering and analysis with the action wing to maximize communication and create an unusually effective little unit we called the *Three Amigos*."

"So, Estelle was right when she said a guy with your background would go into the CIA," Tiffany said.

"Afraid so."

"Holy shit! You were one of the *Three Amigos*?" Lux asked.

"Well, we were three guys who worked for the Agency that called ourselves the *Three Amigos*, but I seriously doubt you've heard of us. Few people knew about our team, and everything we did was obviously top secret."

"What you did might have been top secret, but the Agency likes to celebrate its wins, so rumors of your exploits trickled down through the ranks. There were never any explicit details or names, so most of us assumed it was just bullshit to bolster Agency pride."

"I'm sure there was plenty of bullshit, but the *Three Amigos* actually did exist."

"Jesus, Finn, if those stories were even close to the truth, then you three were doing a lot of good."

"Well, we certainly tried."

"You did a lot more than try, and I have to say that, in spite of not having your two other amigos along on this one, you did one hell of a nice job here as well."

"Don't forget the fact that I had help. I only found the tunnel because of your guy John Parker and his friend John Livingston, and let's face it, I was here for you—and not to uncover some international terrorist plot."

"Well, lucky for everyone, you managed to do it all."

Lux smiled and put her hand on my thigh, and I felt that tingling that you always experienced from the touch of a beautiful woman. Ten years and I was still as smitten as a twelve year old boy with his first crush. How annoying.

"Jesus, if I hadn't intercepted the hundred million, those missile launchers would already be on board that yacht and on their way to their targets."

"Wait a minute—a hundred million dollars? That wouldn't even fit on a semi-truck. There's no way in hell you could have hidden that much money!"

"It's not in actual dollars. It's in rare gems—rubies, emeralds, diamonds, and it's all in an attaché case that we have to go pick up."

"Where did you hide it?" I asked.

"Right under his nose."

"Then I can only assume that French fuck has one hell of a mustache."

"Afraid not, for the real hiding place is the coatcheck of his nightclub," she said, proudly.

"Are you fucking kidding me? A hundred million in gems in a coat check?"

"Yep. I figured no one in the world would ever think to look there."

Actually, it was a pretty clever hiding place.

"Assuming it's still there, do you even have your ticket?"

She unzipped her wetsuit then reached into the front of her bra and pulled out a tiny rolled up piece of paper that she had hidden in the cup. She unrolled it and showed me what was indeed the damp ticket stub in question.

"What self-respecting Frenchmen wouldn't bother to remove a woman's bra?" I asked.

"Babineux, apparently."

"Well, then it's a good thing it wasn't me that captured you, because your bra would have been the first thing I removed."

"Followed by my underwear I imagine."

"Without a doubt, and say what you will about me—I'm extremely thorough."

"I'd have to agree," Tiffany added.

"Well, shit, Pete—I guess we're going back to the island."

CHAPTER NINETEEN
Nights of Future Past

Billings started the boat while I went to the bow and pulled up the anchor, and I wasn't even back to my seat when he throttled up and sent me flying into the open spot next to Lux. I saw the second bottle of wine in the picnic basket and uncorked it and offered it to Lux. She gratefully accepted it and took a long pull before handing it back, so that I could have a drink. We sat there sharing the rest of the wine and enjoying the ride, until she abruptly leaned in close so that I could hear her over the noise of the boat and wind.

"Thank you," she said, before kissing me.

It was kind of bittersweet, and we shared a momentary smile, in spite of the fact that I was still a little irked about the whole Corn thing. Of course, she was probably still mad about her sister, but I suppose we had much bigger problems to worry about at the moment than our interpersonal relationship woes. We raced up the western shore of the island, and it wasn't until we reached the main bay that we encountered other boats that were still ferrying passengers back and forth between the yachts and the island's nightlife. Billings slowed down as we entered the heavier boat traffic, and he was forced to weave through the various yachts and their tenders before going to the same area where I had made my parasailing entrance the night before. He throttled back and brought us down to idling speed so that we could talk.

"So, how do you want to do this, Lux?" he asked.

"Well, they only patrol this area until around nine p.m., so we should be fine just hopping over the breakwater and swimming ashore, though we have another more practical concern, namely my outfit. The nightclub is fairly casual, but I doubt a wetsuit will be appropriate."

"I've got your skirt and dress shirt in my gear bag."

"Yeah, those would be fine except for the whole swimming part."

"Don't worry—I've got you covered, Lux. I always pack an extra bikini in case I go swimming, and, as I have absolutely no intention of diving into a dark ocean, it's yours if you want it," Tiffany said, as she reached into the picnic basket and pulled out the extra swimsuit.

"Thanks! I'll take it!"

Tiffany handed it over, then Lux struggled out of her wetsuit, leaving her clothed in only a bra and underwear. Fortunately, the darkness provided her a moderate amount of modesty as she stripped down in the small space of the boat and proceeded to slip on the bikini. I, of course, once again found myself entranced as I watched the entire process, and could now see, even in the minimal light of the partial moon, that the suit was a perfect fit and made quite a show of her curvaceous figure.

"Aren't you going to change?" Lux asked, breaking me from my stupor.

"Um—yeah, I was just busy finishing up my usual pre-mission meditation."

"Really? Because it pretty much looked as though you were just staring at my boobs."

"Obviously, that's how I get into the zone."

"Well, now that you're in the zone, why don't you do something useful and get out of that wetsuit."

I shimmied out of my wetsuit then grabbed my T-shirt and sat beside her while Billings steered us towards the breakwater.

"After you drop us off you might want to wait a little farther offshore in case they have any unexpected late patrols," Lux said.

Billings stopped the boat right at the breakwater, and Lux and I jumped over then gave him a parting wave, before making our way to the beach. Upon hitting dry land, I slid on my T-shirt, and we headed for the hotel entrance. Only a few steps into our journey, Lux stopped walking then looked over at me with an oddly curious expression on her face.

"What is it?" I asked.

"Did you also hook up with Tiffany?"

"Where in the hell did that come from?"

"I couldn't help but notice the way she responded to your comment about being thorough."

"Being thorough? Seriously? How could that in any way infer we hooked up?"

"I think it's pretty obvious, especially considering that fact that you're new hobby is apparently bedding every woman you meet? Now, why don't you stop stalling and come clean?"

How in the hell could Lux have possibly come up with that little insight? I only got together with Tiffany once, and it was just a rebound thing—more like a mutual kindness between two people who had suffered a similar relationship fate. Fucking Lux had more powerful radar than an E-2C Hawkeye early warning aircraft, and if she'd been this focused on her Soft Taco Island mission, then she'd probably already be back at Langley, celebrating another Agency win with her Deputy Director asshole husband.

"Well?" she asked.

"Well what? It's a ridiculous question, because she's Pete's girlfriend."

"That's not what I asked. I asked if you hooked up with her—

past tense."

"This is neither the time nor place for this discussion, and, honestly, my private life is not your concern anymore."

"So, you're basically admitting that you had sex with her."

"I'm not even going to justify that comment with a response."

Lux stood there, sadly shaking her head side to side as she looked at me.

"Oh, come on!" I said.

"You want to know something, Tag? I have thought about you every day for the last ten years, and you know why? Because you were the best man I ever knew."

"And didn't marry."

She regarded me icily for a moment.

"Irrespective of that one little, insignificant fact..."

"Are you seriously calling marriage an insignificant little fact?"

"In this instance, yes. Now, I want you to know that it hurts me more than you could ever imagine to find out that the man I fell in love with, the man that I've thought about all these years, has become some kind of—fucking—man-whore."

Wonderful. Now even Lux was using that term.

"Look, I've lived a nice quiet monogamous life until a week ago. I'm sorry I've gotten together with a few girls over the last six days, but the one girl I really wanted took off ten years ago and married my best friend."

"I didn't take off, and you didn't know that we were married until an hour ago."

"Whatever, jezebel."

"Whatever, man-whore."

Neither of us spoke as we climbed up the steps and walked through the outdoor bar, passing the few remaining patrons before entering the hotel. The thumping sound of bass-heavy dance music was spilling into the lobby and growing louder as we drew closer to the nightclub. I hazarded a quick glance at Lux only to receive yet another disapproving shake of her head. Ten years apart and we were bickering like a couple that had spent twenty years together. Sure, I had more than my fair share of relations with the opposite sex as of late, but it still didn't seem fair. I was living life as I always had, yet, somehow, the sex-time continuum had been knocked off balance and was throwing beautiful women my way at a breakneck pace. Perhaps fate had decided it was time for me to catch up after all these years.

"Alrighty then, Jugs. Where's the coat check?" I asked.

"Inside the nightclub and over on the lefthand side."

We continued on towards the entrance to find it was bustling with people coming and going, most of them drunk and all of them happy. There was also a security guard scrutinizing the guests, but he seemed less interested in looking for potential dangers than he did ogling the beautiful women. His eyes would go from face to bustline to butt with each female patron who passed. He didn't give the men a second glance, though who could blame him?

"So, we just go in and get it?" I asked.

"Yeah, assuming you haven't had any trouble on the island that might give them a reason to be looking for you."

"Well, I did have a little incident over at the casino, where I ended up knocking out a couple of security guys, but it wasn't a big deal."

"Not a big deal? These assholes won't forget something like that, which means we're going to have to do our best to keep you off the radar if we hope to get this done as quickly and quietly as possible."

"You don't want to dance or maybe grab a drink at the bar for old times' sake?"

"No."

Lux served as my human shield as we moved past the door guard, and, as expected, he spent his time eyeing her curves instead of mine, allowing us to slip into the nightclub without incident. The coat check was, as Lux said, over on the left side while directly ahead was the dance floor and bar. Fortunately for us, the place was crowded and dark, the only light coming from the disco ball and the gigantic screen on the other side of the room. We continued on towards our destination, and it was like trying to move through controlled chaos as people all around danced to the pulsing music, the entire place appearing to undulate like a giant sea anemone in a tidal zone. Suddenly, in the chaos of moving bodies, I was staring at two faces I recognized, and there, directly in front of us, were none other than Isabella and Monique.

"Well, hello again, Tag. Care for a dance?" Isabella asked.

"I'd love one, but I'm afraid I'll have to take a raincheck, as I'm here on official business again."

"Too bad."

"Yeah, it is too bad, but, hopefully I'll run into you some time when I'm not actually working."

"Let's hope so."

"Absolutely, now I'm afraid we must bid you adieu. Cheers, ladies."

"Cheers, Tag," Isabella and Monique said at the exact same time.

We continued on our way, and I could already feel Lux's eyes burning a hole in my head. Running into Isabella and Monique right after our little Tiffany argument was unbelievably bad timing, so I decided it was probably a good thing to clarify that last exchange.

"For the record, Isabella and Monique are just acquaintances."

Just then, Isabella came dashing through the crowd and caught up to us.

"Hey, if you manage to get free later, do you still remember our room number?"

"One-twenty-nine," I responded, without thinking.

She smiled and headed back into the crowd, and I turned to find Lux once again regarding me with utter disdain.

"Acquaintances indeed, man-whore," she grumbled.

We continued on to the coat check and got in the line behind a young couple who were probably from Spain, judging by what I could hear of their accents. We patiently waited our turn, passing the time by watching the spectacle of drunken people, until Lux abruptly tensed and took hold of my arm.

"Oh shit, there are two security guys walking towards us, and they're looking right at you," she said.

"Fuckinzee! What should we do?"

"We need to hide your face. I've got an idea."

She pushed me against the wall and kissed me, as I suppose it was the fastest, easiest way to obscure my face. It worked perfectly, and the two guys moved past us, but the kiss didn't stop after they were out of view. It continued, and now our lips were entwined in an epic battle, our tongues the foot soldiers that met head on at the front line, and what started as a clever ruse became something real and passionate, once again transporting me back ten years to that airfield in Afghanistan. A floodgate of emotion had officially been opened, and I found myself reaching out and pulling her into my arms—only to feel her join my efforts by pressing her hips against mine. My head was clouded with desire, and there were so many things I wanted to touch, that I had to split my attention by moving my left hand down to her buttocks, while I slipped my right up her stomach and under her bikini top. There, I played my finger tips over one breast then the other, feeling her nipples instantly harden at my touch as though there were electric shocks of sexual energy arcing between our bodies. The longer we remained in contact, the more frantic our yearning became, and it wasn't long before she slid her hands down into my shorts and started stroking my manhood, her efforts making it swell and grow hard. We were completely oblivious to the world around us and on the cusp of making sweet love right there on the spot—that is, until we heard the coat check girl say the words next, please. Sweet forces of foreplay—it was like waking up from a really awesome sex dream only to find yourself in the middle of an anxiety dream. We pulled away from each other and shared an embarrassed smile before stepping up to the counter to find the girl behind it was extremely pretty and, judging by her nordic features, most likely, Scandinavian. Her gaze went from my eyes to my privates and back, a smile forming on her lips in response to the obvious hard-on pressing angrily against my shorts.

"How are you this evening?" she asked, her accent clearly Swedish.

"I'm very happy, obviously, as I've been named Viagra's spokesmodel of the year."

"They've obviously chosen the right man for the job. Now, how can I help you this evening? Did you need me to perhaps check your package?" she asked, smiling and raising an eyebrow as she gazed at me.

"I'm afraid we're actually here to pick-up. You see, my friend left her package in the coat check a few nights ago, and I'll be even happier than I am right now if you've still got it."

"Well, then I certainly hope I can find it. Do you still have your ticket?"

"I do," Lux said, as she handed it over.

The girl disappeared into the back, and Lux and I shared several nervous glances until the girl finally reappeared carrying a metal attaché case.

"I found your—other—package," she said, as she placed it on the counter.

"*Underbar! Tack så mycket!*" I said, which was Swedish for wonderful, thank you very much.

"*Varsågod*. Now, are you sure there aren't any more packages that I can help you with?" the girl asked, with a little wink.

Lux didn't say it out loud, but I was pretty sure she was silently chastising me for being a man-whore. Oh well, it was better to live dangerously than not at all. I realized, however, that it was time to give my lovely Swedish coat check girl a tip and, luckily, had some cash on me and handed over a wad of damp money. She picked it up and smiled as she cast another glance at my throbbing gentleman sausage.

"Thank you, sir, that's quite a lovely—tip," she said.

"My pleasure, though I would have liked to have given you more. Unfortunately, that's all I've got at the moment."

"Oh, I'd say it's more than enough," she said, with a saucy smile.

"Time to go, man-whore," Lux said, as she took hold of my arm and dragged me away from the counter.

"*Adjö*," I called out over my shoulder, which meant goodbye in Swedish.

I kept the case in front of me to hide my hard-on, then quickly swerved around to the opposite side of Lux just as we passed by the front door security man. He completely ignored me and, better still, couldn't take his eyes off of Lux's very hard nipples. He could thank me for that. We went through the lobby and headed back to the beach, the deep thump of the bass fading with each step we took away from the hotel. It felt good to be out of the heat and noise of the nightclub and back into the cool, quiet night air. We walked down onto the sand, and Lux stopped and sat on the adjacent sea wall, which happened to have some extremely conspicuous tire tracks leading off the edge.

"It looks as though some idiot drove off of here," she said.

"Fucking tourists," I said, leaving out the fact that I was the fucking tourist in question.

Lux was looking oddly introspective and took a moment to collect her thoughts before speaking.

"I'm sorry about what happened back there," she said.

"Sorry about what? I wasn't exactly fighting you off."

"Seeing you again just brings up so many feelings."

"Believe me—I completely understand."

"I still can't help but wonder if things had been different."

"I know. I think about it too. In fact, I've thought about it every day for the last ten years."

I stood there in the quiet solitude of the night staring at Lux, when a question came to mind that I'd been wanting to ask since the final moment we parted in Afghanistan.

"The morning when they were flying me out of Bagram, you paused at the bottom of the plane's ramp and looked as though you wanted to say something. What was it?"

Lux's demeanor changed, her gaze uncomfortable and looking a lot like it did on that day oh so many years ago.

"Why does it matter now?" she asked.

"It doesn't, but I'd still like to know."

She let out a sigh as her gaze drifted skyward, her thoughts apparently a million miles away. After a moment of quiet reflection, she looked back at me, apparently having resolved herself to answer.

"I was going to tell you I love you."

I felt my heart leap out of my chest as all the years of unresolved feelings poured from my mind and filled my body with an odd mixture of relief and regret.

"Fuck. If you'd said it, I would have told you I loved you too."

"That's what I was afraid of, but, as it is, we're long past that time, so none of it matters anymore."

"I know, but it would have mattered back then, and could have made a big difference. Sometimes words lead to actions, and things between us might have turned out differently."

"Perhaps," she said, looking sincerely conflicted.

An awkward silence ensued as we pondered this latest revelation.

"Well, I suppose I should radio Billings," I said.

I pulled out the radio, and, was about to call him, but Lux placed her hand on my forearm.

"Let's not call just yet."

She reached out and pulled me into her arms and looked at me nervously, her heart visibly pounding in her chest as she considered her next words.

"I want to do something we never got to do. Let's pretend it's 2005, and we're back in Afghanistan. The way I see it, the world stole that moment from us, and I want to take it back—just this once," she said.

"We don't have a lot of time or privacy."

"We'll make it fast and discreet."

She pulled me down into her arms and kissed me, and again, I felt those same deep feelings boiling up to the surface of my consciousness. With each passing second, my yearning grew stronger until the years melted away, and we slipped into our own private fold in time. Our kisses were harried, our hands moving frantically over each other's bodies, and every lonely moment I dreamt of holding Lux in my arms was now mine to realize. I pulled off her bathing suit top and took hold of her breasts before leaning down and kissing them, feeling each nipple harden under the firm tutelage of my tongue. Not one to linger, I traveled up and kissed her neck before returning to her lips only to feel her hands slip down my chest and pull off my shorts. My manhood was now standing proudly in the wind, and she began running her fingers up and down its length. I was soon on the cusp of release and, in order to sustain the moment, decided it was time for a little quid pro quo. As I pulled free and slid off her bathing suit bottom, she tried to steer my manhood between her legs, but I resisted her efforts and dropped to my knees.

"What are you doing? I thought we didn't have much time," she said.

"When it counts, a good man will make time."

"But..."

"But, nothing. The way I see it, this is only going to happen once, and, after ten years of fantasizing about this moment, I plan to make the most of it. Now, you might want to brace yourself."

She leaned back on the sea wall and looked ever so subtly nervous as I dragged my lips down across her stomach before reaching her great divide. I could feel her heart start to race as I used my tongue to survey the region, tracing the outer dimensions of her essence before traveling straight up the middle to find my destination. She immediately gasped and arched her back, and, in order to steady her hips, I reached around, took hold of her buttocks, and pulled her pelvis to my mouth, making her clitoris a virtual prisoner to the whim of my tongue. I slid up, down, over, and around it until Lux's frantic cries filled the night.

"Oh fuck! Oh fuck! Oh my fucking God!" she screamed.

I had barely reached my stride when she violently and unexpectedly climaxed, her body shaking uncontrollably until the wave of pleasure passed, and I withdrew my mouth. In the following silence, we both took a quick look around to make sure we were still alone.

"Sweet mother of cunnilingus! That was fast and loud, and not exactly discreet," I said

"Give me a break. I've spent ten years fantasizing about this moment, and I had no idea you were going to be so fucking good with your tongue."

"You know, I can't help but wonder if now might be the time to voice any regrets you might have concerning your choice of husband."

"It is absolutely not fair to ask me that right now, so, unless you want this little time bubble to pop, you better stop talking and start fucking my brains out."

"OK, but, as I'm more of a romantic, I prefer to think that I'm making sweet love to you until your head explodes."

"Whatever it takes," she said, as she pulled me in close and kissed me.

She was obviously done talking, for she reached down and took hold of my tiller and steered me into her port. I pressed all the way in to the hilt, and the pleasure was enough to part our lips as we both uttered a soft moan. This inspired Lux to form a more perfect union by wrapping her legs around my back. We took it slow and savored every second, Lux pulling my hips to hers, while I added a counter clockwise motion at the apex of each thrust to ensure that her clitoris received ample attention. It was the glorious coupling I had always imagined, and every second of contact was making me fall deeper into the madness of lust, our ten years apart transforming every moment of longing into pure action.

"Oh my God! Why in the hell did we wait so long?" Lux muttered, breathlessly.

"Oh, sweet Lord! I don't know!"

On we went in our magical time bubble, our growing desire inspiring us to quicken our pace and move ever closer to climax. Riding on the fine line between bliss and release, we finally lost ourselves to the chaos of pleasure.

"Oh fuck! I can't hold back any longer!" she screamed, breathlessly.

"Me neither! I'll see you on the other side!"

I joined her, and we came together in all ways, passing through sweet climax and into coital nirvana. At long last, we stopped and held each other in the stillness of the night. Ten years had to come to pass in only minutes, and there we were, back in the present, alone on a beach in the Caribbean.

"That was a long time coming."

"So to speak," I responded.

She smiled, but she had the obvious look of uncertainty in her eyes. That was the downside of an unexpected tryst—dealing with the aftermath.

"So, how do we move forward without this being awkward?" she asked.

"I suppose we just go back to the future and finish your mission."

"Yeah, I suppose that's all we can do."

Lux thought for a moment and appeared to reach some kind of resolution.

"Finn, can you promise me that this will be our little secret?"

I thought about Estelle and how unfair it would be to keep this from her, and it instantly made me feel guilty and conflicted. I, therefore, decided to take the diplomatic route and selectively agree to Lux's request.

"Well, I'm certainly not going to tell Corn about any of this."

"Good. I know this situation is a little complicated. There are obviously some unresolved feelings between you and me, but Corn is my husband, and I love him, so, I obviously don't want him to get hurt."

"It's OK, I understand."

"Thank you."

"Yeah, so, I suppose it's time to call Billings," I said, as I pulled out the Radio.

"Pete? You there, over?"

He responded immediately, the worry obvious in his voice.

"Are you two OK? We heard some screaming."

"Yeah, we're fine. It was probably just a couple of mating sea lions."

Lux proceeded to give me a firm backhand to the ribs.

"It didn't sound like mating sea lions, but I guess it doesn't matter as long as you two are OK," Billings responded.

"Yeah, we're OK and ready for a pickup," I said, as I rubbed the spot where she'd slugged me.

"Head on out, we're coming in."

We could hear the boat idling closer as we made our way out to the breakwater. Billings and Tiffany arrived a moment later, then we climbed over and into the cockpit, and Billings handed us each a towel.

"We got it," I said, patting the case.

"Fan-fucking-tastic."

"Hard to believe you're holding a hundred million dollars," Tiffany said, excitedly.

"I know, and it's probably the first, last, and only time it'll ever happen."

We took a seat, and Billings throttled up, leaving the breakwater behind as we headed off across the bay and towards the *Sozo*. It was yet another perfect Caribbean night, the moon lighting our way as we moved over the dark, calm water. We were soon slowing down and idling around to the boat deck, where, strangely, there was no one to greet us.

"I wonder where Kip is?" I asked, secretly wondering if he was off taking a shit on my pillow.

"I radioed and told them all the good news, so I imagine he and the others are probably already celebrating our successful mission," he said.

I jumped aboard and tied off the lines, then Lux grabbed the attaché case, and the four of us headed up the aft stairs to find no one frolicking on the stern deck. Obviously, they must have taken the party inside, but, when we entered the main salon, everyone was sitting around quietly, and not even Brett was smiling.

"What's up? You all look so glum. We should be celebrating!"

"I agree," came a man's voice bearing a distinctly French accent.

I looked to where the voice originated, and, there, sitting at the bar, I spied a man in a finely tailored white linen suit. He was good-looking and had a shaggy mane of dark hair that made him look like a soap opera hunk, though it was his bearing that was his most unique feature. He oozed smugness and had a distinguished confidence that gave me the impression he was a man who was used to getting what he wanted, and I, of course, recognized the fucker immediately. He stepped down off his stool and walked over, so I drew both of my pistols and aimed them at his groin.

"Interesting choice of target," he said.

"I find a man responds more readily when he has a couple of pistols aimed at his Bilbo and Baggins."

"Indeed, Monsieur Finn, but I'm afraid it's a little late for that," he said, as he snapped his fingers.

Apparently, it was a signal, because Soft Taco Island security men came rushing into the room, four from behind us, and four from the far door. Apparently, this was an extremely clever and well-executed trap. Lovely.

"I suggest you drop your weapons and remove your tactical vest," he said.

I did as instructed, and one of the nearby men scooped them up then stepped back to give some space to the man in charge.

"It's nice to finally meet you, President Babineux," I said.

"Oh, the pleasure is all mine, but let's keep it informal, and, please, just call me Mr. President."

At least he had a sense humor.

"How about *Monsieur Con?*" I suggested, which basically meant Mr. Asshole in French.

He smiled.

"Mr. President will be fine. Now, I must say—I really can't thank you enough for bringing me back my jewels. Speaking of which, would you mind?" he asked, as he pointed at the attaché case in Lux's hand.

One of his men came over, and Lux, to her credit, didn't give it up easily, and the guy had to work pretty hard to twist it free from her grasp. He immediately handed it over to Babineux, and, while our favorite French president took a second to inspect its contents, I decided to have a look around and see how everyone was holding up. Most of the *Sozo's* crewmembers appeared to be scared, though Brett and Kip looked oddly composed considering the situation. Estelle, however, seemed more pensive than frightened. I gave her a reassuring nod, but it didn't seem to help, which was understandable, as it was never a fun experience being held at gunpoint. Babineux closed the case then smiled and turned his attention back to me.

"Mr. Finn, might I say, you have proved to be both a formidable enemy and a tremendous help."

"I guess I'm complicated that way. Now, do you mind explaining what the hell you mean by that statement?"

"Not at all. You see, when Lux refused to tell me what happened to my case, I really wasn't sure what to do. She is strong willed and torturing her would have taken weeks."

"Months," Lux interjected, angrily.

"Perhaps, but then I learned that a man with—how do you say—exceptional qualifications was coming to rescue her."

I guess his intel wasn't that great, as I hardly considered finding lost cats and taking pictures of adulterous spouses as exceptional, but he was French, and, therefore, might have a different opinion on the matter.

"Suddenly, I had a new problem, and I must admit that the way you dealt with my men on Martinique had me worried. In spite of what you may think, they were highly trained operatives and you made them look like idiots."

"Only because they were idiots."

"They are now. After your little—stunt."

Lux looked at me accusingly, obviously wondering what the hell I had done. I responded with an innocent shrug, but it didn't appear to assail her fears. Thankfully, Babineux continued speaking, inadvertently giving me a reprieve from Lux's scrutiny.

"I, therefore, came up with a new plan which was to just sit back and let you do what you do. I didn't even warn any of my men, because I wanted to make sure it appeared legitimate so that you wouldn't get suspicious and figure out it was a trap. Once you rescued Lux, I knew she would take you right to the missing attache case. Excellent job, Mr. Finn! You went against all my Island security and still managed to rescue your girlfriend and get the jewels."

"Ex-girlfriend, and, unfortunately, I didn't manage to keep those jewels out of your grubby little French fingers," I said.

"Either way, you are a man of extraordinary talents."

"Well, thank you, though I can't say the same about a man who is willing to supply terrorists with the tools to kill innocent people."

"Everyone needs to make a living. Now, I am afraid we must get going, and I'll be taking some of you with me to the island as a precaution."

Billings, who was just behind me, stepped forward.

"If you hurt any member of this crew..."

"It's quite all right, Captain. There is no need to get excited. Your crew has not been harmed, nor will they be. I have my property, so you will only be detained until I can complete my business. Now, who shall we bring along?" he said, aloud, as he looked around the room.

He pointed at me, then Lux, Billings, Brett, Tiffany, Estelle, and finally Kip. Goddammit! Why Kip? Perhaps he sensed that it would annoy me and did it out of spite for calling him Mr. Asshole. He left the rest of our crew under armed guard in the main salon then led us out onto the rear deck.

"Where the hell is Bridgette?" Lux asked, angrily.

"She's already there," Babineux said.

"The casino?"

"No, my official residence. Do you think me uncivilized? You are special guests of the president, now."

He continued walking, and we were all made to follow him down to the boat deck, where, out in the darkness I could hear a boat approaching and soon saw the *Sozo's* official tender coming alongside. Strangely, I hadn't noticed it was gone until now, and I looked at Billings and was pretty sure he was thinking the same thing, which made me wonder if perhaps all the rum was impairing our cognitive abilities.

We loaded into the boat along with Babineux's men, and it got crowded fast with all of us crammed in like cattle. We pulled away from the larger yacht, and the powerful twin engines of the tender strained against the excess weight of the extra passengers. Still, the boat soldiered on towards shore, the night just as beautiful, though it no longer had the same magic when you were stuffed into a cockpit with a bunch of heavily armed French mercenaries smelling of garlic and red wine. We docked a few minutes later, and I finally got to see what I had managed to avoid thus far—the official Soft Taco Island port of entry. It was actually quite nice and looked more like a glorified yacht harbor. There was a main pier in the center, and around it extended a number of smaller docks where the visiting vessels could tie up and unload their passengers. Up at the top resided a turnstile and a little kiosk where guests checked in on their way ashore. Beyond that was a restaurant with a deck that sat on the water's edge. During normal hours, they probably had beautiful women in tiny little bikinis to greet all the guests with leis—or did they only do that on the islands in the Pacific? Either way, I didn't care as I had already gotten my lei on the island tonight.

We went past the check-in and there were three small vehicles waiting for us on the pier. They were similar to the truck Estelle and I had driven the day before, except that they had two extra rows of seating instead of a flatbed. We were all separated and seated amongst Babineux's security men who remained ever watchful with their weapons at the ready. Babineux gave a signal, and the little caravan set off along the access road. The first landmark to come into view was the casino, and, soon thereafter, we passed the distillery. A short distance later, we turned right and headed east across the interior of the island until coming to a little three way intersection with a guardhouse. The gates were up and a lone guard waved us through, allowing us to continue on into some densely forested foothills. The going was mostly straight except for a section with some sharp curves that eventually led to an uphill grade. We were obviously getting close to Babineux's residence, as it sat on the high bluff on the southern tip of the island. Sure enough, we came around a final turn, and there, bathed in dramatic lighting, was the presidential palace. It was quite a sight with three of its four stories visible from this side, and, while I had originally thought it was basic white, I could now see it was painted more of a light eggshell color. Combine that with the architectural style and it looked more like the imaginary home of some children's story book Raja. Sadly, our story was more adult in nature and would probably have lots of violence and, hopefully, sex before it was over.

We entered the official compound, and passed a smaller structure that was probably for staff, then the road looped around and formed a circular driveway. In the middle of that circle was a manicured garden and lawn along with a tall white flagpole, and, looking up at the official flag of Soft Taco Island, I had to laugh. The main body was light blue, but in the center was a taco shaped wedge with three vertical stripes in the colors of the French flag—namely blue, white and red. Classy. It was a perfect metaphor for the island itself—a little touch of France in the middle of the Caribbean.

They led us through the front door, and I found the place was even more spectacular on the inside. The foyer had twenty-foot ceilings, white marble floors, and a custom embroidered circular rug with the same graphic as the flag. On the wall to the right was a painted portrait of Babineux looking particularly pompous and stately as he posed with some grey colored hunting dogs. We continued on into the spacious living room to find it had a lovely terra cotta colored tile floor and was furnished with white throw rugs and plush leather couches and chairs. On the main wall resided an enormous fireplace that added generous portions of majesty to the room, though I'm sure it saw little use in the hot Caribbean climate. The other walls were, of course, covered with an array of paintings, while sculptures dotted the various shelves and tables. My eyes were suddenly drawn away from the artworks and over to the arrival of two absolutely stunning women. They were tall and had beautiful dark skin and supple figures, and even better was the fact that they were carrying trays loaded with glasses of Soft Taco Island rum.

"Please enjoy a taste of the island's finest export," Babineux said.

When one of the girls approached, I got a close look at the bottle on the tray. It was the same stuff Estelle and I had gotten from John Stanton back at *Le Cochon Ivre*, which meant President Babineux served only the very best to his so-called guests. He might have been an asshole, but at least he was both a gracious and particularly generous asshole.

"Hello, I'm Tag," I said, gazing into the rum girl's deep, dark sparkling brown eyes.

"Hello, Tag, I'm Camille," the girl responded, with a distinctly French accent, as she smiled and handed me a glass of rum.

"Thank you," I said.

"You're welcome, though I must say that I'm sorry you are here under such circumstances."

"Is this an unusual occurrence?"

"Yes, as no one has ever arrived at gun point before, and those who do come here are generally only his wealthy friends, dignitaries, or celebrities."

"Well, I'm definitely not in any of those categories, but I suppose I should feel lucky that I get to sip his rum and hang out with you."

Camille smiled.

"I would have to agree," she said, picking up a glass off the tray and clinking it to mine before taking a sip.

At that moment, Babineux moved to the center of the room and smiled warmly as he raised his glass to toast.

"You come as strangers, but may you leave as friends," he said.

He was the consummate politician, and, even as he held us at gunpoint, he still offered the illusion that this was all just another state function. I sipped my rum and enjoyed the brief respite it provided as it tickled my palette and slipped down my throat—every second making me feel oddly comforted in spite of our situation. Camille stayed nearby and refilled my glass whenever she saw that it was empty, and I was getting the feeling this incarceration might not be so bad. I've certainly been in worse places. I sensed movement and turned to see Lux looking mildly perturbed as she joined me.

"What is it?" I asked.

"You don't have to enjoy yourself so much."

"I'm biding my time."

"Really? You look like you're just getting drunk and flirting with the rum girl."

"We all bide differently, and I'm just trying to appear to be acquiescing in order to lure them into a false sense of complacency."

She grumbled and went back to sipping her drink, so I decided to put a little distance between myself and her scrutiny, and walked over to join Estelle. She tried to smile, but I think the craziness of the night was starting to wear on her.

"It's going to be OK. I promise," I said.

"I know, and if anyone can get us out of this, it's you."

"Then why do you seem so uneasy?"

"I'm not uneasy—I'm just curious how it went with Lux tonight."

Shit. Could she somehow sense in my demeanor that I had been copulating with Lux on the beach? Did I smell of sex, sand, and guilt, and, if so, how could she be more worried about potential matters of the heart and flesh than of our very survival?

"It went really well, and, as you can see, I got her out and now we're all fucked."

"And?"

"And what?"

"And what happened when you saw each other tonight?"

"Well, it was—um—weird."

"Weird? That's all you can say? Come on, Tag! You have a history with Lux, and according to your earlier discussion with President Babineux, apparently, had a relationship, so I can't imagine that was the entirety of your interaction."

Shit. Technically, she was correct, though how in the hell could I explain what happened without sounding like a complete asshole. Lux had sugar coated our brief tryst by calling it two people taking back a lost moment in time, but none of that changed the fact that we were two people getting together who were otherwise involved. I'd never cheated on a single girlfriend, and, while I wasn't sure where Estelle and I technically stood, it still seemed as though I was in the middle of an ethical minefield. At least I had only selectively agreed to Lux's pledge of non-disclosure, thus allowing me a little wiggle room in terms of what I could disclose to Estelle.

"OK, I suppose you deserve to know the whole story, so here it is. Lux and I did, indeed, have a thing ten years ago, and, to be perfectly honest, I was very much in love with her, but, because I got wounded, we never actually consummated our relationship."

"Meaning you never had sex?"

"Yeah."

"So, what happened tonight?"

There was no reason to beat around the bush, and my only hope of salvaging a relationship with Estelle would entail full disclosure.

"This is going to sound really shitty, but, when we were on the beach earlier, we—um—finally consummated it."

"You're right. That definitely sounds shitty."

"Yeah, but it was a one time thing, and it'll never happen again. Honestly, we were just two people taking back a moment in time that fate had stolen," I said, more or less quoting Lux's words in a desperate attempt to give our tryst a slightly better ring.

"Honestly, I don't even know what to say."

"I understand, and I'm sorry. I am officially a man-whore, but what happened tonight in no way has any bearing on my feelings for you."

"How can you say that?"

"This might sound like a lame excuse, but you have to understand that I spent ten years thinking about Lux every day, wondering what might have become of us had the circumstances been different. And then, when I saw her tonight, it all just came rushing back, and it was like 2005 all over again. There were a lot of regrets and unfinished feelings that I still needed to process—though I probably should have found a better way than making love to her on a beach. Unfortunately, that's how it happened, and, regardless of what you most certainly think, whatever Lux and I had is over, and I've officially let go of that part of my life. I have closure now, and the only woman I have any serious interest in is you. I know we've only known each other a couple days, and we have some serious obstacles, number one being that I'm a man-whore, and number two being geography. You work on a boat in the Caribbean, and I live in northern California, but, I think there's something real—something special, and, while I may have already fucked up any chance of that happening, I'm willing to do whatever it takes to regain your trust and find a way to make this work."

Estelle stood there ruminating for some time.

"Ten years is a long time to pine for someone, and the fact that we've only been dating for about two days, means I shouldn't be totally without understanding of your situation. And, let's face it—I knew going in that you were a man-whore, and it probably didn't help matters that I sent you off on that rescue mission half-cocked, so to speak."

"Yeah, that might have been a contributing factor, but regardless, I still feel like a dick, which means I'm ready to leave my man-whoring days behind me and focus on only one woman."

"I'm happy to hear that, but I'm still going to need to process all this, so, in the meantime, I sincerely hope you can abstain from taking back any more lost moments."

"There's nothing to worry about, as I'm pretty sure I don't have any more."

"Good, then we'll just have to see what happens."

Estelle finally appeared to relax a little, but I could still see anger and hurt simmering behind her beautiful eyes. I suppose I had just potentially brought to an end, the first decent relationship that I had experienced in a long time. This was all getting very complicated, and I was starting to miss my simple life of abstinence back in Sausalito. Thankfully, I had the rum to drown my sorrows as I lamented the loss of both the former and potential future love of my life.

CHAPTER TWENTY
The Gilded Cage

The welcoming party finally came to an end when Camille and her fellow rum matron disappeared, and Babineux and his guards herded us down a flight of stairs and through a particularly secure looking door to the bottom level. This part of the palace was built directly into the cliff, and the entire area overlooked a several hundred foot drop, so there was little or no chance of escape. The view was absolutely spectacular, though it didn't change the fact that we were thoroughly trapped. The upside was that we got the nicest level in the house, but the downside was that we were stuck here until Babineux decided to either kill or release us. President Asshole's men filed back out and remained just beyond the door while the man of the house gave us some parting words in his usual gracious manner.

"My friends—it's late, and I suspect everyone is tired, so I will see you all in the morning. Please relax and enjoy my home."

"Where the hell is my sister? You said she was here," Lux said, angrily.

"She is here, and she is being treated well, but I'm keeping her separate as a little extra measure of insurance until my business is concluded. You may rest assured she is quite comfortable. *Bonsoir, mes amis*," he said.

"*Bonsoir, vous merde putain de grenouille*," I responded.

He let out a small laugh.

"Your French is not bad, but I think you might have been a little redundant with your use of profanity."

I knew exactly what I had said—goodnight shit fuck frog. It was a stupid insult, but it was the best I could do having only been able to remember a limited amount of French profanity. He joined his security detail then closed the door, an audible click signaling that we were officially locked in for the night. I went and took a closer look at the door and frame to see if it had any weaknesses, but I would have no such luck. It was solid, probably even bomb proof, which meant no one was getting out this way unless someone let him or her out from the other side. Shit—this was going be a little harder than I thought, and I, therefore, needed to talk to Lux to find out more about Babineux's missile deal and, in turn, how soon we needed to bust out of Soft Taco Manor.

The others had already dispersed as I left the entrance and walked down the main hallway, checking the various rooms until reaching the main deck. There, I spied Lux sitting by herself at the poolside bar, and I stepped outside and realized that it was too bad we were prisoners, because it would have been a pretty damn nice place to hang out and have a cocktail. The entire level had obviously been carved directly out of the rock, and its location afforded an amazing view of the ocean below. Beyond that, however, were the amenities. It had a Jacuzzi and pool taking up most of the deck, while the bar resided along the edge, where its seats conveniently faced the ocean. I stopped and had a look up at the house and noticed there was a balcony on the very top level. There was light spilling from the windows and sliding glass door, and, considering its lofty position, I was pretty sure it was the lord of the manor's bedroom. I turned my attention back to Lux, and saw that she was gazing intently down towards the *Sarsarun*.

"Hello, Jugs. I see you're enjoying the view," I said.

She turned to me, and I could see the desperation in her eyes.

"Do you think you can get us out of this one, Finn?" she asked.

"Of course—how hard could it be to escape from a fucking palace?"

"Pretty hard considering the only way out seems to be over the side of this fucking cliff."

"Trust me. There's always a way."

"Well, at least one of us thinks so."

"So, how soon do you think this deal is going down?" I asked.

"I delayed it a week, so I'd guess it's going down tonight, probably as we speak, which means those missile launchers will be long gone before morning."

"Then, we need to get the hell out of here right now if we're going to have any chance of heading off those asshole terrorists."

"Pretty much."

I slapped my hand on the bar in frustration.

"I'd sure like to know how that fucking Babineux has managed to stay ahead of us every step of the way. There's definitely something we're missing."

"Yeah, I agree, but it doesn't matter anymore, because he's got us exactly where he wants us."

Lux looked upset, so I put a comforting hand on her shoulder.

"Don't worry, we're going to get out of here and complete your mission," I said.

"I know, but I'm also worried about Bridgette. I dragged her into this mess, so it's my fault if anything happens to her."

"Trust me. She's a very resourceful girl, and I can say with a fair amount of certainty that she's probably holding her own at the moment."

"I know that you're trying to help, but whenever you talk about her, it just reminds me that you two had sex."

"Look, I'm sorry I had sex with your sister. Maybe I should have been a little stronger, but, honestly, how can it possibly be any worse than you marrying my best friend?"

"That is a totally different situation."

"To you, but not me."

Neither of us spoke another word, and we stood there in awk-ward silence until Billings thankfully came out and joined us at the bar. He had obviously heard the tale end of our bickering and figured we needed a little intervention. To that end, he poured all of us a shot of rum then held up his glass to toast.

"I imagine tensions are running a little high, so let's take this moment to regroup and focus on what really matters—namely, thwarting that smug French fucker and saving the free world from some major league assholes. Cheers!" he said.

We all clinked glasses then sipped our drinks. It would have been more dramatic to down our entire shots in one gulp, but we were all obviously taking it slow in order to maintain a clearer head.

"So, where do we stand at the moment?" Billings asked.

Lux pointed down to the *Sarsarun*.

"The missile launchers are probably on their way to the yacht at this very moment, so we need to get our asses out of here and back to the *Sozo* if we want to have any chance of intercepting them before they leave the island."

"Any ideas?" Billings asked.

"Not yet, but I'm working on it," I said.

"Well, I have complete faith in you, my friend. Any man who can use a parasailing rig to successfully infiltrate an island can surely get us the fuck out of this place."

"I appreciate your vote of confidence, Pete."

He smiled.

"I'm going to check on the others and see how they're holding up. Come get me if you need any help."

He finished his rum, poured two more, and took them with him as he left. The extra glass was obviously for Tiffany, and, I must say, Billings certainly got the better job tonight, as com-forting her sounded like a lot more fun than figuring out how to escape from the presidential palace. Oh well, I suppose we all had our crosses to bear, though mine was obviously a tad bit more difficult at the moment. It was therefore time to focus on the task at hand, and I turned my attention to the cliff below and instantly realized that going down wasn't possible. If not down, then why not up? I did an about-face and cast my gaze up at the house. There were four stories and plenty of windows, but the only viable option appeared to be the balcony on the top level. Reaching it meant getting to the white brickwork on one of the outermost corners, and reaching one of those meant getting to a ledge that ran just above this one. Getting to that fucking ledge meant defeating the improbable architectural puzzle that was the pool deck. The area was a rectangular notch in an otherwise rectangular floor, and where the two inside walls came together to form a corner, I might be able to wedge my legs out to either side to create enough grip to climb up to the ledge. Unfortunately, Babineux's architect, in a cruel twist of design fate, had placed the pool directly up against the windows with no walkway on the inner sides—apparently to create a kind of infinity pool effect to those on the inside of the glass. Worse still, the corner sat over the deep end, and if I could manifest a superpower at this very moment, other than flight, it would be the ability to have a super slapping power, so that I could slap the shit out of Babineux's architect for sacrificing practicality for aesthetics. Oh well, there was a workaround, but it entailed going hand over hand along a piece of horizontal trim. The only bright side was that the very same pool I was trying to bypass would also provide a soft, though wet, landing in the event I fell. That is—until I started climbing the outer corner brickwork, at which point I would be beyond the deck and in very real danger of falling to my death. But, what was life without challenges, especially when the fate of thousands of innocent lives were on the line? Fuck it! It was worth a try, though I would need to get a little creative in order reach the trim piece.

"W-T-F-W-M-D?" I said, aloud.

"Excuse me?" Lux asked.

"What the fuck would *MacGyver* do?" I said, as I gazed around the pool area.

MacGyver was a mid nineteen-eighties and currently rebooted television show based around a particularly clever secret agent type guy who could diffuse nuclear bombs with chewing gum and build a hang glider out of tampons and rubber bands. Embodying that same spirit of invention, I grabbed one of the deck loungers and carried it over to where the piece of trim extended past the pool and over the patio.

"Seriously now, Finn—what are you doing?" Lux asked.

"I'm trying to get some trim."

"I take it that's a joke?"

"Well, not if you had to ask."

"Exactly, so, why don't you drop the cutesy euphemisms and explain how you plan to kill yourself?"

"Alrighty then, my beautiful hater—I'm going to shimmy along that piece of trim to the corner, where I'll be able to climb up to the next level. From there, I'll walk back along the ledge to the white brickwork section on the outer edge and use it like a ladder to make my way up to that balcony. Once there, I will enter Babineux's bedroom, overpower him, then come back down and open the door to the lower level, so I can release everyone and be overwhelmed with praise."

"You do realize that once you're out on the brickwork, you'll be beyond this patio and in real jeopardy of falling hundreds of feet to your death?"

"It's an acceptable risk."

"Yeah, if you're insane."

"You're obviously not looking at the alternatives. What happens if we stay here in our lovely accommodations? I'll tell you what—terrorists potentially kill a bunch of innocent people."

"What if you fall and get splattered on some rocks?" she countered.

"What if I'm successful?"

"What if you're not?"

"What if you and Corn get divorced?"

"What if I swing my knee up into your nut sack?"

"You'd only be hurting the best thing that ever happened to you."

"Look, Tag, I don't want you to do this."

"I have to, though I might reconsider if you officially acknowledge that it was a mistake to marry Corn."

I realized she wasn't willing to do that when she reached down and helped steady the chair.

"Last chance," I said.

"Fuck off and start climbing."

I climbed on to the upended lounger and spent a second getting my balance. Thank God Babineux was a choosy shopper and bought sturdy furniture, as the stuff that most people kept around their pool or back patio would have never stood up to this kind of abuse. I reached up and realized that, even on the lounger, I was still a few inches short of the trim piece, and, seeing no alternative, steadied my nerves and jumped. I managed to get my fingers barely over the edge, but the move made the lounger fall over. Fortunately, Lux caught it and kept it from crashing down onto the patio, where it would have made a shitload of noise. I started going to my left, inch by inch, making my way towards the corner, but my fingers were straining, and it was hard to maintain my grip. I had learned rock climbing as part of my training back in the day, but this was specialized and required maintaining the small muscles in the hands. Regular masturbating sometimes worked those muscles, but I had been too sexually active with the opposite sex as of late, and my fingers had apparently gotten flabby. I was almost to the corner when I hit a slippery spot, and realized I couldn't hold on any longer. I brought my feet to the wall and kicked out, sending me falling safely into the deep end of the pool. I hit the water in a sort of backwards belly flop that made more noise than a breaching blue whale, and the minute I popped up, I yelled to Lux.

"Get in the pool and frolic!"

"Why?"

"Goddammit! Get in the pool and frolic!"

She looked perplexed but thankfully jumped in despite her obvious reservations.

"Good, now you need to frolic."

"Seriously now, what the fuck do you mean by frolic?"

I splashed her with water, and, judging by the look on her face, it didn't go over well, because she angrily splashed water back at me. Perfect. I moved closer and pulled her underwater, and she responded by punching me in the stomach. It wasn't exactly frolicking, but it would do. She popped up, wiped the water from her eyes, and looked as though she was about to say something off-colored, when Babineux suddenly stepped out onto the upper balcony.

"I am glad you two are enjoying yourselves, but it really is getting late," he said.

"No problem. We were about to go to bed. *Bonsoir mon petit cochon endormi*," I said, which translated as goodnight my sleepy little pig.

He went back inside, and I smiled at Lux, hoping she finally understood that I was trying to hide the real reason for all the noise. She, apparently got it, because she smiled and sent a playful splash of water towards my face. I splashed her back, then we both laughed. Movement to the side of the pool caught my attention, and I looked over to see Estelle standing there with her hands on her hips and, worse still, a frown on her lips. Shit. She must have thought that we were sincerely frolicking in the pool.

"Over? It sure doesn't look like it, man-whore," she said, angrily, as she turned to leave.

"Wait! It's not what you think."

She stormed off the deck, and Lux immediately cast her scrutinizing gaze in my direction.

"Sweet Lord! You also had sex with Estelle? How in the fuck

did you manage to hook up with so many women in such a short period of time?"

"As a man-whore, I obviously have super man-whoring powers."

"Finn, I'm officially stunned beyond belief."

"Yeah, yeah, I know—but, before you give me any more shit, I'd like to say that this wasn't just a casual hookup and could have been serious—could have being the operative words."

"Well, in that case, I'm sorry," she said.

"It's OK. You shouldn't blame yourself entirely. Sure, you hooked up with Corn, broke my heart, and turned me into a man-whore, but I suppose this current mess is at least partially my fault."

"That's really big of you to admit that," she said, in a sarcastic tone.

"Admitting our faults is how we grow as people. Now, back to the problem at hand," I said, as I climbed out of the pool and put the lounger back up on its end.

"Please don't tell me you're going to try that stupid stunt again!"

"I was almost there."

"Yeah—then you fell, idiot. Your chances of making it up to that balcony are about a hundred to one while your chances of falling and breaking your neck are about ninety-nine point nine out of a hundred."

"Never tell me the odds!" I bellowed, doing my best *Han Solo* imitation.

"Well, look here, Solo, you don't have *Chewie* and the *Millennium Falcon* to catch you if you fall, so you might want to rethink your plan."

"I think I can make it this time—with a little help from the bar."

The ambient light around the pool suddenly diminished a wee bit, and I looked up to see that our host had finally turned out his lights and gone to bed. Nice! It would be a hell of a lot easier to focus on getting past that slippery section if I didn't have to worry about his highness sticking his head out every time he heard a little noise. I walked over to the bar and rummaged around until I found some Cointreau—which I was pretty sure would do the trick.

"You're having another cocktail?" Lux asked, angrily, as she climbed out of the pool.

"No, just a liqueur."

"Same thing, jackass."

I ignored Lux and poured the orange flavored liqueur on my hands and rubbed them together. As the alcohol dried up, the sugary liqueur left a sticky film, and I went back to the chair and climbed onto the upturned lounger for the second time of the night. Lux followed me over and helped to keep the wobbling chair steady as I made the jump and managed to again get hold of the piece of trim. I moved left, only now the muscles in my hands were especially tired having already done this once, and I knew that I didn't have a lot of strength remaining before my fingers gave out. I came upon the slippery spot, but the Cointreau did its job, and I continued past it and reached the corner. There, I wedged my feet out to each of the walls and used my legs and arms together to climb up onto the higher ledge. It was welcome relief to finally get a break, and, as I took a minute to rest and regain my strength, I looked down and saw that Lux was anxiously monitoring my progress.

"Told you I could do it!" I said.

"You've still got a long way to go, cowboy," she responded.

"Anyone ever tell you that you're hard to please?"

"No—nor did I hear that complaint from you earlier on the beach tonight."

I would have given her the finger, but I thought it would be more prudent to keep all my digits firmly attached to the side of the building. I set off, snaking my way along the ledge and out towards the far corner, where I would be leaving the relative safety of the pool area and moving out over the cliff. It was the only way up to the top level, and, if I fell here, there would be no more frolicking in the pool or anywhere else for that matter—ever again. As I had a closer look at the brick section on the corner, I was pretty certain it would provide decent climbing holds and make it possible to reach Babineux's balcony—hopefully, anyway. I started making my way up the wall but took it slow and maintained three points of contact at all times. I wasn't a big fan of heights unless I was wearing a parachute, so I had to put a lot of thought into not thinking about how far it was to the rocks below. Of course, the process of not thinking about something was the best way to end up thinking about it—which meant I was thinking a whole lot about the fact I was one small slip away from my imminent demise. Still, I kept climbing, being careful to move one limb at a time, thankfully reaching the balcony and feeling particularly relieved as I shimmied over the railing and took a moment to rest and recuperate. I exhaled a great sigh of relief then looked back to see how far I had come and felt an instant twinge of vertigo and had to steady myself. Lux was right—I was insane. I gave her a wave then wiped the sweat off my brow and turned around and looked at the curtains gently billowing in the doorway to Babineux's bedroom. I sure hope he's in the mood for company.

I silently moved to the open doorway and hid behind the curtain to listen for any sound from inside the room. I expected to at least hear breathing, snoring, flatulence, discussions of fine cheeses, or any number of noises a Frenchman might make in the middle of the night, but there was nothing to fill the air except for the sound of the crashing waves hundreds of feet below. I slipped inside and spent a tense few seconds as I waited for my eyes to adjust to the dim light before seeing that the king sized four-poster bed was empty. Strange. I decided to check the bathroom, and, finding no one on the toilet, went back to the bedroom and turned on the lights. Where in the hell was Babineux? He had said only minutes ago that he was going to sleep, but there was no sign of the wily Frenchman. I locked the bedroom door and decided to give the place a quick search. The bed was made and the room was mostly tidy except for some female undergarments on the floor over by the closet. Apparently, Babineux recently had some female company though that was pretty much a given considering he was good-looking, French, and owned his own tropical island. I searched the bedside table and found a 9mm Beretta pistol, a pair of reading glasses, and a book about cheese. I have twenty-twenty vision, and I didn't have enough time for any casual reading, so I left the book and glasses, and took the pistol.

Next, I went to the bathroom and turned on the light. Wow. This place would have given me the greatest dump of my life, the view alone through the floor to ceiling windows enough to negate any reason to read on the toilet. Hell, I could live in this bathroom. As I stood there admiring the toilet, I realized how badly I needed to urinate. I'd had at least three snifters of rum, and my bladder was about to burst. I lifted the seat, and gratefully opened up the tap, producing a healthy stream that would have made any urologist proud. I should have pissed all over Babineux's toilet seat, but I just couldn't desecrate such a beautiful bathroom. Therefore, I kept my aim straight and true to the center of the bowl, and I was pretty certain my mother would be very proud of me at this moment.

While I stood there peeing out what felt like an entire bottle's worth of rum, I couldn't help but look around at the accoutrements. The bathroom was stocked with a lot of high-end, name brand grooming products that you'd only find in expensive department stores. There were also female things like tampons, hairbrushes, and cosmetics. Babineux wasn't married as far as I knew, so he either had a vagina or a steady flow of female companions. I finished, flushed, and turned around and noticed he had a laptop sitting on a stand that was built into the wall—the setup similar to the one in my bathroom on the *Sozo*. Apparently, it was a common convenience of the super wealthy. The laptop was the smaller thirteen inch version of my own MacBook pro, and, when I flipped it open, it came out of sleep mode, and his calendar application was filling the screen. I looked at today's date and saw the words, *carburant et fournir le Soft Taco III*, which translated as fuel and provision the *Soft Taco III*. That sounded as though the fucker was provisioning his yacht, and, as it wasn't relevant to our current predicament, I clicked on the next day and saw the words Martinique Aimé Césaire International Airport written in the five p.m. slot. Interesting! It would appear that Babineux was planning a little trip, and now the previous day's note made sense. He was obviously getting his yacht ready so that he could take it to Martinique in order to catch tomorrow's five p.m. flight—which would also explain his current absence from his presidential palace.

I left the bathroom, turned out all the lights, and went to the door to listen for any sign of Babineux's security people. All I could hear was the welcoming sound of silence, so I eased the door open a crack and peered outside to find an empty hallway. Left went to the stairs while right went towards some closed doors. I decided to go right and conduct a little recon of the house and find out who and what we were up against while I could. I slowly opened the first door and discovered it was just an empty guest room. The next door went into a giant linen closet that wasn't too exciting unless you had a thing for sheets and towels. That left door number three which turned out to be Babineux's office. It was a lovely space with polished hardwood floors covered by a Persian rug large enough to nearly stretch to all four walls, which left plenty of snuggle room in front of the fireplace—not that any sane human would light a fire in a climate where the year round temperatures averaged over eighty degrees. The focal point of the room, however, was a Louis XIV desk, which I imagine must be customary for every Frenchman—along with a mistress, of course. It sat in the center of the room and had very little clutter to mar its elegance except for an understated brass desk lamp and a twenty-seven inch iMac. The only other furniture was a warm, comfortable looking leather sofa and file cabinet that looked custom made to match the desk.

There were paintings on the walls from impressionist to modern, and I would be disappointed if there wasn't a wall safe hidden behind one of them. I was doubtful I would find anything more useful than the calendar I'd discovered on his bathroom laptop, but still had to look behind the paintings—primarily, for my own personal gratification. The wall safe ended up being behind a sad painting of a clown. It had a combination lock, and, as I wasn't exactly a safe cracker, I decided to, instead, focus my attention on the desk. In the top drawer I found another Beretta pistol with a fully loaded clip, and I had to admit that it was starting to feel a lot like Christmas. As I turned and left the office, only one more thing was still bothering me—namely, where were Camille and her fellow rum girl? If I were an eccentric French billionaire, I'd want them as close as possible—along with a plentiful stash of rum, of course.

I headed downstairs to the next floor, hopeful that the house would be as empty and uneventful as it had been thus far. I found three more guest rooms, a bathroom, family room, and another linen closet, but there wasn't a person, or even a firearm, in any of them. That just left the ground floor, which had to have someone, maybe even the rum girls if I were lucky. I descended the stairs and arrived in the main foyer, where I was happy to at last be in familiar territory. I heard noise coming from the living room and moved through the doorway, taking up residence behind a large leafy houseplant where I could see without being seen. One of the guards from earlier was asleep on the couch in front of a flat screen television that I hadn't noticed earlier in the evening. It must have been hidden in a cabinet or behind a painting, as wealthy people apparently took a lot of pride in hiding their televisions. I ventured down a nearby hallway and discovered the kitchen.

It was outfitted like a restaurant, and had a professional-grade Wolf range, two double door refrigerators, shitloads of counter space, and every cooking accessory imaginable. Off to the side there was a lovely little breakfast nook, and beyond it was a sliding glass door that led to a quaint little patio area, which would be perfect for croissants and coffee if we were unlucky enough to still be here in the morning. I was still in scavenger mode so I did a quick search of the kitchen drawers and found a roll of duct tape. It was no longer starting to feel like Christmas—it fucking was Christmas!

My preliminary search of the house was officially complete, and it would appear that it was mostly empty. Still, it was possible more guards might arrive at any moment, so I decided I should take care of the guy in the living room sooner than later. One opponent was fairly manageable, but two or more was at least twice as much trouble and, therefore, half the fun. I went back to the living room to size up Mr. Sleepy and saw that he was still passed out cold on the couch. He looked to be a little bit on the heavy out of shape side, though Island life could do that to a person, what with all the good food and rum. As I got closer, I could smell the alcohol emanating from his body and realized that if he was as drunk as he seemed, then taking care of him should be a simple task. I made my way closer, slipping along with the quiet purposeful movements of a jungle cat, but paused when the grandfather clock abruptly went off at eleven. Mr. Sleepy opened his eyes and caught me standing right in front of him. He didn't move for some time and, judging by his drunken expression, was having some difficulty trying to figure out who the hell I might be. He blinked and continued to stare, his brain likely short-circuiting as it was obviously floating in a sea of rum.

"*Attendez une minute,*" he finally said, his French almost imperceptible through his drunken slur.

I believe he asked me to wait a minute, so I responded by asking him a silly question.

"Bonjour, avez-vous plus de rhum?"

I just asked if he had any more rum which would, hopefully, give him pause for thought. He looked a little confused, but then he pointed across the room towards the bar, his arm wobbling and barely able to remain aloft. One of his eyes started to close, but he did his best to keep his other eye focused on me as I walked over and grabbed a bottle of the premium rum and two glasses before returning to sit next to my new drinking buddy. I could have easily overpowered him and knocked him out, but, some- times, problems could be solved with less violent means—and why not indulge in a little snifter of the good stuff. I poured him a generous glass and a tiny one for myself. He smiled and held up his rum to toast, but his hand was wobbling so much that it took three tries before we finally managed to bump glasses and get a decent clinking sound.

"À votre santé," to your health, I said.

"À la votre," to yours, he responded.

He drank it down in one gulp, and I immediately refilled his glass and watched him guzzle another while I made a point of barely sipping at my own. The guy was obviously a tank, and I was relieved, after refilling his glass four times, when he finally passed out completely. I gave him a quick pat down, found his pistol, then poured some more rum in my glass and set off towards the stairway that would take me to the lower levels. Thus far, I had managed to avoid any major confrontations and found myself smiling at having miraculously found the path of least resistance. Or so I thought, until two men unexpectedly appeared from a side room I hadn't yet seen. Shit! I kept smiling and tried to play it off as though I was just another guest enjoying a cocktail, but they were sharp and knew that I wasn't supposed to be there. The nearest one drew his pistol, so I stayed nice and still, hoping to keep him calm. His partner moved closer and pulled out a pair of handcuffs, but there was no way I could let them put those on me if I hoped to have any chance of getting the hell out of this place. When he was close enough to reach my hand, I threw the remaining rum in his face, temporarily blinding him and allowing me to slip my arm between his body and his bicep, then spin him around and apply a judo lock. It was a hold that could hurt like hell, especially when the elbow was torqued backward and away from the shoulder joint. He tried to break free, but it only caused more pain, and, now, I had him in front of me as my human shield. If the other guy decided to shoot, my French friend would take the bullet or at least slow it down.

"Let him go!" the other guard said, in a thick French accent.

Shit! I needed some time to figure out how to deal with this situation, so I decided to initiate a little friendly conversation.

"Fine, but first you have to admit that we saved your asses in World War II."

"*Vas te faire encule!*" he said, which basically meant fuck you.

Oh well—that little piece of history would just have to remain unresolved for the moment. Meanwhile, I had achieved my goal, for as I held the Frenchman in place, I realized he was wearing a bulletproof vest. That meant his friend with the gun would be wearing one as well. Fantastique! Now, I had an idea for how to deal with my two unwelcome French intruders. I placed my empty rum glass on the table behind me then slipped one of the Beretta pistols out of my waistband. The gun was hidden from view, and while it wasn't cocked, it was double action, so all I had to do was thumb the safety off and pull the trigger. Of course, this plan hinged on whether or not there was a bullet already in the chamber, and, if not, then I would have to pull back the slide while simultaneously maintaining my judo hold—an action which would pretty much completely take away the element of surprise. So, first and foremost, I needed to know if the gun was ready to fire, and thankfully I had one very unique little piece of engineering working in my favor. The designers of the Beretta 92 intended it to be used by soldiers and police, and therefore it had to be reliable, accurate, and useful in all conditions—especially low light or complete darkness. To that end they placed a little metal tab just above the trigger that sticks out whenever there's a round in the chamber. That way, the person holding the gun always knew when their weapon was safe or in firing mode. I slipped my finger up and over the little metal tab and all but came in my pants when I realized I was locked and loaded and ready for action.

My nemesis was starting to get antsy, and that meant that I needed to act before he did something rash. I shoved the guy I was holding towards his friend, making the gunman temporarily lower his weapon and take his eyes off of me for a second. It was the break I needed to step sideways and shoot him twice in the chest. He dropped like a rock, and I turned my aim to the other guy, waiting until he turned around before putting the next two bullets square in his chest. Now, both guys were on the floor, but I only had a small window of opportunity before their minds caught up with their bodies, and they realized they weren't dead but temporarily incapacitated by the force of the bullets impacting their vests and knocking the wind from their lungs. As they lay there recovering I moved in and quickly secured their hands and feet using their handcuffs and the duct tape, and, when I was done, they didn't look too happy. They would also be sore as hell, but shooting them in their vests was, ironically, the easiest way to keep all three of us alive. I grabbed their pistols and walked back to the couch to check on the boozehound and found him still asleep. The sound of four gunshots at close range wasn't even enough to wake him, which made me think that he was probably going to feel a lot worse than his two friends in the morning. I grabbed one of their radios, put in the earpiece, then poured myself a couple fingers of rum and headed down the stairs to the lowest level. I reached the security door and realized my earlier summation that it was solid enough to withstand a small explosion was correct, though the lock was something you'd buy at a local hardware store. It didn't require an electronic number pad or special magnetic key, for all it had was a simple bolt. I unlocked the door and opened it to find everyone anxiously waiting on the other side.

"We heard all the shooting! Are you all right?" Estelle asked.

"Not a scratch!" I said, holding up my arms.

Lux, who was standing beside Estelle, cast me a rather scrutinizing gaze.

"Are you seriously drinking another cocktail right now?" she asked.

"This? No, it's just rum."

"Same thing, jackass," Lux responded.

"Whatever—I believe I earned it, having just taken care of the remainder of Babineux's guards."

"And what about Babineux?"

"There was no sign of him, so he's obviously aboard his yacht and on his way to Martinique."

"Why Martinique?"

"Because the fucker plans to fly out of there tomorrow at five o'clock in the evening."

Lux thought for a moment.

"That doesn't make any sense. Are you sure about this information?"

"Of course, I'm sure. I'm a professional, and I just happened to have gotten it from his laptop, which you'll possibly be interested to learn, was in his bathroom—next to the toilet, no less."

"Really—and what exactly was a professional doing searching a bathroom?"

"Looking for his laptop, obviously."

"Men always say they have a hard time understanding women, but it's moments like this that prove it's the other way around."

"Hey, I was mostly there to pee, but, say what you will about the man, he knows how to dump in style, and I now have a major case of bathroom envy."

"Only you could fall in love with a bathroom."

"True, but who is more foolish? The fool who fell in love with a bathroom, or the fool who fell in love with the fool who fell in love with a bathroom?"

Lux stared at me, unblinking, refusing to say a single word.

"No response? No witty retort?" I asked.

"No, but I do want to know if you found any sign of Bridgette."

"Sorry, she wasn't in the bathroom—or any other place for that matter. He must have taken her with him."

"Fucking French fuck."

"It's OK, we'll get her back after we take care of the missile launchers. Everyone ready to go, or do you want a quick tour of the presidential palace? It's really quite lovely."

Apparently, everyone was ready to go, as they practically knocked me down in a stampede to get out the door. Estelle stayed behind and looked at me with concern in her eyes.

"I'm glad you're safe, and I'm sorry I kind of freaked out at the pool."

"It's OK. It's been a hell of a day."

She hugged me, then we headed up the stairs to find everyone waiting for us on the main level.

"Oh, before we continue, I should tell you that I found a few extra pistols for those of you handy with a gun."

Lux, Billings, and Brett gave me a nod so I gave each a pistol but still had one left over.

"Anyone else?" I asked, as I looked at the group.

Estelle raised her hand.

"You really want a gun?"

"Yeah, I feel I should do my part to help us get the hell out of here."

"OK, but..."

"Don't worry. My dad taught me to shoot when I was a little girl. Been doing it my entire life. Pistols, rifles—just about anything with a barrel and a trigger."

"No shit? And you really grew up in Berkeley?"

"I sure did."

I handed her a Beretta, and she expertly inspected it before pulling back the slide and chambering a round. Watching her handle the pistol was actually kind of sexy and gave me some instantaneous pangs of regret at the recent setbacks in our relationship. Where the hell had this girl been all my life?

"All right, fuckers! Lets blow this soft taco stand!" I said.

CHAPTER TWENTY-ONE
The Long and Winding Road Less Traveled

We moved towards the front door, and I paused to listen to the radio I had taken from the guard. All appeared quiet, so it would appear that no alerts had gone out that the rude Americans were trying to escape. I took a quick glance out one of the windows beside the front door and saw that the driveway appeared to be clear of the French menace. Better still, one of the small vehicles that had brought us here was parked off to the side, which meant we had a ride! I eased open the door and walked out onto the stone entryway, carefully looking for any movement. I heard footsteps on the other side of the courtyard and looked over to see a guard with a gun. I jumped back into the doorway just as he fired, and the bullet struck the front wall only inches from where I had been standing. The presidential palace obviously wasn't soundproof, and someone had heard my earlier gunfire and been waiting for us. That meant the front door was officially useless for the moment, and we needed to come up with an alternative plan.

"Alrighty then, I'm going to sneak out of the house through a different door and take care of the lone gunman, but, to do that, I'm going to need someone to create a little diversion by firing a couple shots from here," I said.

"I'll do it," Lux responded.

"Cool. Give me about five minutes and then fire two shots. Wait fifteen seconds and repeat. Oh, and you might want to show a hint of nipple."

"Only a hint?" Lux asked, sarcastically.

"Yeah, as we're operating under the why buy the cow when you get the milk for free rules of engagement."

"Honestly, I have no idea what the hell that means."

"That's fine, because neither do I, but that's what happens when you mix anxiety, adrenaline, and rum."

I headed for the other side of the house, and passed through the living room to see my drinking buddy was still sleeping like a log, his gentle snoring the only sound other than the constant ticking of the grandfather clock. I reached the kitchen, opened the sliding glass door as quietly as possible, then slipped outside and took a second to wait for my eyes to adjust to the darkness. Just as faint shapes started to appear in my field of vision, a fist suddenly came crashing down onto my hand, sending my gun clattering onto the patio tiles. I turned to see that my attacker had been lying in wait to the side of the door, and, now, he was directly behind me with his pistol aimed at my head.

"Oh, would you be trying to escape?" the man asked, in French accented English.

He had the drop on me, but his close proximity was actually an advantage, because it meant that I had a chance of disarming him and getting hold of his weapon.

"Oh relax, I was just out for a little fresh air and a stroll in the garden."

"Carrying a pistol?"

"You're one to talk."

"Enough of your bullshit. Time to head back into the house," he ordered.

"Do you mind giving me a second? I've been in polite company all night, and the actual reason I'm out here is that I really need to fart."

That was a purposeful deception based on the truth that I did indeed have a formidable fart simmering in the breach.

"Forget about farting and start walking."

"Fine, but don't say I didn't warn you."

I turned towards the door and waited until the guy was right behind me, then let loose the great white whale of farts, the violence of its arrival actually startling the guy enough to give me a brief window of opportunity. I twisted around and trapped his gun with my left hand, and, as we struggled for control of the weapon, he inadvertently pulled the trigger. The bullet went harmlessly off to the side of the patio and beheaded a ceramic garden gnome—the little fellow dying quickly, though nobly. The sound of the gunshot wasn't exactly improving my stealthiness, so I needed to get this resolved before any of his friends showed up to help. I reached up with my right hand and took hold of his head, pulled him down into a knee strike to loosen him up, then twisted the pistol back towards his body and out of his hand. With the weapon free, I stepped back, smiled, and wafted the air towards my face.

"Can you smell that? It's the sweet smell of victory."

He stared at me, his bloodied face a visage of menace.

"More like the rank smell of an asshole," he responded.

"Do you mean that literally or figuratively?"

"Both."

"Well, sorry my friend, but only the man with the gun gets to make that call."

"Oh, you are so American with your tough talk, but you would be nothing without that pistol in your hand!"

"Oh, really?"

"Yeah, and if you had any fucking balls, you would put it down and fight me like a man."

I was getting the impression my French adversary was trying to use some very rudimentary psychology to get me to relinquish the upper hand. A bullet might have been the fastest way to deal with him, but my deep inner humanitarian decided to play along.

"Fine, give me your best shot," I said, sliding the gun back into my waistband.

He clenched his fists, gritted his teeth, and came at me like a charging feral pig. I waited until he was just in range then threw a low, hard front kick straight to his groin, and the blow stopped him instantly in his tracks.

"Oh, *mes testicules! Vous fils de pute!*" he said, as he buckled over and dropped onto his knees.

I'm pretty sure he just said oh, my testicles, you son of a bitch, which was completely understandable given the nature of the strike.

"Now—we can do this the hard way or the easy way."

"Fuck you," he uttered.

"OK, hard way, it is," I said, kicking him in the chest and knocking him to the ground.

I rolled him onto his stomach then cuffed him with his own handcuffs before taping up his feet and mouth. With yet another French obstacle out of the way, it was time to get back on track. I moved towards the edge of the patio and found a door in the fence that went in the direction of the driveway. The problem now, however, was that the gunshot just gave away my position, but, hopefully, the guy in the driveway will just think his friend shot me. Either way, it was going to be a lot harder to catch him off guard, as he knew that someone would be coming. Thankfully, I had Lux, and, when she started shooting, the lone gunman would be at a major disadvantage having to fight on two fronts. That would provide me with the second of two advantages—the first already in play. Most people didn't know that the person actively seeking a target has a small reaction time edge over the person waiting for a target. Always better to be the hunter than the hunted. Lux's shots rang out right on time, and the guy returned fire, giving me my opening to go through the gate.

There was an unlit path lined with tree's and hedges, and I stayed low and moved fast, sweeping my weapon across my field of fire as I looked for any kind of movement. I reached the low stone walls of the parking area just in time to hear Lux's second round of shots ring out. There was no return fire or any sign of the shooter, so he had, apparently, moved on to a new location. Just then, a cry came from off to my right, and I looked over to see that the man in question was holding Camille as a human shield. She was dressed in a frilly little teddy and must have left her bedroom in the guest house to come out and see what all the commotion was about and, inadvertently, got drawn into the action. Shit, the last thing I wanted was to have an innocent in the middle of this mess, but the gunman felt otherwise. He had one arm around her throat and held her tightly in order to keep as much of his body behind her as possible. In his other hand, was his pistol, which he had pointed directly at me.

"Drop your gun!" he yelled.

I was a good enough shot that I might be able to take out the guy with a well-placed headshot, but I looked at Camille's face and saw that she was terrified, and decided having a man's head obliterated in front of her was probably a bad idea for her long-term mental health. That meant I had to come up with another way.

"OK, but you have to let her go," I responded.

"You first."

"How about we do it at the same time?"

"Not a chance," he said, having already deduced that I wouldn't do anything to endanger Camille.

"Fine, but I hope you know this makes me the bigger man."

I slowly leaned down and set my gun on the ground, knowing full well it was a terrible tactical move. You never surrendered your weapon—unless, of course, you had another trick up your sleeve.

"Happy now?" I asked.

"No. Kick it away."

I kicked it about five feet away, and my French nemesis was now officially happy and smiled at his little victory.

"Put your hands on your head," he said.

"I will, once you let her go."

He released his grip on her throat, and Camille practically leapt from his arm in an attempt to gain as much distance as possible from her captor. He turned his gaze back to me, his smile now transforming into a smug sneer of victory as I placed my hands on my head.

"Time for you to go back inside," he said.

"Actually, it's time for you to drop your weapon, because there's a particularly beautiful woman with bodacious ta-tas and an itchy trigger finger aiming a pistol at you," I responded.

That statement was not entirely a fabrication, as Lux was nearby holding a gun, and she also had some seriously bodacious ta-tas.

"You Americans are so ridiculous. Do you really think I am so stupid as to fall for your ruse?" he asked, in a condescending tone.

"I'm counting on it," I said, using the brief exchange to dive forward into an aikido shoulder roll.

Like the *porcelet* back on Martinique, just thinking about me trying to trick him was enough to fill his mind and slow his reaction time. He was caught off guard and fired too late—his shot going high and allowing me time to grab my pistol, complete the roll and pop up onto one knee, and put three shots in the center of his chest. He was wearing a bullet proof vest, so the impacts knocked the wind from his lungs and put him on his back and left him gasping for air.

"No one fucks with my rum girl, motherfucker!" I said, as I closed the distance and gave him a hard kick to his jaw that put him out cold.

Camille was standing there in shock, unable to move from her spot, so I went over to comfort her, knowing that there was nothing that could prepare a person for what she had just experienced. She wrapped her arms around me, sobbing as both shock and relief flooded her mind. I stroked her hair and whispered softly into her ear.

"Don't worry. You're safe now."

She held me tightly and was the fourth beautiful woman I'd had in my arms in as many days. The others came out the front door at that moment and joined us, and both Estelle and Lux ignored the guy on the ground and, of course, only focused on the fact that I was holding a beautiful half naked woman in my arms. They both gave me a disapproving look, which was starting to be the rule rather than the exception. You just can't please all the people all the time. I took Camille back into the house, poured her a drink to steady her nerves, then made sure she was OK before telling her it was time for me to leave. She smiled resolutely, kissed me, then we parted ways so that I could rejoin the others. I sure hoped Babineux kept a therapist on staff, as she would most certainly suffer from some post-traumatic stress disorder after tonight. Perhaps her equally beautiful co-worker from earlier would join her in her bed to comfort her. Throw in a bottle of rum and that scenario sounded pretty interesting. Oh well, my male fantasy life would have to wait until my real life was a little less hectic.

I walked back through the living room, and, as I was passing the bar, I realized I needed a souvenir, and what could possibly be better than a bottle or two of Babineux's finest rum? I squeezed in between two stools and leaned over and looked behind the bar and spied a wooden case on the floor in the corner. Sweet mother of goats! I'd hit the mother lode! It was an unopened case of the Island's Special Edition rum, and, in my humble opinion, it deserved a better home. I picked it up and carried it outside to find everyone was waiting for me in the little vehicle. Tiffany was beside Pete riding bitch in the middle of the front, while Kip and Brett were in the second seat. Estelle and Lux were in the third row, and I found their seating arrangement to be more than a little bit disconcerting, as it was never a good idea to place current and former girlfriends in close proximity for fear they might fight or, worse still, bond. There was nothing I could do about it at the moment, so it was time to climb aboard and, fortunately for me, they had left the right front seat open, which meant I didn't even need to call shotgun.

"What have you got with you?" Lux asked.

"A souvenir."

"I'm asking you seriously."

"And I'm answering you seriously. It's a souvenir."

"It looks like a case of booze."

"Good God, woman! This is more than just booze! It's a case of Soft Taco Island's finest rum!"

"I'm honestly starting to wonder if you have a problem."

"Yeah, no shit! Do you know that when the Soft Taco Security forces were combing Old Town for us, Betty Ford here wouldn't leave until he grabbed his four bottles from the storage room of the bar."

"Seriously, Finn? What were you thinking?" Lux added.

"They were a gift. It would have been rude not to accept them."

"We were on the run for our lives!" Estelle responded.

Sweet Lord of lover's triangles! My fear had become reality, and, now, I officially had the Ghost of Girlfriend Past bonding with the Ghost of Girlfriend Present, which begged the question of who in the hell would end up as the Ghost of Girlfriend Future. As usual, life was doing its best to test my resolve, but we had bigger fish to fry—namely escaping from this fucking island. I sat down and placed the case on the floor between my feet then pulled out the extra pistols.

"I managed to snag two more pistols, so if anyone else wants one, or those of you who already have one want to get all *John*

Woo, now is your chance," I said.

The term, John Woo, obviously referred to the famous Hong Kong movie director who had a propensity for having his characters brandish two pistols.

"I'll take one," Kip said.

"OK, but have you ever handled a firearm?"

"I graduated from West Point and was on the Army national rifle team. What do you think?"

"I think you should have told me that little fact a lot sooner."

"I don't like to brag."

I couldn't help but wonder if he might end up using it on me, but I decided to throw caution to the wind and handed over a pistol to my nemesis.

"Back to the *Sozo*, Pete. We have a pirate raid to conduct."

"Arrrrrr, just hold on tight," he said.

"Arrrrrr!" I responded.

The rest of the passengers remained quiet, so it would appear that only Pete and I liked to make pirate sounds.

"Don't any of you fuckers have any pirate spirit? Come on. Let's hear it all together now!"

"Arrrrrr!" Everyone but Lux and Estelle yelled out.

"Come on girls!"

"Ar," they both said, with a distinct disinterest.

"Good enough. Let's roll, Pete!"

He slammed his foot down on the accelerator, and we took off, the tires chirping on the pavement as we left the presidential palace and headed down the hill. We reached the rolling foothills and, with Pete driving at full speed, branches and insects appeared to leap out into the path of our headlights. Up ahead was the section with the series of tight turns, but Billings kept the gas pedal firmly planted on the floor. Everyone held on for dear life as he expertly navigated the curves, and it was all I could do to keep both myself and the rum from flying out of the little vehicle.

"Sweet Lord of the *Nürburgring*! Where did you learn to drive like that, Pete?" I asked.

"Sports Car Club of America. When I'm not behind the helm of the *Sozo*, you'll find me on the track behind the wheel of my 1995 BMW M3 race car."

"I knew there was something special about you the moment we met," I said.

"I take it you're into cars?" he asked.

"Isn't every man?"

"Only if he truly is a man."

"Words to live by."

"I believe we're in the opening moments of a burgeoning bromance. Do you want me to hold the wheel so you two can hug it out?" Tiffany asked.

Pete and I shared a smile, but it quickly faded when we turned our gazes back to the road ahead and noticed that we were rapidly approaching the little guardhouse we had passed on our way in to the presidential palace. If I remembered correctly, it was kind of a flimsy looking little structure with gates that were probably more of a psychological ploy to keep the riffraff away from the president. The lights were on, so someone was obviously home, and Pete slowed down and looked at me.

"Any suggestions?" he asked.

Fortunately, I had already memorized the Soft Taco Island map when I was browsing their official website—bringing credence to the saying that failing to prepare was preparing to fail. In this instance, I was prepared to succeed.

"As I recall, the guardhouse controls access to two different routes. Both take us back to the resort side of the island, but the shortest route is the one we took here, while the other is the scenic way that loops through Old Town. I guess we'll have to go whichever way is clear, but, no matter what happens, keep going and let me worry about any hostiles. You're the wheelman and I'm the triggerman."

"And the bromance continues," Estelle muttered, from the

back seat.

Pete slammed his foot down on the gas pedal, and we raced towards the checkpoint. As we got closer, I noticed that both gates were down and the left hand route was blocked by a jeep and a lone guard armed with a submachine gun. So much for the short cut. The guard brought his weapon up to fire, but I was quicker and fired off three rounds. It was hard to get an accurate shot firing a pistol from a moving vehicle at this range, but it was enough to send the guy running for cover behind the jeep. I fired two more times just to keep his head down, while Billings steered to the right and crashed through the wooden gate. It was, as I already suspected, more of a psychological barrier, and it broke into several pieces, with a large section landing in my lap—thankfully missing my precious manhood by mere inches. Pete looked over and grimaced.

"Oh shit, are you OK?" he asked.

"As you can see, I've got some serious wood here between my legs—obviously, as a result of your driving."

"Then I'll just have to—keep it up," he said, with a smile.

Tiffany decided to make fun of our bromance yet again, only this time, by singing the opening line of that old cheesy nineteen seventies disco song *Love is in the Air*.

"*Love is in the air*—everywhere I look around," she sang.

At that point the others joined in for the next line.

"*Love is in the air*—every sight and every sound," they sang.

Had this been a movie, the actual song would have faded up and started playing, thus giving us a lovely musical accompaniment as we sped off into the night. In reality, the song petered out at that point as no one could remember the next line, but I was still damn proud of my fellow pirates.

"Arrrrrr! Breaking into song shows some fucking serious pirate spirit!" I yelled, out.

I turned my attention back to our immediate problem and pressed the radio earpiece to my ear to listen for chatter, but still only heard static. I was getting the feeling that they might have switched to a different frequency, so I changed channels and listened at each click of the dial. Four clicks up, I heard frantic French being spoken, which meant that I was right, and now they were warning all their friends up ahead that we were out and on the run.

"Shit! It sounds like the frogs know the chickens have flown the coup! Things are probably going to get a little hairy, so everyone needs to be on the lookout for island security."

I turned to the dark road that loomed ahead and watched as the jungle gave way to open land and houses as we entered the south end of Old Town. Estelle and I hadn't seen this section on the first visit, and I was reminded again of why I liked this part of the island more than the resort side. This was where real people lived, and the homes were rustic and had that unique island character native to the Caribbean. Four more blocks and we were entering the little downtown area, and I could see that the Drunken Pig was still open—several of its customers milling around in front as the sound of Reggae music spilled out onto the street. I wonder if the Johns were in there right now, drinking rum and smoking the reefer? Ahhh—good times.

Headlights appeared ahead of us on the other side of town, and I told Billings about the back street that ran parallel to the main drag. He made a quick left and then a right onto the quiet alley, and our headlights suddenly illuminated a plus sized alley cat lounging in the middle of the road. He was no Mr. Pickles, but his size made him slow, and Billings's evasive driving maneuver to avoid the portly pet practically sent me and my precious case of rum flying out the side of the vehicle. I caught the case and averted a minor catastrophe, and we continued without incident down the alley and onto the next block. It was more of a residential area, and the houses were dark and the streets empty at such a late hour, which made it that much easier for us to keep an eye out for any island security. At the end of town, Billings turned right and then left to bring us back onto the main street, and all appeared quiet.

"So far, so good," he said.

Suddenly, a pair of headlights appeared behind us, and, a moment later, there was a flash, followed by the sound of a gunshot—the bullet coming so close that we could feel its shockwave as it raced past our vehicle.

"Or, perhaps not so good," I responded.

Billings began steering in an erratic serpentine manner to make us less of an easy target, and the next two shots thankfully missed. Eventually they would get lucky, and that meant we needed to get them off our tail. I leaned out to fire back but couldn't get a clear shot with our vehicle swerving left and right.

"You guys in the back have the best vantage point, so, one, or all, of you is going to have to shoot at those fuckers and get them off our ass!" I yelled.

No one looked very excited about my words, but at least Lux, Brett, and Kip had served in the military in some capacity and wouldn't be a complete stranger to this kind of task. Still, it was never fun to fire a weapon at a fellow human being, but Lux, knowing our safety was on the line, got the ball rolling by aiming and squeezing off a round. Her shot hit their left headlight and caused the driver to swerve right, where he narrowly missed a parked pickup truck before steering back onto the road. The little jeep immediately sped up and closed the distance, allowing the man in the passenger seat to lean out the side and prepare to fire his pistol. This time, Kip fired, and his shots impacted the jeep's right side mirror, forcing the man to retreat back into the jeep. Holy shit! Gymnast gopher really was a shooter.

I decided to join the fight and leaned out, waiting for the moment when I had a clear shot. Billings swerved right, giving me my opening, but, just as I pulled the trigger, we hit a bump in the road, and my shot went high and missed the jeep entirely. As I prepared to shoot again, Estelle fired off a round, and her bullet impacted the center of the jeep's windshield, causing the driver to panic and swerve. He lost control of the vehicle and it flew off the road and came to an unceremonious stop in a drainage ditch.

"Nice shooting, hippy!" I called out.

Estelle turned to me and blew the smoke from the tip of her barrel.

"I told you—my momma didn't raise no hippy."

Shortly thereafter, I heard more frantic French being spoken on the radio, and I was pretty sure it was the men in the jeep warning their friends that we were still on the loose. We reached the end of town and were soon on the same road Estelle and I had been on just the night before. It was, of course, a lot easier to navigate, as we were using the headlights, and the road was quiet and deserted for the moment. Of course, the French menace would surely be waiting for us somewhere up ahead, probably near the official port of entry.

"We should ditch the car when we get close and go the rest of the way on foot," I said, to Billings.

"Good idea. I'll stop the minute I see a place where we can pull off the road and hide the vehicle."

Billings slowed down, and we soon spied an opening up ahead on the left. We cut off the road and bumped over a small dirt berm and onto what appeared to be an old access road that had become partially overgrown by the surrounding jungle. It was clear enough for us to keep going, and we continued west, free of the French menace for the moment. The road finally became too dense, and Billings stopped the car and shut down the engine. Our surroundings were suddenly dark and quiet, the only illumination being the smattering of moonlight that made it through the jungle canopy above, and the only sound was the buzzing insects and the waves gently breaking on the nearby shoreline. I grabbed the case of Rum, and we headed towards the water. It was slow going as we picked our way through the dense foliage, but, after ten slow minutes of progress, I could see a light up ahead and realized we were approaching the beach access road. It ran parallel to the walking path that went from the hotels to the casino, and that meant we just happened to be in close proximity to my favorite landmark on the island—the rum distillery! Lux came up alongside me and delivered another of her scrutinizing looks.

"I can't believe that you're still carrying that case."

"It's a memento, like a T-shirt, only better."

"You're retarded."

"You're not allowed to use that word anymore."

"Oh, yes I can, because I'm using it properly."

"Oh, were you an English major? Do you happen to know the official definition of every word in the English language?"

She regarded me a moment with a holier than though look in her eyes before she answered.

"Retarded—adjective meaning a person less advanced in mental, physical, or social development than is usual for one's age."

As I quietly pondered her little victory and tried to think of a witty retort, the Ghost of Girlfriend Present decided to join the *let's give Tag some shit* party.

"I believe, Tag, that you lugging that case around is the equivalent of a teenager raiding his parent's liquor cabinet, and, as you're an adult, it means that you embody the exact meaning of the word retarded," Estelle said.

"Damn right, sister!" Lux said, holding up her hand for a high five.

The two completed the gesture then shared a laugh, the exchange a sign that my earlier fears were coming to fruition. It was bad enough that Lux pulled the proper definition of retarded out of her magnificent ass, but it was even worse that Estelle had come in for the assist—the two of them working together to take those words and shove them right up my butter maker. Clearly, the camaraderie between the ghosts of girlfriends past and present was alive and well.

"Well then, my walking talking dictionary and her beautiful

sidekick—we'll see who's retarded when we're back on the *Sozo*, and I'm making the best rum drinks you've ever had—drinks so good they'll make you *plotz*."

CHAPTER TWENTY-TWO
A Boat Too Far

We reached the road, and it was nice to finally be free of the jungle as we crossed over the short patch of asphalt and continued our journey on the walking path. We soon arrived at the little bridge where I'd rendezvoused with Estelle in her spectacular red dress, and there wasn't a security person in sight. That meant they were, as I suspected, waiting for us at the port of entry—or so it seemed, until the peaceful silence of the Caribbean night was interrupted by the sound of a vehicle coming up the path. I motioned for everyone to jump off the bridge and hide in the man-made river while we waited for it to pass. It turned out to be two guards in a little security jeep heading north towards the hotels, and, once they were gone, we decided that staying on the path was too risky and opted to head for the beach. There, we stayed in the shadows of a line of palm trees that bordered the shore then continued on until we were at last in sight of the official port of entry. The bad news was that there were two vehicles and at least eight guards forming a checkpoint to screen everyone attempting to leave the island. The good news was that the *Sozo's* tender was still tied up at the end of the harbor in the same spot, which meant that we had a ride home if we could just reach it without getting caught. I motioned for everyone to take cover behind a lifeguard shack, so that we could talk and form a plan.

"So, I'm thinking the best way past the guards is to swim out to the tender."

"What about your case of rum?" Lux asked.

"Alcohol is lighter than water, so it'll float," Kip said.

Holy shit. I'd hardly heard a single peep out of Kip the entire night, and his first words were in my defense. Perhaps I had misjudged the fucker.

"Thanks, Kip."

"You're still a jackass to be lugging that case around," Lux said.

"I agree," Estelle added.

"Can we talk about something else for a change? Perhaps, Brett's teeth, or what a good job I did getting all of us out of Babineux's presidential palace."

"No—not as long as you keep wasting your energy carrying around that case of booze."

"Do I seriously have to keep reminding you people that this is Soft Taco Island premium rum?"

I patted my precious wooden case, then we headed down to the water and continued out until it was shoulder deep. From there, we moved parallel to the shore until reaching the main pier, at which point we turned and headed out, careful to stay out of view of the guards. It only took a minute to swim to the end of the guest docks, which were particularly quiet at this hour. I heaved the case up onto the dock then climbed out and turned to help the others. Once we were all out of the water and huddled together, I gave the group a quick lesson on hand signals so that we could proceed without needing to speak. Keeping it simple, I showed them the signal for freeze. It was a closed fist, and the gesture inexplicably made Brett giggle. Fucking pilots. They probably had their own lame-ass hand signals. Rub your tummy if you wanted more pie, and hold up your fist if you needed to make a poopy. Basic pilot speak.

We started making our way out towards the *Sozo's* tender, and covered the distance without incident until I spied a person standing in the cockpit. He was facing the dock, and that meant it would be mostly impossible to sneak up on him from this side, so I held up a closed fist to signal everyone to stop, hopeful that Brett wouldn't take a shit. He did, however, let out a tiny snicker, so I extended my middle finger, giving him the one hand signal I knew he would understand. I imagine the tan wonder would have been taking this all a lot more seriously had we been fighting plaque. I put down the case of rum and turned to my merry band of pirates for a quick briefing.

"As you can see, we only have one final obstacle between us and freedom, but we need to take him out as quietly as possible so as not to alert his friends up on the pier."

"We get it, Captain Obvious. Now, what's your plan?" Lux asked.

"We need a distraction—preferably a lovely female one if you catch my drift. I'm thinking that one or all of you ladies can go over and talk to the French menace while I swim around and sneak up behind the fucker."

"So, you seriously want us to just walk over there and start talking to the guy? Are you forgetting that Soft Taco Island's security force is out looking for us?"

"Not at all, and the key word here is us. They're looking for seven people all traveling together—not three insanely beautiful, lonely women looking for a little action on the docks."

"Yeah, but I still think it'll seem a little suspicious."

"Not really. Even at this hour, people are going back and forth between the yachts and the island."

"Have you looked around? There's not a single person in sight."

"Don't worry. Even if he does get suspicious, I only need a small window of opportunity."

"OK, fine, I'll do it," Lux said.

"And I'll go with you," Estelle added.

"Me too," Tiffany chimed in.

"Even better, and remember, girls—your breasts are your

weapons."

The three of them stood up and started walking towards the boat, and I was happy to see that the pale light of the moon would be more than enough to illuminate their lovely curves. It certainly didn't hurt that all three were scantily dressed in bikinis. They stepped into the guard's view, and I couldn't help but imagine there were little pink hearts flowing out of his loins and encircling all four of them in a great big tornado of love.

"Excusez-moi, est-ce le ferry pour Martinique?" Lux asked, in a sultry voice.

That was my cue to slip into the water and make my way around the boat. I reached the stern of the tender and eased myself up onto the swim platform, careful not to create any undue noise. The boat shifted slightly under my weight, but the girls were doing a good job of keeping the man's attention. This allowed me to slip into the cockpit and prepare to take out our final obstacle. He was, as expected, totally enraptured by the girls, and he was talking and nodding his head so enthusiastically, that his thick mop of curly hair was dancing about his ears. As I stepped closer, I passed over a hatch in the floor, and it elicited a high pitched creaking sound that made me freeze in my tracks. The guard stopped talking and was turning his head in my direction when Estelle, apparently, remembered my fateful words.

"Hey!" she said, as she pulled open her bikini top.

Lux and Tiffany followed her lead, and now all three sets of their exposed breasts took firm hold of the man's attention. Unfortunately, I too was caught up in the moment and proceeded to stare in wonder at all three pairs of my beloved lifelong obsessions. Sure, I'd seen all of their bosoms fairly recently, but it was oddly more exciting to see them all together in a glorious six-boob chorus line. Estelle, Lux, and Tiffany all caught me staring and yelled in perfect unison.

"Tag!" they called out.

I broke from my stupor and reached over and stripped the

French guard's assault rifle off his shoulder and tossed it out of reach. Now that he was safely unarmed, I reached one hand around his throat while I used the other to place the barrel of my pistol against his head.

"You're mine, Goldilocks," I whispered, ominously into his ear.

He was in an odd state of mental incapacitation as his mind shifted from the gleeful joy of gazing at boobs to the sad contemplation of the potential of his premature demise, but, after a moment, he regained his wits enough to respond.

"My hair is dark brown you stupid asshole!"

"Yeah, but it's unnaturally curly."

"Well, fuck you, because I got my hair from my father."

"No, fuck you because you got it from a salon, and I get the last word because I'm the one with the gun pointed at your head."

"Whatever, I know you're not going to pull that trigger, as it will alert all my fellow security men on the shore."

"Are you willing to risk your life and that expensive perm on that possibility?"

The man thought for a moment then let out a frustrated sigh.

"Ah fuck it! They don't pay me enough for this shit, and, for the record, my hair really is this naturally curly," he said, as he acquiesced.

"Barring the expert opinion of a proper stylist, I suppose I'll just have to take your word for it. Now, ladies, would you come over and perform a little moonlight bondage on our French hair model here?"

The three of them started to readjust their clothing.

"Oh, there's no need to cover up just yet, as I think it's the least we could do to show our new friend a little kindness for making the right decision just now."

Unfortunately, Lux, Estelle, and Tiffany ignored my suggestion and proceeded to cover up their lovely bosoms.

"Oh well, I tried," I said, to the Frenchman.

"*Oui, merci*," he responded.

The girls came over, and we set about securing the Frenchman's hands, feet, and mouth with duct tape. When we finished Lux looked over and smiled at me.

"I hate to admit it, Finn, but you were right. Apparently, our breasts really are our weapons," she said.

The others rushed over, Kip now acting as the official bearer of my case of rum. He handed it over to me, then he and the others stepped into the cockpit of the tender. Brett and Kip helped me lift the bound Frenchman onto the dock, then we took a moment to discuss our next move.

"OK, fellow pirates, let's see how far we can drift before we start the engines. The longer we can wait, the less likely the security men on the shore will hear us," Billings said.

"Good idea, Pete. You take the helm, and we'll give the boat a push to get it going," I said.

Billings went to the helm, while Kip, Brett, and I undid the lines then pushed as hard as we could on the hull before jumping onto the swim platform. The boat slipped away from the dock, and, with our job done, the three of us climbed into the cockpit to join the others. We were fortunate that the current was flowing offshore, and, soon, we were more than fifty meters away from the dock.

"Time to take back our ship," Billings said.

"Yep, and there's only one way for our small but hearty band of pirates to deal with the French menace," I responded.

"Harrrrrrshly," he said.

"Damn right!"

He fired up the engines and eased them into gear without letting them warm up. It went against his nature to treat his boat this way, but it was a necessary evil. The tender started moving forward, and he steered us towards the *Sozo*, the pier thankfully remaining quiet and my radio free of French chatter. I looked down at my case of rum and felt a brief moment of satisfaction as I gently patted it, ever hopeful that our luck would hold out until we took back the *Sozo*.

"You'll be home soon, my darling," I said.

"I'd call you a jackass again, but it would obviously be redundant at this point," Lux said.

"Maybe we should find a new word to describe him," Estelle added.

"No, I have a better idea. Why don't we stick to the original word, but, this time, the two of you say it together so that I can enjoy it in stereo?"

It would have showed some real pirate spirit if they had actually done it, but they chose to remain quiet—probably just to spite me. Billings, meanwhile, steered the big tender gingerly up to the side of the *Sozo*, keeping the engines barely above an idle. Hopefully, if any of the French menace did hear us, they'd just assume that it was more of their friends coming to join the party. I jumped out and performed a quick sweep of the deck, and, finding it empty, returned to tie off the bowline. Kip got the stern and, once the boat was secure, we huddled up to figure out our next move.

"Pete, as we're on your territory, I figure it's up to you to decide how we proceed," I said.

"Well, first and foremost we need to know where our people are being held. If we're lucky, they're still in the main salon, but, Tag, I think you should do a little recon to be sure. Once we have the intel, we'll form a plan and proceed from there. Sound OK?"

"Yeah, but keep the rum safe. It's come a long way, and I'd hate to lose it now."

"As far as I'm concerned this case is our lovechild, and I intend to guard it with my life," Billings said.

"Good, and if for any reason I don't make it back, I want you to think of me fondly while you drink it."

"That goes without saying," he said, as he held up his right hand for a fist bump.

We completed the gesture and, once again, Tiffany decided to make fun of us.

"Should we break into another round of Love is in the Air?" she asked.

"Only if you can sing it very quietly."

I set off for the forward stairs, as they would allow me to recon the boat from the bow to the stern and, hopefully, stop by my cabin for some extra goodies. I came out in the crew's quarters, and, as I did a quick sweep of the rooms, heard a muffled cry from somewhere ahead. I walked by each cabin until finding the one where the noise originated, then placed my ear against the door and heard what sounded like a struggle. I checked the handle and, finding it was unlocked, quietly slipped inside. The lights were low, but it didn't hide the fact that one of the French guards was trying to force himself on Brett's new squeeze. She was stripped down to her bathing suit bottom, and he was clothed in only a wife beater tank top and bright blue butt hugger bikini underwear as he writhed atop her like a great big hairy octopus. He was nuzzling her neck and using his left hand to fondle her breasts, while he used his right to try and free his manhood by sliding off his obnoxious briefs. He couldn't seem to get them past his chubby thighs and, thankfully, was stuck in a kind of rapist's limbo.

The girl looked over, saw me at the door, and started to say something, but I put my finger to my lips to signal for her to stay silent. Unlike Brett, she understood hand signals and quietly waited for me to make my move. Fortunately, the scumbag was so engrossed in his unsavory sexual assault that he never heard me coming. With my anger at full tilt and my adrenaline pumping, I grabbed the French octopus by his shirt and underwear, and yanked him backwards off of the frightened girl. He flew like a rag doll and landed roughly on the floor then rolled onto his back, his member still hard as he tried to recover. I thought about kicking his boner, but, instead, carefully stepped past the appendage then punched him in the face. His head flew back and hit the floor, leaving him dazed enough, that I decided that he'd had enough for the moment, and I would finish him off by securing his hands and feet with duct tape. As I reached into my pocket, the fucker made two consecutive and unforgivable mistakes—the first being his smile and the second his words.

"Fuck you, asshole! She wanted it," he muttered.

It was time for a change of plans, as a statement that insulting deserved a proper response—and the only proper response I could think of at the moment was to kick him in the groin. My heel struck his testicles while the ball of my foot hit the tip of his penis, and it was officially the first time in my life that I had kicked the entirety of man's reproductive system. Sure, I'd kicked plenty of balls but this moment was special because it was my first boner. He cried out like a child and rolled onto his side, but he recovered quickly enough to reach for his rifle, which he'd carelessly left beside his shoes at the foot of the bed. I was quicker, however, and managed to step on his hand, pinning it and the weapon to the floor.

"Alrighty then, I can take the rifle and break your finger in the process, or you can release your grip, and save yourself a lot of pain. You make the call, shitbag."

He acquiesced and released his grip, allowing me to take the rifle from his hand.

"Good choice, my friend, but it still doesn't change what happened here," I said, as I threw a front kick straight to his face that knocked him out cold.

He would be out for some time, but a slippery sexual predator of his magnitude should always be properly restrained. I set about taping up his hands and feet, and, the minute I was done, the girl came over and hugged me. Her heart was pounding and tears were rolling down her cheeks as I held her in my arms, keenly aware of the fact that she was practically naked. I, therefore, prayed to God that Estelle and Lux didn't come walking in—although it certainly seemed like a real possibility considering my luck as of late. Eventually the girl pulled away and looked at me with the most grateful blue eyes I'd ever seen.

"Thank you," she said.

"You're welcome, but I'm really sorry you had to deal with this asshole."

"Yeah, but I'm not sorry with how you dealt with him."

I smiled and placed my hand on her shoulder.

"Extreme assholes require extreme measures. Now, I need to check on the others. Will you be OK?"

"Yeah, but I won't stay in here with that piece of shit."

"I understand. You can wait in my cabin."

I turned to go to the door, and she followed me, slipping her arm through mine, where I paused and thought about the fact that she was practically naked.

"Oh shit! I'm sorry—do you want to grab some clothes first?"

"I just want to get the hell out of here."

"Are you sure?"

"Pretty fucking sure."

"I completely understand, and my name's Tag, by the way. We haven't met, but I've seen you around the *Sozo*—though obviously not quite like this."

She shrugged and smiled shyly as she acknowledged her partial nudity.

"I'm Yvonne, and I'm really happy we finally met when we did."

I nodded, and she followed me out the door, taking firm hold of my hand as we walked up the hallway, keeping vigilant watch for any more of the French menace. We made it to my cabin, and I was happy to discover that it hadn't been disturbed, and all my things were just as I had left them—most important being the re-mainder of my weapons and equipment. I led Yvonne to the bed, covered her up with a blanket, then took a moment to comfort her by running my fingers through her hair as I told her everything was going to be OK. She had been through a traumatic encounter and needed as much positive reinforcement as possible in order deal with the shock. Unfortunately, I had to momentarily leave her to go to my gear bag to grab the two remaining flashbangs. Goodies in hand, I returned to her side to give her some final reassurance.

"This will all be over soon, so just stay here, and you'll be safe," I said, as I held her hand.

She smiled, and I could see relief in her eyes, so I was confident she'd be all right on her own for the moment. I left the room and moved down the hall towards the main salon, where I could hear the sound of some kind of sporting event on the television. I stopped just outside the doorway and gazed inside to see that the *Sozo's* crew and the guards were all there, the crew sitting on the floor while the guards were occupying the couches, two on the left and two more on the right. The noise I had heard was indeed a sporting event, and, now, I could see that all four guards had their eyes glued to a soccer game on the television. As Frenchmen, I would have thought that they'd be engrossed in some existential period romance or an old Jerry Lewis movie, but, alas, they had fallen prey to the curse that plagued nearly all men from every culture—the curse of watching sports on television. With my recon complete, I backtracked to the forward stairs and went down to the boat deck, where everyone reacted by bringing their weapons to bear on me with the speed of a nest of deadly pit vipers.

"Easy there, my wily pirates—it's only me."

They all lowered their weapons and relaxed.

"How's it look?" Billings asked.

"Not too bad, and I already managed to take care of one of them, but we've got four more in the main salon—two on the starboard side and two on the port, and all four of them are watching a soccer game. It shouldn't be too difficult, especially since I managed to stop by my cabin and pick up some goodies that will be a big help," I said, as I showed them the flashbangs.

"What are you going to do with grenades?" Estelle asked.

"They're flashbangs. They make a loud noise and send out an

incredibly bright blast of light that temporarily stuns and blinds anyone in the immediate vicinity. It's standard issue for any hostage rescue team."

She nodded in understanding, but I'm pretty sure that she thought I was a lunatic to have such items in my possession. Perhaps she would be happier if I collected stamps—and used them to stamp out injustice everywhere I went.

"Based on the layout of the room, it would be safest to split up into three fire teams. We go in after the flashbang with team one taking the left side and team two the right side, while team three holds at the door to watch our six and intercede should either team need assistance. We take the bad guys down hard and fast and, hopefully, won't even have to fire a shot."

"Sounds good to me," Billings said.

"Me too," Lux added.

"Oh, one final thing. It would be extremely convenient if you had some duct tape around here for the second team."

"Duct tape?" Estelle asked.

"Apparently, it's Finn's go-to accessory for every occasion," Lux responded.

"True, but in this particular instance, it's the easiest way to tag and bag the bad guys," I said.

"We have some," Kip said, as he walked over and grabbed a roll from the boat deck's utility closet.

With that problem solved, we divided up into our teams. Team one consisted of Lux and me, and we would take the left side of the room. Team two was Billings and Brett, and they would take the right side, while team three was Estelle, Kip, and Tiffany. With the planning faze completed, we went to the forward stairway and headed up to the next level, walking single file as we made our way to the main salon's entrance. Once there, I glanced inside and hoped to make eye contact with at least one of the crew, so that I could pass on the message for our people to prepare for the flashbang. Unfortunately, most of them were sleeping or keeping to themselves, so this called for a little field improvisation.

"Hold on—I'll be right back," I said, as I made my way to the galley.

Once there, I went to the bank of drawers that sat beside the sink then searched for the two items that I desperately needed to complete our assault on the main salon. They both turned out to be in the bottom of the third drawer. Perfect, I now had a rubber band and a paper clip—two more unlikely items that I considered indispensable to have on my person during a covert operation. Of course, I had both of those items in my tactical vest, but that fucker Babineux had been particularly thorough when he'd taken it during our little meeting earlier in the night. I rejoined the others then took a second to straighten the paperclip into a little arrow of sorts, completing the task by bending the end back to form a little hook.

"Dare I ask, *MacGyver?*" Lux whispered, as she regarded me with a skeptical look on her face.

"You'll see," I whispered back.

Stretching the rubber band between my thumb and forefinger, I created a little slingshot, then launched the paperclip at the nearest crewmember. It hit him in the arm, and he glanced in our direction, immediately smiling as he realized that we were there to take back the *Sozo.* I showed him the grenade and motioned for him to plug his ears, close his eyes, and open his mouth. He understood and then quietly passed on the news to the rest of the crew. Now that we had the home team on board with the plan, it was time to act.

I counted down from three with my fingers, and, when I reached one, everyone assumed the ready position, then I threw in the flashbang. There was a great blast of light and sound, then Lux and I went left while Billings and Brett went right. Our two guys each had their hands to their ears and were writhing around on the floor, which made them fairly manageable. I grabbed my guy and rolled him onto his stomach, jamming my knee into his back, while I taped his hands and feet. Once done, I looked over to check on Lux and saw that her guy had trapped her foot between his thighs, and he was doing his best to take her down— well, either that or he was trying to dry hump her leg. In either case, Lux didn't look too happy.

"Need a little help?" I asked.

She proceeded to pull her foot free and deliver a swift kick to the man's balls.

He immediately acquiesced, and Lux looked over and smiled at me as she responded.

"Do I look like I need help?"

Sweet fires of estrogen! I knew she was a badass pilot, but I had to admit that she was also pretty damn good with her hands, or, should I say, feet. After wrapping her guy up better than a Christmas present, I searched him for additional weapons and found my Walther PPK and Glock tucked inside his flak jacket. I was wondering if we'd ever be reunited, and saw this little twist of fate as an omen of good things to come. We moved over to see how Billings and Brett had faired, and discovered them looking perplexed as they stood over a lone, bound guard.

"Where's the other one?" I asked.

"We only had one guy on our side," Billings said.

"Shit."

I scanned the room, curious if he had somehow managed to crawl into a corner, but there was no trace of the elusive fourth guard. At that moment, Kip, Estelle, and Tiffany came in to check on the situation.

"How did it go?" Estelle asked.

"Good, except that we're missing a guard."

There was the sound of a door opening, and everyone looked over to see our missing fourth guard come casually strolling out of the main salon's bathroom. His assault rifle was slung over his shoulder, and, as he took in the scene, he stopped cold in his tracks and quickly brought his rifle around into firing position. I drew my pistol and prepared to act, but Kip moved in on the man with the swiftness of a wraith and used his left hand to drive the aim of the barrel down towards the floor. With the rifle pointed in a safe direction, he wrapped his right arm around the man's back and performed a hip throw that sent the Frenchman flying head over heals. He landed on the floor with a dull thud, and Kip, now holding the rifle, slid back the bolt, chambered a round, and pointed it at the man before casually smiling and turning his gaze to me.

"It's OK, Tag. I've got this," he said.

"Sweet burning fire of Chuck Norris's loins! I had no idea you were so good with your hands!" I blurted out.

"Oh, I'm that good all right. It's just too bad I didn't get the opportunity to give you a more hands-on demonstration before now."

Fuck! Kip was indeed my Kato, though far more skilled in the art of hand to hand combat, and this revelation would do very little to help me sleep in the coming nights.

"Alrighty then, Pete, what do you want to do with these guys?" I asked.

"For the moment, we'll stick them down on the boat deck."

"Good idea, and the guy I already took out is in crew cabin four, all packaged and ready to go."

"I'll send some crewman to get him and put him under the tree with the other presents."

We shared a little laugh, then Billings's look turned serious.

"How soon will you be ready to move on the *Sarsarun*?"

"Apparently, there ain't no rest for the wicked, so I'm going to stop by my cabin to grab a few things, then I'll be ready to roll in about ten minutes."

"Good! I'll be ready when you are," he said.

As I turned to go, my gaze unintentionally fell upon the bar, where I spied my beloved tactical vest still packed with all of its goodies. Sweet hot, deep fried peanut butter and banana sandwiches! Things were definitely looking up!

CHAPTER TWENTY-THREE
The Sarsarun

I was just passing the galley, heading aft when Lux caught up to me and proceeded to follow me to my cabin. She was looking particularly nervous and wanted to talk about how we were going to take down the *Sarsarun*. This entire operation had been hers from the start, so I could understand why she might be especially eager to make sure we were successful. I opened the door to my room, and, Yvonne, who I had completely forgotten about in all the excitement, popped her head up and smiled with relief as she regarded me.

"There you are!" she said, excitedly.

I could already feel Lux's scornful gaze as Yvonne, still wearing only her bikini bottom, leapt out of my bed and hugged me, pressing her bare breasts against my chest and practically squeezing the air from my lungs. I hugged her back, as it was only polite considering what she had been through, though I knew full well that I would have some serious explaining to do. Then, as if it couldn't get any worse, Estelle and Brett came strolling into my cabin. Apparently, my open door policy was still in effect, as neither bothered to knock or wait for an invitation. Thankfully, I was only harboring a beautiful naked woman and not taking a dump. The room became uncomfortably quiet as Brett, Lux, and Estelle all looked at me with a colorful blend of scorn and curiosity. They were obviously waiting for me to explain this awkward turn of events, but I wasn't sure where to begin.

"So, Tag, would you like to explain why Yvonne is naked and in your arms?" Estelle asked.

"Yeah, I'd kind of like to know the answer to that question as well," Brett said.

"Me too," Lux added.

"She's only half naked, and seriously now, people. When doesn't a beautiful woman, partially naked or otherwise, end up in my arms?"

No one found that particularly funny, but, thankfully, Yvonne interceded and told them the entire story in all its glorious detail. By the time she finished talking, tears had welled up in her eyes, and she continued to hug me, thanking me once again for coming to her rescue. At that point, Estelle wrapped Yvonne up in a blanket, then she and Brett led her out of the room. A second later the door opened a crack and Brett leaned his head back inside.

"Oh, hey—thanks, Tag," he said.

"You're welcome."

He closed the door, and I turned to see Lux regarding me with a peculiar smile.

"Just when I thought you couldn't possibly be a bigger manwhore, you returned to being the Finn I knew and fell in love with back in Afghanistan," Lux said.

"Oh, are we back in the time bubble again?" I asked, as I pointed at the bed.

"Unfortunately, we need to come up with a plan for the *Sarsarun*." she said, though there was a sparkle in her eye that told me she was at least pondering that thought.

"Well, in that case, I'm thinking we should let our fingers do the walking by conducting a little online research about the yacht and its owners. I find that it's always nice to know even a little about the people you might have to kill."

"That's a pretty grim sentiment."

"Yeah, but it's a pretty grim business."

"It certainly is at times like this."

"Alrighty then, I know the Agency already investigated these fuckers, but I figure at the very least we might find out something about the boat and its layout."

I took out my laptop, brought up Google, and typed in *Sarsarun*. Several hits came up including the meaning of the name, which was Arabic in origin and translated as fast wind in English. The fourth on the list was an article about the yacht, which belonged to the thirty-second wealthiest person in the world. He was a Saudi businessman named Habib Mubarak, and there was even a picture of him and his family. He had a pretty wife named Amira, two pretty teenage daughters, Adina and Feliz, and one son, Nadir, who was a good-looking twenty something. The article was mostly a puff piece with some nice photos, but it didn't give a clear picture of the interior layout of the *Sarsarun*. Oh well, at least I had names and faces.

"It's a lovely yacht, and they appear to be a nice family and, honestly, it's hard to imagine Habib firing off a missile at an airliner or building, which means he's either really good at hiding his illicit activities, or he loans out his boat to some pretty unsavory friends," I said.

"Yeah, and I can see why the Agency came to the conclusion they did. He certainly doesn't look like a terrorist."

"None of them do until they pull the trigger, but I imagine there's probably a lot more to this story, and we'll find out the rest when we take down the yacht."

"Speaking of which, any ideas yet about how we how we should do it?" she asked.

"I'm thinking it'll be easiest if I sneak aboard and try to take them out one at a time—ninja style. That way, we can avoid any kind of all-out fire fight, and hopefully end up with more than a few Chatty Cathies to spill their guts about their terrorist organization and its various members."

"That's it?"

"That's it. Simple, stupid, and effective."

"Just like you."

"Yeah, me—the guy you didn't marry, but call when you're in real trouble."

Lux smiled.

"Sorry—sometimes I can't help myself," she said.

"Don't I know it."

She smiled and gave me a playful hit to the bicep, but then her look turned serious.

"So, that really is the entirety of your plan?"

"Yep."

Lux didn't look entirely convinced, but desperate times called for desperate measures, and it was officially time to pick out equipment for the mission. I opened the closet and rustled around in my equipment bags looking for the toys I'd need to take down the *Sarsarun*. I pulled out my bulletproof vest and weapons then placed the latter on the bed. Now, I had a difficult decision to make, like trying to choose between a blond, a brunette, or a redhead. After a moment of thought, I decided on the M4 Rifle, the HK94 submachine gun, and two pistols, which was sort of like having a blond, a brunette, and two redheads. Boats, even large ones, had a lot of different sized areas where the shooting could take place. In close quarters it was better to have the maneuverability of the smaller weapons like the pistols or the submachine gun, but, on the deck or in any of the larger spaces, it might be better to have the accuracy and added firepower of the rifle—especially considering the disposition of my potential targets. They were likely extremists and more than willing to die for their cause, and that meant I needed to be prepared. Of course, if they were that eager to go to heaven, then I'd be more than happy to help send them on their way. I put the stuff I didn't need back in the closet then sat down on the bed beside Lux to find her looking a wee bit concerned.

"Are you worried about Bridgette?" I asked.

"That's part of it, but, now I'm worried about you. You shouldn't do this alone."

"I'm not, I'm bringing two good friends along. Heckler and Koch."

"That's not funny."

"Well—Heckler is, but Koch is the quiet type."

I thought it was a good pun on the names of the founders of HK, but Lux didn't look amused.

"I didn't save your ass all those years ago to send you off on a suicide mission because I screwed up my own assignment."

"You said it yourself. There are thousands of lives at stake. We don't have time to wait for reinforcements."

"Then I'm coming with you."

"Do you honestly think that's a good idea?"

"As a matter of fact, I do. I'm a fully trained field operative so, technically, I'm the most capable person here to back you up."

"Well, other than Kip, apparently, though I couldn't be entirely certain he wouldn't end up shooting me instead of the terrorists."

Lux appeared to be confused by my statement and obviously thought it was a joke.

"Come on, Tag! Stop fucking around and admit that you need me on this one."

Lux stared intently at me as I sat there thinking, and I could tell from her expression that she wasn't going to take no for an answer. Unfortunately, the sad truth was that she was right, and I could use another person. Teams worked better than loners, as it enabled you to cover more angles of fire and you had someone to watch your back. I looked up into her beautiful blue eyes and melted like butter on a hot griddle.

"OK, fine, but I have one condition."

"What?"

"It's a matter of principle."

"What?" she asked again, sounding annoyed.

"You have to admit that marrying Corn was a mistake."

"Fuck you. You've slept with everyone on this boat except for Billings and Brett."

"It's not my fault that those two turned me down."

"It's not funny."

"It's kind of funny."

"Fuck you. You fucked my sister."

"Fuck you. She fucked me."

"Same difference."

I guess she was still a little sensitive about the whole I slept with your sister thing. I didn't get it. She married my best friend behind my back, and, in my book, we were more than even. Unfortunately, women had their own unique set of laws regarding relationships, and the majority of them existed in stark contrast to men's ideas of justice. Apparently, my offense was worse in her estrogen fueled legal system, so, instead of continuing the conversation and making her more angry, it seemed safer to change the subject by discussing the disbursement of equipment for the mission. I gave her the bulletproof vest, but I kept the tactical one. She also got one of my silenced pistols, and I thought about whether or not I should give her the M4 assault rifle. Its high energy rounds could tear through fiberglass and man alike, which could be useful if we ended up needing a higher powered weapon. But, it was a lot to carry, so, for the moment, I just slung it over my shoulder with the HK, and we left my cabin and found Billings in the main salon.

"I just came from the bridge, and, according to the radar report, Babineux's yacht, the Soft Taco III, has left the island and is heading south towards Martinique, which means your intel was likely accurate."

"Good to know," I said.

"Yeah, but we'll have to deal with that problem after we get the missile launchers," Lux said.

"Speaking of which, Pete, we're going to need the fastest, quietest way to board the *Sarsarun*. Any ideas?" I asked.

"I'd take the Jet Ski. It's small, fast, maneuverable, practically no radar signature, and has room for three."

"Three?"

"You, Lux and I. You won't have time to mess around with your ride. You need a fast insertion, and it'll be a lot faster if I drive in and drop you off."

"Good thinking."

"I'll have Kip get it ready," Billings said, as he left the bridge.

The pre-mission adrenaline rush was starting to kick in and make me a feel a little giddy.

"I must admit—I'm kind of excited to be back in the game again," I said.

"If you enjoy it that much, then why did you leave?"

"It's kind of a long story."

"Does it involve the other two amigos?"

"No, we'd already disbanded by then, so I was a lone wolf amigo when I made the decision to leave the Agency. When we're done with all this, we'll have to have a drink, and I'll tell you all about it."

"It's a date."

"A date? That sounds a little risqué for a married woman."

"Friends can go out on dates."

"Sure, but what happens if they end up having sex on a beach?"

"That's not funny—and, technically, it wasn't a date."

"Then it was one of the best non-dates I've ever had."

Billings announced over the *Sozo's* intercom system that everything was ready, so Lux and I headed to the aft boat deck. As we stepped off the stairs, Kip smiled and said hello, which wasn't his usual greeting, but then I wasn't half naked and having sex with Estelle at the moment. He set about fueling up the Jet Ski, while Lux and I headed into the dive room to pick out wetsuits. We decided on the shorty kind which were designed for warmer weather with their short sleeves and equally short pant legs. Once again, Lux was struggling to squeeze her ample breasts into the suit, and this time I managed not to mention her sister, though I did giggle.

"Oh, are you enjoying the view, man-whore?" she asked.

"I am, actually."

"Well, avert your eyes, because this ship has sailed."

"Oh, come now, Lux, if you're going to put pudding on a shelf, then someone is going to eat it."

"Did you seriously just say that?"

I smiled.

"Of course. I love that classic old saying."

"Classic, my ass. That was obviously something stupid you just made up."

"Well, technically that's true, but even old sayings had to start somewhere."

"Yeah, but I seriously doubt that one is going to get any traction, so it'll never make it beyond this boat deck to become a classic."

"Are you kidding? It has the open ended universality that is the cornerstone of all great sayings. Can't you see it could be applied to any body part on display—your lovely backside, for instance."

"I think we're officially back to the whole retarded thing, so it's probably a good idea for you to shut the fuck up and help me get this thing on."

Seeing she was legitimately frustrated, I dropped the subject and reached over and zipped the suit up the rest of the way. She thanked me in spite of her frustration, and we put on the rest of our gear in silence. Once finished, I checked to make sure she had put on the bulletproof vest properly, but she swatted me away.

"I know how to put one of these on," she said, testily.

"It's not a reflection on you. I always check my team members before an op," I said.

"Fine."

I checked to make sure she had it buckled correctly, and everything looked shipshape, so maybe she was right, and I was just being over protective. Whatever—I didn't get her off of Soft Taco Island to get her killed raiding a terrorist pleasure yacht. She gave me a smug smile, knowing she had done a good job, so I moved around to inspect the back.

"Everything looks good here too," I said, giving her rear end a firm smack.

"Do you always smack your team members on the ass as well?"

"Absolutely. It's a tradition in special operations. We do it for good luck," I said, as I turned and prepared to leave the dive room.

"Well, then here's to good luck," she said, as she slipped up behind me and smacked my ass with the ferocity a farmer might utilize when coaxing an obstinate heifer into the barn.

The blow was loud enough to make my ears ring, and sent me bounding out the door, where I practically fell into the arms of Billings who was just coming in to change.

"Hey! Easy there, Peter Pan! Save a little for the terrorists," he said, as he helped me back up to my feet.

"I was just giving Tag's ass a good luck slap. He said it was a tradition in special operations. Is that true, Pete?" Lux asked.

Billings turned to her and answered in a serious and authoritative tone.

"Absolutely," he said, before patting me on the ass.

"Men," Lux grumbled.

Billings went into the dive room and changed into a shorty wetsuit then called up to the bridge to get a radar report on the *Sarsarun*. Our target was still at anchor down in the cove by Babineux's villa, which meant we finally had some good news. We all moved to the side, and, while Kip used the davit to lower the Jet Ski into the water, I had a moment to reconsider my equipment choices. The M4 was probably a little bulky for our purposes and the HK, while smaller, would also hinder our maneuverability. I, therefore, decided to give both to Billings in the event we needed some serious backup. With my last minute weapon plans resolved, it was time to board the Jet Ski. Billings climbed on first, then me, and finally Lux. Personally, I would have rather had Lux in the middle, but it came down to the best position for boarding the *Sarsarun*. Being closer to the front would allow me to go first then help Lux get aboard if need be. Billings started the engine, and I settled in, placing my hands around his waist.

"Comfortable?" he asked.

"Absolutely. What man isn't comfortable wearing a tight rubber suit while holding another man in an equally tight rubber suit?"

Lux climbed aboard, completing our awkward threesome, her arms wrapped around my waist and her chin resting on my shoulder. Truth be told, it felt good to have her that close, but it also made it clear what an emotional roller coaster my personal life had become. At least the fact that she was married to Corn, and I was dating Estelle kept things simple—in a twisted, complicated sort of way. Kip let us loose, then Billings gunned the powerful motor, and, within seconds, we were skimming the waves at a conservative sixty miles per hour. The Jet Ski would do eighty, but he wanted to be careful about how much noise we made. We sped through the night, and, even though we weren't close to full throttle, it felt like trying to reign in a racehorse. Thank God Billings knew what he was doing and managed to zigzag around the anchored yachts and boat traffic using only moonlight to navigate the island's busy waterways. We left the main bay behind and only minutes passed before we saw the lights of the *Sarsarun* in the distance. Billings slowed down to an idle to quiet our approach then did a wide loop around the stern to see if they had any sentries on deck. It was pretty much deserted except for a single guy on the transom who was stowing some inflatable boat bumpers in a compartment below the aft deck. That was actually a very ominous sign, as those bumpers were put out when you had another vessel rafted up alongside—in this case it was most likely a submarine with a load of shoulder-fired missiles. That meant our transaction was indeed complete, and we were just in time. The man closed the hatch then walked inside the yacht, leaving the deck deserted.

"Don't seem to be keeping much of a watch," Billings said.

"Might as well take us all the way in on the port side."

Billings gave it a little throttle, and we rapidly closed the distance to the stern of the boat. This was the critical window where we would be the most visible to the people aboard, although that would change once we were close enough to be hidden by the towering sides of the hull. We made it without incident, but the current around the boat made it difficult to keep the Jet Ski steady. Fortunately, Billings was a good helmsman and got us right up to the swim platform. I jumped across then turned and held Lux's hand as she made the leap. With both of us safely aboard, I held my hand to my ear to symbolize that I'd radio him when we were done. He nodded solemnly, swerved hard to port, and idled away from the hulking yacht. Lux and I looked at each other, and took a final moment of calm before heading into the unknown dangers of the *Sarsarun*.

The boat's lights were all on, so it was safe to assume that everyone was up and probably getting ready to set sail. We climbed up a short staircase to reach the stern deck then took cover to the side of the sliding glass doors that led into the yacht's main salon. I peered around the edge of the doorframe and saw that the room was empty, and not a single person was taking advantage of the plush leather furniture, massive dining table, or full bar. We, therefore, stepped inside and made our way across the room, but paused when we heard the sound of voices coming from the forward passageway.

"Shit, we better hide. I'm thinking behind the bar is our best option," I said.

"This seriously better not be about you trying to score more alcohol."

"Don't be silly. It's a strategic choice. If these are true Muslims, then it'll be the safest hiding place on the boat."

"Let's hope so," she said, as we raced over and ducked down behind the bar.

We listened as the voices drew closer, and, interestingly, they were speaking English with a slight British accent, which meant our visitors had likely spent a fair amount of time in England.

"Yousef, would you get us a scotch and meet me in my cabin? I could use something to steady my nerves," one of the men said.

"Of course, Nadir," the other guy responded.

Interesting—Nadir was the yacht owner's son, so this may very well be a family affair, or, more likely, the little fucker was secretly moonlighting as a jihadist. Lux looked at me nervously as we listened to the guy named Yousef making his way ever closer to our hiding spot.

"What do we do?" she whispered.

"This," I said, waiting until I knew Yousef was right on the other side of the bar before I abruptly stood up and placed the barrel of my pistol against his forehead.

"You can be a good Muslim or a booze hound, but you can't be both. Are you going to heaven or hell, fuckface?"

He was probably in his middle twenties, had the soft look of a person who had been raised in extreme privilege, and was particularly plump and devoid of any muscle tone. Combine all that with the fact he was wearing brown pants and a red shirt, and he looked more like a man-sized *Winnie the Pooh*. He stared wide-eyed in terror, unable to speak, and appeared as though he might shit his pants at any moment. I'd seen the look before, and it wasn't pretty, especially if the person in question actually did shit his pants.

"Well? What's your answer, *Winnie*?" I asked.

"Um..."

I thought about what the little shit was involved in, and I found my anger rising up inside of me and decided the terrorist needed to experience a little terror of his own.

"Hell, it is," I said, in my best *Clint Eastwood* voice, as I cocked my pistol.

Before I could complete my little show of farce, his eyes rolled into the back of his head, and he inexplicably passed out, apparently, from fear. His limp body flopped down onto the bar then slid backwards onto the floor.

"That was a little extreme," Lux said.

"Not for an extremist," I countered.

We moved around to the other side of the bar, and saw that he was laid out flat on his back and looked particularly peaceful in his current state.

"Why did you call him *Winnie?*" she asked.

"I thought the combination of his brown pants, red shirt, and pudgy body made him look like *Winnie the Pooh.*"

She gazed at him for a moment then nodded.

"I hate to admit it, but I can totally see it."

As I stood there gazing at the young man, I thought he seemed a little too soft to be an adequate terrorist, as a lot of the guys I had encountered back in Afghanistan were pretty hardened individuals. *Winnie the Pooh* here wouldn't have lasted more than ten minutes over there before he'd be calling his parents and requesting a first class flight home so he could be reunited with *Tigger, Eeyore,* and *Piglet.* With Lux's help, I duct taped his hands and feet, then we dragged him onto the back deck to the very same hatch where he'd stored the bumpers. I opened it and discovered a large storage room beneath the deck. Perfect. We dropped Winnie through the opening, and his slack body inadvertently missed the soft rubber bumpers and hit the hard floor. Oops. He'd have a few extra bruises, but those were the breaks when you became a terrorist. We headed back inside, and I went to the bar and filled a glass with scotch.

"Don't tell me you're having another cocktail right now," Lux said, looking irritated.

"Of course not! I'm just getting Nadir his scotch."

With the cocktail in my left hand and my gun in my right, I led the way as we headed for the passageway at the other end of the salon. First up was the galley and next were the cabins—the layout fairly similar to the *Sozo,* which made me suspect there was some kind of logic or tradition that naval architects followed when they designed mega-yachts. I heard music coming from behind the first door and suspected it was probably the owner's stateroom, only in this case, it was apparently occupied by his wayward son. As we got closer I whispered in Lux's ear.

"Time to meet Nadir, the thirty-second wealthiest man in the world's piece of shit son."

"Shit—the analysts at Langley never even considered him and primarily screened his father."

"Personally, I find it unlikely that the dad would be involved, as he has way too much to lose—and, I'd be willing to bet a lot of money that he has no idea how his son is using the family yacht."

"Ahh, kids," Lux muttered.

"Yeah, and seriously now, what in the hell makes a billionaire's son choose this path? Was the little prick bored with his idyllic life of privilege and decided it would be fun and exciting to become a terrorist?"

"God only knows, but do you think the little shit is actually dangerous?"

"Only when he has a video game controller in his hands but not in the real world."

"Maybe he makes up for it with intelligence."

"Maybe, though I can't imagine he's all that bright if he's mixed up in this shit."

"True."

Upon reaching the door, I knocked, and we waited for a response, something no one ever did outside my cabin. We heard the words come in, so we walked inside and found Nadir sitting in front of a laptop, where he was typing in his status on Facebook. What had the world come to when terrorists actually updated their nefarious activities? I wouldn't be surprised if Nadir had just written fighting the great Satan, so that his asshole jihadist friends could *like it* or *comment*. I brought the drink over and set it on the desk beside him. He glanced up to thank me and realized that I wasn't Yousef, and he froze with his eyes wide in terror—the only movement being his beating heart. He closed his laptop then turned around to face us, and, gazing at him head on, I could see he looked pretty much exactly as he had in his picture, though he now sported a scant amount of facial hair that may have been purposeful or the result of some lazy grooming standards.

"Who the hell are you?" he asked, trying desperately to sound authoritative.

In reality, he sounded like the frightened twenty something he really was.

"We're from *Tali-Beard*. I believe you called our company about wanting to have a fuller and more radical beard."

"I don't understand."

"It's a joke, Nadir, and you'll be very unhappy to know that we're from the United States government. Did you think you'd buy a hundred million dollars in Russian shoulder-fired missiles and get away with it?"

He sat there unable to speak, looking as though he was having a painful bowel movement until words started to come from his mouth.

"I have nothing to do with the arms deal. The men behind it forced me to give them access to the yacht by threatening to hurt me and my family. I can show you—I have proof of it right here."

He turned and reached down into the top drawer of the desk and pulled out a chrome plated Desert Eagle Fifty caliber pistol. Clearly, this kid was new to this kind of thing, as no one but a spoiled brat, raised on video games and bad movies, would carry a piece like that. Still, it was a lot of firepower, and could blow my head clean off more efficiently than *Dirty Harry's* 357 Magnum. Of course, I also knew that it was a real pisser to aim and fire accurately, as the recoil was enough to separate your arms from your shoulders—inspiring the Israelis who'd created the monster to develop a special technique just to fire the damn thing.

"You're here to kill me aren't you?" he bellowed.

"No, we're just here to stop you."

I lowered my voice and tried to sound consoling.

"Look shithead, you're way out of your league here. Don't waste your Oxford education on a bullet to the brain."

"You know nothing about me—about any of this!"

"I know you're the son of the thirty-second wealthiest person in the world, and your father Habib has no idea what you're really doing with the family yacht. I'm also pretty sure that your mother Amira and your two sisters, Adina and Feliz would not be very proud of you at the moment."

He was shocked, and I could see him desperately trying to understand how I could know so much about him. To his credit, he tried again to sound confident, but his voice kept breaking each time he spoke.

"I don't understand how you know..."

"Oh, we know everything, Nadir."

The gun stayed pointed at my head, but I could see the strain in both his arm and his will. The Desert Eagle was extremely heavy and his hand was shaking, partially from fear, but mostly from the weight. Even the bullets were heavy and eventually he'd wish he had a nice light 9MM or even a 22. If he didn't willingly lower his weapon soon, I might have to lower it for him, but it would be a good, if not painful, way to teach him about the consequences and punishment for making bad life choices. Once again, I had to wonder what brought this kid to this moment? Were his parents too harsh and he was rebelling, or were they too soft and he was just a spoiled, bored brat, too lazy to go into the family business? Now, his gun hand was really starting to sag, and I saw my opening. I stepped right and grabbed the weapon with my left hand and twisted it out of his grip, lightly pistol-whipping him with my own gun. He cried out and dropped his head into his hands and began to sob. I grabbed him firmly by the collar and gave him a little shake to get his attention.

"All right, pussy, you can cry later, but right now we need to know how many people are on the boat?"

"Tag!" Lux exclaimed.

"What? He's a terrorist."

"He's a kid."

"He's over eighteen. That makes him a full fledged terrorist and, more importantly, an asshole."

Lux stepped in and pushed me aside, apparently unhappy with my version of the ol' feel-good approach. She knelt down so that she was face to face with the kid then placed her hands on his thighs and spoke with a soft soothing voice. She certainly didn't speak that way to me—not since I had sex with her sister, anyway. The boy's crying got worse and soon Lux had him completely in her arms. Of course, it was my theory that the little shit probably just wanted to get a closer look at her breasts. Hell—if I had known that would work, I would have cried in front of her a long time ago. The longer she held Nadir, the more he relaxed, so I guess she was correct in using her gentle loving approach to interrogation. He became nothing more than a puppet in her arms as he remained glued to her chest. Eventually, Lux eased his head away, so that she could look at him with her endearing blue eyes that no man could resist.

"Why would you get involved in all this? I know you don't really want the deaths of thousands of innocent people on your conscience," Lux said.

"You're correct, and I don't know what the hell I'm doing here, as it all happened so quickly. A friend from my university brought me to a party, and the host spoke about the importance of saving our culture from the West. He tried to make it all sound very heroic, but I wasn't interested and tried to leave. That's when they took me to a private room and told me they needed to use the *Sarsarun* to complete an upcoming attack. I refused to agree to their demands, so, as I told you before, they forced me to help them by threatening to hurt me and my family."

"You've been dragged into a bad situation with some bad people, and in order for us to help you and take care of all this, we're going to need you to tell us as much as you can about the rest of the men on this yacht."

He wiped his eyes and seemed to perk up a little.

"There are seven more men on the boat, including the captain, who you should know is being forced to help against his will. Of the other six, one of them is my friend Yousef, but he's a good person and only here because I dragged him into this. I don't want him to get hurt because of me."

Lux glanced over at me with a disapproving look on her face, and I responded with a shrug, as it wasn't my fault his fucking friend passed out from fear.

"Well, then there are five men left, as I've already taken care of your friend, and he's safe and unharmed—mostly, anyway," I said, muttering the last two words under my breath.

"These men are fanatics, and their leader Jael is the worst of them and is said to kill men, women, and children without remorse."

"I assume you know that the minute they delivered the missile launchers, you and your friend Yousef would have become liabilities and been eliminated," Lux said.

"Yes, but we were hoping to have escaped by then."

"Well, then thank your lucky stars, because the cavalry have arrived," I said.

"The cavalry? I don't understand," Nadir responded, looking confused.

Apparently, he'd never heard that expression.

"The cavalry were a mounted military unit in old western movies that would ride in at the last moment and save the day. In this instance, we're the cavalry, and if we're going to save the day, then we're going to need to know where the bad guys are at the moment."

"I believe they are all in the upper lounge, as Jael wanted to have some kind of private meeting."

"Perhaps to discuss how to deal with you and your friend."

"Perhaps," he said, gravely.

"Are they armed?"

"I'm not sure about the others, but Jael always carries a pistol."

"Nadir, can we trust you to stay here, out of the way? It's for your own safety," Lux said.

"Yes, I'll stay here."

He rubbed his red eyes and appeared distraught as he stared at the floor. I looked at Lux and showed her the roll of duct tape, but she shook her head and whispered that we could skip that part. I guess she trusted the little fucker and thought he would stay put, though I still had my doubts.

CHAPTER TWENTY-FOUR
The Ace in the Hole

We left Nadir in his cabin and moved quietly down the passage-way, and I quickly realized that carrying the Desert Eagle pistol was a major nuisance. It was heavy as hell, and we had a lot of boat to cover with five hostile fanatics still at large—one of them a ruthless killer, so I, therefore, decided it was more of a hindrance than a help and tossed it into a linen closet. We continued on and found the stairs and moved quietly upward, the tension increasing with every step as we looked and listened for any sign of our targets. I had a passing thought and decided to stop and have a quick word with Lux.

"What is it?" she asked.

"I was just thinking that if we didn't manage to survive this little encounter that now might be a good time to finally acknowledge that you made a mistake when you married Corn."

"Shut up. This is stressful enough without your shitty attempts at humor," she said, sounding annoyed.

"OK, then we'll just leave it unsaid."

"Good—now, get going."

I continued on and suddenly felt the powerful slap of Lux's

hand on my backside, the lasting sting making me seriously consider the fact that my little joke in the dive room was coming back to bite me in the ass—literally. We arrived at the top of the stairs to find ourselves in a sort of anteroom that resided between the bridge and the aft upper lounge Nadir had mentioned. There were four doors, one to the bridge, one to the lounge, and one on each side of the boat that accessed the deck that encircled the entire upper level. We needed to do a little recon first, and that entailed using one of the outer doors to go onto the deck and look through the windows of the two compartments. We headed outside and crept over to the bridge first and looked inside to see a man in his middle fifties with salt and pepper grey hair and the weathered skin of someone who had lived his life at sea. He was obviously the captain, and the fact that he wasn't looking particularly happy meant that Nadir had likely been telling us the truth—at least about him, anyway. With that room clear, we went to the window outside the aft lounge and looked in to see there were four people seated inside, and they appeared to be having a rather serious conversation. Unfortunately, we couldn't see the entire room, so all we could do was hope that our fifth man was also in there. We slipped back out of view to take a moment to discuss our game plan.

"I say we throw in a flashbang and anybody who resists, goes strait to Allah," I said.

"That's it?"

"That's it."

"And what about the fifth guy?"

"Let's just hope he's in there. Now, for the breach—I'll go in first. You hang back at the door and keep an eye on our six in case number five isn't in there and decides to crash the party late."

"I got it. Keep an eye on your six."

"Our six—which includes your backside as well," I said, reaching down and giving her buttocks a solid pat.

"You'll come up with any excuse to touch my ass, won't you?"

"Pretty much, now let's do this."

We walked back into the hallway, stood at the door, and took a second to ready ourselves. It sure would be convenient if all five were in there, as it was never as much fun as you'd think having a stray fanatic sneak up behind you. I eased open the door and threw the flashbang into the center of the room, where it went off with the usual ear splitting bang and blinding flash of light. I burst through the doorway and converged on the men to find them all holding their ears and writhing around in agony on the floor. Unfortunately, there were only four of them, which meant our mysterious fifth terrorist wasn't here. Oh well, we'd deal with these fuckers first then go find lucky number five when we were done.

I had a moment to take a closer look at our merry band of terrorists and could see they were all Middle Eastern, middle aged, and a bit thick in the middle. In my opinion, they were a little too soft and clean-shaven for extremists, but their appearance was probably purposeful so they could blend in better with us smooth shaven infidels. The first two guys were easy to take down, as the combination of the shock of the flashbang and me shoving a pistol in their faces made them particularly malleable—thus allowing me to quickly secure them before moving on to my next target. The third guy had his wits about him, however, and rolled over and kicked me hard in the stomach—the only upside being that he'd missed my groin. It knocked a little of the wind out of me, but, fortunately, I had exhaled and tightened my stomach muscles just as he landed his foot. It still hurt, but I ignored the pain and managed to trap the fucker's ankle and throw my kick to his groin. The blow made him grunt in pain and lurch forward, setting him up for the next kick, which I delivered straight to his face, knocking him back onto the floor and leaving him incapacitated enough to allow me to tape up his hands and feet.

There was only one more fanatic to go, and, having finished with number three, I looked over to find number four about ten feet away, crawling on his hands and knees toward a small end table that held a lamp and some books. As I got hold of his foot, he grabbed the lamp, twisted around, and bashed it across my head, destroying the shade and shattering the bulb in the process. I faired a bit better than the lamp, but it was a solid hit and knocked me to the ground. I doubted that breaking Nadir's father's shit was going to make him very happy—but it wasn't going to be anywhere near as shocking as the rest of this story. As I recovered from the hit, I realized I had somehow lost my pistol, but, before I could search for it, the guy came at me again, a manic look in his eyes as he prepared to attack me with the remains of the lamp. He might not have the beard, but he sure as hell had the fanaticism, which meant I would have to take care of him the old fashioned way—with my hands or, more specifically, my foot. I stayed where I was until he got close enough to swing at me, then I twisted sideways at the last second and back kicked him up under his throat. It was a good way to strike someone you didn't particularly like, and a great way to strike someone you absolutely detested. Now, he was on his back, clutching his neck and trying desperately to breathe. He would have died had I kicked him with full power, but I wanted to keep him alive so he could spill his guts in a more meaningful way—namely by revealing the names and addresses of his fellow terrorists. I pulled out the roll of tape and secured unhappy tango number four then called out to Lux.

"All clear, but, unfortunately, there's no sign of our fifth man," I said.

She stole a glance away from the door and saw that most of the fun was thankfully over.

"You never cease to amaze me," she said.

A man suddenly appeared behind her, and, before I could utter a word to warn Lux, he placed the barrel of his silenced pistol against her head.

"I'll take that," he said, as he casually reached out and took hold of her weapon.

I could tell this was the infamous Jael, as he had the stone cold demeanor of a killer, his unblinking eyes devoid of any kind of soul. As expected, he was Middle Eastern, and like his friends was mostly beardless, though he did have that purposeful scruff that every two-bit hipster seemed to have these days. Even worse than his menacing expression and bad facial hair, was the fact that he was tall, well muscled, and obviously pretty experienced at being a world class asshole.

"Oh, hello, Jael. I was wondering when you were going to join the party."

"No need to wonder anymore. Here I am," he said, as he shoved Lux over towards me, smiling cruelly as he regarded us.

"It seems I have you at a disadvantage. What a shame for you, yet wonderful for me, as I'll have two more entries on the list of all the infidels I've killed."

"Yeah, but it won't even come close to the number of goats you've fucked."

He didn't find my quip very funny and proceeded to cock his pistol, the simple action of his thumb now giving it a hair trigger. Shit! We were totally fucked unless I could think of a way out of this situation, but everything that came to mind would be a lot more effective if I could just find my damn gun. I glanced around the room, but there was no trace of it, which meant I needed to employ a little psychological warfare in hopes of buying us some time.

"Jael, as we speak, a SEAL team is boarding the yacht, so your only hope of survival is to keep us alive and use us as hostages to bargain for your freedom."

"I think I'd prefer you dead."

"Face it, a dead hostage isn't worth shit."

"I think you're lying to save your ass, but even if you aren't, I am prepared to sacrifice my life for Allah."

He was trying to sound noble, but the truth was that he was a selfish asshole, and he and the rest of his kind would never will-

ingly sacrifice their own lives. Rather, they would send off the ignorant, the young, or the mentally challenged to die for the cause.
Thus, my ruse about using us as hostages just might keep us alive
until I could find my gun.

"Come now, Jael. A man as important as you need not die in
vain."

There was a noise out in the passageway, and I could see that
Jael was starting to grow anxious as he considered my words.
Unfortunately, the longer he stewed, the more agitated he was
becoming, and worse still, his finger was hovering ominously over
the trigger. I needed to do something, but what? At that moment,
we finally had some good luck when I spied my gun lying on the
floor beneath a nearby chair—too far to reach before I got shot,
but close enough to make me want to try. A distraction would
certainly help, but, barring one, things were looking dire.

Somehow, at that moment, fate, or, perhaps, Lux's karma for
being a warm and innately understanding person, decided to intervene. The noise in the hall turned out to be Nadir, and, at that
exact moment, he came racing through the doorway and took
hold of Jael's gun hand—leaving the two men engaged in a deadly
game of tug of war for control of the pistol. I dropped to the floor,
and, as I crawled over to grab my own weapon, heard a shot ring
out from Jael's gun—the bullet missing my head by mere inches.
I glanced over to see that Nadir and Jael's struggle for control of
the pistol was sending the barrel sweeping back and forth across
the room, making an already dangerous situation even more challenging. The weapon discharged again, this time the bullet nearly
hitting Lux's leg as it embedded into the nearby sofa. Goddammit!
I needed to finish this before someone got seriously hurt, but, as
usual, fate decided to throw me a curveball. Jael's experience won
out over Nadir's enthusiasm, and he managed to land an elbow to
the ribs of his younger opponent, allowing the more seasoned jihadist to take back his pistol. Nadir was quick to recover, but Jael
was quicker and, now, had the gun aimed at the young man's head.

"I guess I'm going to have to kill you sooner than I planned," Jael said, with a menacing smile on his face.

Nadir looked terrified, but something in his expression changed, and I saw a look of determination that made me instantly respect the little fucker. He was about to give his life to try and save ours, which meant I needed to return the favor.

"Goat fucker!" I yelled, as I made a last second dive for my pistol.

Jael turned his attention to me and fired, his shot, thankfully, missing me, but still close enough that I could feel the wind from the bullet as it passed by my face. That was it—the last straw. I was done fucking around with this fucker. I had lived by several rules during the course of my unusual life, and one of the top three was not to get shot in the face, least of all, by a complete asshole. I landed and managed to grab my pistol then roll onto my back and put two tightly grouped shots into Jael's forehead. His body went slack, and he was officially dead and probably introducing himself to his seventy-two virgins before he even hit the floor. Hopefully, God, in his infinite wisdom would, instead, take them away and give him seventy-two goats. Wait—I take that back, as it would be way too mean to the goats, so, instead, he should be given seventy-two pieces of fifty grit sandpaper and be forced to masturbate with them for all of eternity. With Jael's fate sealed, Lux turned her big beautiful blue eyes to Nadir and smiled.

"Nadir, you saved us!" she said.

"So, I was like the cavalry you mentioned?"

"You bet your sweet ass!" I said.

"Yes, but what now? Look at what I have been a part of. How can I ever face my family?"

"You weren't exactly a willing participant and, more importantly, you risked your own life to save ours. You'll, of course, need to answer some questions and name some names, but we'll make sure you're free to go when it's all over."

Nadir turned and stared at Jael's body, obviously still trying to come to terms with all that had occurred in the last two minutes. He was obviously in shock and appeared as though he might fall down at any moment, so I led him over to the nearest sofa and he sat down, placed his head in his hands, and began to weep. Being a terrorist wasn't as much fun as the brochures made it out to be, and our young friend was learning a valuable life lesson about being more selective in choosing his social engagements. I placed my hand on his shoulder to get his attention.

"Nadir, I was wrong about you. You're a good kid, and you did something incredibly brave just now."

He looked at me for a moment, but all he could muster in return was a nod. I decided he needed something to get his mind back on track and came up with the perfect task.

"Your friend Yousef is down in the aft storage locker. You should probably go check on him."

"Yes, that's a good idea," he said, perking up a bit.

He left to find his friend, and I used the time to radio Billings.

"Arrrrrr! The *Sarsarun* is ours!" I said.

"Arrrrrr! When do you need me to come in for a pickup?" he asked.

"It'll take us a few minutes to get things in order, though I think you might need a vessel a little bigger than the Jet Ski, as we have some items to transport to the *Sozo*."

"Roger that. I'll be back with the *Sozo's* tender."

I clicked off and saw that Lux was staring at me.

"What is it?" I asked.

She didn't answer and, instead, came over and wrapped her arms around me. It had been quite an emotional couple of minutes, and we stood there and held each other, silently thankful that we were both still alive. A moment later, Nadir returned with his friend, Yousef, who didn't seem entirely comfortable around me—regardless of the fact that I never actually laid a hand on him. We all walked across to the bridge to inform the captain that he could officially take back control of his ship, and he was particularly relieved the job was done, as he too had been planning his own mutiny. His name was Nelson Williams, and he wasn't your typical pleasure yacht captain and was, in fact, a retired officer of the British Royal Navy. His first desire was to go pick up his crew, who had been off-loaded in Martinique by Jael and his band of terrorist shitbags. They probably would have off-loaded Captain Williams as well except that they needed his skills to pilot the *Sarsarun* and its cargo to its next destination. Needless to say, the good captain was thoroughly disgusted to learn the entirety of what Jael and his cronies had been planning, and he thanked us profusely for having resolved the situation and taken care of his unwelcome guests.

Lux used the *Sarsarun's* radio to contact Langley and made arrangements for Captain Williams to rendezvous with a nearby Coast Guard Cutter to off-load the terrorists and their dead leader. After that, he'd be free to sail to Martinique to pick up his crew, and Nadir and Yousef would stay aboard the *Sarsarun* for the moment then come in for a debrief of their own volition. That just left the missile launchers, which were stowed in the *Sarsarun's* aft cargo hold. Everyone worked together to carry them onto the back deck, and, by the time we had moved the entire stack, I heard a vessel approaching and looked out to see Billings come speeding out of the night. He glided up to the port side of the *Sarsarun*, his glowing smile of excitement bright enough to penetrate the darkness like a searchlight.

"Ahoy mateys! Anyone here know where I can get me some Russian shoulder-fired missiles?" he asked.

"Arrrrrr—I might just have a few for sale."

We made a quick round of introductions then all worked together once again to move the missile launchers from the *Sarsarun* to the *Sozo's* tender. Ten long minutes later, we said goodbye to our new friends then idled away into the darkness, the first half of our mission complete.

"So farrrrrr, so good," I said, to Billings.

"Arrrrrr!" he responded.

I think he was extra excited, because he gave us a devilish grin then opened the throttles all the way up for the ride back, sending us rocketing over the water at a brisk seventy-five miles per hour. We made it to the *Sozo* in six minutes flat—six of the most terrifying minutes of my life, which was saying a lot considering I used to jump out of airplanes for a living. Lux, too, must have been equally terrified for she held me in a vice-like embrace until we finally slowed down as we neared the *Sozo*. We had to make a subtle detour at the last minute to make our way around one of those large circular rafts you pulled behind a speedboat. This one's occupants were the five captured Soft Taco Security men, and they didn't look as happy as the people who were usually riding on them. Kip, who was standing guard over our unwelcome guests, came over and tied off the tender.

"I see you've brought some presents," he said, as he looked at the stack of crates.

"We sure have, though we could use a little help off-loading them," I responded.

He made a quick announcement on the *Sozo's* intercom system and, soon, more crewmembers arrived, allowing us to quickly unload the missile launchers and bring the tender aboard and secure the boat deck.

"Now, it's time to once and for all blow this fucking soft taco stand and go to Martinique and get your sister," I said.

"It's also time to say bon voyage to our French guests here," Billings added.

"*Oui*," I said.

Billings tossed them a paddle, untied the line holding them to the boat, then used his foot to shove them off towards the shore.

"Nobody fucks with my crew," he said.

Good thing he said fucks with, and not just fucks, or I'd be on the raft with the frogs considering my very intimate relationship with Estelle. He went to a control panel and closed the giant side hatch, then Lux, Kip, and I followed him up to the bridge, where we joined Brett, Estelle, and a number of the other crewmembers who were preparing the *Sozo* to get underway. The entire place was aglow in the customary red night light that was commonly used on boats, and it had the unintended side effect of making the bridge look like the inside of a space ship. Billings gave the order to weigh anchor, and the large yacht started moving forward as the bow winch brought in the great expanse of chain. It was only a matter of minutes before the *Sozo* was free and moving slowly out of the bay. We cleared the other boats, and the powerful engines roared to life, bringing us up to a top speed of forty-one knots. All we could do now was stare at the dark horizon as we headed south, ever hopeful to at last be free of Soft Taco Island. Billings told the first mate to kill all running lights and watch the radar for any contacts following our course.

"There's not much for us to do other than watch and wait to see if they send anyone after us, so I suggest everyone adjourn to the upper lounge to get a little rest," Billings said.

The six of us walked into the lounge behind the bridge and spread out around the room. Kip, Estelle, and I took one couch, while Brett and Lux took up residence on the other. Billings and Tiffany disappeared into his private cabin, and minutes later, all was silent as we drifted off to sleep, our bodies spent from a night of far too much excitement.

I was in the middle of a glorious dream where I was swimming in a pool full of rum when I awoke to Billings gently tapping me on my shoulder.

"What's up?" I asked.

"I've got bad news."

"Let me guess—the pool isn't full of rum?"

"Afraid not, and radar shows we have a contact closing fast."

"Shit. How long have I been asleep?"

"Same as me—about five minutes. I guess they figured out we've taken back the *Sozo*."

"Then, I guess we still have some work to do."

"The night that just won't end," Billings muttered.

"No shit, so it's about time we ended it."

We woke the others and gave them the news then headed down to my cabin to get properly armed. We were going to need long range weapons, so I laid out all the rifles on the bed. There was my DSR-1 sniper rifle, M4, and the five French FAMAS assault rifles we'd taken from the Soft Taco security forces. Everyone stood around, staring at the array of weapons, unsure what to do.

"I know—they're all so beautiful, you're having a hard time choosing, so, I'll get things going by taking the sniper rifle. That makes it easier because now you only have two choices left. In my opinion, the M4 is slightly more accurate, but those FAMAS rifles will also get the job done."

That seemed to do the trick, for Lux reached down and picked up the M4, leaving the FAMAS G2's for Kip, Brett, Estelle, and Billings.

"Now, if everyone will follow me to the main salon, I'll give each of you a radio so we can all stay in contact," Billings said.

We filed out of my room, and seeing Kip holding the assault rifle made me wonder if I was once again arming the object of my eventual demise, but desperate times called for desperate measures. Once we had assembled in the main salon and everyone had a radio, Billings decided it would be prudent to have a last minute strategy meeting.

"So, Tag, as the person with the most combat experience here—do you have any thoughts on how we should do this?" Billings asked.

I took a moment to look around at my team and think about their various strengths before answering.

"Alrighty then, Pete, as you're a former Cyclone Class Patrol

Boat captain, I'm thinking it would be extremely useful to have you up on the bridge, so that you can use the radar to keep track of the incoming vessel's position and then coordinate the rest of our efforts. Everyone else pretty much needs to fan out across the main deck and find cover behind anything large and metallic that'll stop any incoming bullets. We don't know what we're up against yet, so it's better to be safe than sorry."

"OK, and what about you?" Lux asked.

"Well, as I have the extra long range weapon, I'm going to need a place with plenty of visibility, so I think I should probably set up my sniper's nest in the aft deck bar," I said.

"Nice try, jackass, but shouldn't you actually be up high where you'll have the best vantage point?" Lux asked.

"Fine, I'll just put some rum in a to-go cup and take up position on the *Sozo's* helicopter pad."

We all headed off to our respective positions, and only had to wait a minute before Billings came over the radio to tell us that our target was about three hundred meters off the stern and closing fast. I braced the rifle and set the scope for night vision then scanned the horizon behind us, and, there, exactly as Billings had said, was our pursuer. It was moving fast, gaining on us quickly, and my heart sank as I realized what we were up against. I was hoping it would be some dilapidated third world hulk, but, instead, I was looking at a state of the art patrol boat. It was fast, maneuverable, and armored, but the most worrisome feature was the fifty-caliber turret mounted machine gun on the bow. With the right shells, that thing could do some serious damage to the *Sozo*.

The best option we had would be for me to take out the boat long before it got into range, and, for the first time on this trip, I was feeling as though I had distinctly under-packed. I was really wishing I had brought the Barret Light Fifty sniper rifle, which could penetrate armor and take out the patrol boat as easily as if it were a child's toy floating in a bathtub. With my current rifle, it would come down to accuracy and putting enough well-placed shots around their vessel to scare them into calling off the chase. Of course, this would be no easy task when both the shooter and the target were bobbing around on the surface of the ocean.

A person appeared in the gun turret, and it turned until it was aimed directly at the *Sozo's* stern. I saw the flash before I heard the shots, and suddenly a number of bullets were flying overhead, and at least one embedded into our radar mast. So much for a warning shot.

"Attention, *Sozo*, you will come to a full stop, or we will open fire on your vessel," came a French accented voice over a loud speaker.

"What the hell do they call that last round?" I said, over the radio.

"No shit. Any thoughts?" Billings responded.

"Let's show those assholes we're armed and dangerous."

I chambered a round and prepared to return fire, hopeful to show the French menace we had no intention of following their orders. PJ's rarely, if ever, got to attend sniper school, but I'd had the unique opportunity of doing so before deploying to Afghanistan. I wasn't number one in my class, but I was in the top two, which meant I had a pretty damn good shot—at a pretty damn good shot—so to speak. I relaxed and controlled my breathing, as I focused on the movement of my target, waiting for it to cross my aim point. Several tense seconds passed, and I squeezed off a round. It went a little high and right, hitting the steel armor plate in front of the gunner, the impact making him jump and inadvertently turn the turret off to his left. As he rotated the gun back towards the boat, I adjusted my aim, hoping to pull the trigger before he did. We both shot at the same time, and his bullets hit the upper deck to my left while mine struck the same armor plate. Apparently, some of the fragments reached my nemesis, because he vacated the turret seat while another crewmember took his place. Bursts of light erupted from the barrel, and, while the new gunner was firing wild, he got lucky, and a number of his rounds struck the lower deck and main salon. Damn it! I should have already put down some suppressive fire.

"Is everyone OK?" I asked, over the radio.

The others came back saying they were fine, but I could hear the anxiety in their voices. It was time to get this done. I took aim then fired, and my shot impacted the upper edge of the gun's armor plating, sending the guy out of the turret seat as he ducked for cover. He climbed back in, and I fired again, the bullet hitting the same general area and sending him fleeing to safety, except, this time, he didn't return. It was a smart move, as it was only a matter of time before I got lucky and hit flesh. As I sought out a new target, the boat veered abruptly out of my sights, following an erratic course, obviously trying to be less of an enticing target. Several flashes erupted from the fifty, and bullets were whizzing overhead, a few impacting the upper deck. They obviously had a new gunner, but it was going to be a lot harder to hit him now, so, instead of focusing on the weapon, I decided to focus on the head of the beast by turning my sights to the man at the helm. I wasn't sure if the windshield was bulletproof, but there was only one way to find out. I followed the left and right movement of the boat and fired, my shot hitting the glass just left of his head. It was hard to tell in the night vision scope, but it looked as though the bullet's impact had created the telltale spider web pattern of bullet resistant glass. Either way, it scared the helmsman enough that he turned the boat hard to starboard and veered off at a forty-five degree angle from our course. Now, I could see the port side of the boat and there were men staying low in the cockpit, their heads barely visible above the deck. Muzzle flashes appeared, followed by the sound of their shots as the bullets impacted into the *Sozo*. The men were firing assault rifles, and, though they weren't as lethal as the fifty-caliber, they were still plenty capable of delivering deadly force.

I radioed for the others to open fire, then I sighted in on the men in the stern. I squeezed off a round and my bullet impacted the side of their boat causing them all to duck out of sight. The rest of my team were now shooting, peppering the patrol boat with hot lead, and it only took a second before the helmsman throttled back and veered off course, obviously unwilling to risk any more harm to his crew or his vessel. We had won our little sea battle, so I cued my radio and called for a ceasefire, and the shooting stopped and was replaced by the sound of cheering voices from all around the *Sozo*. We left our firing positions and headed for the bridge to join Billings and celebrate yet another victory. Everyone was happy, especially Estelle who was obviously still high on the adrenal rush of combat. The others had been through it before, so it was easier for them to come down and relax.

"Nice job, everyone! The *Sozo* and everyone aboard are safe. Only one of the crew was hurt, but it was just a small cut from some flying glass during that last barrage," Billings said.

"Thank God," Lux responded.

"We'll keep an eye on the radar to be safe, but we'll be in international waters in less than a minute, so I suggest everyone go back to their cabins to get some sleep, and we'll regroup in the morning."

Lux asked if I could stay behind to talk, so I told Estelle I'd meet her back in my cabin. Everyone headed off to bed for the night, and we went down to the main salon, where Lux poured us each a shot of Ketel One Vodka. This particular spirit had nostalgic meaning for us, as we had shared a bottle of it during our first Christmas together in Afghanistan. She handed me my glass then held up hers to toast.

"Here's to you—for saving my operation and my ass."

"Well, then here's to both—with the emphasis being on the latter."

We clinked glasses then drank, and I had a quiet moment to reflect before I spoke.

"Honestly, tonight really was a team effort, so you can thank yourself and everyone on this boat for our success," I said.

"Yeah, maybe, but you brought that team together."

"Hardly. It was already here when I arrived."

She smiled as she regarded me.

"I'm happy to see you're still humble as ever."

"For a reason."

"What reason? I don't know what you've been doing since you left the Agency, but you've clearly still got it, Finn."

"Then working shitty divorce cases and finding lost cats apparently keeps me in tip-top shape."

"Lost cats? I seriously doubt that."

"Remind me to show you a picture of Mr. Pickles."

"Why? Is he a former client?"

"Yeah, but he's a cat. A big, fat cuddly cat."

She didn't appear to believe me and, instead, poured us each one more shot and held up her glass, staring for a long moment before a conspiratorial smile appeared on her lovely lips.

"To a lost moment in time," she said.

"Lost, but not forgotten," I added.

We both smiled as we clinked glasses and sipped our vodka, though a distinct silence overtook the room at the mention of our little tryst. When Lux finished her glass, she placed it on the bar and looked over at me with a subtly bittersweet gaze.

"I must say, Tag, Estelle is quite a woman, so I sincerely hope that you two work out."

"Thanks, and I hope so as well, though only time will tell."

"I'm off to bed. I'll see you in the morning," she said, as she turned and headed for her stateroom.

"Late morning," I added.

I went back to my cabin to find Estelle eagerly awaiting my return.

"So, any more lost moments with Lux that I should know

about?" she asked.

"No, but she did just say that you're quite a woman, and she hopes we work out."

Estelle smiled.

"Well, she's also quite a woman, so at least I know you have good taste."

"Yeah, but what I had with Lux is all in the past now—and you're the future."

"I certainly hope so," Estelle said, as she yawned.

I could see she was starting to fade, her eyes telling the true extent of her exhaustion.

"How about a shower before bed?" she asked.

"With a man-whore?"

"A dirty man-whore."

"A dirty man-whore who would love a lost moment in the shower with you."

We undressed and headed for the bathroom, and the shower was just like heaven, the hot water feeling like a thousand little fingers massaging my sore muscles. Estelle and I lathered each other up and spent a few moments frolicking in our private little fish bowl.

"I must say that I'm a little surprised that you're even talking to me, let alone showering with me."

"Well, I'm not happy about what you did, but, at least, now, I can understand why it happened. Plus, I want you to get a really good look at what you're going to be missing," she said, with a wicked smile.

I gazed at Estelle and knew, right then and there, that I would indeed be missing her, and I had to admit that, in spite of all that had transpired, I was more than a little relieved to be back with the same woman, however short, or limited our time together might be. I didn't know if Estelle would ever forgive me, but I was happy for the moment and would do my best to make amends. We rinsed off the soap, toweled dry, and climbed into bed and turned off the light.

"Is your life always like this?" she asked.

"Yep—boring as fuck."

Estelle laughed and snuggled up close to my side, slipping her long leg over mine. I closed my eyes and felt the slow rhythm of the *Sozo* as it churned through the waves, my mind emptying of all worry as I drifted off into a deep slumber, saying goodnight to yet another glorious, albeit challenging, day in the Caribbean.

CHAPTER TWENTY-FIVE
A Better Tomorrow Today

It was the third day in a row that I'd woken up with the same woman, and it felt particularly good to lay there together, enjoying the quiet solitude of morning. Estelle was curled up against me, and I could feel the subtle movement of the *Sozo* as it powered through the waves on its way to Martinique. I got up, brushed my teeth, and had two cups of coffee with cream ready before Estelle even opened her eyes. I set her cup on the bedside table and let the heavenly aroma gently dig into her olfactory senses and bring her out of a deep slumber. She smiled as she sat up and picked up the cup to enjoy her first sip of the day. After taking a nice long pull, she lowered the mug down until it was residing between her bare breasts, the gesture unintentionally presenting me with the holy trinity of a perfect morning.

"So, where am I on the man-whore meter today?" I asked, as I sat down beside her on the bed.

"I'd say you're down to about a four, but it doesn't mean that I've forgiven you yet."

"I know, but it gives me hope."

I decided to pour myself a second cup, and, after finishing

nearly half, felt a familiar pressure in my lower abdomen. I had gotten cocky and thought I could handle more coffee, but now there was a serious number two knocking on my back door. Estelle got up and headed for the bathroom, and I started to panic. Oh God! Please, not now!

"I'm going to shower, do you want to join me? Might be the last time you see me naked," she joked.

"Um—well. You see—I—um..."

"Are you OK? You look like you're in pain."

"I'm fine. It's just that..."

"Actually, you look like you have to take a shit."

"No, it's nothing like that."

"It's OK. Everybody poops. Now go into that bathroom and make momma proud."

"I can't. Not with you here. It's too soon."

"People do this every day. It's a fact of life."

"I know, but..."

She led me into the bathroom, set my coffee cup on the counter next to the sink, then left for a moment only to return with a car magazine from the stack on the corner table in my room. I guess she figured I'd like some manly literature, but, realistically, content was secondary to the mere presence of words. I'd read everything from novels to aspirin containers while on the toilet, so my only real problem in this scenario was having a beautiful woman just outside the door. Estelle sensed my unease and smiled reassuringly.

"How the hell can you be the same guy who jumps out of planes, rescues a damsel in distress, and saves a ship's crew from ruthless French mercenaries?"

"I never shit while I'm doing those things."

She shook her head, frowned, and closed the door. I wanted to get up and lock it to guarantee my privacy, but it seemed like some kind of test—and probably part of my probation. I took a sip of coffee and tried to relax, as there was a lot of pressure in my abdomen, and I really needed to go, but I suppose this moment came down to trust. Picking up the magazine, I took yet another sip of my favorite beverage then started reading a story about an exotic new supercar. By the second paragraph, I was busy at God's work, and about halfway through the article, I was done and feeling a whole lot better. I finished up, washed my hands, and took my now empty cup with me as I left the bathroom. Estelle was waiting patiently on the bed and stood up and clapped as I came out.

"Congratulations!" she said.

"Thank you, but I think I need a hug. That was a big step for me."

She smiled as she prepared to leave.

"Where are you going?" I asked.

"To my cabin, as I realize that I also need to—um—freshen up."

"You mean take a shit?"

"Yeah."

"Why not use my bathroom?"

"Are you kidding? It's way too early in our relationship for that."

She was out the door and gone before I could even call her a coward. I can't believe she tricked me like that then fled like a skittish little dear. Screw her. Victory was mine. I went back into the bathroom, looked in the mirror, and smiled as I thought about what I had accomplished in the last few days. I'd rescued the love of my life, saved the crew of the *Sozo*, thwarted a dastardly terrorist plot, and, most important of all, managed to shit in the same vicinity of a woman I'd only known for three days. I was all that was man. I proudly refilled my coffee cup, took a sip, then stepped into the shower. Sure, I didn't have Estelle's agile hands enthusiastically soaping my privates or her slippery breasts pressing against my chest, but I was content. I had faced one of my lifelong demons and shit in its face—so to speak. I performed my final rinse, dried off, then dressed in my usual tropical attire of shorts and T-shirt before heading out to the main salon. Only Lux,

Tiffany, and Billings were there as I sat and poured myself yet another cup of coffee. I looked across the table at Lux, and found it hard to believe all that had transpired the night before, especially our little lustful entanglement on the beach. She seemed to know what I was thinking, because she gave me the subtlest of smiles.

"You'll be happy to know that I got an update from the Agency this morning, and we now have official confirmation that our intel was indeed accurate, because the *Soft Taco III* just docked in Fort De France, Martinique."

"So, what is the Agency doing about it?"

"Apparently, the mission has expanded a bit."

"Meaning?"

"Meaning, they've now decided they want to bring Babineux in, so they can interrogate the fucker and get all of the information he has on his terrorist clients."

"So, it's officially a rescue and a snatch and grab."

"Yeah, and they're sending someone to meet us in Martinique to take over the operation, but he won't get there until three this afternoon."

"Babineux is supposedly leaving at five, so that seems to me to be cutting it a little close."

"Yeah, typical Agency maneuver."

"No doubt, and I'd bet good money the agent coming to join us is probably some out of shape desk jockey who's never spent any real time in the field."

Lux shrugged, looking a bit uncomfortable, as it wasn't cool to talk shit about a fellow agent, regardless how inept he might be.

"Honestly, I'm not too thrilled about this latest turn of events either," she said.

"Well, rather than sit around with our thumbs up our asses, I think we should get proactive."

"And just how in the hell do you expect us to accomplish that when we're not even in Martinique yet?"

"You'll be happy to learn that I have a guy on the island who would be perfect for a little surveillance. We can have him go to the harbor and keep tabs on Babs—actual eyes on our guy."

Lux didn't look very excited about my ability to rhyme, or my potential operative.

"How exactly do you know this person?"

"He was my waiter at a lovely café on Martinique."

"Oh—your waiter. Sounds like the perfect agent. Maybe he could bring along the busboy and the barista, and, that way, we'd have an entire surveillance team."

"Even better!"

"Are you crazy? This is a top secret, priority anti-terrorism operation and you want to trust a waiter?"

"Hell yeah! He made me the best café au lait I've ever had, and he gave me a tropezienne."

"Oh, well in that case I guess it's safe to trust him with our national security."

"I know what you're thinking, Jugs, but that waiter also happens to be ex-Australian SASR, so I don't think we can find anyone better."

Lux stewed for a minute, tapping her hand on the table as she thought about my potential asset.

"OK, fine, but keep our operational details to a minimum."

"That won't be a problem, because I have no idea what our operational details are."

Lux didn't look happy, but she had no other choice at the moment. I raced off to my cabin to retrieve the card Mick had given me and felt mildly annoyed that I hadn't already bothered to memorize the number—a simple chore that would have been standard operating procedure back during my days with the Agency. As I'd been a civilian for the last five years, I'd let some of the habits of my former life slip into obscurity—memorizing Australian waiter's numbers, apparently, being at the top of the list. I returned to the main salon and used Billings's satellite phone to call Mick, who finally managed to answer after five rings.

"Hello?" he said, sounding a little sleepy.

"Hey, Mick, it's Tag."

I heard a female voice in the background, then Mick said something unintelligible to her before coming back on the line.

"Say that again, mate?"

"I said, it's Tag. I'm not sure if you remember me, but we met at your café a couple days ago."

He was quiet a moment, obviously trying to put a face to the name.

"You're not calling because I had a thing with your wife or girlfriend are you?"

I laughed.

"Definitely not, but it might help you remember me if I mentioned that you helped me deal with a couple of Frenchman behind the café where you work."

"*Oi*! Yeah, I remember you. What's up mate?"

"Well, if you're free today, I have a little surveillance job for you—and it's extremely important."

"How important?"

"Life and death and national security important."

"Ah, bloody hell. What do you need?"

"A big ass yacht called the *Soft Taco III* is docked in Fort De France, and I need you to keep a close eye on its occupants—specifically the owner and a woman he's holding prisoner. You'll be paid well, of course—even more than I tipped you at the café."

He was quiet a moment as he thought about my offer.

"Ah, fuck it. I don't care about the money. I'll do it for fun."

"I appreciate the offer, but I'll make sure you get paid."

"Whatever, I'll shower and head over. Be there in half an hour."

"Perfect, and you can reach me on this number. Now, tell your lady friend I say hello."

"I will. Cheers, mate."

He hung up, and I put down the phone and smiled.

"We'll soon have eyes on Babineux."

"I hope we can trust your waiter."

"Your operation isn't exactly air tight at this point, so we certainly couldn't do any worse."

"Maybe Mick can bring us a tropezienne when we get to port," Lux said, sarcastically.

"Don't knock it. It really was that good."

Estelle and Brett came strolling in at that moment, and, shortly thereafter, crewmembers brought in trays of scrambled eggs, pancakes, and bacon. We all dug in and ate like pigs, for there was nothing like a late night of shooting, fighting, and fornicating to stir up the ol' appetite. Brett, after swallowing his last bite, used his knife as mirror to check his teeth then got the post breakfast conversation going by asking about the day's plans. Lux told him we were in a kind of limbo, as we were waiting for someone from the agency to arrive in Martinique and take over control of the operation.

"So, we're not doing shit?" he asked.

"Not really, though we are conducting some active surveillance through a contact of Tag's on Martinique."

"Who the hell would that be?" he asked.

"Mick, his waiter from some café he visited."

"Oh, yeah, I remember that dick. He made fun of me for ordering mineral water."

"Well, in that case, I'm starting to think Mick might be an OK guy," Lux said.

By the time the table was cleared away of dishes, the phone rang, and I looked down, saw it was Mick, and hit the accept button.

"I'm down by the water in Fort De France and officially have my eyes on the prize. Bloody hell, mate! You didn't tell me she was going to be so fucking hot."

"I wanted it to be a surprise. Now, can you tell how's she holding up at the moment?"

"Well, she and the man in charge are sitting on the aft deck, and he's got an entire contingent of serious looking security men all around her, so, other than being around those fuckers, I guess she's OK."

"That's good, now just keep an eye on them, and call if it looks as though they might be getting ready to leave."

"No problem," he said, before hanging up.

"What's the good news?" Lux asked.

"Mick has the *Soft Taco III* under surveillance, and he says your sister appears to be just fine."

The news was good, but Lux still looked anxious.

"It'll work out, Lux. I promise."

"I hope you're right."

"Am I ever wrong?"

"Surprisingly, not very often."

"Exactly! Now, Pete, how long until we reach Martinique?"

"We'll be in Fort De France in a little less than an hour."

I chugged the last of my coffee and got up from the table and headed to my cabin to think about the next phase of our mission. At the moment we were in a kind of limbo, and I found that to be more stressful than having a clear plan. I, therefore, decided I needed some kind of meditative activity to ease my troubled mind. One thing I always found cathartic was breaking down my weapons and making sure they were in perfect functioning order. It might sound a bit morbid, but, for me, the process was probably the adult equivalent of a child playing with Legos. I disassembled each one down to its most basic parts then oiled and reassembled it before placing it on the bed. When I was done, I gazed at the vast assortment of weaponry, and had my usual conflicting thoughts about what I was doing with such a collection. They were the tools of my trade, and I appreciated the precise engineering involved in their creation and function, but I also understood that they were designed with one purpose in mind—to kill. In a perfect world, we wouldn't need these, or any other weapons, but human beings were still imperfect, so, at the moment they were a necessary evil. Of course, I did enjoy the zen-like experience of target shooting, something my father had passed on when he first took me out to fire his .22 caliber Colt Woodsman pistol. I was hooked, and the following day, he bought me a Daisy Red Ryder BB gun with the provision that if I ever shot at a living thing, he'd take it away and I'd never see it again. I religiously adhered to that rule until I entered the service, whereupon I added human beings to the list of appropriate targets—a list that, until then, included only bottles, cans, and paper targets. Once my moment of nostalgic reflection and mild inner conflict passed, I headed up to the bridge to see Billings and check on our progress. He was standing at the helm, his gaze fixed so intently on the horizon that I thought he might be able to bridge the distance with his eyes alone. After a long moment, he realized I was there and looked over and gave me a nod.

"I've got her up to forty-five knots," he said.

"Plenty of time, Pete. Don't break her before we get her there."

"She can take it. This girl was born to run."

Lux joined us on the bridge a moment later and told us that she had just spoken with the Agency and had some good news.

"Do tell," I said.

"Well, first of all, the Coast Guard already rendezvoused with the *Sarsarun* and took the terrorists into custody."

"Nice! Job one is complete."

"Yeah—and there's more. It turns out the Agency has a SEAL Team en route to help with the final part of the operation."

"Even better! When do they arrive?"

"Three o' clock—same as the Agency guy."

The bridge grew quiet and, sensing Lux's uneasiness, I placed a reassuring hand on her shoulder.

"It's OK, Lux. We're going to nab Babineux and get your sister safely back."

She turned and wrapped her arms around me and buried her face in the crux of my neck. It wasn't a sexual hug, but it would be enough to bother Estelle if she happened to walk onto the bridge at this moment.

"I don't know what I'd do without you here," she said.

"You'd hug Billings instead."

"Very funny, asshole."

We headed downstairs to get coffee and kill some time in the main salon until we reached Martinique. The situation was feeling a bit tense, but, overall, things seemed to be looking up. We sipped our lovely caffeinated beverages and engaged in small talk as the *Sozo* blazed along at full speed, and it wasn't long before Billings came over the yacht's intercom system with the good news that we were entering the Fort De France bay. We anchored on the northern end, well out of view of the *Soft Taco III*, then Billings's phone rang, and I looked down to see it was Mick calling yet again. I hit the accept-button, but I could hardly understand him, as it sounded as though he was eating and trying to talk at the same time.

"*Oi*, just a second," he said.

I heard him swallow, and he came back on the line.

"*G'day*, mate."

"Your breakfast sounded delicious."

"It was. Fresh baked Almond Croissant and a coffee."

"Ah, the breakfast of champions."

"French champions, anyway."

"So, what's the latest, Mick?" I asked.

"Your guy is heading out with the girl and at least half a dozen men."

"Do they have any baggage with them?"

"Nah, looks pretty casual, so I'm pretty sure they're going to brunch. Damn, that is one beautiful hostage. Are you sure I shouldn't go down there and rescue her right now, so I can offer her a little thunder from down under?"

"Not yet, magic Mick. Just follow them and keep an eye on the French guy and the beautiful girl."

"No worries. Cheers, mate."

I hung up and saw that Lux was anxiously awaiting news of her sister.

"Bridgette's fine, and it sounds as though they're heading out to brunch."

"Why doesn't that prick just let her go if he's going to waste time wining and dining her?" she asked, sounding irritated.

"He's French, and they obviously have a very differently philosophy when it comes to handling their captives. Instead of torture and confinement, they keep them pacified with fine food and drink."

"I'm starting to think we might be on the wrong team."

"I pretty much knew it the minute the rum matrons appeared at the presidential palace."

We went outside and stood by the railing on the back deck while down below us Kip was refueling all of the various watercraft. I had to admit that the *Sozo*, in spite of being a pleasure craft, had quite an efficient crew, and it felt more like an actual military operation. I looked at my watch and saw that it was almost eleven a.m., which meant we had four long hours to sit and stew until our help arrived. At that moment, a crewman came walking onto the deck carrying a satellite phone.

"Sorry to interrupt, but you have a call," he said, to Lux.

She looked mildly concerned as she took hold of the phone and said hello. She listened for a moment then walked a few steps away before continuing the conversation. She apparently wanted some privacy, so it was likely someone from the Agency. More words were exchanged, then she looked a wee bit concerned as she reached down and hit the end button.

"Now, I have some bad news," she said, as she rejoined me.

"How bad?"

"Fairly bad. It seems that Babineux filed a new flight plan and is now set to depart at three o'clock."

"Lovely. That fucker will be leaving just as our help arrives."

"Yep, so now it's all back on us."

"Well, that certainly sucks a goodly amount of dick."

"It sure does."

I had a moment to think about our situation, and realized this turn of events might not be such a bad thing.

"You know what? I think it's good for us to do this ourselves. We already know the target and the hostage, and who better than us to make sure that no one gets hurt in the crossfire?"

Lux thought for a moment.

"I suppose you're right."

"You bet your big boobs I'm right. We've been kicking ass and taking names ever since we escaped from Soft Taco Island, and, now, Bridgette and Babineux are just another name and an ass on that list."

"I must say, Finn—I like your enthusiasm."

"And, I like that you like my enthusiasm."

We had a moment of silence where I was secretly hoping that Lux would say the next logical progression to my statement, but she remained particularly quiet as she crossed her arms over her chest and regarded me with a questioning look on her face.

"Well?" I asked.

"If you think that I'm going to say that I like, that you like, that I like your enthusiasm, then you're going to be sorely disappointed."

"Technically, you just did."

"Anyone ever tell you that you're like a seven year old James Bond?"

"No, but I think that's the nicest compliment you've ever given me."

Billings appeared on the deck and walked over and joined us.

"What's the latest?" he asked.

"Babineux moved up his flight to three o'clock, so now we're on our own."

He thought for a moment then smiled.

"Fuck it! I think it's better if we do this ourselves. That way, we make sure Bridgette doesn't get hurt in the crossfire!" Billings said.

"That's pretty much exactly what I said, Pete."

"Of course, because great minds think alike."

"And the bromance begins yet again," Lux said.

"Don't be ridiculous. It never ended," I responded.

"Damn straight! Now, how are we going to proceed?" Billings asked.

"That's an excellent question, especially considering our latest intel from Mick is that Babineux, Bridgette, and several of his men just left the *Soft Taco III*—apparently to go to brunch."

"Are they coming back or going straight to the airport?" he asked.

"They didn't have any luggage with them, so it would be safe to assume they're coming back to the yacht."

"So, the *Soft Taco III* is particularly vulnerable at the moment," he said.

"Yes it is—which means it would be an excellent time to sneak aboard and do a little reconnaissance."

"To what end?" Lux asked.

"First of all, it beats going back to sitting around with our thumbs up our asses, and second, it would allow us to do a little recon and gain some first hand knowledge of the yacht in the event we have to conduct a raid. Thirdly, and most important of all, we might even figure out a way to hide in Babineux's stateroom and ambush him when he comes in to take a shit."

"What makes you think he's going to take a shit when he gets back to the yacht?"

"Everybody shits after brunch."

"Wouldn't that depend on what you eat?"

"No, it doesn't matter if you have eggs Benedict or waffles—everyone shits after brunch."

"Anyone ever tell you that you might be a little fucked in the head?"

There was something familiar about our exchange, and I found myself smiling when I remembered what it was.

"What's so funny?" she asked.

"I said the exact same thing to Corn ten years ago, and he pretty much responded with the exact same words."

"So, he obviously would agree with me that you're a twisted fucker."

"Yeah, though I would counter by saying I'm insightful."

"And you wonder why I married him instead of you," she said.

"Not really, as I think the answer is obvious. You see, it's an accepted truth that women marry a man in hopes that they can change him—improve, or fix him. With me, you already had the perfect guy, so where's the fun in that?"

Lux shook her head in dismay.

"I'll take your silence as agreement," I said.

Billings interrupted our banter looking rather excited.

"I have to say—I think doing some recon of Babineux's yacht is a great idea," he said.

"Well? What do you think Lux? This is your operation, which means you have the final say."

"Fuck it! Let's do it. I'm tired of having my thumb up my ass."

"Arrrrrr! Now, that's pirate spirit!"

"Hell yeah, it is! Now, how do you want to get there? The Jet Ski?" Billings asked.

"I'm thinking the ski boat and some dive gear. We'll get close and then swim the rest of the way under water. The *Soft Taco III* won't have too many people still on board, but I think we should be as stealthy as possible."

Billings got a conspiratorial look in his eye.

"I wonder if there's any chance you'll find more rum?" he asked.

"We can always hope, my friend, for the world, as cruel as it can be, can never strip us of that."

Lux rolled her eyes at me, then the three of us headed down

to the boat deck to prepare for the mission. Billings worked with Kip to get the ski boat ready, while Lux and I entered the dive room to pick out our scuba gear. We grabbed the Draeger bubble-less re-breathers, masks, fins, and regulators, then finished up by putting on shorty wetsuits. Dressed and ready for our aquatic adventure, we joined Billings, who was already eagerly waiting at the helm of the ski boat. He started the engine and, after letting it warm up for a minute, gave Kip a nod, and my nemesis undid the lines and set the boat free. As Billings put it in gear and steered us away from the *Sozo*, I glanced back and saw Kip wave, so I returned the gesture, completing one of the friendliest interactions we'd yet been able to share. Strangely, it would appear that he had finally accepted me, which meant no more checking under the bed or in the closet every time I returned to my cabin. I saw this as an omen of good things to come and couldn't help but feel a bit optimistic as I turned my attention to Billings.

"I won't lie Pete. This is nice, but I kind of miss the intimacy of the Jet Ski."

He smiled and patted the open space beside him on the front seat as he looked back at me over his shoulder.

"I've got a place for you right here, sailor," he said.

He turned his gaze back towards the bow of the boat and pushed the throttle all the way forward to full speed, sending us careening southeast across the bay. It was yet another beautiful day in the Caribbean, and Lux and I spent the time gazing out at the waterfront of Fort De France. About a mile later, the *Soft Taco III* came into view, and Billings slowed the boat and steered us closer to shore before coming to a full stop.

"I suspect we shouldn't go any closer," he said.

"I agree. We'll get out here."

I used Billing's phone to call Mick.

"G'day," I said, with an Australian accent.

"G'day, mate."

"Anything new?"

"Yeah, they're having brunch at *La Belle Epoque*—a posh place up on the hill above Fort De France. It's pricey, like all things French, but has good food and an even better wine list. Do you want to hear the dessert menu?"

"I'll wait until after they've eaten brunch, as we're about to do some recon on the yacht. Needless to say, I'd appreciate a call when they leave."

"No problem."

"Oh, and just out of curiosity—do you happen to have a gun on you in the event that things get a little ugly?"

"No worries, mate, I've got seven and a half inches of hard steel right here in my hand."

"Good, I've got a little over eight, but, apparently, size doesn't matter."

"True, as it's more about the width of your barrel," he responded.

I hung up and stuck the phone in my waterproof gear bag, then noticed that Lux was staring at me.

"What?" I asked.

"Penis jokes? Now?" she muttered, with a scowl.

"If not now, then when?"

Lux and I put on our diving gear, then I took a moment to make sure that she had everything on correctly. She didn't like that I was doting on her again and gave me the same angry glare. Before she could utter a complaint, I spun her around, checked her tank and regulator, then gave her backside a friendly smack—the rubber of her shorty wetsuit, greatly magnifying the sound and startling the shit out of her. I prepared for the worst, but when she turned around, she smiled and motioned me on towards the swim platform. I had just stepped out onto it when I felt a solid smack on my own backside and learned, at that moment, that revenge was a dish best served by a scorned woman. The combination of the rubbery elasticity of the shorty wetsuit and Lux's substantial upper body strength magnified her blow, thus launching me pre-

maturely into the drink. Clearly, she was missing the joyous camaraderie component of the rear end smack. My hits were playful
and fun, while hers showed a real mean streak and propensity for
deadly force. I was a little annoyed as I looked back at her, and,
even more so, after she gave me a winning smile. Bitch.

Lux stepped over the rail and dropped into the water beside
me, creating a series of small waves that splashed up into my face,
thereby adding insult to injury. She surfaced, gave me a thumbs up,
and we slipped on our regulators and swam down about fifteen feet
then set off towards the *Soft Taco III*. The water clarity in the busy
bay was surprisingly good, and we encountered an abundance of
rich corals and tropical fish to mark our passage as we swam along
over the bottom. It took us a good ten minutes before we crossed
beneath the large ominous shadow of the *Soft Taco III* and began
our slow ascent. We surfaced just off the stern of the yacht, and
I finally had a good look at our French nemesis's floating palace
and was thoroughly impressed. It was nearly as large as the *Sozo*,
but it was brilliantly white from waterline to bridge, and, like our
mega yacht, had all the accouterments a cheeky billionaire could
want—the most obvious being the helicopter on the upper deck.
I guess wealthy people got bored of taking their luxurious Italian
speedboats to shore and decided to mix it up by taking the chopper. It certainly was a big boat, but, luckily for us, it didn't appear
to have a big crew, as there wasn't a single person in sight. Still,
I tapped Lux and directed her to move closer to the side of the
hull, where we would be less visible from both the main and upper
decks. It was always better to be safe than sorry.

We worked our way to the swim ladder, slipped off our tanks,
then climbed out and placed our dive equipment on the stern
platform. I pulled my gun, Billings's phone, and the radio out of
the waterproof gear bag, then we moved onto the aft deck and
discovered a door and three large oval shaped portholes. I had a
look through the nearest one and realized we were directly outside what I was pretty sure was the master stateroom. Before I

could go over and check to see if the door was unlocked, we heard the voices of a couple of Babineux's crewmen walking in our direction up on the upper deck. Unfortunately, we would soon be visible in our current location, so we needed to find a hiding place. I spied an alcove a few feet away, and we raced over and squeezed into the space, which was barely big enough for one person, let alone two. Our close proximity meant that I could feel every inch of Lux's body pressing against me, and, while it provided certain obvious benefits, it was a torturous test of my resolve to stay true to Estelle and not get aroused by Lux's womanly goodies. Of course, my gaze soon fell upon her bosoms, which were hard to ignore as they were mere inches below my eyes. She caught me looking and proceeded to wiggle them against me, the movement causing a distinct stirring in my happy place.

"Are you seriously doing that right now?" I whispered.

"If not now, then when?"

"*Touché*," I said, acknowledging Lux's excellent ability to turn my own words against me.

"Good, now quit your bitching, as I'm just trying to get comfortable."

"Well, I'll be more comfortable if you stop wiggling."

"Why? Are you worried you're going to get a boner?" she asked, with an annoying smile.

"No," I lied.

"Really? Because I'm pretty sure I feel something pressing against me," she said, as she slipped her hand down between us and ran her fingers over the front of my wetsuit.

"If you don't mind, we should stop fooling around, so we can try and understand what they're saying. It could be important."

The men were directly above us on the upper deck now and speaking French so rapidly, that I could barely understand a single word of their conversation.

"Well, super spy, I certainly haven't heard them mention anything super important yet," Lux said.

"Just a second—their conversation is going in an interesting direction, and I have a feeling that one of them is about to reveal something potentially relevant to our situation."

Lux and I listened intently, and, a second later, the conversation stopped and one of the men let loose a very loud and impressively long fart. Had I been on the upper deck, I would already be giving him a high five, but, as it stood, all I could do was deliver my silent praise. The two men started laughing, and I hazarded a glance at Lux to find her regarding me with a scornful stare.

"What?" I asked, desperately trying not to join in the laughter.

"Clearly, you're a master linguist," she said.

"More of a cunning-linguist, but I suppose you already know that after last night."

"It always comes back to the ladies, doesn't it, man-whore?"

I ignored her comment for the moment and decided to focus my attention on my fellow fart enthusiasts. Their footsteps sounded as though they were continuing on their way, which meant it was time to get back to the task at hand—namely, penetrating the *Soft Taco III*. We slid out of the alcove and walked back to the door that accessed the master stateroom. I turned the handle and discovered it was unlocked, which meant we had found a nice easy way to get inside the yacht.

"Lux, I need you to watch the door, while I recon the boat."

"Why can't I go with you?"

"Because I need you to watch my back like you did on the *Sarsarun*—only this time you can't let your guard down."

"I thought we were going to do this together."

"We are, and that means you keeping your eyes peeled for the French menace."

"I swear to God—this better not be about you sneaking off to look for more rum."

Fuck! Lux obviously remembered my little exchange with Billings, and she was now keenly aware that my secondary mission was indeed to procure more rum.

"Lux! Come on! This is about saving Bridgette and nabbing Babineux and, honestly, I'm a little hurt that you would even say such a thing."

"Fine, Tag, but if you come out that door with a bottle of rum in your hand, I will work your ballsack like a speedbag," she said, as she rolled her hands like a boxer to emphasize her point.

This mission just got a wee bit harder, but what was life without challenges? I put Lux's threat out of my mind, slipped through the door, and instantly realized that Babineux had an excellent eye for interior design. There was no doubt in my mind that this was the master stateroom, and, while I thought it would be hard to top his home, his yacht came pretty damn close. The overall theme was a combination of modern styling and classic materials. The floors were polished hardwood, but they were covered by fancy-pants fluffy white throw rugs. The furniture was also made of wood, but it was blocky and minimalist, and obviously custom made for the room. To maximize the feeling of space the walls were almost completely covered in mirrors, making it feel as though I was walking through a nautical version of the halls of Versailles. The single most amazing feature of the room, however, was a huge fish tank built into the wall behind the stately king sized bed.

I moved closer and saw that the tank was filled with a variety of exotic saltwater fish, all swimming around props including a sunken galleon and a faux reef. Below all this, the entire sea floor was made up of realistic looking emeralds, rubies, and diamonds that appeared to flow out from a little pirate treasure chest in the corner. Oh to be an eccentric French billionaire. A small crustacean ambled by and broke me from my reverie, its interruption reminding me to turn my attention back to reconnoitering the boat, and, more importantly, finding more rum!

After a quick search, I discovered nothing of interest except a pair of frilly undergarments that either belonged to a very sexy woman or a very effeminate French man—which meant I basically had nothing. I left Babineux's cabin and headed down the passageway, where I discovered a number of staterooms. I checked all of them, but only one showed the signs of being occupied. There were a number of female clothing items, so I was pretty sure this was where they were keeping Bridgette. I closed the door, moved on, and found a stairway and took it up to the next level. This was the main deck and was similar to the *Sozo's* in that it was all about entertaining the guests. There was a lounge, bar, dining room, dance floor, and a kitchen with enough appliances and cooking implements that it could rival any five star restaurant. It seemed a bit excessive, but that's what happened when a Frenchman outfitted his yacht. As I completed my covert recon, I heard the voices of the same two men from earlier and realized they were coming down to the main deck. I had seen enough of the yacht's layout and decided it was time to leave.

I went down to the bottom level and returned to Babineux's cabin, where, on a whim, I decided, to check out the bathroom. I walked in through the double doors and stopped dead in my tracks. Sweet mother of porcelain, stainless steel, and tile! I wouldn't have thought it was possible to upstage his home bathroom, but this one came pretty damn close. The place was the size of an average person's living room, but its interior was all about bathing and shitting. The shower had room for six and beside it was a Jacuzzi tub where those same six people could engage in a game of Marco Polo that had the very real possibility of never having a winner. Just ahead was the main counter which had two large sinks and enough personal grooming products to get a gaggle of models ready for a runway show. To the right, and taking up the back corner, was the pièce de résistance—the toilet. It was beautiful, sleek, modern, and begged for a test sitting. I placed my backside upon its glorious seat and breathed out a sigh of sweet relief. It was as comfortable as any toilet I'd ever experienced and instantly gave me the desire to read—a thought which made me wonder where Babineux kept his reading material. I hadn't seen any in his bathroom back in the presidential palace, so perhaps he relied on his laptop or smartphone. That seemed doubtful, however, so I did a quick search of the surrounding area and discovered the outline of a good sized cabinet beside the toilet. Unfortunately, it didn't have a latch like most boat cabinets, so I, instead, pressed on it and voila! It snapped open, and I looked inside and nearly pooped in my suit. In addition to a number of magazines, there was an unexpected bounty—namely the case of jewels! It might seem kind of strange to find them here, but most men, myself included, saw the bathroom as a kind of temple, holy ground, and, therefore, a place where it should be safe to leave something valuable—though we usually left something else entirely. Still, I never imagined I would find a hundred million dollars worth of jewels hidden beside a commode.

I pulled the case up onto my lap and decided to look inside, curious to see if Babineux had already moved its contents to a new location. I undid the latches, lifted the lid, and felt a little like the bad guy in *Raiders of the Lost Ark* when he opened the Ark of the Covenant. In this case, I was the good guy, and beams of godly retribution didn't melt my face. Instead, I saw that its contents were still there, which made this the first time I'd seen a hundred million dollars in jewels—an event I never expected to experience, least of all, while sitting on a toilet. The case had a black foam interior and the emeralds, rubies, and diamonds were all neatly organized into little plastic bags. Sweet buttered monkey balls! These gems were worth the kind of money that could alter the course of history, save people's lives, or potentially even destroy them I suppose. I closed the case and sat there on the toilet thinking, my gaze directed out the door where it fell upon Babineux's bed and fish tank. Somewhere deep in my subconscious there was an idea brewing, but it took a moment for it to surface, and when it did, I couldn't stop smiling—well, that is, until Billings's phone vibrated. Fuck! What was it about the combination of toilets and me that always brought about unexpected calls? I looked at the screen and saw that it was Mick.

"Oi!" I said.

"Oi, mate. Just giving you a heads up. Your guy is on his way back. He'll be there any minute."

"Can you slow him down?"

"Bloody hell! I'll do what I can, but I suggest you hide or get the fuck out of there."

"Thanks, mate," I said.

Shit, I didn't have a lot of time to put my plan into action, but it was worth a try, as I had a strong feeling it might all pay off in the end. I took the case and went back out into the bedroom, where I quickly got everything together and properly packaged for the underwater journey back to the ski boat. Finished, I went back into the bathroom and completed the affair by writing the letters *IOU* on the toilet paper roll that sat directly above the now empty cabinet. I headed out into the bedroom and noticed an odd section of wall that I had missed on my first pass. On closer inspection, I realized it was yet another hidden cabinet, and I pressed on the panel, and it opened up to reveal a lovely minibar stocked with several bottles of Soft Taco Island's finest! Apparently, that French fuck liked to hide all of his treasure. I thought about Lux and the continuing sanctity of my ballsack, but decided that life was too short not to grab some more of that delicious rum. I nabbed a bottle, headed for the door, and popped my head out of the master stateroom to find Lux anxiously awaiting my arrival.

"All done!" I said.

"What's the plan? Are we going to hide out and grab him when he comes to take a shit, or are we going to use all your precious recon and come back later?"

"Neither," I said, stepping completely outside, keeping the case in front of me and the bottle behind my back in the event that she lived up to her earlier promise.

"No fucking way! You found the jewels!"

"I sure did, and you'll never guess where they were!"

"Where?" she asked, curiously.

"In a hidden cabinet beside the toilet!"

"You're kidding, right?"

"Nope."

"Well, thank God for your bathroom fetish!"

"No shit, and I assume you know what this means?"

"I believe I do. We don't have to storm this fucking yacht. Now that we have the jewels, we can make that French fucker come to us!"

"Damn straight!"

Lux looked too happy to use my ballsack as a speedbag, so I brought my other arm around and revealed the bottle of rum.

"I also found this," I said, proudly.

"Another bottle? Seriously?" she asked.

"You bet your sweet ass!"

She looked down at my arm and noticed it was wet.

"Why is your arm all wet? Wait—never mind, you were just in a bathroom, so I'd rather not know."

"It's not what you think."

"Doesn't matter."

"Fine—then let's get the fuck out of here."

Lux started to head for the swim platform but paused and turned around to regard me with a rather curious look on her face.

"What is it?" I asked.

"I was just wondering if you came here with the intention of finding that case—or was it just blind, dumb luck?"

I hadn't intended to find the case, although it might have been a subconscious thing as Mick did say that they didn't have any kind of luggage when they left for brunch. That would have been a pretty good indicator that the jewels could still be aboard the yacht.

"They say we make our own luck," I responded.

"Then you made yourself a whole shitload today, Tag Finn, which is why I'm going to leave your ballsack in peace."

I radioed Billings that we were heading back, then Lux and I went to the swim platform and started putting on our gear. We had just finished when Babineux, Bridgette, and his contingent of mercenaries arrived and began walking towards the yacht. I motioned to Lux that we should get into the water, and she acquiesced but didn't look too happy to be leaving her little sister behind yet again. I had a last look at the scene then took Lux by the hand, and we began our descent. We reached the bottom and started swimming west back towards the ski boat, eventually surfacing a few feet from the swim platform. I handed the tanks up to Billings, then Lux and I climbed out and joined him in the cockpit, where he smiled when he saw the attache case and bottle of rum.

"I'm happy to see you've got the jewels back, but I'm a little sad you only found one bottle of rum."

"True, but now we can afford to buy the entire distillery," I said, as I patted the case.

He slid behind the controls, fired up the engine, and hit the throttles, sending me flying back into the seat beside Lux. The afternoon heat felt good, and she looked particularly beautiful with her long hair billowing in the wind. She smiled at me, and I smiled back a little sadly as I thought about how our lives had been changed by that one bullet back in Afghanistan. Shit happened, but it sure seemed like it happened a lot more often to me.

CHAPTER TWENTY-SIX
The French Connection

We arrived back at the *Sozo*, and Kip secured the boat as we climbed aboard and went into the dive room to stow our gear and change. It was never easy to get out of a wetsuit, and it took me a minute to wriggle out of the top part, and it would probably take twice that time to get free of the bottom. I, therefore, wasn't too surprised to see that Lux was struggling and unable to get free of her top. I reached over and helped her get the zipper past her sizable breasts, and, with a quick tug, she was finally able to slip her arms free, but the effort accidentaly took her bikini top off with it. I tried to do the gentlemanly thing and look away, but I was, as expected, hypnotically drawn to the bounty of her beautiful bosoms. She caught me before I could look away, and I smiled dumbly, feeling like a teenage boy gazing at his first set of real life boobies.

"For Christ's sake—they're just breasts," she said.

"And what were they a half an hour ago when you were shoving them in my face?"

"Still just breasts."

"More like tools of torment. Obviously, as a cold hearted woman, you don't understand the importance of breasts in a man's psyche. To us, they are the pillows of life, and it's in our DNA to hold, kiss, and caress them," I said, as I slid my legs out of the bottom of my wetsuit, only to catch Lux smiling as she regarded me.

"What?" I asked.

"I guess you weren't just talking out of your ass," she said, pointing at Tag Junior.

Shit. Now, that I was free of the compression of the wetsuit, it was pretty obvious that my manhood was saying hello in its primitive penile language. There weren't any actual words or sounds, as it was entirely a physical thing—mainly swelling.

"Oh, this? It's probably just from friction," I said, as I tried to ignore her while I looked for my shirt.

I felt eyes on me and looked over to see Lux was still staring.

"What now?" I asked.

An oddly self-satisfied smile appeared on her lips as she responded.

"You know Tag, if you're going to put pudding on a shelf, then someone is going to eat it."

Now, we had officially come full circle, and, while I didn't want to smile at her victory, I did want to smile, for I had thought of a witty retort.

"Are you offering to eat my pudding?" I asked.

"No, but I am going to clear up the question of whether or not that boner was actually from friction—or me."

Lux decided to test her little hypothesis by coming over and standing directly in front of me, her lips hovering only inches away from mine as she took hold of my hands and placed them upon her bare breasts. It had been hard to ignore her earlier assault against my resolve in that little alcove on the *Soft Taco III*, and, now, it was downright impossible.

"So, Tag, does this take you back to our little moment on the beach where you fucked my brains out?" she asked.

"Honestly, I'm trying not to think about it, but if I did, I would correct you by saying that I had been making sweet love to you until your head exploded."

"Close enough."

There wasn't a penis on earth that could have remained flaccid after such an onslaught of feminine guile, and, now, my member was literally about to burst as it strained against the fabric of my shorts. Lux looked down to admire her work then smiled smugly.

"You're right. It must be the friction," she said, as she reached down and gave my manhood a playful squeeze.

"Fuck you. That totally counts as eating my pudding."

"Maybe—but, now, I'm thinking that your stupid saying might just have enough universality to gain some traction after all," she said, as stepped back and put on her bikini top.

It was annoying to have my own silly words used against me yet again, but, deep down, I couldn't help but admire her clever victory. At least, that was the case until she walked past me and gave me a solid slap on the ass. Oh well, I suppose I had made my bed, so all I could do was lie in it. I grabbed my gear, but, just as I was about to follow her outside, I heard Billings on the other side of the door. Wonderful, now I would have a witness to my weakness. I thought about staying in the dive room until my boner subsided, but he was eagerly waiting and would probably just come in if I didn't go out. I, therefore, decided to use the same technique I had used when I exited the nightclub on Soft Taco Island and carried the case in front of me as a veritable boner shield. Billings saw the discomfort in my gait and looked concerned.

"Are you OK? You're moving like you have a pulled groin muscle," he said.

"I'm fine, it's just a little—swelling."

Estelle suddenly came bounding down the stairs looking excited to hear the news of our recon operation.

"What's up?" she asked.

Lux stifled a laugh, and I glared at her a moment before turning my attention back to Estelle.

"Nothing," I said, innocently.

"I wouldn't exactly say nothing," Lux responded, as she glanced towards the case that blocked Estelle's view of my raging boner.

"Come on! I'm dying to hear how it went!" Estelle said, excitedly.

"A lot better than expected, as I just happened to find this while I was on Babineux's yacht," I said, turning my gaze down to the case.

Estelle stared at it, a longing in her eyes proving that Diamonds just might be a girl's best friend.

"Holy shit! You stole them back!" she said.

"Sure did."

"Can I see the jewels?" Estelle asked, as she reached towards the case.

"Not yet," I said, as I panicked and stepped back.

She looked a little offended as she regarded me.

"Why not?" she asked.

"Unfortunately, we have some major preparations to make, but I promise I'll show them to you in a little bit."

"Well, OK," she said, perking up.

Fuck! The last thing I needed at the moment was to compound my troubles with Estelle, but Lux was apparently intent on making my personal life inordinately more complicated—a point proved all too true by her next statement.

"Do you want me to take care of the jewels?" Lux asked, reaching down towards the case.

"I think it's best if I keep my hands on them for the moment. Now, if you don't mind, I need to rinse off, so why don't we all meet in the main salon in fifteen minutes," I suggested.

Before anyone could answer, I turned tail and raced from the boat deck, taking the stairs two at a time, hoping to get as much distance between my boner and Estelle as possible—which was particularly ironic, because I generally liked having my boner as close to her as possible. This particular instance, however, I was dealing with an especially tenacious hard-on that I had no chance of adequately explaining.

I continued on, my penis pointing the way, like a unicorn's glorious horn until I reached the landing at the halfway point only to collide with a very startled Kip. The case flew from my hands, leaving my boner waving in the wind like the proud prow of a majestic sailing ship. Kip glanced down and smiled awkwardly.

"Well now—I don't believe I've ever seen you this happy to see me," he said, before continuing on his way.

I heard footsteps coming from below and frantically picked up the case and continued on, trying to make sure I stayed well ahead of my pursuer who, almost certainly, had to be Estelle. I reached the main deck, and it seemed as though the entire crew had decided to come out and bask in the sunshine. Wonderful—it was as though I was traversing a human obstacle course, but I ran through them as quickly as I could, weaving left and right, desperately trying to reach the privacy of my cabin. I had made it through the main salon, and was only ten feet short of my door, when Estelle finally caught up to me, grabbed my shoulder, and swung me around—the jarring movement sending the case flying out of my hand and onto the floor. Fearing she was about to ask me the most awkward of questions, I looked down and breathed a sweet sigh of relief as I realized that my brief jog had deflated my manhood to a manageable size, and it now hung quietly behind the nylon fabric of my board shorts.

"Are you OK?" she asked.

"I'm fine," I said, still a little breathless from the chase.

"You seemed a little tense downstairs."

That was an excellent unintentional double entendre about my penis, and quite possibly the understatement of the year.

"No, not at all—I was just excited that we got the jewels back."

"Well, good. I just wanted to check on you—make sure you're OK."

I suddenly thought back to my little incident on the stairs with

Kip.

"I'm fine, but I do have one little concern."

"What is it?"

"Kip has been giving me the evil eye ever since you and I got together, but now, he's all smiles. I don't get it."

Estelle smiled and looked around awkwardly for a moment.

"I thought that you would have already figured it out considering you're a detective and all."

"What?"

"Isn't it obvious? Kip likes men."

"Ohhhhh."

"Yeah, he's been angry with me, because he has a little crush on you."

"So, he doesn't want to kill me?"

"No, kill is definitely not the correct word."

Now that I thought about it, it made perfect sense! Aggression and lust could look identical, and I had obviously misinterpreted the signals, and all of Kip's snarky comments weren't threats, but clever sexual innuendos.

"Shit, I feel a little silly now."

"Don't worry. We just had a nice long talk, and he's cool with everything. Besides, you're straight and things probably weren't going to work out the way he wanted."

"What do you mean, probably?"

"Face it, Tag, you're a man-whore, which means your life is open to a myriad of potential sexual encounters."

Just then, Kip came around the corner.

"Oh Estelle, give Tag a break. He's had a very—hard—day," he said, with a wink before disappearing down the passageway.

"What was that supposed to mean?" Estelle asked.

"Probably nothing, as I suppose a crush will turn any man into a blathering idiot."

She shrugged then turned and headed back towards the main salon, while I went inside my cabin, sat on the bed, and took a moment to put the universe back together. I was relieved to finally reach some peace with Kip, but Lux was an entirely different and confusing matter. It was weird being around her again after all these years, and obviously I was still coming to terms with my feelings for her—the little exchange on the boat deck not making my life any easier. I undressed and headed into the bathroom and figured I had just enough time for a quick shower, perhaps a cold one. I stepped inside, happy to have a little alone time to unwind as I washed off the saltwater. When I was done, I emerged ready to face the world. A shower could work like a cup of coffee to invigorate the soul, and now feeling fresh, clean, and boner free, I dressed and took a moment to get everything ready for the big exchange. Satisfied, I grabbed two pistols and the case then headed to the main salon to find everyone patiently waiting for me.

"Alrighty then! Now, that we have such a valuable bargaining chip, we have an entirely new plan on the table. Instead of storming his yacht, we're going to contact Babineux and arrange a nice little meeting to make the big exchange. Of course, another viable option in my mind would be that we forget about both him and Bridgette all together, and keep the jewels. A hundred million, even split ten ways, is plenty for all of us."

"Not funny," Lux said.

"Oh well—it was worth a shot."

Lux glared at me, so I decided it was time to continue on with the discussion.

"OK, as we're going with the original plan to rescue Bridgette and snatch Babineux, then I suppose we need to figure out how to conduct this meeting in such a way that we isolate our two objectives from his little army of mercenaries. To that end, I'm thinking we could probably just stage the meeting via helicopter."

"Good idea, as that will obviously limit the amount of his people he can bring along," Lux said.

"Exactly, though we'll, of course, make it a caveat that he can only bring Bridgette."

Lux took a moment to think before posing another concern.

"What if he finds another way to get his men to the meeting place?"

"He won't be able to because we're only going to give him the coordinates at the last minute. It puts everyone an even playing field and makes it a hell of a lot safer for us."

"Sounds good. Let's figure out where to do this."

"I'll bring up Martinique on the satellite feed," Estelle said.

She went to a console on the wall and pressed a button, and it was amazing to actually see the entire transformation take place. The last time we used the screens, they were already setup, but, now, right before my eyes, I realized the paintings were, in actuality, high definition monitors. It must be nice to be super wealthy and have all this cool gadgetry at your disposal. Come to think of it, I remembered reading that one of the big software billionaires in Seattle had similar screens throughout his home that allowed him to display whatever art met his fancy at any particular moment. The art in my houseboat was quite the opposite, however, and consisted of some crappy paintings I had procured at my local art festival. Worse still, I had only purchased them because they were painted by a neighbor who brow beat me into the sale in hopes of stirring up the other onlookers. Estelle hit another button, and the keyboard and trackpad slid out from underneath the table—the experience making me feel as though I were living in a James Bond movie. She took a seat, tapped the spacebar, and the dancing V logo on the center screen disappeared and was replaced by a satellite feed of Martinique.

"So, we obviously need a place big enough to land two helicopters," Estelle said.

"Are there any nice wide open beaches nearby—preferably nude?" I asked.

Estelle gave me a disapproving look.

"Hey, if everyone is nude, it'll be a lot safer, as no one can smuggle in any hidden weapons."

"Well, in that case, I do know of one, but it's all male," she responded.

"Never mind. Better keep looking."

"Oh well," Kip muttered.

Estelle turned her attention to the screen and scanned the Island, zooming in whenever she saw a place of interest. She covered almost every square inch before finally settling on the municipal stadium parking lot near Fort De France. It was a large open area and not too close to any residential dwellings.

"That'll work," I said.

Billings, deep in thought, looked up excitedly.

"Fuck it! Why don't you have him come to us? He can land on the *Sozo's* bow, and then we'll have the home field advantage."

"I like it! Good idea, Pete."

"Let's call the prick and set it up," Lux said.

"All right, how do we get in touch with Babineux? Cell phone or radio his yacht?"

"I know his cell phone number," Lux said.

"Interesting—is there something else you haven't told us about your relationship with President Babineux?" I said, giving her a questioning look.

"Fuck you, its standard procedure to memorize your subject's key information. I would have thought you already knew that, Amigo," Lux said.

"Whatever, let's give your boyfriend a call."

Lux glared at me, then she keyed in his cell number and hit send before handing me back the phone. He picked up on the third ring.

"Bonjour, cici est Babineux," he said.

"Bon après-midi de pamplemousse puante," I said, which translated roughly as good afternoon you smelly grapefruit.

I always loved the word, pamplemousse, because it sounded so fanciful and even more so when combined with the adjective smelly. It was stupid, but it gave me a great deal of pleasure crafting such creative French insults.

"Bon après-midi vous piquer indignes de confiance," he responded.

Not surprisingly, he called me an untrustworthy prick.

"Speaking of which, I wanted to thank you for the case of rum I found in your palace. I must say, I'm feeling a little guilty, as I haven't gotten you a single thing in return."

"Well, you did provide me with a beautiful female hostage, though I am a little saddened by the fact that you did not take me up on my gracious hospitality. You should have considered it a rare pleasure to have been invited into my home. Few people, other than celebrities or heads of state have ever been to my presidential palace."

"I know, and while the accommodations were spectacular, we really had some more pressing engagements—namely, a little stopover on the *Sarsarun*. Lovely yacht by the way, and we managed to get our hands on some Russian shoulder-fired missiles for an excellent price. Practically stole them."

Babineux was quiet for a moment, as I assume he was telling one of his men to contact the *Sarsarun*. He had to be nervous, but he was still maintaining his composure like a pro.

"Oh really, Monsieur Finn?"

"Yeah, though the reason I actually called is that I'm curious if you've been to your yacht's bathroom recently. I had to use it, and, instead of taking a shit, I took something else."

I heard Babineux get up and say something to one of his men, but I couldn't understand it, because he had covered the phone with his hand. When he came back on the line, I could tell by his breathing that he was walking—probably to his bathroom.

"Whatever do you mean, Monsieur Finn? I am sure that whatever I may have put in my bathroom is exactly where I left it."

"I hope you're not referring to your morning dump, because that should have been flushed—as leaving a deuce in the bowl would go against the rules of the International Accord on Bathroom Etiquette. Trust me, I know my shit when it comes to shit."

"You're a funny man, Finn, but I seriously doubt you have been on my yacht and seen my bathroom."

"Oh no, I have, and I must say, it's easily as nice as the one in your home. Of course, I have to admit that your entire stateroom is lovely, especially the fish tank behind the bed. It's a wonderful way to capture your Versailles meets the sea interior design scheme."

He stopped talking, and his breathing became even more labored as he picked up his pace. I heard a door open and imagined that he must be in his cabin. A moment later, he let out a long uncomfortable sounding groan that had the distinctive echo of having been uttered in a bathroom.

"Oh, was that the sound of you beginning your post-brunch dump?" I asked.

"No. Now, what is it that you want, Monsieur Finn?"

"Bridgette, in exchange for the jewels."

"That's all?"

"That's all."

"When and where?"

"Today—I'll call and give you the location, then you'll have ten minutes to fly there by helicopter."

"Easy enough."

"Good, and make sure it's just you, Bridgette, and the pilot."

"I'll fly my own helicopter if you don't mind."

"Even better, and, for your information, we have you under satellite surveillance, so we'll know if you bring any extra help along."

We, of course, had actual eyes on Babineux, but there was no reason to reveal Mick's existence and put him in any kind of danger. Of course, Mick being ex-SASR, meant he was probably more than capable of dealing with any threat to his personal safety.

"What can I say—it's a deal."

"Good, and Lux would like to talk to her sister."

"Fine."

I hit the speaker button and held out the phone to Lux.

"Bridgette?"

"Yeah, it's me. I'm OK. Babineux is treating me well, but you have to give him the jewels, or he will hurt me. I'm serious, Lux."

"Don't worry, he'll get them, but, more importantly, I want you to know that I love you, and you're going to be OK. I'm going to get you out of this. I promise."

"I know you will. I love you too."

Babineux came back on the line, so I took it off speaker.

"Satisfied?" he asked.

"Oui—I'll be in touch. Au revoir mon petit chou," I said.

"You might want to take a French refresher course unless you really do think of me as your little cabbage."

"You're right, I'll have to work on my French."

"Oui, now, au revoir mon petit trou du cul," Babineux said.

"Wait, what does trou du cul mean?"

"Asshole," he said, before hanging up.

I laughed as I hit the end button.

"What's so funny?" Lux asked.

"He called me an asshole."

"Well, you have stolen his shit and fucked up his arms deal."

"True, but I did it for you."

"So, I guess we're both assholes," Lux said, her expression turning anxious.

I suppose she wouldn't be happy until she had her little sister safely back aboard the *Sozo*, and who could blame her? It's not every day that your sibling ends up in the hands of a French arms dealer with his own private army. Still, I was confident it would all work out in the end. I went to my cabin, grabbed a pistol, then headed back out to the main salon to find that everyone was still sitting around the table.

"Alrighty, Estelle, you said you wanted to get a look at the jewels, so I'd suggest you do it now in case our exchange doesn't go as planned," I said, as I reached over and opened the case, which was sitting in the center of the table.

Estelle and the others all came around and gazed longingly at the contents.

"So, that's what a hundred million dollars in gems looks like," she said.

"Yeah, and it's too bad the government will probably end up with them in the end."

Lux reached over and inspected the jewels, looking at several of the bags before placing them back in the case and closing the lid.

"OK then, let's talk about how we're going to do this," she said.

"Well, our first goal is to exchange the jewels for Bridgette, and, once she's free and clear, we'll make our move on Babineux."

"That kind of sounds as though we're winging it again."

"Yeah—pretty much, but we'll also post a backup shooter somewhere on the bridge, so, if everything really goes to hell, he, or she, could, potentially, use a well placed bullet to disable the helicopter and make sure Babineux doesn't get away."

"I'll do it," Kip said.

"Good, but remember—don't pull the trigger unless Lux gives the official OK. We want Bridgette safe and Babineux alive."

Everyone knew the plan, so it was time to check in one more time with our man on the ground. It took Mick five rings to answer the phone, and, when he did, his voice had a strange echo.

"Bloody hell, mate. I'm taking a piss in a porta potty on the pier."

"I know. I can tell by the acoustics, and I must say, I'm surprised you answered your phone."

"Can't help it. It's an obsessive compulsive thing."

"I completely understand. So, look, we're almost done with this business, which means I just need you to keep an eye on our guy a little longer and call me to verify that only he and the girl board his helicopter."

"Got it. We're hoping for a twosome. Cheers, mate," he said, hanging up.

I dialed Babineux next, and he picked up on the second ring.

"Bonjour trou du cul," he said.

"Bonjour merde chou," I responded, which meant shit cabbage.

He laughed, and I had to admit that I kind of admired Babineux's composure. I had stolen a hundred million dollars from him, and he was acting as though we were setting up a casual lunch date.

"Excellent—I see you have expanded your French vocabulary since we last spoke."

"Oui."

"So, my friend, where do we meet?"

"The bow of the *Sozo*. We are moored on the north side of the Fort De France bay. The *Sozo* is big enough that I'm pretty sure you'll be able to find it."

"All right then, but no funny business, funny man, or Bridgette gets hurt."

"No problem. We'll see you in ten minutes. Au revoir."

He hung up without another word, and I told Lux they were coming. She was nervous, but she tried her best to look confident as we left the lounge and walked out to the bow of the boat to wait for Babineux. It was yet another lovely day in paradise, the wind calm, and the water even calmer with hardly a ripple to mar its surface. After a few moments of quiet reflection, Lux turned and looked into my eyes.

"Thanks, Finn—for everything."

"It's not a problem, and let's face it—I owe you more than I can ever repay. I wouldn't be here if it weren't for you."

"I know, but I've been giving you a lot of shit, and it's probably not fair."

"You're under a lot of stress. Plus, you're coming to terms with the fact that you chose the wrong guy ten years ago, and it's obvious that you're dying on the inside."

"I'm trying to be serious you asshole, so, please just shut up and listen. I want you to know your help means a lot to me, and I'm sorry I never got in touch before now, and I'm also sorry I never told you anything about my family. It's just that mentioning the Vandenberg name has a strange effect on people, and, back in Afghanistan, I wanted a clean slate, so I never told anyone—not even you."

"I wouldn't have given a shit about your family and all their money. All I really cared about were your looks."

"Fuck you. I'm trying to tell you something serious," she said, as she delivered a friendly backhand to my ribs.

"I know, and I'm sorry, but, as a man, it's my sworn duty to use evasion and humor to hide my feelings."

She smiled, but her eyes told the true tale of her growing unease. She was stressed and needed a little comfort, so I reached out, and, just like our moment on the bridge, she melted into my arms. Lux was a tough cookie who never lost her composure, even in the heat of combat, which meant this business with her sister was pushing her to her breaking point. I, therefore, did the only thing I could at that point, which was to continue to hold her for as long as she needed me. Her heart was beating hard in her chest, and, when she eventually pulled away, her eyes were wet with the beginning of tears.

"Don't worry. I'll make sure nothing happens to Bridgette," I said.

"I know, but I just can't help feeling so awful about all of this. You know, ever since our parents passed away, it's been my responsibility to take care of her—and I totally fucked it all up when I got her into this mess."

"You're a good sister, and everything will work out. I promise."

"I hope you're right," she said, as she wiped her eyes with her sleeve.

"I know I'm right."

Just then, the phone rang, and I looked down to see it was Mick calling, so I hit the accept-button.

"Oi," I said.

"Oi, mate, I got word on your guy. He and my future wife just took off in his helicopter."

"And no one else snuck aboard?"

"Nope, definitely a twosome."

"Thanks, Mick. You'll be getting a big fat check and a hug for all your help."

"Is the hug coming from you or the girl I'm watching?"

"The girl—and her equally hot sister."

"Best surveillance job I've ever had."

"Well then, G'day Mick,"

"G'day, mate," he said, before ending the call.

We stood there and waited until we could hear the faint sound of Babineux's helicopter approaching from the east. At first, it was just a spec in the sky but quickly grew as it neared the *Sozo*, and I could see it was a Eurocopter. His particular model seated six, but I was happy to already know that it was carrying only two at the moment, as a violent gun battle against a team of French mercenaries wouldn't exactly be the best addition to the day. The helicopter swooped over the bow and descended slowly to the foredeck, where I finally had a good view inside and was relieved to see that Mick was correct, and only Babineux and Bridgette were aboard. So far, the Frenchman had kept his word. Lux and I shielded our eyes from the rotor wash as the helicopter dropped the last few feet and touched down gently onto the deck—the blades still spinning as the engine wound down. Bridgette stepped out and Babineux followed close behind with his gun trained on her as they moved closer. Lux and I walked forward to meet them then stopped about ten feet away, all the while keeping our pistols at the ready.

"Bon après-midi de la merde mangeur," I said, which translated as good afternoon shit eater.

"Most impressive! You're still expanding your French vocabulary."

"I think it's important to be well versed in the language of my adversary."

"Well, then let me greet you with this little gem—bonjour dugland," he said.

"And that means?" I asked.

"Hello, fuckface."

"I like it—though I must admit that fuckface definitely sounds better in French."

"Of course, because everything sounds better in French."

"Except farts—and they certainly don't smell better."

"Says the man raised on burgers and hotdogs."

"To the man raised on garlic, cheese, and onions."

"*Touché.*"

I couldn't help but smile at our little exchange.

"What has the world come to when I've inspired a member of the French aristocracy to engage in tough talk about flatulence?" I asked.

"Excellent point. So, if we are done talking like children, I would appreciate getting my property back. To that end, I want Bridgette to open the case and show me the contents, and, once I know the jewels are there, we can part ways for good, dugland."

I walked forward with the case, and Bridgette came out and met me halfway, and I had to admit that she was doing a good job of maintaining her composure in the face of adversity—even giving me a little wink that I desperately hoped Lux didn't see. I handed the case over, and she opened it and peered inside before showing it to Babineux. He nodded, and she closed it and smiled at me.

"Thank you, Tag. I knew you'd come through for me," she said.

Lux came forward and hugged Bridgette.

"I'm so sorry for dragging you into this mess," Lux said.

"It's OK, Lux. Everything is fine now."

They held each other, and Lux looked ever relieved to have her little sister in her arms. At long last they parted, but, when Bridgette stepped back, she had a pistol in her hand, and, worse still, she was aiming it at us.

"Now, I'm the one who's sorry, Lux," she said.

"What's going on, Bridgette?"

"I'm taking the jewels and leaving with Adrien."

Adrien? That sounded awfully chummy, though it certainly explained some things—especially this latest turn of events.

"No, you're not. Now, put down the gun," Lux said.

"Sorry. No can do, Lux."

"I don't understand."

"You will one day—I promise."

Bridgette kept the gun aimed at us as she backed up and joined Babineux, which left us all armed and aiming guns at each other. Considering both sides had a family member they would rather not see get shot, we were in a kind of Mexican standoff, and it certainly didn't get any more fucked up than this scenario.

"This is a family reunion for the record books," I said.

Babineux smiled then glanced down at his watch before turning his gaze back to us.

"Yes, indeed, but I'm afraid we must go, as we have a flight to catch, but, perhaps, we can all get together again for Christmas," he said.

"Sounds lovely," I responded.

They climbed into the helicopter and Babineux started the engine and the blades began to turn. The noise and wind gradually increased, but Lux didn't move an inch and, instead, continued to stare unflinching at Bridgette. My radio crackled and I heard Kip.

"What's the plan, over? Do I try and disable the helicopter?" he asked.

"Negative. It's too risky," I said.

Technically, it was Lux's call, but I already knew she wouldn't green light any shooting as long as Bridgette was aboard the helicopter. Fuck—this wasn't exactly how I hoped this day would come to a close, but life, as usual, tended to have its own plan far beyond the wishes of us tiny insignificant mortals. I put my arm around Lux and held her as we watched the helicopter continue to throttle up—the wash from the rotors encircling the front deck of the *Sozo* and making it feel as though we were standing in the middle of a tornado. Lux's hair was billowing and whipping her face in the powerful currents, but she remained unmoved, stoically watching as Babineux adjusted the collective and brought the helicopter up off the deck. He steered it around to the left on a course for Martinique then gave a parting wave while Bridgette mouthed one final word—sorry.

CHAPTER TWENTY-SEVEN
Ugly Americans

We stood on the bow and silently watched the helicopter disappear into the distance, the distinctive roar of its powerful jet engine and the wup wup sound of the blades cutting through the air finally diminishing until all we could hear were the waves gently lapping up against the *Sozo's* hull.

"Fucking Bridgette! I can't believe that just happened," Lux said.

"I can."

"Why do you say that?"

Before I could answer, the stillness of the moment was suddenly interrupted by the loud bellow of an air horn, and we looked back towards the stern to see a French Navy patrol boat approaching from the south.

"Is this your agency guy?"

"Doubtful, as I'm pretty sure the French Navy isn't working cooperatively on this operation, so I have no fucking idea why they're here."

The patrol boat came ever closer, and my unease was growing with each passing second.

"I really hope this has nothing to do with an assault on some federal employees on Martinique."

"What the hell are you talking about?"

"Remember when Babineux said I made some of his men look like idiots?"

"Yeah."

"Well, those idiots also happened to be agents of the DGSE."

"There's no way they would send a navy patrol boat out here for that."

"I certainly hope not, but you better promise to bail me out of jail if that turns out to be the case."

The Patrol Boat tied up to the starboard side of the *Sozo's* stern, then armed men started clambering aboard.

"This really is one of those days that just won't end," Lux said.

"This is what happens after a hard day's night turns into an even shittier next day."

This certainly didn't look like a friendly visit, and I could see the concern in Lux's eyes as we walked back along the deck and headed inside the *Sozo*. The boat was eerily quiet and devoid of activity until we reached the main salon and experienced yet another moment of déjà vu. French seamen armed with assault rifles were taking everyone into custody, and, the minute Lux and I appeared, we were grabbed and had our hands bound behind our backs with zip ties. Once secured, we were roughly ushered over to one of the couches and forced to take a seat beside Billings, who was not looking happy to have his boat boarded yet again. At that moment, the French Navy captain in charge of this little operation made his appearance. He was probably around forty, had a mustache and, oddly, kind of resembled a real life *Inspector Clousseau*—minus the trench coat and woolen hat, of course. I never smelled *Clousseau*, but I seriously doubted he wreaked of cologne as badly as our French captain.

"I don't think you should speak any of your French to him," Lux said, as he approached.

"Hello, I'm Captain Jaques, and you have all been detained because we have received reports that this vessel and its crew are believed to have been engaged in acts of terrorism."

"How stupid can you be?" Lux asked, angrily.

"Do not take that tone with me madam. I am an officer of the French Navy, and you will give me the proper respect."

"Maybe I should try some of my French now," I said.

"Absolutely not," Lux countered.

I ignored Lux and spoke anyway.

"Bonjour, Captain Jackass. Je m'appelle Finn," I said.

The captain didn't look very happy to hear my interpretation of his name, and he proceeded to lean down and get in my face.

"Well now, Monsieur Finn, since you are American and your kind never bother to learn any language other than English, I will assume you are too ignorant to properly pronounce my name, so I would officially advise you to remain silent for the moment."

"Look here, Captain Jackass," Billings interrupted, impatiently.

"Goddammit! It's Jaques."

"Fine, Jaques—if you would just listen for a moment, I could tell you that I'm a retired United States Navy Captain, and, from one captain to another, you should know that this vessel is, at this very moment, being used by the United States government for a top priority anti-terrorism operation."

Jaques scrutinized Billings, one eyebrow raised as he looked at his fellow captain.

"I'm sorry, Captain, but I'm just following the orders that I have been given. Of course, I find your statement somewhat contradictory considering the cargo we discovered down on your lower boat deck."

Shit, I had completely forgotten about the missile launchers, and only now realized that their untimely presence would do nothing to help us out of this predicament.

"We just commandeered those missile launchers from actual terrorists," Billings countered.

"Regardless the circumstances, the rest of this affair will be left up to the proper authorities to resolve."

"Do you realize that while you dick us around, the real bad guy in this situation is flying away with my sister and a hundred million dollars of terrorist money," Lux added, leaving out the fact that Bridgette wasn't exactly a prisoner.

"Please, save your comments for the formal inquiry. Your yacht will be impounded, and all of you will be brought ashore for processing."

Jaques walked away leaving a very angry Billings and Lux fuming beside me.

"Goddammit, this is the second time my ship has been taken over in less than a week. What the fuck is going on here?"

"I wish I knew, Pete, but I have a strong feeling that Babineux arranged this little speed bump to keep us off his ass."

"Then, let's hope the agency guy gets here in time to clear all this up," Billings said.

"Yeah, though that would constitute a miracle," I added.

"True, but maybe, just maybe, you should have called Babineux Mr. President instead of shit eater, and none of this would be happening right now," Lux added.

"He called me fuckface. What can I say?"

The captain came over with several of his soldiers and told us to get up. It wasn't easy with our hands secured behind our backs, but we all eventually managed to stand, and Lux and I ended up at the back of the group. They started herding us towards the aft deck, and, as I passed the bar, I saw a bottle of Soft Taco Island rum and couldn't help but think about the case in my room. I hadn't even opened it yet, and, the way things were going, it would all likely end up impounded in some French evidence locker. Goddammit! That fucker Babineux had outplayed us yet again, and now we were back to being held captive by the French menace. Lux fell behind a step, and the soldier behind her gave her a rough shove that sent her stumbling into me, the collision nearly knocking both of us to the floor. That was it. I'd had my fill of French hospitality and was officially at my breaking point. I turned to face the man, only to discover that he was a little over six feet tall, muscular, and had breath that still smelled of his onion-laden lunch. Worse still, he was definitely one of those assholes who seemed to be angry at the world and enjoyed pushing people around—his turned-down mouth and dour expression a perfect accompaniment to his unpleasant demeanor. Lux seemed to sense my mood and looked worried.

"Finn, please don't do anything stupid and get yourself hurt," she said.

"Don't worry—I won't."

"Promise?"

"I promise."

"Good, now, I'm sure our French friend here will be civil to us as long as we're civil to him—considering we're all technically on the same side," Lux said, as she turned her gaze to the man.

He leaned in close as he responded.

"But of course, now why don't you shut the fuck up and keep moving you bitch!" the man growled, the anger behind his words making spittle fly from his mouth and land on Lux's face.

That was one-third rude and two-thirds disgusting, which meant I was exactly one hundred percent incapable of remaining civil with our French captor.

"I know you enjoy being an asshole and all, but I'd really appreciate it if you would abstain from pushing my friend or calling her a bitch."

His sour expression turned into a cruel smile as he spoke.

"Oh, I see, you are a gentleman. Is this better?" he asked, as he slammed the butt of his rifle into my stomach.

It hurt, but I was expecting the hit and managed to stay upright.

"No, and I'm afraid it makes you an even bigger asshole," I responded.

His smile disappeared, and he slammed the butt of his rifle into my stomach yet again, only, this time, I played along by buckling over and acting as though I'd had the wind knocked out of me.

"Oh, perhaps you have something else you want to say? How about an apology for calling me an asshole?" he suggested.

"Fine, I apologize," I said, in a barely audible whisper.

"Oh, I'm sorry. What was that? I couldn't hear you properly," he said, holding his left hand up to his ear as he smiled triumphantly.

I made a point of moving slowly and looking pained as I tried to straighten up.

"I said that I apologize—for knocking you the fuck out."

He looked confused as I proceeded to slam my forehead into the crown of his nose. I felt and heard the cartilage snap as his head jerked back, and this allowed me to step forward and swing my knee up into his groin. He grunted in pain as his head dropped down, and I landed another knee, but this one was to his face. He was dazed, and he staggered backward giving me just enough room to throw a high right rear-leg roundhouse kick. I was breaking my cardinal rule by kicking above the waist, but I needed a headshot if I wanted a knockout. I adjusted my stance then swung my foot, all the while letting my anger fuel my effort as I hit the side of his head and knocked him out cold. He collapsed to the ground, and I scrambled down and turned my back towards him, so I could slip his utility knife off his belt. It wasn't easy working behind my back, but I eventually got the blade out and cut the cable tie off my hands—barely missing my radial artery in the process. Once free, I looked around to do a quick threat assessment and was amazed that no one had seen our little mutiny.

"Vive la révolution!" I muttered, quietly.

I cut Lux's hands free then grabbed the man's Beretta pistol and FAMAS assault rifle, which meant we were now officially armed and dangerous.

"You promised you wouldn't do anything stupid," Lux said.

"I didn't think that was stupid, and, regardless, I wasn't about the stand by and let any more French seamen get in your face."

"I'm not even going to justify that attempt at humor with a response."

"Well, technically, you just did," I said, smiling.

"Do you ever get tired of using that line?"

"Not as long as you keep giving me the opportunity to use it."

The rest of the soldiers were busy at the front of the group, and no one paid us any attention as we slipped out of the main salon and into the forward passageway.

"So, what now, Houdini? Hide out until they're gone and hope they don't realize we're missing?" Lux asked.

I looked out beyond the main salon, and saw that the French captain was on the other end of the deck, and his close proximity to the rear stairwell gave me an idea.

"No, we need to take Captain Jackass hostage."

"Are you crazy? He's got at least eight armed soldiers with him on that deck."

"It doesn't matter, as right now we need to buy some time until your Agency guy arrives and clears all this up."

"I assume you understand that this could constitute an act of war."

"Not if they're our allies. Now, come on, Jugs—we'll use the back stairs and sneak right up behind Captain Jackass."

Lux wasn't entirely convinced, but she followed me as I ran forward past the crew's quarters and headed for the forward stairwell. Upon reaching the lower level we headed aft to the boat deck, but Lux grabbed me by the shoulder and stopped me in my tracks.

"Hold up. I'm having doubts about this plan. We really shouldn't take a French Navy captain hostage."

"Do you have a better idea?"

"No, but I'm afraid we're going to make this situation a lot worse."

"Worse than all of us ending up in a French prison?"

"Yeah—what if someone get's seriously hurt or killed, and we escalate this into an international incident?"

"Oh come on, do you remember World War II? I think we have

really excellent odds they might just peacefully surrender."

I turned and headed up the back stairs and spied Captain Jackass droning on in his nasal voice as he asked the *Sozo's* crew-members for their names before writing them into some kind of official ledger. Lux joined me, and we quietly made our way closer until he was no more than a couple feet away—his sickly sweet French cologne engulfing us like tear gas and practically making our eyes water. Lux leaned in and whispered in my ear.

"This would be a lot easier if we had a distraction."

"Don't worry—we are the distraction. The minute they find out that their fellow cheese eater has been knocked out cold, all their attention will be focused on him and who the hell assaulted him."

"Which would be us."

"Exactly, so all we have to do is wait and then use the confusion to grab Captain Jackass."

Lux and I only had to wait another minute until they had gotten to the end of the line, then the hysterical cries of French soldiers filled the air. They had found their fellow frog bloodied and knocked unconscious, and, now, they were looking for the people who had done it—namely us. Just as planned, everyone's attention turned towards the main salon, and the French soldiers raced inside to investigate, thus giving us the opportunity to move in on Captain Jackass. I slipped up behind him and placed the barrel of the pistol against his head.

"We meet again, Captain Jackass," I whispered into his ear.

I couldn't see his eyes, but I would imagine that they were probably as big as a bullfrog's at the moment. Lux slid his pistol out of his holster, and we moved away from the stairwell and backed up against the aft railing. I raised the pistol up and fired a shot into the air, and the scene went quiet as everyone turned and looked at us with panicked expressions. Shortly thereafter, the French soldiers came rushing out of the main salon and joined the crowd of stunned gawkers—realization slowly sinking in that we had taken the French captain hostage. The *Sozo's* crew, unlike the soldiers, looked pretty excited, though Billings was the first to vocalize his enthusiasm.

"Arrrrrr!" he exclaimed, loudly.

"Arrrrrr!" I responded.

Now that we had officially celebrated our moment of glory, it was time to deal with the situation.

"Bonjour, effectuez l'une des idiots vous parler anglais? Levez vos mains," I said.

I just asked if any of the idiots spoke English, and, if so, to raise their hand. My French was not good enough for a prolonged or meaningful hostage situation, so I was relieved when at least half of them raised a hand.

"Alrighty then, mes amis. Now, that I have your attention, let me explain something. We are agents of the United States government working on a large scale counter terrorism operation, and all of you idiots have boarded this vessel under false pretenses. Comprendre?"

No one nodded, but I continued on anyway.

"At this very moment, our government is sending a liaison and, as soon as he arrives, we'll release Captain Jackass unharmed, and all of us can celebrate our new found friendship with Chèvre cheese, Champagne, and kisses."

The French soldiers stared incredulously.

"I think this was a bad idea," Lux whispered.

"It doesn't matter—we're just buying time and giving them something to think about while we wait for the cavalry."

At that moment, the soldiers all chambered rounds and aimed their weapons at Lux and me.

"I don't think it's working."

"Look, mes amis, there is no need for anyone to get hurt. We are all friends here—or at least we were during World War II, and, while I have no idea what happened after that to make you hate us so much, I wish to extend my desire for us to create an atmosphere of joyous diplomacy."

"Joyous diplomacy? Seriously?" Lux asked, quietly.

"Give me a break, I'm trying to improvise here."

Captain Jackass was starting to look nervous, and he had beads of sweat trickling down his forehead.

"Don't listen to him. He is obviously a stupid American!" he yelled, to his men.

"Silence, Jackass."

"It's Jacques you illiterate ass! Jacques!"

Meanwhile, the French soldiers kept their rifles dutifully aimed in our general direction.

"Any idea how long you think you can stall them before they shoot us?" Lux asked, quietly.

"No, but if all else fails, you could try doing a little striptease as a show of good faith. Remember, your breasts are your..."

"Yeah yeah, I know, they're my weapons, but it's still a stupid idea."

The French captain turned toward Lux and his eyes fell upon her substantial bosom.

"Eyes forward, Captain," she said, jabbing him with her elbow.

"Obviously my stupid idea has some merit," I said.

"It's not going to happen, asshole, so you better start praying that our people make it out here before this situation gets out of control."

Just then, came the sound of another air horn, and I looked over to see a United States Navy Patrol Boat coming in quickly from the east. Everyone's gaze turned to the approaching vessel, and we all watched as it stopped just off our stern. The crew lowered a rigid inflatable into the water, then at least ten to twelve people boarded the smaller boat, before it sped over and tied up to the *Sozo's* starboard side. Seconds later, a group of armed American soldiers came clambering onto the deck, all of them wearing full combat gear and fanning out and taking up strategic positions all around us. I knew the uniforms and weapons, and instantly realized that it was a SEAL team. Hot diggity dog! The cavalry had arrived, and, as if that weren't enough, behind them were three men, one I had never seen before and two I instantly recognized though never expected to see in a million years.

CHAPTER TWENTY-EIGHT
Old Friends New Beginnings

I stared at the men on the other side of the deck and felt a great welling of emotion, as two of them were close friends who I hadn't seen in person in about ten years. One was John Matheson, the current Vice President of the United States of America, while the other was Cornelius Wallace, or, as I called him, Corn—a man who was apparently the current Deputy Director of the CIA. They were both smiling smugly, though Corn appeared to be harboring just a touch of guilt in his expression, or perhaps I was just projecting what I wanted to see. Oh well, I was still happy to see the fucker. The third guy, judging by his rank insignia, was a French admiral, and, after all three of them exchanged some words, they proceeded to walk over and join us.

"What the fuck brings such esteemed assholes as yourselves all the way out here?" I asked.

"We heard the French authorities had boarded an American vessel, so we decided to come out here and save your ass. How does it feel?" John asked.

"Humiliating, but maybe if you carried me around the ship for a few hours, we could call it even."

"You can release the captain, now," John said, smiling as he gave me a reassuring nod.

I lowered my weapon and let the captain loose. He quickly stepped away and joined his men, but proceeded to leer menacingly at me from across the deck of the *Sozo*. The third man, who had come aboard with John and Corn, at last introduced himself.

"Hello, I am Admiral Jules Bertrand, and I'm here to clear up our little problem," he said, in accented, although excellent, English as we shook hands.

"Nice to meet you, Admiral, though I'm sorry about the little misunderstanding with your men here."

"No, it is I who apologize. Sometimes, shit happens and the wrong orders reach the wrong person," he said.

He turned to address Captain Jaques and his troops.

"Vous, les hommes sont sommés de se retirer et revenir à votre vessal," he said.

I'm pretty sure he told them to fuck off and go back to their vessel—although maybe not in those exact words.

"Oui," Captain Jaques said, with a smart salute.

Jaques, his pride somewhat diminished, quietly excused himself, bowed his head, and ordered his men to form up and return to their vessel. Three of the men picked up their unconscious friend and proceeded to grumble at me as they carried him past us and left the deck. The French menace now gone, the SEALs went around and cut the wrist ties off of the crew, freeing them, and allowing everyone to breathe a sigh of relief. With our little drama at an end, the SEALs and the crew dispersed, leaving me and my three old friends alone to conduct our impromptu reunion. Corn turned his gaze to me, stepped closer, and smiled shyly as he held open his burly arms for a hug. I begrudgingly opened my arms, and he squeezed me the way a two year old squeezed his first teddy bear—though my stuffing thankfully remained intact. He was still strong but definitely looking quite a bit soft in the middle from his years away from active duty. He stepped back, his gaze shifting uncomfortably between me and the deck.

"I assume you know about Lux and me?" he asked, sheepishly.

"Yeah."

"Well, I just wanted you to know that I'm sorry we didn't tell you sooner," he said.

"It's not a problem—life moved on for all of us."

We all stood for a moment, no one quite sure what to say, until, John, who had just said goodbye to the French Admiral, came over and joined us. I realized the fucker was looking good, a lot better than he had lying in that hospital bed back in Afghanistan, though, now, he was obviously a bit older, his dark brown hair showing hints of grey at the temples. Over the past few years, I'd only seen him on television and the internet, and it was hard to believe that he was now the second most powerful man in the free world and a veritable celebrity. He smiled warmly, looking every bit the politician, as he offered me his hand.

"A handshake for the man who saved your life? What's the problem? Does your blue blood make you too good to hug a member of the proletariat?" I asked.

"No. But I wanted to know who you voted for before I got that close."

"Nobody, I'm an independent."

He stepped forward, and we hugged like a couple of long lost sorority sisters.

"I've missed you, Finn."

"I've missed you too, Sasquatch."

"I told you, its Yeti."

We finished our hug and stood back, all of us looking shocked to be together again after so many years.

"So, how did it go?" John asked.

"Not exactly as planned. Babineux and Bridgette escaped," Lux said.

"I don't understand?" John said, looking a little confused.

"Me neither," Corn added.

"Bridgette left with Babineux—willingly, I'm afraid. She was the leak in my operation."

"Well, that certainly complicates things," Corn said.

"Yeah, I imagine it does," I said, as I went to the bar, grabbed four glasses and a bottle of Soft Taco Island Rum, then motioned for them to join me at a nearby table.

"So, John—Vice President? Honestly, I expected more from you. I didn't save your ass so you could end up as a number two."

He laughed and shook his head.

"Ahh—you haven't changed! You're still an asshole," he said, before taking a sip of rum.

"How about a quick debrief," Corn said.

"As you already know, we got the missile launchers and the buyers, and figured out how Babineux is conducting his illicit arms dealing business, but we obviously didn't capture the fucker," Lux said.

"The lucky bastard got the money and the girl," Corn responded.

Lux glared at Corn.

"What?" he asked, innocently.

That was a weird exchange. A little jealousy perhaps? Maybe there was trouble in paradise.

"So, Babineux is the big winner, I guess," John said, somberly.

"Not exactly," I responded.

Everyone looked at me.

"He only got the girl."

"Excuse me. I saw him leave with the case," Lux said, a bit curtly.

"You saw him get a case full of pretty glass. The real jewels are safely hidden in my room."

The three of them looked at me with blank stares, so, apparently, I needed to use smaller words.

"I switched out the jewels for fakes."

"When the hell did you do that?" Lux asked.

"Do you remember asking me about why my arm was wet back when we were on Babineux's yacht."

"Yeah, but you'd just come from the bathroom, so I didn't want to know the details."

"Well, that's, more or less, when it happened."

"OK—but would you mind clarifying?" she asked.

"Yeah, I'd also love some clarity here," John said, looking confused.

"It's elementary my dear friends. You see, while Babineux was off enjoying a Champagne brunch, Lux and I decided to conduct a little reconnaissance of his yacht."

"He means he did some recon, while I got stuck standing guard outside," Lux added.

"Which is an equally important job. Anyway, I went through most of the boat to memorize the layout in case we needed to conduct a raid, and, on my way out, I decided to take a look at his bathroom."

"For what purpose?" John asked.

"To admire it, obviously."

"Seriously?"

"How could you forget Finn's whole bathroom fetish?" Corn asked.

"It's not a fetish—I just enjoy a good dump, so I, in turn, appreciate a nice bathroom, and, having fallen in love with the *baño* in his presidential palace, I was more than a little curious how his yacht's would measure up."

Lux was, apparently, a little annoyed at how long my explanation was taking.

"Finn, I know you found the case of jewels in the fucking bathroom, so do you mind getting to the part about switching them out with fakes?" she asked.

"Hey, we haven't heard any of this yet," Corn complained.

"Yeah, and wait a minute. You seriously found the jewels in his bathroom?" John asked.

"I sure did, and, believe it or not, they were in a kind of hidden cabinet right next to the toilet."

"I bet Babineux probably never imagined anyone would find his booty in there—so to speak," John said.

"Nice one. I see politics hasn't taken away your sense of humor."

"Quite the contrary, I'm afraid."

"Seriously now, Tag, I checked that case, and those jewels didn't look like fakes."

"They were fakes all right, and you'll all be really surprised to learn that I dredged them from the bottom of the coolest fish tank you've ever seen."

"And this fish tank was in Babineux's bathroom?" Corn asked.

"No, the fish tank was built into the wall directly behind his bed."

"And it was full of fake jewels?"

"Yeah, it was pirate themed, and the jewels were meant to look like a pirate's treasure instead of the typical crappy colored rocks you get at your local pet store."

"So, you basically used fake pirate treasure to steal real pirate treasure," John said.

"Arrrrrr—you got it matey. I snagged several handfuls and threw them in the case, then, when I was back on the *Sozo*, I switched them out with the originals in the little plastic bags."

"Pretty sneaky fucking move," John said.

"Well, that French fucker had been ahead of us at every turn, so this was a little insurance policy to make sure we finally got the last laugh."

"What if Babineux looked more closely and realized they were fakes?" Lux asked.

"I figured those little plastic bags would be more than enough to disguise their appearance, and I had already put that theory to the test when you checked them out for yourself. If they got past a blue blood like you, then Babineux would be none the wiser."

"And what if it didn't work? Weren't you worried about Bridgette?" Lux asked, angrily.

"No."

"How can you say that?" she asked.

"Two reasons—the first being the nature of our meeting. It was quick and dirty, so he wouldn't have time out on the windy deck of the *Sozo* to pull out a jeweler's magnifying glass and do any kind of thorough examination."

"And the second?"

"I had a pretty good suspicion at that point that Bridgette wasn't in any real harm, because there was a fairly good possibility that she was playing for the other team."

"And how exactly did you know this?"

"A little basic inductive reasoning."

"Oh, well would you care to elaborate, Sherlock?" Lux asked, sounding a wee bit skeptical.

"Funny you should mention the great progenitor of deductive reasoning, for he was, in truth, more akin to the use of inductive reasoning—the very same reasoning that allowed me to eventually unearth our unlikely bad girl."

"Whatever, just get to the point," Lux said.

"Alrighty then, but I suppose, in the interest of clarity, I should start at the beginning—namely when you became Soft Taco Island's public enemy number one. There was obviously a serious leak in your operation, but was it electronic or human, and if the latter, then who? Assuming you took the appropriate precautions then your leak was indeed human, and to that end, Bridgette was the only central figure who had the means and opportunity to bring about the events as they occurred. Still, it was too early to make any concrete conclusion, as most of the events had yet to occur, and she was doing a damn good job of playing the concerned sister."

"Yeah, but that makes sense, as Bridgette was a drama major in college."

"She certainly managed to put on a very convincing show, especially during our first meeting, where she shed some rather conspicuous tears in an effort to pull on the old heartstrings."

"Well, don't feel too bad, Tag, as she obviously had all of us fooled," Lux said.

"Yeah, she did, and, honestly, a lot of the clues were pretty damn subtle, and only seem obvious in hindsight—case in point being the first one, which was the simple fact that Bridgette was texting someone after we landed in Martinique."

"Texting certainly isn't a nefarious or unusual activity these days."

"Definitely not, but it turned out to be, when, ten minutes later, I was accosted by two French DGSE agents in the part of town that Bridgette suggested we visit for a little last minute shopping."

"I see your point," Corn said.

"Yeah, and after I took care of the DGSE agents, Bridgette looked oddly surprised to see me, which would infer she knew about their plan to kidnap me and spirit me the fuck off the island. It would also explain why she was texting shortly there-after—obviously reporting back to her boyfriend, Babineux, that his plan had failed."

"It would appear that the clues aren't looking too subtle any-more," Lux said.

"Yeah, and there's more. You see, I also saw Bridgette talking on her phone on two rather auspicious occasions, the first time being the morning before Estelle and I met with John Parker, while the second was right before I busted you out of the Soft Taco holding cells. I had wondered who in the hell she could be talking to, but it's fairly obvious now that she was relaying our plans to our favorite French arms dealer—which also explains how that fucker managed to stay ahead of us at every turn."

"So, is that the end of your glorious recap, Sherlock?" John asked.

"Actually, there was one final obvious lynchpin that brought it all together," I said, looking triumphantly around the table.

"Which was?" Lux asked, impatiently.

"Bridgette's underwear," I said, with glowing pride.

Lux groaned.

"Excuse me?" John asked.

"I finally put it all together when I realized the underwear I saw in Babineux's palace and on his yacht were Bridgette's."

"Wait a minute. How in the hell would you know they were Bridgette's underwear?" Corn asked, with a little too much enthusiasm.

Lux gave Corn another icy glare before turning her scrutinizing gaze back to me. I decided I needed a little liquid courage to finish the story and downed the last sip of rum in my glass. As I went to pour myself a little more, Lux, John, and Corn held their glasses in my face to signal they were eagerly awaiting refills. I topped off their glasses, then we all took a swig of our drinks.

"Well, what's the story with Bridgette's underwear?" John asked.

"A gentleman never tells," I responded.

"He fucked her," Lux said.

"She seduced me."

"Same difference," Lux muttered.

"And equally favorable either way," John said, clinking his glass to mine.

He took a sip, and I could see he was lost in thought as he apparently imagined the event that I had experienced firsthand.

"It would have been nice if you'd told me all this sooner for fuck's sake. I could have spent a lot less time worrying about Bridgette's welfare and more time worrying about how we were going to snatch Babineux."

"I know, and I'm sorry, but I was really hoping I was wrong, and to be perfectly honest, I wasn't a hundred percent certain myself until she pulled the gun on us."

Everyone drank quietly, obviously deep in thought about all that had occurred.

"So, what the hell happens now?" I asked.

"We still need to bring in Babineux. I'm not exaggerating when I say he'll be the single greatest intelligence asset we've yet been able to acquire in the war on terror. He's been supplying ISIS, Al Qaeda, and a number of the other terrorist factions for quite a while, so he'll know names, faces, and details we could only dream about."

"Do you think he'll be cooperative, and, if not, what happens if the French government steps in and demands his release?"

"That's the interesting part. Initially, we weren't sure how all this would play out, but, now that you've sabotaged the arms deal and he's on the run, things have changed a bit—for the better."

"How so?" I asked.

"The failed arms deal is going to bring some serious retribution. His clients just got fucked, and they're going to be out for blood. He's going to need serious protection, and, before it's over, he'll be begging to come in."

"You don't think he'll just go back and hide out on his Island?"

"He can't hide from people like that forever. They'll eventually get him."

John's phone rang, and he excused himself and stepped away from the table. Corn and Lux refilled their glasses, and the three of us quietly waited for John to return. There was definitely something odd going on between Lux and Corn, and a tiny little vindictive part of me was enjoying their discomfort. John eventually finished his call and came back to the table.

"That was the director of the Agency. They've got confirmation on Babineux's flight plan. It turns out he's bound for Zurich, Switzerland which makes sense, as it's an excellent place to liquidate the jewels."

"If he had them," I said.

"True," John responded.

"Well, then that should make it easy for you guys. The Swiss authorities can grab them at the airport and hand them over to the Agency. Everybody wins," I said.

"Afraid not. There are too many issues regarding extradition, especially since neither Babineux or Bridgette have even officially been charged with a crime."

"So, what are you going to do?"

"That's the million dollar question at the moment."

John asked Corn if he would join him for a minute so that they could talk privately.

"That's fine—leave us out. We're obviously not as important as you two fucks."

Corn grabbed his glass and followed John over to the railing, where the two of them talked for several minutes, occasionally throwing a glance our way. I generally didn't like being left out of important conversations, as it often meant they concerned you—a fact which wasn't making my rum go down very easily at the moment. The fuckers finally finished their little chitchat and came back over and sat down at the table. John smiled and looked at Corn who smiled back at him, before they both turned and smiled at me. I stopped smiling and got nervous wondering what the hell they were smiling about.

"What's up? Why are you two assholes smiling?"

"We have a proposition for you, Finn," John said.

"Oh fuck—what now?"

"Don't worry. I think you're going to like it—unless you're too busy with your work in the private sector."

I had the distinct feeling that they knew exactly how much work I didn't have, but they were at least nice enough not to rub it in my face. The CIA liked to know everything about everyone, and sometimes it actually did, so it was entirely possible that the fuckers knew how desperately I needed a paying job.

"As you know, Babineux and Bridgette are on their way to Zurich, but the Swiss authorities will not provide any direct interdiction, which means it is entirely up to us to get them back to the States. This is Lux's operation, but she could use the help of an experienced operator, someone who has worked all over the world and can deal with some potentially serious shit—someone who can think on his feet and adapt to any situation. I happen to know from personal experience that you are that person," John said, looking me directly in the eye, his head cocked slightly to the side, as he delivered his best politician's voice.

I sat there, feeling a little conflicted as I finished my glass of rum and poured another. The others held out their glasses as well, and it was definitely feeling a lot like old times, the only thing missing being the deck of cards.

"So, you want me to rejoin the agency? Honestly, I can't imagine going back. I wasn't too happy when I left the first time."

"You'll be an independent contractor. No strings attached," Corn said.

"What's the pay? It would have to be good, because I make a lot of money in the private sector, and I have a heavy caseload at the moment."

"How about you keep the jewels? Who's to say they weren't lost at sea," John said.

I drank the last of my rum in one gulp, still trying to process what I'd just heard. I refilled my glass with only a splash realizing that I probably needed a clearer head at the moment. John, Corn, and Lux held out their glasses for another refill, and I realized that if we kept drinking at this pace, the four of us would be passed out drunk on the deck within the hour.

"Jesus, guys! Take it slow—this stuff is expensive."

"I think you can afford it."

"I haven't said yes yet, and let's be honest—why the hell wouldn't you assholes just take the jewels for yourselves? Why give me a hundred million dollars? I'm a nobody."

"Good question, and one I can answer very easily with another question. How in the hell does the vice president of the United

States explain the sudden addition of a hundred million dollars to his personal net worth?"

"True, it might be a little sticky for you, but what about Corn?"

"Same boat, but believe me I'm tempted. Unfortunately, my position as the Deputy Director of the CIA puts my finances under just as much scrutiny as John."

"Seriously, guys, people get killed every day for a lot less money than this. I can't accept it," I said.

"Think about it, Finn. The important thing here is that the terrorists are a hundred million dollars poorer, and, if we get Babineux, we'll have the whole enchilada. A hundred million dollars is nothing compared to ridding the world of terrorists and potentially saving the lives of millions of innocent people."

I suppose that a case of jewels would sure be a bright ray of sunlight to the black hole that was my current financial state. I, therefore, eyed my friends curiously and tried to get a better read on the situation. John was sitting calmly, his hands entwined on the table while Corn was leaning forward, staring at me with the nervous intensity of a man about to propose. Lux, who was also a newcomer to this latest development, also watched me closely as she waited for my response. John, sensing I might be a little reluctant, thought I needed a little more encouragement.

"Finn, we don't care about the money. The real issue now is that Bridgette is involved, and it's become a personal matter, and that means we can't use the usual Agency resources. We need someone from the outside who we can trust to bring them back safely. That someone is you," he said.

"He's right, we need you—but, more importantly, I need you," Lux added.

I closed my eyes and rubbed the sides of my head, partially believing this might all be some kind of drunken dream. The problem, however, was that I was awake.

"We need your skills on this one, Finn. You're the best man we've got for the job."

I had a sip of my rum and took a moment to reflect on the past week and realized it had probably been the best time of my life. I'd spent it with amazing people in amazing places, all the while enjoying the comfort of private jets, mega yachts, and fine food and drink. Perhaps it was time to leave behind the days of lost cats and libidinous adulterers, and I could certainly do with a little trip to Europe, so why not do it on the Agency's dime?

"You can quit blowing smoke up my ass. I'll do it for fuck's sake, though I'm going to need an expense card and a guarantee that any travel will be first class."

"No need to worry about that, as you'll have the Vandenberg Jet and the *Sozo* at your disposal."

I looked at my old friends, and it was hard to believe how far we had come from those crazy days in Afghanistan. Somehow, fate had decided to bring us all back together again—the love of my life, the Senator's son, and the corn fed farm boy. It was quite a reunion, and I could only imagine what adventure lay ahead. Still, deep down, I knew things were never as simple as they appeared, though, as usual, only time would tell. John, looking relieved that I had taken the job, held up his drink to toast. The rest of us lifted our glasses and joined in.

"To old friends," he said.

"And new beginnings," I added.

TAG FINN WILL BE CONTINUING HIS ADVENTURES IN

TOPLESS AGENDA

Tag Finn, an elite CIA operative turned private investigator, just managed to save the former love of his life and thwart an arms deal that would have facilitated the largest terrorist attack since September 11. But, the man behind the arms deal, Adrien Babineux, managed to escape and is on the run in Europe, and the CIA needs Finn to bring him in. What begins as a routine snatch and grab, gets complicated quickly when the arms dealer's terrorist clients and an unknown black ops team come looking to exact some revenge.

Finn is now on his own as he, Babineux, and their small band of compatriots race across Europe and try to stay one step ahead of their ruthless enemies. They're out-gunned and out-manned and only have their wits and their will to help them survive, so, buckle up, because this shit is about to get real!

THE MANTASY SERIES:

SOFT TACO ISLAND

TOPLESS AGENDA

GORDITA CONSPIRACY

MR PICKLES

STRIPPER BOAT

POI PREDICAMENT

CHALUPA CONUNDRUM

PROMETHEUS PROTOCOL

ACKNOWLEDGEMENTS

I suspect every writer has a large list of people who make their work possible, and mine begins with my wife, who hears every one of my idiotic ideas and gives her opinion freely and without fear that I might get offended and stop helping with the housework. Next, would be my editors, Ruth A. Bright, Chris Cooper, and Aria Pearson who have generously given their time to comb the book for mistakes and keep me grammatically, if not politically or morally correct. After editors, comes my army of proofreaders, namely Matt Zeeman, Chris Imlay, Bob Horton, Katherine Gundling, and Jason Bright. Following them is my family, especially my father Fred Christie, who has always believed in my artistic endeavors and supported them both figuratively and literally. Next would be my mother Jane Christie (Posthumously), who definitely played a roll in my odd sense of humor. Also in the family category, is my pushy sister Sheree Wilson who helped get me into a posh New York Literary Agency, as well as my less pushy sister, Shelly Hall. From there, it continues on to two special friends who helped in a very unusual way, namely securing the Macbook Pro laptop that I would use to write while incarcerated at Stanford Hospital. Those two generous souls, inadvertently responsible for the proliferation of the Mantasy Genre, are Michele and Dan Scanlon. Next is my oldest friend and layout expert Chris Imlay followed by Dianna Woods, Jimmy and Jodie Woods, as well as Robert O'Brien and Elizabeth "highbeams" Machado, all of whom have been willing to suffer through early drafts, mistakes, inaccuracies, and a vast number of unusual sexual metaphors.

Another special thank you goes out to Greg Owens, good friend and international man of business acumen, who passed on the following advice from his mentor George Leonard—take the hit. Which means: should you ever be sidelined with something such as five years of cancer treatment, do something positive with the time—in my case writing a bunch of escapist, erotic, adventure novels.

I'd also like to thank Mike Rowe and his *Dirty Jobs* show, Tom Selleck and the creators of *Magnum PI*, Jeremy Clarkson, James May, and Richard Hammond and their show *Top Gear* (which is now more or less the *Grand Tour* on Amazon), and, last but not least, J.K. Rowling and her *Harry Potter* book series. All four would make an unbearable time more bearable, and, in the case of when I finally left the hospital, I had a new immune system and more or less was the equivalent of an adult newborn and therefore had to avoid the public and its various viruses, bacteria, and germs. To that end, I was home all day every day, and the only way to keep from going totally bonzo when I was writing was to have a show on in the background. With *Dirty Jobs* I found the perfect everyman in host Mike Rowe, whose filthy exploits and double entendres kept me feeling connected to the "dirty" world beyond my room. *Top Gear* and its wacky hosts and scenic locations kept me fully entertained and desperate to get well and make it back out to the world at large. *Magnum PI*, however, was a different experience, for it brought me back to one of my beloved childhood shows, and its characters and setting served as a kind of comfort food during the anxiety filled hours of treatment. In the early stages of treatment, however, I started reading J.K. Rowling's *Harry Potter*. Nothing was better at taking my mind off the chemo drip, and it was actually the void I felt after finishing the series that helped inspire me to create my own literary world in which to escape—though mine would obviously be for adults and contain a shitload of profanity, humor, and sex. We often underestimate the value of entertainment and its unique ability to take us away from our problems, and so, to all four entities and all those involved—you have my gratitude!

My final word of thanks goes out to my vast martial arts community, all of whom helped keep me alive and well throughout the dark days of cancer treatment. At the top of that group, and requiring special thanks, are Matt Thomas, Rick Alemany, and Margaret Alemany whose wisdom and teaching helped inspire many of the techniques in the book. Beyond them and within our own karate community is Lauren and Rob Sandusky, Thandi Guile, Aria and Daniel Pearson, Tom Jacoby and Jennifer Solow, John Hedlund, Michele & Dan Scanlon, Katherine Gundling, Bob Horton, Sue Fox and J.T. Meade, Mark, Matt, Brad, and Jade Zeeman, Ted Hatch, James Parks, Rob Capps, Mari Sciabica, Jeremy Holt and the Holt Family, Sabrina Haechler, Jonathan Johnson, Brannon Beliso, Catherine and Eric Engelbrecht, Catherine and Ian Moore, Tamera Blake, the families and students of Christie Kenpo Karate, Michael Mason MD, Natalya Greyz MD, Sally Arai MD, and the Stanford University BMT Unit & ITA. If you don't see your name here, don't worry—there is a more comprehensive list of the karate community on the Thank You page of my website.

To all of you, I say be well—and more importantly—dump well.

ORIGIN OF THE MANTASY GENRE

In 2010, I was diagnosed with Stage 4 Non-Hodgkins T-Cell Lymphoma Cancer, and, with only weeks before my imminent demise, began rigorous dose dense chemotherapy. With an extremely low survival rate, about one in five, I was particularly lucky to achieve a full remission in just over two months. I went on to receive a stem cell, and eventual bone marrow transplant at Stanford University, the last procedure being the most effective treatment for a lifelong cure.

So, what exactly does a person do when faced with extreme isolation and the fear of a potentially premature demise? Well, I started reading Harry Potter and filled many long hours hooked up to a chemo drip, spending my time with the life and adventures of the boy who lived—hoping, in my case, to be the man who survived. There aren't many books more removed from the doldrums of cancer, so it became the perfect escape. The problem, however, was that I tore through them so quickly that I was soon on my own again—desperately in need of something to fill my long, anxiety filled days.

I tried several popular novels and authors I liked but couldn't find anything to adequately fill the endless hours of isolation. Of course, I could have wallowed in self pity, but I really didn't want the months of downtime to be meaningless. If I was forced to sit around like a piece of shit, then I wanted to do something with the time. I immediately decided that I should turn my screenplay writing skills into the ultimate, tell-all cancer book, but, five pages in, I realized the topic was too depressing and decided to instead write a novel. It was going to be the book I desperately wanted to read and would include all the things I lacked at that moment—namely sex, alcohol, adventure, travel, and privacy in the bathroom—the key elements for a truly rewarding existence.

I finished chemo at Kaiser then headed south to the Stanford University Hospital and quickly realized that I would have nothing but a window and the internet for a companion in the coming months. Worse still were the medical horrors that would soon become a part of my daily existence. My morning nurse, concerned about the debilitating physical effects of intense chemo, entered my room each day with the following words:

"What would you like me to check first? Your balls or your butt hole?"

"Um—neither?" I responded.

At that point, all I desired went into my writing, first and foremost being a little privacy in the ol' baño. The nurses had an annoying habit of always wanting to weigh my stools—something to do with keeping track of fluid and food intake and the subsequent amount of release. My bathroom contained what I called the cowboy hat, a plastic insert to catch waste entering the toilet. Peeing in the little urinal was enough indignity, so whenever possible, I woke up early and dumped before they could make their rounds. Every day that I sent a number two un-accosted down the drain was a small, though cherished victory. I felt like a prisoner—a veritable Count of Monte Cristo, though my prison was a hospital and my battles were waged over porcelain.

Continuing with the theme of writing about all I lacked meant that the book would sizzle with sex, adventure, and humor. Three months later, I would complete book one and within the year, finish two more—completing what I called at the time, The Mantasy Trilogy—the word Mantasy, being the combination of Male and Fantasy. The following year, I managed to write five more follow ups, all with the same character and eccentricities but with new and exciting storylines and locations. Now, I had a Mantasy Series. Or, if I wanted to follow in Douglas Adam's footsteps, I would say—books four, five, six, seven, and eight in the Mantasy Trilogy. I'm currently finishing books nine, ten, and eleven.

Writing has always been one of my great loves but sadly, it took a life threatening illness to bring us back together full-time. I have written a number of screenplays and had two optioned for motion pictures, but traditional writing is more complicated and requires a hell of a lot more work. It is, however, more rewarding because you have the ability to deliver your story directly to an audience, whether it's your friends, the woman at the Post Office, or the thousands of potential readers trolling the online eBooks. It doesn't need a fifty million dollar budget, a production team, distribution, and funding for it to reach an audience—and that is pretty awesome.

ABOUT THE AUTHOR

Lyle Christie was born in San Francisco, raised in Marin County, and attended the University of Kentfield, San Francisco State University, the Academy of Art College, and Dominican University, where he majored in film and social psychology, and minored in Philosophy, Anthropology, and Human Sexuality—all of which gave him the diverse educational background to become a writer and director. In addition, he holds a fifth degree black belt and teaches Kenpo Karate, Jujitsu, Arnis, and Wing Chun. During his lifetime in the martial arts, he has taught civilians as well as police and military personnel and has the unique pleasure of training with elite members of the United States and international defense and intelligence community.

He also teaches firearms, swords, sticks, and knives, though he is equally deadly with the nunchaku, machete, goat, tether ball, and skin flute—the last perhaps being his greatest skill set. Above all else, he maintains excellent, if not grey, hair and lives aboard a yacht in Sausalito with his wife, French Bulldog, and Miniature

Dachshund. When he's not writing, directing, teaching martial arts, or training with the real life James Bonds of the world, you'll find him fighting injustice, cherishing a number two, working out, or riding his mountain bike through the scenic hills of Marin County.

You can learn more at www.lylechristie.com

Made in the USA
Monee, IL
24 March 2021